SILVER
AND LEAD

BY THE SAME AUTHOR

Deadlands: Boneyard
Dusk or Dark or Dawn or Day
Dying with Her Cheer Pants On
Laughter at the Academy
Letters to the Pumpkin King

Overwatch: Declassified:
An Official History of Overwatch
The Proper Thing and Other Stories
Velveteen vs. The Early Adventures
What If... Wanda Maximoff and
Peter Parker Were Siblings?

THE OCTOBER DAYE SERIES

Rosemary and Rue
A Local Habitation
An Artificial Night
Late Eclipses
One Salt Sea
Ashes of Honor
Chimes at Midnight

The Winter Long
A Red-Rose Chain
Once Broken Faith
The Brightest Fell
Night and Silence
The Unkindest Tide

A Killing Frost
When Sorrows Come
Be the Serpent
Sleep No More
The Innocent Sleep
Silver and Lead

THE INCRYPTID SERIES

Discount Armageddon
Midnight Blue-Light Special
Half-Off Ragnarok
Pocket Apocalypse
Chaos Choreography
Magic for Nothing
Tricks for Free

That Ain't Witchcraft
Imaginary Numbers
Calculated Risks
Spelunking Through Hell
Backpacking Through Bedlam
Aftermarket Afterlife
Installment Immortality

THE GHOST ROADS SERIES

Sparrow Hill Road
The Girl in the Green Silk Gown
Angel of the Overpass

THE ALCHEMICAL JOURNEYS SERIES

Middlegame
Seasonal Fears
Tidal Creatures

THE WAYWARD CHILDREN SERIES

Every Heart a Doorway *Across the Green Grass Fields*
Down Among the Sticks and Bones *Where the Drowned Girls Go*
Beneath the Sugar Sky *Lost in the Moment and Found*
In an Absent Dream *Mislaid in Parts Half-Known*
Come Tumbling Down *Adrift in Currents Clean and Clear*

Seanan McGuire's Wayward Children, Volumes 1–3 (boxed set)
Be Sure: Wayward Children, Books 1–3

THE INDEXING SERIES

Indexing
Indexing: Reflections

AS A. DEBORAH BAKER

THE UP-AND-UNDER SERIES

Over the Woodward Wall *Into the Windwracked Wilds*
Along the Saltwise Sea *Under the Smokestrewn Sky*

AS MIRA GRANT

THE NEWSFLESH SERIES

Feed *Blackout*
Deadline *Feedback*

Rise: The Complete Newsflesh Collection (short stories)
The Rising: The Newsflesh Trilogy

THE PARASITOLOGY SERIES

Parasite
Symbiont
Chimera

Rolling in the Deep
Into the Drowning Deep

Overgrowth *In the Shadow of Spindrift House*
Final Girls *Square³*
Kingdom of Needle and Bone *Unbreakable*

SEANAN McGUIRE

SILVER AND LEAD

TOR PUBLISHING GROUP
NEW YORK

This is a work of fiction. All of the characters, organizations, and events portrayed in this novel are either products of the author's imagination or are used fictitiously.

SILVER AND LEAD

Copyright © 2025 by Seanan McGuire

All rights reserved.

Interior art by Tara O'Shea
Map by Priscilla Spencer

A Tor Book
Published by Tom Doherty Associates / Tor Publishing Group
120 Broadway
New York, NY 10271

www.torpublishinggroup.com

Tor® is a registered trademark of Macmillan Publishing Group, LLC.

EU Representative: Macmillan Publishers Ireland Ltd, 1st Floor, The Liffey Trust Centre, 117–126 Sheriff Street Upper, Dublin 1, DO1 YC43

The Library of Congress Cataloging-in-Publication Data is available upon request.

ISBN 978-1-250-37519-3 (hardcover)
ISBN 978-1-250-37523-0 (ebook)

The publisher of this book does not authorize the use or reproduction of any part of this book in any manner for the purpose of training artificial intelligence technologies or systems. The publisher of this book expressly reserves this book from the Text and Data Mining exception in accordance with Article 4(3) of the European Union Digital Single Market Directive 2019/790.

Our books may be purchased in bulk for specialty retail/wholesale, literacy, corporate/premium, educational, and subscription box use. Please contact MacmillanSpecialMarkets@macmillan.com.

First Edition: 2025

Printed in the United States of America

10 9 8 7 6 5 4 3 2 1

For Mike and Marnie
Chicago to Glasgow, where you are, I'm home

Kingdoms of the Westlands

- Kingdom of Frozen Winds
- Kingdom of Warm Skies
- Kingdom of Evergreen
- Kingdom of Leucothea
- Kingdom of Silences
- Kingdom of Starfall
- Battle of Silences
- Kingdom of the Mists
- Kingdom of Painted Skies
- Kingdom on the Golden Shore
- Kingdom of Angels
- Kingdom of Copper

Priscilla Spencer

OCTOBER DAYE PRONUNCIATION GUIDE
THROUGH *SILVER AND LEAD*

All pronunciations are given strictly phonetically. This only covers types of fae explicitly named in the first nineteen books, omitting Undersea fae not appearing or mentioned in the current volume.

Adhene: aad-heene. Plural is "Adhene."
Aes Sidhe: eys shee. Plural is "Aes Sidhe."
Afanc: ah-fank. Plural is "Afanc."
Annwn: ah-noon. No plural exists.
Arkan sonney: are-can saw-ney. Plural is "arkan sonney."
Bannick: ban-nick. Plural is "Bannicks."
Baobhan Sith: baa-vaan shee. Plural is "Baobhan Sith," diminutive is "Baobhan."
Barghest: bar-guy-st. Plural is "Barghests."
Blodynbryd: blow-din-brid. Plural is "Blodynbryds."
Cait Sidhe: kay-th shee. Plural is "Cait Sidhe."
Candela: can-dee-la. Plural is "Candela."
Coblynau: cob-lee-now. Plural is "Coblynau."
Cu Sidhe: coo shee. Plural is "Cu Sidhe."
Daoine Sidhe: doon-ya shee. Plural is "Daoine Sidhe," diminutive is "Daoine."
Djinn: jin. Plural is "Djinn."
Dóchas Sidhe: doe-sh-as shee. Plural is "Dóchas Sidhe."
Ellyllon: el-lee-lawn. Plural is "Ellyllon."
Folletti: foe-let-tea. Plural is "Folletti."
Gean-Cannah: gee-ann can-na. Plural is "Gean-Cannah."
Glastig: glass-tig. Plural is "Glastigs."
Gwragen: guh-war-a-gen. Plural is "Gwragen."
Hamadryad: ha-ma-dry-add. Plural is "Hamadryads."
Hippocampus: hip-po-cam-pus. Plural is "Hippocampi."
Kelpie: kel-pee. Plural is "Kelpies."

Kitsune: kit-soo-nay. Plural is "Kitsune."
Lamia: lay-me-a. Plural is "Lamia."
The Luidaeg: the lou-sha-k. No plural exists.
Manticore: man-tee-core. Plural is "Manticores."
Naiad: nigh-add. Plural is "Naiads."
Nixie: nix-ee. Plural is "Nixen."
Peri: pear-ee. Plural is "Peri."
Piskie: piss-key. Plural is "Piskies."
Puca: puh-ca. Plural is "Pucas."
Roane: row-n. Plural is "Roane."
Satyr: say-tur. Plural is "Satyrs."
Selkie: sell-key. Plural is "Selkies."
Shyi Shuai: shh-yee shh-why. Plural is "Shyi Shuai."
Silene: sigh-lean. Plural is "Silene."
Tuatha de Dannan: tooth-a day du-non. Plural is "Tuatha de Dannan," diminutive is "Tuatha."
Tylwyth Teg: till-with teeg. Plural is "Tylwyth Teg," diminutive is "Tylwyth."
Urisk: you-risk. Plural is "Urisk."

ONE

February 21, 2016

Therefore the lottery,
that he hath devised in these three chests of gold,
silver and lead, whereof who chooses his meaning
chooses you, will, no doubt, never be chosen by any
rightly but one who shall rightly love.
—William Shakespeare, *The Merchant of Venice*

I SAT ON THE living room couch with my feet propped up on a pile of pillows and a version of *Much Ado About Nothing* I'd already seen a dozen times playing on the television, and all I could think was that if I didn't get to do something—pretty much anything—soon, I was going to start screaming, and I might never stop.

My name is October Christine Daye. I am a trained knight, a private detective, and a named and known Hero of the Realm. I can take care of myself. And yet none of the people in my family seemed to believe that just now, as they were intent on keeping me locked in the house while I went slowly out of my mind from boredom.

Oh, yeah. Being back in the real world was definitely better than being trapped in Titania's toxically idealized version of what Faerie should have been. But honestly, both of them sucked.

I could hear people rattling around in the kitchen, and knew that if I tried to get off the couch or made any sort of noise, someone would immediately head into the living room to make sure I was okay and take care of anything I might need. That was why I was holding as still as I possibly could, barely even breathing. I did *not* want another supportive round of "what can I do for you, October? How can I make things better? How can I convince you to keep acting like a houseplant instead of a person?"

It's rude to throw things at your family, and I didn't want to start, except for the part where I absolutely *did*.

Important piece of information I may have omitted before: everything I said about who I am is true. I just happen to also be a little over eight months pregnant, and married to a man whose first wife died due to complications in childbirth. I should probably have considered what that was going to mean during my own pregnancy before I agreed to have kids with him. I didn't. That's my bad.

Not my bad, exactly, is the fact that almost as soon as we'd realized I was pregnant, Titania, the Summer Queen of Faerie, had decided to throw a Kingdom-spanning enchantment over everything I knew and loved, transforming us into alternate versions of ourselves and locking us into her ideas of what Faerie *should* have been from the beginning. I'd been trapped there for four months, unaware that I was pregnant—unaware that I'd ever done anything that could have *made* me pregnant—while my husband searched for me, coming up with endless nightmare scenarios of things that could have gone wrong while I was enchanted and barely aware of them.

Lots of things went wrong while we were all Titania's captives. Titania is kind of the worst. But nothing terrible happened to the baby, and after tearing her enchantment down, we'd finally been free to return home and get back to our lives. I'd been excited about that, right up until I discovered that "getting back to my life" meant effectively going into lockdown. I'd been trying to deal with the transition from "surprise, you're pregnant" to "you're four months along and your normally reasonable husband looks like he wants to vomit every time you mention leaving his line of sight," while he'd been trying to deal with the fact that I was still me, no matter what I'd been living through for the previous four months without him, and he was going to have serious trouble keeping me completely stationary.

I'd actually said as much to him, during one of the brief quiet moments after our return home, when our collection of random teenagers had been sleeping and my Fetch, May, had been upstairs with her girlfriend. His response had been that the Luidaeg could probably turn me into a tree of some sort without harming the baby, and then remaining stationary would be easy.

To make matters worse, he'd repeated this suggestion to the Luidaeg when she'd dropped by a few days later, and she had not only laughed, but agreed that it was wholly possible. I'd reminded them both that I don't care for involuntary transformation, and the Luidaeg, looking me dead in the eye, had answered, "If you force the issue, I won't regard it as involuntary."

The Luidaeg can't lie. I'd changed the subject quickly after that, and spent the next few months doing my level best to take it easy. I was allowed out for short walks around the park, but never unaccompanied, and never if it looked like there might be anything remotely dangerous going on—a list which included "light rain," "large dogs," and "human teenagers being too rowdy while they played games of Frisbee."

Tybalt and the Luidaeg were the loudest voices encouraging me to stay safe at home, but they weren't the only ones. I am not a patient woman. What I am is a woman who desperately loves her husband and family, and doesn't want to hurt them when I don't have to. Tybalt's concern was clear enough, and obviously rooted in his own past traumas, and so I did my best. But I'd come home not just to Tybalt, but to a collection of heavily traumatized teens who all seemed to be convinced that I would disappear again if they let me out of their sight. I couldn't entirely blame them for that: I'd spent the last six years of my life mostly trying to *stay* alive, not get transformed into anything unpleasant, and not overthrow any monarchies that didn't already deserve it. That didn't mean I was enjoying my time as a functional prisoner in my own home.

Still, if it had just been Tybalt, and if he hadn't been reeling from the effects of a major trauma, I could probably have found a way to talk him into the idea that I at least needed to be allowed to go to the grocery store and visit my liege. Sylvester and I hadn't been on the best terms for quite a while, but we had been close when under Titania's enchantment, and the twisted life she'd created for him had to have reminded him how much he needed his family. As long as he and I were semi-estranged, he wouldn't have his brother, or either of his nieces. The immediate aftermath of breaking the spell would have been the perfect time to start rebuilding some bridges.

And yet, while I'm not always the most emotionally intelligent person in the room, I knew that forcing the issue while Tybalt was barely sleeping out of sheer anxiety would make what he was already going through much worse than it already is, and I loved him far too much to hurt him like that. I just needed to keep trying to make him understand that at a certain point, his concern had started hurting me.

The rattling from the kitchen was getting louder. I decided to risk swinging my feet around to the floor and sitting up, only slightly hampered by the size of my midsection. I wasn't as large as I'd been with Gillian, but I was large enough to be inconvenienced by my own body. That was only fair. I inconvenience my body enough, after all.

I've mentioned Faerie a lot, so here's the brief: it's real, the fae are real, and they live alongside humanity, hidden by illusions and veils of otherworldly distance. I'm what's called a changeling—fae mother, human father. My first child, Gillian, was born a thin-blooded changeling: her own father, Cliff, was fully human. For most of her life, she lived with him and his wife, Miranda, who was perfectly human, but under an unbreakable enchantment spun by Maeve. She's actually my maternal grandmother, Janet Carter of the old ballad. Because once you add magic and curses that can extend people's lives by centuries, nothing gets to stay simple.

Not that things are particularly simple for humans, either. Gillian thought she was one, but when Faerie came calling for her, she lost her humanity and became one of the skin-shifting Selkies, only to lose that as well and become a shapeshifting Roane. She had barely spoken to me since then, and I couldn't entirely blame her.

I wrapped one arm around the sphere of my belly, addressing my next words to the child inside. "I'll do better by you," I promised. An unkeepable pledge, maybe, but in the moment, I more than meant it. Carefully, I pushed myself off the couch, grunting slightly, and started toward the living room door.

For a moment, I thought I was going to get away with it. Then I opened the door to find Raj already waiting there, a perkily helpful expression on his face. I groaned.

"Oak and ash, Raj, aren't you supposed to be running the Court of Cats right now?" I asked.

"Tybalt's there, checking in with Ginevra," he said brightly. "Which means I get to be on Toby duty. Why are you up? What do you need?"

"I'm *pregnant*, not an *invalid*," I snapped. And as pregnant women go, I was in remarkably good health, as long as you ignored the constant hunger and all the vomiting. My size was a problem, and my knees—which had never quite recovered from the way I treated them when I was younger—sometimes complained, but that was about it.

My type of faerie heals like it's our job. I can literally slice my hand open and be healed less than ten seconds later. My knees would probably fix themselves if I was willing to start hacking at them and giving the tendons and cartilage an opportunity to self-repair. So yeah, I was more than a little tired of people acting like being pregnant meant that I was suddenly breakable. It wasn't even like it was my first time.

"Yeah, but your husband is still my uncle, and that makes him the boss of me until he fully steps down," said Raj. "Can I get you anything?"

"I am *going* to the kitchen," I snarled, pushing past him.

One small advantage to the way everyone was treating me: he couldn't stop me without touching me, and so he let me pass, following me to the kitchen.

It wasn't far—just the other side of the hall. I tried to pretend I wasn't annoyed at how close Raj was on my heels as I stepped into the room, which was warm and smelled like fresh baked goods.

May, my live-in death omen and, more importantly, my sister, looked up from the tray of scones she was pulling out of the oven, flashing me a quick smile. As a Fetch, she had all my memories up to the moment of her creation, including my first pregnancy. She knew, more intimately than anyone else, that the more time I spent sitting around watching dust settle on the walls, the more convinced my entire body became that this was a trap and we were about to be eaten by something large and full of far too many teeth.

Unfortunately for me, the thing with far too many teeth was plural.

Tybalt had plenty on his own, and my maternal aunt, the literal sea witch, had a seemingly infinite number of teeth, which she could summon at will. Both of them were highly invested in me staying safe, indoors, and bored out of my mind.

I had made the choice to go along with their overprotectiveness rather than doing more damage than had already been done. I still felt pretty damn ganged up on. May straightened, removing her oven mitts, and said, "Hey, Toby. Can I get you anything?"

"My car keys and a fast route to anywhere but here?" I offered, not remotely joking.

My squire, Quentin, who had apparently been on baking duty with her, frowned at me. "Are you really sure you should be leaving the house right now?"

I started to reply, then caught myself and counted to three, breathing in through my nose and out through my mouth. Titania's spell had turned Quentin into the worst version of himself, and he was still haunted by the memory of who he had been capable of becoming. He had developed a tendency to take any argument as a criticism of who he was as a person, which wasn't fair on either side.

Normally I would have reminded him that I am a whole-ass adult, and that means I can go where I please, whether it be down to the grocery store for milk or out to Half Moon Bay to visit my semi-estranged daughter. And to be fair, normally my family wouldn't be doing this. We were all still bruised and recovering, and it wasn't entirely their fault that their trying to take care of me was driving me out of my mind.

I managed to scrape up a smile for Quentin. It must not have been too terrifying, because he hesitantly answered it with a smile of his own. "I'm still a person, not an incubator, and I can go for a little drive if I want to," I said, in the sweetest tone I could muster. "I'm not due for another two weeks."

"My mom said—"

"Your mother doesn't heal the way I do," I said, before he could go any further. "I'm in perfect health. A little worried about my pants splitting, but that's fine. I can buy new pants. What I can't buy is a new brain if I break this one by staying inside for very much longer."

"Come on, Toby, you promised Tybalt you wouldn't attempt a jailbreak while he's at the Court of Cats," said May.

"I feel like someone promised that on my behalf. I don't feel like I made that promise."

"Come on, Toby," said Quentin, plaintively. "Just stay home. Please? Like you said, you're due in two weeks. We're almost at the finish line."

"Pregnancy is neither a race nor an excuse for house arrest," I said. "I am going to start climbing the walls soon. Possibly literally. Do you want me to climb the walls? I could fall and hurt myself. Much safer to give me back my car keys and let me go on my way."

"Uncle Tybalt will *kill* us if we let you go," protested Raj.

"I may kill you if you keep me here," I replied.

The doorbell saved him from needing to reply. I turned as quickly as my current condition would allow, taking advantage of my size to block the entire doorway as I got myself oriented and then waddled toward the front door, bound and determined to get there before any of my self-appointed protectors could beat me to the punch.

They didn't try that hard to stop me, possibly out of the fear that they'd have to put their hands on me to do it, possibly out of self-preservation: none of the people I liked to surround myself with were fools, and they could all see just how close to the end of my rope I really was.

I wrenched the door open, and the teenage girl standing on the porch shot me a sly smile, clearly amused all out of proportion with everything that was happening around her.

"You wanna buy some Girl Scout cookies?" she asked.

"Okay, one, it's not Girl Scout cookie season," I said. "Even if it were, they have an age cutoff, and you'd never qualify. Two, if you were selling cookies, you'd have a backpack or a little red wagon or something, and you're empty-handed." I sighed, then smiled. "Hello, Luidaeg. What's new?"

Her smile winked out like a candle being snuffed. "A little overfamiliar, don't you think?"

"You just tried to sell me out-of-season cookies. I can be familiar if I want."

She snorted. "Guess that's so. You going to ask me in?"

"Do I have to?" My wards were good, but not *that* good. Then again, I'm not sure anyone in Faerie can cast wards solid enough to keep out one of the Firstborn.

"Have to, no. I can come in whenever I want. But it's polite, and the longer you make me stand out here on the porch, the more likely it is your neighbors decide you've kicked out one of your resident teenagers." She looked at me, eyes suddenly wide and filled with tears, lip wobbling. "Do you not love us anymore, Auntie Toby?"

"You're my aunt, not the other way around, and random house calls don't require civility on my part, but sure, Luidaeg, come on in."

"Great." She grinned, displaying too many teeth for the shape of her jaw, and walked easily inside. "I appreciate the hospitality. Do I smell scones?"

"Yes, you do, and I *do* have manners when it's important. What's going on?"

She sobered, looking me up and down. I held my tongue, waiting for her to finish. The Luidaeg, also known as Antigone of Albany, is the oldest person I really know. She's the eldest of the Firstborn, first daughter of Oberon himself, and better known as "the sea witch" in most circles. I grew up thinking of her as an untouchable water demon, and while the truth is a lot more complicated, she's still scary when she wants to be, and I try not to upset her if I have any choice in the matter.

"Can't I visit my favorite niece?" she asked finally, looking back at my face.

"You can, but you generally *don't*," I said. "Did you need something right now?"

"I always need something," she said. "Right now, I need one of those scones."

There are a lot of things to be said for the way I take care of the various teenagers who swarm around my house like pixies around a leaking Slurpee machine. Many of those things are bad ones. But probably my worst crime is that after a few months with me, none of them have any remaining fear of the Luidaeg. In short order, she was settled at the kitchen table with a plate of scones and a mug of some sort of sharp-smelling herbal tea, while Quentin and Raj sat across from her, both of them beaming like it was suddenly Christmas morning and she was there to deliver all their gifts. I leaned against the counter next to May, watching them.

"Boys seem happy," she observed.

"They like the Luidaeg," I said.

"Think we should call Raysel down?"

Raysel—my liege's daughter—wasn't technically a teenager, although she had more in common with them than with any of the resident adults, and she wasn't nearly as comfortable with the Luidaeg as the rest of the kids. She'd get there, she just needed . . . time, and understanding, and to be allowed to come around to things at her own pace.

"Probably not the best plan," I said.

"Fair enough," agreed May. "Any idea why she's here?"

"For scones, apparently." There was definitely something else going on, but for the moment, scones were keeping her occupied, and I was willing to let her stay distracted as long as she wanted to. When the Luidaeg appears, things tend to get complicated, fast.

I was bored, but was I "the Luidaeg has a problem for me" levels of bored? And even if I was, would Tybalt let me do anything about it? I rubbed my stomach with one hand, almost automatically, as if reminding myself why I'd been on such a tight leash for the past four months. Sometimes the thought of a baby at the end of all this difficulty made things better.

Not this time. I sighed, and the Luidaeg looked around at me, eyes slightly narrowed as she took me in.

"Cargo's almost ready to be dropped off, isn't it?" she asked.

"It is, and please don't tell me that one of the bargains I made with you secretly involved my baby," I said. "I really don't think I could handle that right now."

"I don't trade in children if there's any evading it," said the Luidaeg. "No matter what some of my stepmother's descendants will try to say, I've never taken in a foundling who had somewhere else to safely go, and I've never based a price on the life of a child. I know you were joking, but please. No jokes about that."

". . . sorry," I said.

"It's cool," she replied. "Can I have another scone?"

"Sure," said May.

While she was getting the Luidaeg her scone, I stayed where I was, feeling worse and worse about my clumsy attempt at humor. We called the Luidaeg "the sea witch" in part because she was under a geas set by her stepmother, Titania, which forced her to do whatever she was asked, but allowed her to charge whatever price she saw fit for her help. I had been in and out of her debt since we first met. But because of that geas, she didn't have a choice: if she was asked, she *had* to intercede, or at least set the price she'd accept for intercession. She was trapped, just as much as any prisoner in Faerie.

My stomach growled, and I paused in my woolgathering to glare at it. This needing to eat all the time nonsense was getting old. "I can't wait to be done being pregnant," I muttered.

"Could be worse," said the Luidaeg. "Pinniped pregnancies last for eleven months."

"You're kidding," I said flatly.

She grinned, showing a flash of fang in the process. "Can't lie, remember? Eleven months, and every one of the Roane I carried with my own body took that long to come into the world. They weren't in any hurry at all."

"That's horrifying," I said.

"Even worse, when they started having kids of their own, they only had to be pregnant for nine months. Little brats." She smiled as she spoke, like she was remembering those pregnancies with fondness.

She'd been doing that more often since the Convocation of Changes returned the Roane to the sea—talking about them, and reminiscing about the good things that had happened before they died.

Before they were murdered.

I rubbed my stomach again, trying to imagine how I would react if someone hurt my children the way hers had been hurt. I hadn't reacted well when Gillian had been in danger, and I couldn't imagine I'd handle it any better with this baby. Even thinking about it was making me antsy. I shoved the thoughts aside and focused on the Luidaeg.

I don't know what she really looks like. I'm not sure anybody does. I'm not sure *she* does. She's a true shapeshifter, completely protean, and her form shifts to suit her mood and needs. At the moment, she looked like a human teenager with a dusting of acne scars on her cheeks, curly black hair pulled into thick ponytails and tied off with strips of electrical tape. Her eyes were a nondescript dark blue, unremarkable. If not for the fact that sometimes her smile contained too many teeth, it would have been easy to dismiss her.

Easy, and stupid.

The Luidaeg was nothing to dismiss: she was older than the modern arrangement of the continents. She had seen empires rise and fall, been present for the birth of fairy tales and legends, and was as close as it comes in this world to unkillable. She didn't need to look fae. Our foundations were in her bones, and our borders were in her blood. Leave the pointed ears and unearthly beauty to the ones who needed to wear their alliances on their sleeves; she walked the world as she saw fit.

Taking her second scone from May, she flashed my Fetch a toothy smile. "Can we have the room?" she asked.

"Oh," said May. "Oh! Sure. Quentin, Raj, come on, boys. Raysel's probably wondering where we are."

The three of them bustled out of the kitchen without looking back, and the Luidaeg and I were alone. She watched them go, then turned her toothy smile on me.

"Looks like it's just us girls for right now," she said. "You are a difficult lady to catch without a crowd."

The air in the room felt suddenly cooler. I swallowed hard. "I guess I'm just lucky that way," I said. "And does it really count as catching me without a crowd if you have to send everyone else away?"

"Still. You've come a long way from the mewling little exile who insisted no one would ever care enough about her to notice if she lived or died. From sitting alone in your apartment with your sad little secondhand coffee maker to two sisters, a squire who may as well be a son, a nephew by marriage who might as well be a squire, a husband, and so many others that it would insult us both to stand here listing them all. You've done well for yourself, niece. But we both know it's not going to last forever. It never does for people in your line of work. One day, it's all going to catch up with you."

"Is this where you kill me?" I asked, mouth going dry. "I know you've always said you were going to."

"Not yet," she said. "I keep my word, and when you die, it'll be at my hand if there's any possible way of it, but that isn't yet. That is still far enough in the future as not to matter now. I'm not here to speak of murder."

"Then why are you here?"

"The tides told me now was the appropriate time to come, although I was hoping to catch the kitty-cat at the same time. Oh, well, I guess. I'm here about your child."

"The baby?" My voice squeaked, breaking unsteadily, and I abandoned rubbing my belly as I wrapped both arms around my midsection. There was nothing I could do that would hold the sea witch back if she wanted to attack me. I had to hope it was hormones making her seem threatening, and that the years of tentative friendship and ever-changing debt between us were heavy enough to counterbalance her current strangeness.

"Yes, the baby. Child of Miles Cross and the Shadow Roads united, first of their kind in all of Faerie. They'll be Dóchas Sidhe, and with their birth, the line is true. Firstborn begin the line, but its continuance is down to those born to it. I'm not saying your baby will have some terrible fate or grow up to be a hero like their mother; for all I know, they're to be spared all the worst horrors of Faerie. But those horrors are coming, and one day you may not be able to protect them."

I clutched my stomach tighter and just stared at her.

"We steal words and concepts from the human world like candy from cradles," she said. "We never took their gods—we have our own, and some of theirs are shadows of our stories, but we took everything else from them."

"And?" I asked warily.

"I would like to offer to stand as your child's fairy godmother," said the Luidaeg, bowing her head. "No divinity about it, only a promise that should anything happen to you, I'll care for them as if they were my own. They'll want for nothing, need for nothing, and walk the halls of our kind free of all fear."

I blinked at her. "You . . . want to be the godmother."

"Yes."

"To *my* child."

"My great-niece or nephew, yes."

"I thought we didn't do..." I paused, trying to gather my thoughts. Faerie did fosterage, yes, children sent to live with other households for their education or protection. Faerie did adoption when something happened to a child's parents before they were old enough to live on their own—both the simple sort of names and contracts, and the more complicated sort, with bloodlines and lineages, children sworn into lines that weren't previously their own but would be considered true thereafter. Maybe once upon a time, when the world had been more dangerous for us, when more of us had risked the end to our dancing, Faerie had done godparents as well, sworn guardians standing watch in case something happened. In case the worst came to pass.

"I thought we didn't do that anymore," I said, voice breaking again. "Luidaeg, have you Seen something?"

"You walk too close to my father—you walk too close to me," she said. "Your future has always been a hazy beast, too changeable for me to pin down, although the tides offer me little things, such as the best time to come and visit. But I know you're a hero married to a king, and I know he's in the process of setting his throne aside. Kings who give up their crowns don't tend to live for long. Neither do heroes. Amandine's line is meant to save Faerie. Gillian is no longer a member of that line."

"Neither am I," I protested. "I chose Simon in the divorce."

"Legally, you're not. But your blood remembers where it began, and for the purposes of prophecy, you qualify. Prophecies have never cared about the law. They're much more interested in reality. When it comes to matters of line, you and August are all we have. This baby will shoulder the same burden until the deed is done, and I doubt you're going to let the weight of it fall upon your child. So the chances that something will happen to you are far higher than I'm comfortable with."

"I..." When the Luidaeg makes that sort of huge, impossible offer, there's really only one answer that can be given. No matter how much I stalled and questioned, I already knew what I was going to say.

She looked at me expectantly. I glanced at my hands, unable to face the weight of her gaze. The deep blue she'd worn when she arrived had bled out of her eyes, leaving them green as glass, save for a ring of black around the edges. Somehow, that made it worse to try and face her. I was good at facing down the sea witch, good at staring into the eyes of a monster and refusing to be cowed. I wasn't so good at looking into the eyes of a friend.

"I'll have to ask Tybalt when he gets home." I glanced up again. "I can't make a decision this big without his input."

"You know he'll agree. Only a foolish man would refuse the kind regard of one among the Firstborn, and he's less a fool than you are."

"Maybe, but I promised to stop rushing into danger without giving him a chance to say something about it, and you can't really pretend that letting you stand as godmother wouldn't be dangerous."

"You're right." She shrugged. "I can't. Offer stands, though, and if you want to be the mother of a child that lives, you'd do well to take me up on it."

"I promise to talk to Tybalt as soon as I can," I said gravely.

She nodded. "Good. Good. That baby has enough stacked against them. They deserve the chance to thrive, and that can come from me, if you allow it. I'm sure I'm not the only offer you're going to receive. I hope I'll be the one you entertain."

I opened my mouth to answer, and stopped as she rose, leaving her half-eaten scone behind. "Arden's going to send a messenger to see you soon," she said, and as if on cue, someone rang the doorbell. We both turned toward the sound, the Luidaeg pursing her lips in mild annoyance. I could tell it was mild because while her eyes darkened by a few degrees, they stayed green, rather than bleeding entirely black. The longer I've known her, the more I've learned to read her mood by her eyes.

The doorbell rang again. I pushed away from the counter and moved in that direction as fast as my current state allowed, the Luidaeg following close behind. When I reached the front door, I paused, grabbing a handful of air and beginning to mutter under my breath.

"Let me," said the Luidaeg.

She snapped her fingers, and I felt the illusion settle over me like a thin layer of dust sticking to my skin. I glanced at her. She was looking at the door, seeming to ignore me. Right. Confident that I at least looked human now, even if I wasn't, I opened the door.

There was a short, unfamiliar man on the porch, looking at the clipboard in his hands. I blinked, pulling the door open a little wider. "Can I help you?" I asked.

"Yes," he said, looking up. "I'm here to see Miss Octavia Daye?"

"It's October, actually," I said. "And whatever you're selling, we don't need any. Have a great day."

"I'm not selling anything," he said, and blinked deliberately. When he opened his eyes again, his pupils had gone horizontal, like a goat's. "Just making sure I had the right house. You're Sir October Daye?"

"Yes," I said, more warily. "Who are you?"

"I work for the queen," he said, which wasn't a name, but was almost good enough. "She sent me to let you know that court will be called tonight at sundown, and she wants both you and your husband in attendance."

"Am I invited?" asked the Luidaeg sweetly.

"I don't know who you are," he said. "You'd have to ask Her Majesty. But it's not a closed court, so the chances are she'll let you in. Sundown, Muir Woods. I hope you both have a pleasant afternoon."

Then he was gone, and we were alone, and silently watching him walk away, right up until the Luidaeg sighed, heavy as a crashing wave.

"Guess the tides gave me the right time," she said. "Better go get ready."

I closed the door.

TWO

MUIR WOODS IS A series of hills and trails, and the two are frequently combined. Not frequently enough for fae needs: Arden's knowe was located at the top of a hill that was inaccessible by official means, since the park rangers got upset when they saw people hiking outside the designated areas. Normally, I would have been complaining about the need to climb the hill in court attire. My current condition meant I didn't need to.

Tybalt climbed the hillside easily, holding me against his chest in a perfect bridal carry. The air changed as we reached the top of the hill and transitioned into the Summerlands, becoming sweeter and cleaner, losing the distant taste of petrochemicals. Even the cleanest air in the mortal world had nothing on Faerie.

I exhaled as Tybalt set me gently on my feet, holding my arms until he was sure I had my balance. Irritated as I was at the continual coddling, I was grateful for the assist. I've never been as graceful as a pureblood, much less one of the Cait Sidhe, but pregnancy had changed my center of balance enough to make me worry about falling. His eyes searched my face, looking for any sign of distress. I smiled warmly at him, even as I pushed his hands gently down.

"I've got another few weeks of this, you know," I said. "You don't want to use up all your fretting on me before the baby even gets here."

"I promise, I have more fretting in me than you can imagine," he said.

I laughed as I took his arm and turned us toward the knowe. "I don't know," I teased. "I have a pretty solid imagination." Was he going to fret more or less when I had a chance to sit down with him and tell him about the Luidaeg's offer? A godmother was no small thing, and a Firstborn godmother . . . it spoke to more concern on her part for our child's safety than I was entirely comfortable with. But if it kept our baby safe, I'd accept it.

Tybalt didn't dignify my teasing with a response. I hugged his arm, taking a moment to enjoy the silence as we approached the knowe that served as the royal seat of the Kingdom in the Mists.

The doors were already open, tall, elegant impossibilities set into the trunk of a towering redwood. They revealed a long hallway winding deeper into the structure, far too long for the tree to have contained, and well-lit by some unseen source. I hugged Tybalt's arm tighter, bracing myself for the transition.

We had already stepped onto the edge of the Summerlands when we reached the top of the hill. Stepping into the knowe was something different. It marked the point where we passed beyond the reach of the mortal world, crossing fully into Faerie. My human blood meant that it could be difficult for me to make the transition, and indeed, my stomach felt like it flipped as we crossed the threshold, nausea washing over me.

I swallowed bile, forcing myself to keep smiling. Pregnancy is an endless parade of wonders, and no two women experience it exactly the same. I missed out on a lot of the back pain and general exhaustion, thanks to the way I healed, but I didn't get morning sickness so much as I got "frequent and unpredictable nausea with no identifiable triggers." Honestly, the best thing about having this baby would be keeping dinner down for more than an hour.

I looked around the entrance hall to distract myself as we walked, studying the carved panels lining the walls. They showed important moments from the Kingdom's history, and they tended to change depending on what was going on around them. Sometimes they would show scenes that didn't seem important at all, but became endlessly relevant after they were put into context. Other times they would focus on births and coronations, all the important milestones a kingdom lives and dies by.

Tonight, they were a mixture of recent events and ancient history. They all appeared to have been carved by the same hand, even though that was patently impossible. Some of these panels had been here since Arden had reclaimed her throne and reopened the knowe, while others depicted events from the past four months. I saw the Selkies and Roane returning to the Duchy of Ships, from which they had been exiled by Titania's spell. I saw changelings running back to their families, some of them people I recognized, some of them people I didn't.

And I saw myself, pregnant, standing with my arms wrapped around my belly and my mother's tower behind me. That, more than anything, confirmed that sometimes the scenes were more representative than literal. I had never been in my mother's tower and aware of my condition. In the carving, I was looking directly at the viewer, and I was alone.

Wait—not alone. In the background, almost lost among the carved foliage of my mother's garden, a tabby cat crouched, watching me even as I watched the person looking at the piece.

I shivered. Tybalt followed the line of eyes, and snorted.

"It's a fine likeness, but a dishonest framing," he said. "We had you well away from that place before your belly was half so big as that."

"Only because babies grow so damn much faster in the second half of a pregnancy," I countered.

"Still. I should have a talk with whichever part of the knowe is providing these images."

"So you agree with me that the knowes are alive?"

He snorted again, but paused before he replied, with absolute care, "I believe you believe that they're alive, and more, that I've seen sufficient evidence of awareness that I can agree it hurts nothing to treat them as individuals worthy of some small respect."

"Huh," I said, feeling unaccountably pleased with myself as we walked onward.

I was wearing a proper gown for a formal occasion. May had produced it from the back of my closet as soon as I'd told her Arden was calling court. It was a rich cherrywood red velvet, shading into more golden tones as it neared the hem, and it wrapped around my protruding belly like a moth's wings, accentuating my size without turning bulky. The skirt extended all the way to the ground, which was doubtless part of why Tybalt had carried me up the hill. I didn't mind. The absence of boning was a relief, and the length of the skirt meant no one would know that I was wearing sneakers.

The sleeves carried on the moth-wing motif, threatening to swallow my hands whole. Three matching hairpins shaped like large silk moths were tucked into my hair, holding it away from my neck and giving it the faint illusion of being something other than utterly stick-straight. It was only the second time I'd worn proper court attire since the end of Titania's enchantment, and the memory of all the balls and courts that had never been felt like they weighed more and more heavily as we neared the closed doors of Arden's throne room. Most of me knew that this was business as usual, and Arden was unlikely to spring anything really shocking on me when I was this close to giving birth—not unless she was really in the mood to go to war with the Court of Cats. Part of me, though, was trying to insist that my appearance here was going to get me thrown into the scullery and punished for impersonating a fine lady.

Quiet, I told that part of me, with all the fierceness I could muster. *I am not impersonating a fine lady. I would never.* And I wasn't, because I have never been a lady, and I wasn't dressed like anyone but myself.

I'm a knight.

I held firmly to that thought as the doors swung open and we stepped into the massive throne room. Like most throne or receiving rooms, Arden had a dais at one end of the space, hers occupied by two thrones—one for her, and one for her brother. Other chairs could be added and removed as necessary. For informal occasions, her seneschal and chatelaine would often sit up there with the Queen and Crown Prince. For this evening, those places had been removed. The windows were open, letting the night air flow freely in, accompanied by brightly colored pixies who flitted to and fro among the rafters. The air was fresh and sweet, smelling of redwoods and rain with a faint undertone of cinnamon.

Arden's coat of arms hung on the wall behind the dais, next to Nolan's. I paused, blinking. While her coat of arms retained its verdant green color, blazoned with star-shaped white blackberry flowers, it had gained a golden bundle of wheat at the bottom, like a foundation under everything else. I glanced at Nolan's coat of arms. They displayed a hoop of blackberry brambles against a silver background, and had acquired the same bundle of wheat, this one at the top of the blazon.

Coats of arms are a noble affectation that can always be changed, but the images generally mean something. I couldn't wait to find out what had triggered this particular transition.

The room was full of people. As this was a court, and not a celebration, there were no refreshment tables; for all of that, servants still circulated with heavy trays laden with drinks and small appetizers, all single-bite and designed to be eaten while standing. My stomach grumbled, and I put a hand over it, like that could be enough to muffle the sound. Tybalt snorted, looking genuinely amused, and proceeded to flag down a passing server, a piebald Silene whose eyes were ringed in stark white, giving her an effortlessly startled expression.

"Sir Daye," she said, correctly interpreting Tybalt's imperious waving as an effort to feed his pregnant wife. She offered me both a half-bow and the tray, holding it out toward me with a clear air of "take whatever you want, fighting a Hero of the Realm is above my pay grade."

I flashed her a smile in place of the thanks I wasn't allowed to offer—Faerie has some weird hangups around the appearance of obligation, which a direct "thank you" can imply—and started to reach for the tray. Then I froze as the smell hit my nose, and clapped my hand over my mouth, swallowing bile.

Being simultaneously hungry *and* intermittently nauseous was pretty definitely the worst part about pregnancy for me. My pants didn't fit and if I dropped something, it lived on the floor, but wanting to eat even while I was throwing up was *awful*.

Tybalt saw my expression change and waved the baffled server away, murmuring a quick "Bring back something blander if you could, please," before he turned his attention on me, moving closer despite the risk that I was going to toss my cookies all over his leather pants. Damn the leather pants. I wouldn't be in this situation if it weren't for the leather pants.

I think. I'm almost sure, anyway. Sure, the leather pants weren't involved with the actual conception, but they did a lot to turn my head in the early days, and that set us on the path that led us here.

Again, I swallowed, doing little to clean away the burning taste of stomach acid.

"Are you all right?" he asked.

"Baby did *not* want a blue cheese and onion tart," I reported, only to have my stomach lurch again, as if saying the words were the same thing as actually *eating* the offending pastry. I clapped my hand back over my mouth.

"I have to go now," I said, voice muffled by my fingers. "Give Arden my apologies if she comes looking for me."

I spun on my heel and ran, heading for one of the doors on the side of the hall. Not only had I been in the knowe enough to be relatively confident that I was heading for the bathroom, I knew Arden wouldn't want me to toss my cookies all over her ballroom floor, which meant the knowe wouldn't want that, which meant my chances of making it were better than they might be otherwise.

Running while extremely pregnant is not an experience I would recommend. But then again, neither is barfing on a Queen's floor, and of those options, I'll take the running.

It was almost funny, in a terrible way. Every type of fae comes with their own magical gifts and inclinations. Dóchas Sidhe are bloodworkers of unparalleled skill, eclipsing the Daoine Sidhe, who were the big rock stars of blood magic before we came along. In me, this expresses mostly by causing me to heal almost faster than I can get injured—and I am very, very good at getting injured. Sometimes there isn't time to pull the knife out before the wound it made has healed around it. I don't get sick, either. My immune system just says "nah, hard pass," and what's circulating leaves me alone.

So being at the mercy of "normal" pregnancy-related nausea would have been hilarious, if it weren't so damn frustrating. It had been the same way with Gillian. Most of my pregnancy had been a breeze, but wow had I gone through a lot of mouthwash.

The door I'd crashed through led to a short hall lined with vases of sunflowers and moonflowers, all enchanted to remain in perfect bloom. There were a few open doorways leading to small foyers with chaise lounges and comfortable-looking leather chairs, and a few closed doors graven with a pattern of asters and moonflowers. I kept running until I reached the first closed door, shoving it roughly open to stumble into the remarkably modern-looking bathroom on the other side.

There were no stalls, which explained the iconography on the door, with a single toilet, sink, and even a small shower tucked into one corner, in case someone's bathroom experience went terribly wrong. I stumbled toward the toilet, not even taking the time to lock the door.

I almost made it, too.

After my dinner was done making a repeat appearance all over the tile floor of Arden's bathroom, I stepped back from the mess and turned to check myself over in the mirror, silently hoping that I'd managed to avoid getting any of it on myself. When I got married, my friends and fiancé conspired to enchant my wedding dress so thoroughly that it could repel anything that might stain it. Sadly, those enchantments are complicated and expensive, and most of my wardrobe is as vulnerable to accidents as anyone else's.

Luck was on my side this time; apart from the burning need to rinse my mouth out, I didn't appear to have suffered anything more dire than the loss of my supper. I turned on the sink, using my hand as a cup, and swished and spat with all the vigor I could muster.

When the taste was gone, I straightened and began splashing water on my face, trying to chase away the lingering nausea. I don't think I was ever a good sick person, but when I was more human, I used to at least *get* sick. I had to imagine I was better about it back then, since otherwise, either Devin or my mother would probably have killed me with their bare hands.

Finally satisfied, I turned away from mirror, yelped, and staggered back against the sink.

"You shouldn't sneak up on people like that!" I said, pressing one hand flat against my chest to try and calm the frantic pounding of my heart. "What if I'd gone into labor?"

"Then you wouldn't have been the first woman to give birth on a bathroom floor, and at least this one's cleaner than most." Arden Windermere, Queen in the Mists, gave the puddle of vomit on her floor a dubious look, wrinkling her nose. She was dressed for court in a long dark silver gown with blackberry canes embroidered around the hems, and she could easily have passed for something out of a Waterhouse painting if she'd wanted to. A silver diadem rested on her brow, completing the appearance of power and poise. None of which went with the way she was eyeing the floor. "I worked San Francisco retail, and even with the current mess, this is still cleaner than most."

"Are you trying to reassure yourself or me?" I took my hand away from my chest and curled it protectively around my stomach. "I am not having this baby on a bathroom floor. Tybalt would kill me."

"Please. He's Cait Sidhe. What, does he expect you to give birth in a box in the closet?"

"What do you want, Your Majesty?"

Tuatha de Dannan—like Arden and her brother, Nolan—are teleporters. Sometimes I think Faerie has a nasty sense of humor when it comes to deciding which descendant line will get which magical abilities. Hey, you over there, you can read memories by drinking people's blood! But if you drink too much, you might die! Oh, and Susie here? She gets to move freely through space, without worrying about what may be in her way!

Faerie has never been particularly concerned with fairness, but there are moments when I have to wonder whether it does things on purpose.

Normally, I can tell when one of the Tuatha enters a room. The portals they use carry the scent of their magic, and Arden's mixture of redwood bark and lightly bruised blackberry flowers is hard to miss. Normally, I'm not trying to breathe through a nose clogged from vomiting, blocking out the scent. Pregnancy is a banquet of endless delights.

Arden lifted an eyebrow. "Do I have to want something? Can't I just be checking on a valued denizen of my kingdom?"

"You could be, but you're not," I said. "If you were, you'd have come through the door, and Tybalt would be with you."

"The King of Cats is presently occupied. My dear brother needed to ask him some very important questions about the Cait Sidhe population. The mortals are stepping up their efforts to thin the feral cat colonies, and we felt it important that none of your husband's subjects be caught in the sweep."

It was my turn to raise my eyebrows. "You had him waylaid so you could get me alone?"

"That would be manipulative and underhanded."

"Uh-huh."

"Not at all befitting a proper queen."

"True enough."

"But I did need to speak with you, and it seemed best to do so in private."

"You're the Queen in the Mists," I said. "You could have just had someone ask me to step out for a moment, instead of ambushing me in the bathroom. Better yet, let me get back to my husband and then ask *him* to let us go off by ourselves."

"I could have, but then people might speculate about why I was summoning you; being able to find you alone like this provided a better opportunity for discretion," she said mildly.

"So glad my needing to toss my cookies was so beneficial for you," I grumbled, without any real heat. I knew when I was beaten.

Arden sighed, moving closer. "Would you like to come with me someplace more comfortable, so the Hobs can clean up this bathroom before someone comes looking for us?"

I never really go anywhere alone, even when I think I am. May and Jasmine had left the house before Tybalt and I did, and were doubtless somewhere in the hall; Quentin was supposed to attend with his boyfriend, Dean Lorden. They weren't the only people who might get concerned if I vanished for too long, but they were the most likely to come looking if they couldn't find me where they thought I should be.

I sighed. "Is there any getting out of this conversation?"

"It may surprise you to hear this, but I wouldn't be sharing this special magic bathroom time with you if it weren't important."

"Fine," I said. "But you'd better have someone tell Tybalt where I am, before he comes looking for me."

"Nolan should be informing him as we speak. Unless you have any other objections?"

I shook my head.

Arden stepped briskly forward, grabbing my upper arm with one hand while she sketched a circle in the air with the other. A portal opened, accompanied by the scent of redwoods and blackberries, and she pulled me through into someplace else.

The portal closed behind us, and I looked quickly around. We were in a small lounge, although I doubted that it was one of the ones attached to the bathrooms: it was too nice for that, and one entire wall was made up of windows, looking out on a trellis dripping with blackberry canes that drooped under the weight of ripe dark purple fruit. A few of the windows were cracked open, allowing the berry-scented air to trickle inside.

A table had been set up at the center of the room, piled with plates of cucumber sandwiches, scones and cream, and blackberry tarts. My stomach growled as uncomplicated hunger washed through me, not a hint of nausea. I glanced to Arden. She nodded.

That was all the permission I needed. I moved toward the table, grabbing a small plate and beginning to fill it with a heavy hand. Arden had more or less admitted that this was an ambush, meaning this food wasn't intended to be shared with anyone I didn't decide to share it with. That was fine by me. If my Queen was going to ambush me, feeding me was really the least that she could do.

Arden waited until my plate was full before she made a small coughing noise to get my attention and said, "It's been hard to get a message to you these past few months. Tybalt and May have been running interference."

"Can you blame them for being a little overprotective?" I asked. "We're all still recovering from what we went through. Poor Rayseline is barely leaving her room."

"Why? I thought she spent the duration of Titania's enchantment in the former Blind Michael's lands, which should have been . . ."

"If you say 'restorative,' I'm going to have to throw a scone at you."

"I wasn't going to say 'restorative.' Just that for someone who has such a complicated relationship with most of Faerie, I can see where being removed from it entirely might be something of a relief, especially since her memories weren't tampered with the way the rest of ours were."

"You'd think. But Blind Michael's lands weren't exactly a nice vacation spot—and remember, we were all enchanted for *four months*."

"What does that have to do with—oh." Arden's eyes widened as the significance of those four months finally hit her.

I nodded. "Yeah. Oh."

Rayseline Torquill is the only daughter of my sworn liege lord, Sylvester Torquill of Shadowed Hills. She's also my cousin, technically, even though we aren't actually related. Family trees can get remarkably complicated in Faerie. When she was born, she was half Daoine Sidhe, and half Blodynbryd laced with Kitsune. Blodynbryd aren't mammals, and Raysel's body had been tearing itself apart from the moment she was conceived. That might have been difficult but survivable, had she not been abducted as a child and grown to adulthood in an enchanted prison, with only darkness and isolation as companions. The trauma of that time had led her to do some pretty awful things, and she'd been elf-shot, meaning she should have slept for a hundred years.

We have a cure for elf-shot now, created by the alchemist Walther Davies, and waking Raysel had become possible. But I had spoken to her while she was sleeping—it's a long story, just go with it for now—and she'd begged me to find a way to get her away from her parents. She needed to rest, recover, and decide how she was going to move forward from everything that had happened, everything that she'd done. She needed to figure out how to be herself, and not the pretty prisoner her mother wanted her to be.

That was something she had in common with me: my biological mother, Amandine, always had firm ideas about what she wanted her children to be, and wasn't inclined to change her ideas just because we turned out to be people rather than pretty dolls for perfect playtimes. But unlike me, Raysel's parents hadn't divorced, and she hadn't been given the opportunity to decide which of them she was going to belong with. She was trapped. I was supposed to be a hero, and so, when she'd finally been woken up, I'd done what I could to save her. I'd claimed offense against her for her crimes, backed by the Duchess Lorden and Tybalt, and I'd managed to get her released to my household for a year's time.

One year. Eight months of which were already gone, four stolen by Titania, the other four spent dealing with what had happened during that ordeal and trying to readjust to the real world.

"There has to be something we can do," said Arden.

"The laws of offense are pretty clear, and strictly time-based," I said grimly. "Four more months and she goes back to Shadowed Hills, whether she's ready or not."

"You know, I'm the Queen in the Mists, and her father is one of my vassals," she said. "I could order him to let her stay with you."

"Can you order her mother? Luna's a duchess by marriage. I'm not sure whether that means she's directly sworn to you."

"She isn't, but her title means I have some authority over her all the same." Arden frowned thoughtfully. "I'll figure out a way we can extend her time in your care. I know she needs your hospitality to help her healing. But Rayseline isn't why I wanted to speak with you. Please, have a seat."

I sank gratefully into one of the chairs next to the refreshment table, noting as I did that my plate was already half empty. I hadn't even noticed eating what I'd chosen. That said something about the care Arden had taken in selecting her high-calorie bribes: none of them were upsetting my newly finicky stomach in the slightest.

"So what *do* you want?" I asked, leaning over to take a few more slices of crostini smeared with a tart mushroom spread and sprinkled with watercress. According to the pregnancy books that May had been reading obsessively, I wasn't supposed to have half the things on this table, but that was in the mortal world. I had every faith that Arden wouldn't serve me anything that could hurt me. Maybe upset my stomach, sure, but hurt me? She would never knowingly do that.

"Titania's enchantment removed several of us from our positions," said Arden, sinking into another of the chairs and choosing a chicken salad sandwich for herself. "Muir Woods was entirely sealed off for the duration of the spell. No one could get in or out."

"Tybalt told me," I said, trying to figure out where she was going with this.

"Did Tybalt tell you that it didn't seal until she removed me from my position?"

I frowned. "Okay, so what?"

"No one was able to get into the knowe after it was sealed." Arden paused, pinching the bridge of her nose with one hand. "But there was a window when they could have, and well, someone did."

I sighed. "I'm guessing I'm not going to like whatever you're about to tell me next, so maybe you should just spit it out."

Arden dropped her hand. "The royal vaults have been raided. Almost everything of any value is missing. Including the hope chest."

THREE

I FROZE WITH A crostini half-raised to my mouth, then slowly lowered it back to my plate. "I'm going to need you to explain what you know to me," I said, voice low and as level as I could possibly make it. "Slowly. Assume the pregnancy has made my thoughts as clumsy as my feet, and use small words."

Arden nodded. "All right. Titania didn't get all the details of her spell right the first time. The Library confirms it, and the Gwragen agree. She was trying to craft her perfect Faerie, and every iteration was a little different than the ones before it. I can't remember any but the last of them—none of us can—but they were all recorded in the Library. And before she realized that getting me and Nolan out of the way required booting us down the coast to the Golden Shore, she tried a few other approaches."

"Meaning what?"

"Well, first, she tried to let me stay Queen while she wiped my mind and made me her obedient little toy. But that apparently destabilized everything, since there was no way to make me Queen *and* let me be the one to kill Oleander. Nolan killed her in that timeline, and it all fell apart when I tracked him down and had him arrested for breaking the Law. Apparently making me try my own brother for murder caused me to rebel and everything went to shit. We didn't even need to bother you to break her toys in that version." Arden smirked, looking obscurely pleased with herself. "So she reset it all, and the second time, she brought back her shitty false Queen, and had me serving as her Chatelaine while Nolan was her Seneschal. I think it was supposed to teach us our place or something. Instead, the false Queen got a little murdery and knocked down the whole house of cards. It wasn't pleasant, and I think I'm glad not to remember it.

The third go-round, we were on the Golden Shore, and Muir Woods was sealed."

"All right," I said, wondering just how much of the four months I remembered were as implanted as the rest of Titania's false memories. May and I had discussed the fact that Titania had revised her enchantment several times, something which most people would never have to know. I certainly hadn't expected it to have actual consequences.

"But the knowe was open and in use during her first two tries; that must have been when whoever it was cleared out the vaults," continued Arden. "They got away with essentially everything."

"Including the hope chest," I said. I was starting to think through the implications of that, and none of them were good.

Hope chests were created by Oberon as a means of turning the changeling children of his descendants fully fae; they were essentially an inanimate version of Amandine's descendant line, with the same magical ability to change the balance of fae blood. Anyone fae could use them—anyone. We even have stories of merlins successfully using hope chests, and merlins have so little fae blood that they age at almost the same rate as humans do. In the wrong hands, a hope chest could be used to change someone against their will, making permanent alterations to their selves. They could do that in the right hands, too, but at least when the hope chest was locked in Arden's vaults, I didn't have to worry that it was being used to torture people.

Faerie is a world made up of hundreds of different, loosely related species. Children of Oberon, Titania, and Maeve, united only in that we're all functionally immortal: if something doesn't come along to kill us, we'll live forever. But we're not human. That may be the most important thing about Faerie: none of its denizens are human.

And yet somehow, through some bizarre twist in an already bizarre biology, we can breed with them.

The offspring of fae-human unions are people like me, changelings, who straddle two worlds without fully belonging to either. If changelings have children with purebloaded fae, their children are still changelings, until enough generations have passed that they breed the mortality back out again. If they have children with humans, those children are still considered changelings for a generation or two. But anyone with a quarter fae blood or less is considered a thin-blooded changeling, and is less likely to be able to perceive or interact with Faerie.

If it stopped there, it might be okay. The pureblooded fae might not hate us as much, and while we'd probably still exist, we'd have an easier time blending into the glorious chaos that is Faerie. But thin-blooded changelings can live entirely in the mortal world, and many of them do, walking away from the rest of us in favor of living in a world that doesn't pity and belittle them for the circumstances of their birth. If they can adjust, they often do better than their more fae counterparts. They're usually a little prettier than the humans around them, a little more compelling, and they can turn that into a good life.

Their children will be more human still, and if *those* children have children, well.

That's when you get merlins. Merlins are still changelings, technically. But they have so little fae blood that they're really just long-lived humans in most ways that matter. Most . . . but not all. Because something about dumping that much humanity on top of a few drops of fae blood has a tendency to unlock power most fae can only dream about. Not most changelings: most *fae*. Merlins have the potential to inherit all the magical strength of their fae ancestors with few, if any, of the limitations. Iron doesn't burn them. Rowan doesn't bind them. And sunrise doesn't tear their towers down.

The first wars in Faerie were fought over the existence of merlins. Changelings were bad enough, but at least we mostly fit into the feudal structure our parents had so painstakingly created. Merlins, though . . . merlins *broke* things.

As a changeling, I could understand the impulse. Faerie is often cruel to her part-human children. We aren't equal to our fully fae relations, we can't hold lands or titles, and worst of all, we die. There's no point in investing in us as friends or allies, because we're always here to go. I tried not to think about that when I didn't have to. Since my return from the pond where Simon had left me, I'd made no new human friends, and very few changeling friends. One day, I was going to die, and everyone I loved was going to have to mourn for me.

A large part of Titania's enchantment had been geared toward making sure the changelings it ensnared knew our place, knew with absolute conviction that we were well below the station of even the lowliest pureblood. We were a servant class in her perfect world. It was a version of the existing system, taken to its absolute extreme, and given that, it wasn't hard to understand why merlins, when they realized how much power they could wield, might decide to burn a corrupt and broken system to the ground.

But when merlins started smashing things, people got hurt, and that mobilized the rest of Faerie against them. The first war against the merlins drew the Firstborn into the conflict. People died, both during the war and after, when the changelings who hadn't rebelled were executed to keep it from all happening again. Did things need to change? Absolutely. And at the same time, I had too many kids and teenagers to take care of to want to see Faerie caught up in another cycle of violence.

"So there's a hope chest somewhere out in the world, and we don't know who has it, or what they're going to do with it," I said. "They could be planning to charge changelings to turn them fully fae. Or to turn them fully human and eject them from Faerie."

"Or they could be planning to tinker with them until they get merlins," said Arden. "Either way, we need it back—and it's not the only thing we're missing. Various pieces of tableware—there are a *lot* of enchanted knives and hampers out there. The fount that treats iron poisoning. Arthur's Mantle, Clydno's Halter, lots of other things that probably shouldn't have been on this continent to begin with. Tudwal's Whetstone, and the scabbard that can transform any metal into iron."

I had never heard of half those things, and I wasn't sure I wanted to. The last item on the list caught my attention above the rest. "Why would something that makes *more* iron even exist?" I asked sourly.

"Gremlins are immune to iron. Coblynau are resistant, and like the challenge of embedding magic into metal. Maybe someone needed a weapon they could count on to protect their holdings. Or maybe they were a serial killer. I don't know *why* the thing exists—I don't even know its name. We found it in the treasury of the false

Queen's knowe, and we locked it away for safekeeping. We locked a lot of things away for safekeeping."

"Not so safe if they're out in the world now."

"No, I guess not." Arden sighed. "I'm sure you know what I'm about to ask."

"Can it wait another few weeks?" It had already waited for months. Maybe this was just a warning of what was to come.

Arden shook her head, looking genuinely miserable. "I wanted to wait, please believe me, I wanted to. And when it looked like this might just have been a thief taking advantage of a great opportunity, I was able to keep pushing back calling for you. I hoped we could reach your due date."

I frowned. "I need you to cut to the chase here."

"Whoever has these items has started either using them, selling them, or both. We don't know if they're all in the same hands. But we do know that someone is using the scabbard to make weapons for criminals," she said. "The first would-be Robin Hood with iron-tipped arrows could have been a fluke. The seventh? Not so much."

"Why haven't I heard anything about this?" I asked. "I know I've been out of the loop, but there still should have been something."

"We've been doing our best to keep it under wraps. People are already unsettled enough about what happened. Having the Queen of Faerie effectively declare war on your kingdom and way of life doesn't leave a lot of confidence in the way things are." Arden sighed. "My guards have been constantly busy, and my vassals are getting overstretched. Duke Torquill wasn't able to attend tonight because he needed to be home with his guards, protecting Shadowed Hills."

"And again, why haven't I heard *anything*? Not even from the Luidaeg."

"It was all little things until this last week, when everything seemed to start collapsing at once. We've had over a dozen muggings, all purebloods, which makes it seem like changelings taking revenge for the way they were treated during the enchantment—understandable, just making things worse right now. Which is probably why we had a Daoine Sidhe highwayman with an iron sword set up by a freeway onramp and start slashing tires on changeling cars. Just two nights ago Dame Altair was attacked on her way home from the Library. That was the first time one of my direct vassals was assaulted."

"Is she all right?"

"She is," said Arden. "One of her footmen, however, is not. The man was cut down with a blade of purest iron, and has stopped his dancing. He's the first so far, but if things continue as they have been, he's not going to be the last. We have to find the stolen artifacts, October. We have to find them soon. I would give you the time you need to birth the baby and recover if I had it to offer, but you're the only Hero I have right now, and I need you to do your duty by the kingdom."

"Can't you name another Hero?" I asked, half-desperately.

Arden sighed again, looking down at the plate in her hands. It was much fuller than mine. Apparently, she didn't have much of an appetite. "I would if I could. I've already had my people searching for what's been lost. Even Nolan's been going out in the city trying to find traces of the artifacts. I've amped up my guard, and set them patrolling as much as their numbers allow. Golden Shore has sent additional guards to bolster their ranks, and I've offered protection to my vassals. Nothing's worked. I really hate to do this while you're expecting, but I don't have a wide variety of heroes to choose from, and you're the best finder in the Kingdom."

"Not because I'm any good at it!" I protested. "I'm not a great detective. I'm just too stubborn to know when I'm past the point of giving up."

"That's good enough for me," she said. "Look, it's not that I want you to charge in knives out and defenses down. I just need you to ask a few questions, see if you can't get me a better shape for the situation. That's all. I'll do everything in my power to make sure you'll never be in danger."

"You just told me a man *died*." No matter how much I wanted to help—and I wanted to help—I would never intentionally do anything to endanger my child.

"Yes, but the woman he was protecting survived. My guards and your household will make sure you do the same."

I fixed her with an unhappy eye. "Leaving aside that the kind of people I'll need to talk to are not going to cooperate if I show up with a bunch of royal guards, my 'household' is never going to allow me to *do* this. Tybalt will disappear me into the Court of Cats until I go into labor if you try to push the issue."

"He'll want to. But he does respect hierarchies, and his subjects are in as much danger as mine if someone's running around out there making iron weapons at will. More, even. Iron pellets for a pellet gun? Iron wire for snares? He'll hate it, but he'll allow it. Believe me."

"I would love to, but I know my husband, and I need you to believe me when I say that you're incredibly mistaken." It didn't matter how much she wanted to be right, or how much I wanted to do as my liege asked—a response born of my upbringing in both this world and Titania's. Faerie is very feudal, and has never encouraged saying no to a queen. "Under normal circumstances, he'd let me do as my queen commanded, because he would expect nothing less from his own subjects. These aren't normal circumstances."

"And he's a King of Cats, under no obligation to comply with my orders," she said mildly. "But if I directly commanded you to do something and he chose to go against it, it could cause a diplomatic incident, which would either make me look weak or make him look unfit to rule. I'd really prefer to avoid that outcome."

A chill swept across my entire body at the thought of how bad things could actually get if my husband and my monarch went to war over whether or not I was allowed to do my job. Carefully, I set my plate aside and sat up straighter, folding my hands together in front of my belly. "I think we would all very much prefer to avoid that outcome, so *please* don't give me any direct orders."

"Why do you think I've been trying so hard to explain my side of things in a way that isn't going to enrage your husband?"

"Okay. So we're on the same page here. Please just let me go home and talk to him alone, in a place where he's not going to feel cornered, and I can call you tomorrow. If you push this the way you are, things are going to get more fucked up than you can possibly imagine, and no one is going to get what they want here. Like, I understand that you're in a difficult position, but it's important that you trust me on this. Please?"

Arden was silent for an uncomfortably long time. "Very well," she said at last. "I can do that. The rest of tonight will be taken up with court anyway, and it will go long—we have the false Queen in custody, and her punishment is one of the things we're going to be discussing."

"Can't you just decide what it's going to be? You're the Queen."

"I could, and technically, if I dug far enough back, I'm sure I could find a violation of the Law that would support my doing whatever I wanted to the woman. But I don't want to be like her. I don't want to be a despot. We don't exactly have a judicial system. Everyone here is either my direct vassal or someone who's been actively harmed by the false Queen. They all have the right to claim offense against her. The least I can do is hear them out before I decide on her sentence."

"That sounds . . . like opening the can of worms with a sledge-hammer and using a spatula to get them all off the floor," I said, dubiously.

"That isn't the only reason," said Arden. "And I know Faerie isn't a democracy. But none of us can claim offense against Titania for what she did to us, or have any recourse against her. The false Queen is a different story. I can not only punish her, I can show people I actually care about what she did by listening to them. Sometimes people just need you to listen to them."

Much as I didn't appreciate any of this, she wasn't wrong. It was almost ironic—I would have been a lot less tempted by her offer of heroism and something to do if the people who loved me had been listening when I told them I needed them to loosen their grip, just a little.

Arden rose. "Are you ready to return to court?"

I stood, more awkwardly than she had, and nodded. "I am."

She offered me her arm, and I took it as she sketched a circle in the air with her free hand, opening a portal that looked into the receiving hall. One of the many advantages of Tuatha teleportation: they can see where they're stepping. It helps them avoid collisions, and means they never appear inside things, which would be uncomfortable at best, fatal at worst.

She looked through, then stepped into the portal. I followed, feeling awkward and immense but doing my game best to match her steps. The quiet of the parlor was replaced by the cacophony of a court gearing up to enter session: while no one was shouting, that many bodies will generate their own symphony of rustles and mutterings, all independent of their intentions.

Arden released my hand and opened another portal, making the shorter hop to the dais where the thrones were. That was sensible. It put her into a position to start court, while leaving me no opportunity to argue further about what she wanted me to do. I remained where I was, waiting for the inevitable.

I didn't have to wait for very long. A hand caught my shoulder, turning me half around as Tybalt pulled me toward him. His cat-slit pupils were blown, turned so wide and dark that they consumed the bulk of his green-banded irises. He looked me up and down with a fierce intensity.

"Where have you been?" he asked, voice pitched low and words spat hastily. He sounded less angry than alarmed. "What happened?"

"I was with the queen," I said, barely resisting the urge to roll my shoulder to break his grasp. "Didn't Nolan tell you?"

He let go of me. "He did, but you were gone for so long that I was starting to get worried."

Meaning he'd been maybe five minutes from coming looking for me. "Arden needed to talk, so she took me to a private lounge to sit down for a minute and eat something. I guess we both lost track of time."

He gave me an anxious look. "But you're all right?"

"I am all right," I assured him.

"What did she want to speak with you about?"

"I'll tell you later," I said. There was no way I was going to start filling him in now, because I meant what I had said to Arden about not wanting to cause a diplomatic incident. Luckily I was saved from having to say anything further as Madden, Arden's Seneschal, stepped to the edge of the dais. Court was going to begin.

Tybalt moved to stand behind me and put his arms around me, positioning them so that they grazed the very top of my stomach. It was the closest and most comfortable way he could come to holding us both. I leaned my head back so that it rested briefly against his chest, then turned my attention to Madden.

Madden shifted his weight from one foot to the other, looking out across the throng that had collected in the hall. Knowing that this was going to be a formal court put the sheer number of people in attendance into a new light. Eira Rosynhwyr, masquerading as Countess Evening Winterrose, had put the false Queen on the throne after the death of Arden's father. Emboldened by the circumstances behind her coronation, the false Queen had never been very careful about who she pissed off. I guess when you're planning to be Queen forever, you stop really paying attention to that sort of thing. During her time on the throne, she had played favorites, enforced rules arbitrarily and with no eye to the future, and honestly, that had been her downfall. I hate to admit that I'm not constantly motivated by the need to make things better for everyone, but I'm not, and if she hadn't targeted me for her cruelties, I would never have gone looking for the true heir to the throne in the Mists.

In a way, Arden owed her position to me, and if she'd wanted it more, she would probably be in my debt. Instead, I get to be the woman who sort of saved and sort of ruined her life, and that was only one of the many reasons we were probably never going to be friends. I leaned back on my heels, resting against Tybalt, and waited for Madden to call the court to order.

The room quieted further. Madden kept standing there in silence, just watching us. He was a striking man in a room full of striking figures, with platinum hair streaked with veins of bloody red. He should have looked like a candy cane with that hair. Instead, he looked like someone who'd just been in a vicious fight, and deserved to be viewed with respect. He was tall and broad-chested, with a fighter's build, dressed in the livery of the Mists. Every scrap of his clothing had been impeccably tailored, lending him an air of luxury and wealth that was only partially true. When not serving in Arden's court, Madden worked at a coffee shop down on Valencia Street, happily making only slightly above minimum wage. He shared an apartment in the Castro with his human boyfriend, Charles, who thought the "queen" Madden served was the drag variety.

The places where Faerie and the human world collide are not always without humor.

Finally, Madden cleared his throat. The sound rolled through the hall, clearly enhanced by some sort of magical effect. I paused, realizing I didn't know all that much about the magic of the Cu Sidhe. They were shapeshifters, switching at will between canine and humanoid forms, and they had sharp senses of smell, but did they have other gifts? Maybe some sort of amplification to help their howls guide the hunts they used to accompany when we had access to the deeper realms of Faerie?

And it didn't matter now, because Madden was speaking. "Hi," he said, sounding only slightly uncomfortable. Behind him, Arden took her throne, and Nolan appeared, doing the same with his own. They were a matched pair, both with purple-black hair and mismatched eyes, one mercury, one pyrite. Looking at them side by side, and having seen the carvings depicting their parents in the main hall, it seemed incredible that the false Queen had ever been able to pursue her claim to the throne. They looked so much like each other, and like their father, that it should have been impossible.

"Welcome to the Court of Arden Windermere, rightful Queen in the Mists, protector of Muir Woods and guardian of the Pacific Coast," said Madden, gesturing vaguely to the thrones behind him. "I am Madden, Seneschal of the Court, and you have been summoned here tonight for the sentencing of the pretender to my liege's throne, the nameless woman known only as the false Queen of the Mists."

There was a commotion on the other side of the ballroom. I straightened, straining to see what was going on. A group of Arden's guards—and she hadn't been exaggerating about expanding her guard; I'd never seen half of these people before—were leading a tall, white-haired woman into the room, her wrists and ankles bound with carved rowan-wood shackles. More ropes of braided yarrow were wrapped around her body and even crowning her head. She looked furious, moon-mad eyes snapping fire as she looked around herself. Her mouth was a thin, hard line behind a muzzle of woven rowan wood, and her hands were clenched into claws that dangled uselessly against her thighs.

Her gown was simple, gray linen, tattered and stained, but I could tell, even from a distance, that she hadn't been exposed to iron. Arden was doing her duty as a queen. She was not embracing the false Queen's cruelty as a torturer.

Tybalt's arms tightened around me. "What is *she* doing here?" he hissed, voice low.

"As far as I know she's been here in the dungeons the whole time. It seems like a waste not to have had her play herself, but apparently Titania doesn't like to reward failure."

"So when I saw her, that was . . . ?"

"Karen Brown, under an illusion. Titania didn't let anything go to waste." The statement might seem strange, but there was an explanation: several other people I really hadn't wanted to deal with had been a part of the enchantment, despite the fact that they were dead or imprisoned or otherwise unavailable. Blind Michael, Devin, they were monsters from my past, and I should never have had cause to fear them again. Titania had accounted for that little hiccup by simply transforming people she didn't need for other purposes into them. Worse, she'd cast her own children, my honorary nieces and nephews, in those roles.

Tybalt snorted, breath warm against my ear. "Naturally. Why use the monster in your pocket when you could abuse a helpless child?"

"That's Titania for you." The guards were continuing to lead the false Queen across the room. She glanced back and forth as she walked, clearly searching for someone who would speak for her. She was met with cold looks and open hostility. Rather than wilting in on herself, she stood up straighter, squaring her shoulders and adopting an expression of frozen unconcern as she kept walking.

When the guards reached the center of the room they pushed her into place, centering her before the dais, and stepped away. This left her still-bound wrists dangling, pulled down by the weight of the rowan chains. I inhaled, and realized part of why they were making such a public spectacle of her condition:

There wasn't a speck of iron on her. Unhappy as she looked with her bonds, they were all good, honest wood and wards. She wasn't being poisoned by her own captivity. By forcing us to acknowledge that, Arden was reminding us all that the false Queen's cruelty had been a choice all along. There had never been any reason to do things the way she had.

"We have asked you your name, repeatedly, that we might seek your next of kin to see if anyone would speak for you," said Arden.

She sounded almost bored, and her voice carried the same way Madden's had. "We have asked, and you have refused to answer. So we call you now before us under the only name we have for you: false Queen of the Mists, you stand before us accused of high treason, kidnapping, unlawful imprisonment, willful distribution of goblin fruit to our changeling subjects, and the assault of the Crown Prince in the Mists. How do you plead?"

The false Queen drew herself up to her full height, which wasn't as great as it had been before I'd been forced to pull the Siren blood from her veins in order to protect my people. She was shorter and frailer now, a blend of Banshee and Sea Wight, and while she was still beautiful, she was less preternaturally compelling. I still felt a little bad for stealing her Siren heritage. I'd done it because I hadn't seen any other way out of the situation she'd had us trapped in: she'd been using her Siren powers to control and harm my allies, and had even forced May to slit her own throat. Leaving her with that power could have resulted in a whole bunch of death, and would definitely have resulted in even more injury. And all that felt like making excuses for having done something truly terrible to her. She may have been a throne-stealing, iron-waving bitch, but she'd still deserved to have her bloodlines left alone.

The silence stretched out. Arden frowned, leaning forward in her throne. "How do you plead?" she repeated.

The false Queen tilted her head gently to the side and smiled, a small, self-satisfied expression.

"Allow the record to show that the accused has pled guilty on all counts," said Arden, leaning back again. The false Queen's expression of satisfaction melted into shock, and then quickly onward to anger.

She took a step forward, wooden chains rattling. "Insolent child, how dare you place words upon my royal tongue?" she demanded. Her voice lacked the rolling acoustics of Arden's, but had a certain sonorous menace to it, like thunder rumbling in distant hills. That was the Banshee in her coming to the fore. Not for the first time, I wondered what could have led a Siren and a Banshee to lie down together. Faerie can make for some strange bedfellows, but we normally have limits.

"You have no royal tongue for us to place words upon," snapped

Arden. "Hold your silence rather than lie; if you lie, this will not go well for you."

"It was never going to go well for me," said the false Queen, voice shaking slightly. "You've already decided that. I had nothing to do with the death of your father, and he had no heirs declared or claimed. When my Lady of the Roses offered me everything I could ever have wanted in exchange for a few meaningless trinkets, I accepted, and she set the crown upon my brow, she settled the mantle over my shoulders. I am as royal as you are, for my title was granted to me by one among the First. Yours comes from what? The rutting of your royal father and your unwed mother? Which of us has the greater claim?"

"That would be the Windermeres," said a new voice, sounding almost bored. The false Queen whirled around so fast that she nearly toppled to the side. Behind her, the crowd that had been summoned to observe parted, revealing the Luidaeg.

She still looked like a human teenager, but she had changed her clothing rather dramatically. Her pigtails were tied off with strips of torn tartan, and she was dressed in a long linen tunic, belted at the waist, with a plaid sash in a tartan I'd never seen before draped over one shoulder and tied at the opposite hip. Her feet were bare, her sleeves long and loose and unornamented. She was watching the false Queen the way I'd seen Tybalt watch a pigeon when he was having a particularly lazy evening, her eyes half-lidded and filled with malicious curiosity.

The false Queen took a step backward, away from her. Not a bad idea when suddenly confronted with the sea witch.

The Luidaeg smiled, showing the full assortment of her teeth, and took a step forward. "When Denley and Nola Windermere came to the Mists, I was here to greet them. They were Scottish. They knew me when they saw me, and they bowed and made the proper obeisances. Nola brought me soda bread and scones. Denley asked me to tell him where he was forbidden to place his knowe. They were good neighbors. Polite. And so I gladly set a kingdom upon them. The first crown in the Mists passed from my hands to the brow of Denley Windermere, and from him to his son. The Windermeres are the only bloodline with claim over the throne in the Mists, because I gave them that claim, and I haven't seen fit to take it back yet."

"You didn't object to my coronation!" wailed the false Queen.

"No, I didn't," agreed the Luidaeg. "My sister desired it, and she was a daughter of Titania. It's often better to let them get their own way, at least in the short term. Arden was too young, Nolan younger still, and I had all faith that one of them would come to find me when they were ready to reclaim their family's throne. Silence is not endorsement. Sometimes it's just silence."

My gut twisted, and I scowled at the Luidaeg. She's been a friend for most of the time I've known her, but she has a tendency to think in almost geological terms. All the damage the false Queen had done had been in service of letting Evening get her own way. People *died* because of the false Queen's behavior! *I* nearly died! Tybalt *did* die—he just got better, a trick royal Cait Sidhe can occasionally pull off. Doesn't mean I liked it.

"The throne is *mine*," said the false Queen.

"No," said the Luidaeg. "The throne was always Arden's. You just borrowed it for a little while."

"Let the court record show that the Windermere line was *also* granted the throne by one among the First, and that as the Luidaeg is here with us tonight, her claim shall be deemed superior," said Arden, sounding faintly choked. "Should the Lady of Roses wish to appear before us, we would be willing to reopen this discussion."

"Be careful what you wish for," said the Luidaeg.

Arden paled, but didn't reply.

"Does the accused wish to say anything in her defense?" she asked, looking at the false Queen.

"Only that I acted to protect the Mists from hostile influences; I served as a Queen, even if you now deem me illegitimate, and I make no apologies for the things I did to preserve our way of life." The false Queen didn't waver as she addressed Arden, only tipped her chin defiantly upward and looked at her through thick white lashes, looking every inch the imperious monarch scolding a recalcitrant child.

Arden inhaled audibly through her nose, then exhaled again and turned to face the court. "If you wish to speak against the false Queen, please approach the dais."

FOUR

PEOPLE WANTED TO SPEAK against the false Queen. More people than I would have dreamed possible wanted to speak against her. I spotted Magdaleana, the Librarian from the Library of Stars, among the throng waiting to make their points, and a few courtiers in the livery of the Kingdom of Silences stood not far behind her. Of course the Kingdom of Silences had sent an envoy, after what she'd done to them—and to their ruling family.

The testimonies to her cruelty went on and on. People were treating this as an airing of their grievances, and boy did they have a lot of grievances to air. Tybalt's arms tightened around me.

"I will have to say my piece, after her transgressions against my Court and against you," he said. "But I think your presence speaks as much as any words you might offer."

"Why, Tybalt, are you saying that I can go sit down if I want to?"

He grimaced but nodded. "If your accounting of anything before her creation is needed, May can speak in your stead," he said. "I would much prefer you rest your feet and perhaps eat something, rather than standing here for what seems to be an unending recitation of wrongs."

"Sadly, Arden's a little busy right now," I said. "And I don't know how to get back to the parlor where we stopped off between the bathroom and here."

Tybalt looked around, arms still tight around me, and I heard his small, pleased exhale. "I adore you," he murmured, letting go of my waist and taking my hand, walking around to face me directly. "You are all my trials and all my treasure, wrapped into a single complicated mess."

I eyed him. "Meaning?"

"Meaning I have spotted someone to whom I can trust your safety, if only for a short time," he said. He let go of my hand, and I turned to follow the angle of his gaze. I nearly laughed when I saw who he was looking at.

Simon Torquill was making his way toward us.

Like his brother, my liege, he was redhaired and golden-eyed, with surprisingly freckle-free skin, given his fair complexion. His ears were sharply pointed, and his features were classically strong, as if he were a work of art that had decided to come to life and walk around for a while. Daoine Sidhe are like that. They specialize in the sort of beauty that can stop a heart, or lift it up, depending on how it's worn.

Simon wore his beauty like an apology, like he wasn't entirely sure where he'd found it, but would be more than happy to return it if given the opportunity. Clothing-wise, he was in breeches and a doublet over a white shirt, with the arms of Saltmist stitched above his heart. He smiled hesitantly when he saw me.

There was nothing hesitant about my answering smile. "Fa—Simon!" I exclaimed, starting toward him.

He startled but only slightly, catching himself before he could commit fully to the gesture. "October," he said, voice warm and reserved at the same time, like he was holding himself back.

Screw *that*. Simon and I had been building a relationship before Titania's enchantment, but he had still been the monster under my bed, even as I'd tried hard to forgive what he'd done. During the enchantment, he'd been my father, beloved and trusted above all others, even my mother. I had four months of earnest, unquestioning love between me and the pains of our past, and I wasn't in any hurry to let those go. It wasn't betraying my human father to let myself love Simon. It wasn't letting Titania win.

It was just letting us both be happy, and we deserved it.

I reached Simon and grabbed his hands in my own, holding them tightly so that he couldn't easily pull away. "Are you here to testify?"

"I am," he replied. "But as there's quite a queue in front of me, it may be some time before I can step forward. It's . . . very nice to see you, my dear." His eyes flicked to the undeniable swell of my midsection, tracing the shape of my stomach with a look.

I smiled indulgently when he looked up again. "You knew I was pregnant when you left for the Undersea," I said. "Is it really a surprise that I've gotten *more* pregnant while you were busy?"

"No," he admitted. "But you weren't showing before, and now, it seems as if you could give birth at any moment."

Tybalt shot us both an alarmed look.

I shook my head, still smiling. "Nope. Baby's still baking, and I'm not having any pains that might progress into labor. I can't be absolutely certain, but I think we're good for now."

"Do you have a birth plan?"

For a moment I paused, savoring the strangeness of being asked that question by Simon Torquill—a man I would have once sworn wanted to see me dead—in front of my husband, the King of Cats. Life has a way of doing whatever the hell it wants, and the rest of us just need to do our best to keep up. "I do," I said. "I'd rather not go into it while the Queen is trying to conduct the sentencing of her predecessor, but I have one."

"I was hoping you might be able to escort October to a lounge where she can rest her feet and have something small to eat," said Tybalt. "I'll come to join you as soon as I've given my testimony."

"I would be honored," said Simon, true gratitude shining in his eyes as he turned and offered me his arm. I took it, and he led me toward another of those open hallways, moving slow and careful in deference to my condition. Tybalt stayed behind, and it was jarring how strange that felt, to have him allow me to walk away without trying to follow.

"We haven't seen you in a while," I said, as we walked.

"No," he agreed. "I've been . . . otherwise occupied."

"Is something going on in the Undersea? August's been awfully quiet about how things are in Saltmist when she's come to visit, and we haven't seen you, Patrick, or Dianda on the surface since Titania's enchantment broke."

"Things are complicated at the moment," said Simon, as we passed from the noise of the main room to the quiet of the hall. "My lady wife dislikes allowing me to leave her sight, and I can't honestly blame her for that. If not for the importance of these proceedings, she would have asked that I remain at home with her and Patrick."

I blinked. "Simon, is Dianda holding you captive in the Undersea?"

He blinked back, then barked laughter, moving smoothly to open a door to another small parlor, near identical to the one where I'd met with Arden. The only difference: the table in this parlor was empty, which was to be expected, but still disappointing.

"No," he said, reassuringly. "Not in the slightest. There are simply matters which require my attention at home in Saltmist, and after a routine trip to land resulted in both my near death and a four-month entrapment at Titania's hands, well. She's a little anxious about my safety."

Put like that, I couldn't blame her, any more than I could blame Tybalt. Still, I had to make one more attempt. "She and Tybalt should form a club. And she lets August leave."

"August is her stepdaughter, not her husband," he said, shutting the door behind me. "August also has a stronger aversion to being kept than I do. She yearns for freedom. I want only for security and a place where I can be truly needed." He turned to re-take my arm and guide me to a chair. "Saltmist affords me both these things."

I looked into his face and saw no deception there, only the honest weariness of a man who'd gone too long looking for a place where he could feel safe and like his welcome wasn't somehow conditional. "Well, we've missed you," I said.

His smile was surprised and clearly involuntary. "Why, October, I have missed you too."

He picked up a small bell resting on the edge of the table and rang it, only once. The sound was sweet and clean, silver against glass. A bare second later the door opened, and several servers entered the room, setting plates and platters on the empty table before leaving again, none of them saying a word.

I looked at Simon. I looked at the food. "I think I love you," I informed him.

His smile turned wavery around the edges, like he was barely managing to hold it in place. "That's all I've ever wanted to hear from you," he said. And then he was crying, and I was crying, and while there are many things about pregnancy that were not my favorite, the hormonal crying was definitely right up there at the top of the list.

Fortunately, I got myself under control before Tybalt could come to join us and this could turn from a sweet family moment into the sort of terrible misunderstanding that got people hurt. I assembled myself a plate while Simon wiped his eyes, then sat back down and looked at him.

"Simon," I said. "When you worked for . . . who you used to work for, did she ever have you dealing in artifacts?"

"Oh, quite regularly," he replied. "She believed items of power crafted by fae hands belonged in *her* hands and hers alone, unless one of her favored pets needed them for one purpose or another. She gave a few to Oleander, a few to her puppet queen, but the bulk of what she sent me to retrieve she kept for herself, adding it to her hoard like a storybook dragon. I have little doubt that her riches exceeded those of the High Kingdoms."

I nodded slowly. "Did she keep those artifacts here in the Mists?"

"She did." He looked at me with grave eyes. "Most of what she'd swindled, stolen, and sought for was recovered after she fell and Arden rose, finding its way into the kingdom's coffers. Why do you ask me these things?"

"Because the royal vaults were looted during the enchantment, and now Queen Windermere needs me to find what's been lost. How dangerous are we talking here?"

Simon blinked, apparently taken aback. "I can't believe she would order you to endanger yourself or your child when you're so close to your time."

"She says she doesn't want me to do anything that would risk our safety, but I don't think my husband will see it that way." That was quite probably the understatement of the century. Tybalt was going to see this as a betrayal.

"You can't refuse her; she's your queen," said Simon, voice going hollow.

"I know," I said. "That's why I'm trying to learn more about what I might be walking into. And you know I'd refuse, queen or not, if I thought there was any real risk to the baby, right? But I'm not sure how to make Tybalt understand that I need to do this if there's any way I can manage it. Especially since . . ." I trailed off. It felt new and a little strange to be confiding in Simon, but a lifetime of memories told me it was the most natural thing in the world.

He watched me with loving, infinite patience, and I found myself continuing: "Even though I know it's going to make him unhappy, I'm looking forward to having something I can't dodge doing. I understand why Tybalt's so protective right now, but I'm about to start climbing the walls."

Simon chuckled. "Ah, yes. That's a familiar sentiment. Why—" He cut himself off.

I frowned, cocking my head and looking at him carefully. "Simon? What aren't you saying?"

"Nothing. Just remembering how when Amy was pregnant, she was unable to stomach the taste of blood," he said. "It turned her stomach dreadfully sour, and as a consequence, her magic was all but unavailable to her during that time."

"That must have been annoying for her."

"So much so that when August was born, she swore she would never carry another child. That was part of why you were such a surprise to me." Simon sipped his drink. "It seemed impossible that she would have voluntarily chosen another pregnancy."

"I'm not entirely sure why she did," I admitted. "She didn't want me to be part of Faerie, and she did her best to hide me until she'd turned me human enough to evade the Choice."

"Then I suppose I owe my brother a debt of gratitude for finding you before she could achieve her ends. I can no longer imagine a world without you in it." He looked at me, pride bright in his eyes. "You are one of the best things I've ever had a part in."

"I share the sentiment, sort of father-of-mine," I said, relaxing now that we were discussing subjects less fraught than my work for the queen. "You said things were complicated in Saltmist. How's Dianda doing? Are the three of you getting along all right?"

Simon's cheeks reddened. "We're getting along marvelously well. Their love brightens my nights and eases my days," he said. "Our love is not the complication. But Dianda isn't currently able to swim as far as she would like, and in the Undersea, that can be taken as a weakness. Patrick stays with her at all times, to be sure she doesn't injure herself in her eagerness to prove her continued fitness to rule. She'd prefer I do the same, but understands that unless I'm willing to surrender all ties to the land, when my queen calls, I answer."

I blinked. What could possibly cause one of the most terrifying women I knew—and I knew a lot of terrifying women—to be worried about admitting weakness?

I glanced down at my own swollen midsection, then gave Simon a sharp look. Pregnancies are rare in Faerie when compared to the mortal world, but they seem to come in clusters, like the world wants to be sure the children we sometimes get preoccupied with making will have people they can play with, peers they can grow up alongside, and not be dropped into a world of eternal adults so much older than they are that nothing will ever make sense.

"Simon," I asked, in a careful tone, "is Dianda pregnant?"

He looked at me, eyes wide and expression guilty.

I frowned. "Why didn't August tell us?"

"It's not common in the Undersea to tell people when you're expecting," he said. "To be pregnant is to be vulnerable, and more than that, not every pregnancy is successful. Do you really want to hand a weapon as well-honed as a parent's grief to your enemies, when you live surrounded by them on all sides?"

"But we're not enemies of Saltmist," I argued. "Dianda married you, and you're legally my father. In the mortal world, that would make her my stepmother. You normally tell your stepkids when you're making them a sibling."

"Even so, I'm expected to hold to the customs of the demesne where I'm dwelling," said Simon. "My lady is going to be quite cross with me when she finds out you know."

"I'm not going to take out a newspaper ad or anything like that."

Simon's lips quirked in a smile. "I think that's a bit old-fashioned, dear. Haven't you heard that print is dead?"

"You don't get to tell me what's old-fashioned, old man," I replied, and grinned. "Seriously, though. Congratulations. That baby is so lucky to have you as a father."

"I'm honored that you would think so, but . . ."

"No buts," I said, shaking my head. "You were never my father by blood, but you were still the best father I could have asked for, even in an enchantment that had been intended to make me miserable. Titania was trying to give you paradise, and what she gave you was the opportunity to raise your daughters with patience and love. That baby is going to get for real what I only got through magic, and I am so happy for them."

Simon looked like he was on the verge of breaking down in tears again, and moved to hug me even as a portal appeared in the air off to the side and Nolan Windermere stepped through, accompanied by the smell of redwood sap and new-picked blackberries. He barely spared me a nod before focusing on Simon.

"Consort Lorden, Arden needs you," he said.

"Pardon?" replied Simon, blinking away his tears.

"Arden? My older sister? Currently in charge of the kingdom we're all chilling in? She's ready for your oh-so-scintillating testimony against the imposter who stole our family's throne." He flashed me a quick, sidelong smile. "She's agreed to speak with October here at the end of the court period, when it can be as non-stressful as possible."

"I didn't ask for that," I objected.

"No, but your husband did, your squire did, and even your liege did," he said. "Duke Torquill appears to be trying to step up and do right by you, and if that takes the form of telling your queen to take it easy on you, I say it's time to allow it."

"Huh," I said, too astonished to say anything else.

Simon turned his face toward Nolan, his body still angled toward me in a clear effort to keep me at ease. "Is he here?" he asked.

I already knew from Arden that he wasn't, and yet I caught my breath, waiting for Nolan's answer. I hadn't realized until that moment just how much I wanted to see Sylvester, to smell the comforting dogwood and daffodil scent of his magic, to feel like I was finally able to go home again. Maybe Shadowed Hills was never going to be the home it had been when I was younger, but for part of me, it would always be the place where I'd been granted my knighthood, something that's supposed to be impossible for changelings. The place that had taken me in when no one thought I was worth taking.

Even if we were never close again the way we had once been, he would always be a part of who I was. He had been kind to me when no one else was or needed to be, and I'd always believed it was because he somehow saw something in me that no one else did, something worth caring about. The worst part of learning that Simon was legally my father had been discovering that I was technically Sylvester's niece, and he might have been kind to me for reasons I had no control over.

Nolan shook his head. "I'm sorry, but no," he said. "He sent word through one of his vassals. Sir Etienne?"

"I know him," said Simon.

"He was my knight," I said, surprising sorrow washing through me.

Finding out that Sylvester might have only cared about me at first because of his brother had been a shock that I was still recovering from. At least I knew Tybalt loved me because of who I was. There was no other explanation for him deciding to stick around, much less marry me. Not that marrying a walking disaster said much about his taste in women, but hey.

"Is Etienne still here?" I asked, when the silence got to be too heavy and needed to be set aside. "I haven't seen him since we all got back."

"I believe he's returned to Shadowed Hills, as he had no direct business here and was needed there," said Nolan. "If I see him, I'll tell him you asked after him? Perhaps he can be enticed to return."

"It's all right," I said. "I'm just glad to hear that Sylvester spoke for me."

Things had been strained enough between us for the last few years that I'd been half-expecting him to release my fealty. I wouldn't be an unsworn knight for long, even if that happened. Arden would be happy to take my oaths, and if for some reason I didn't want to pledge to her, January or Li Qin, in Tamed Lightning and Dreamer's Glass, respectively, would be thrilled to have the opportunity to claim me. I had choices now, options, and Sylvester wasn't the only game in town.

But he was finally making an effort after too long spent in silence, and if I could forgive him enough to stay with my original liege, that would absolutely be my preference.

Simon rose, shooting me an apologetic look. "Forgive me, my flower, but it seems my presence is required," he said. "I'll return if I can."

"I'll hold you to that," I said, as lightly as I could manage.

He smiled, and stepped through the portal Nolan had opened

in the air, vanishing as the portal closed and Nolan and I were left alone.

He looked around the small parlor, then walked over to take an éclair from the table. "Sorry to steal your dad," he said.

"He's not my dad," I protested. "Father, yes, but 'dad' is different, at least in the human world."

"Still."

"It's okay. We both knew we weren't coming to a social event before we got here." I watched Nolan carefully, trying to gauge his mood. He looked reasonably relaxed. "I was talking to your sister earlier."

"She told you about what's been going on?"

"She did, and I just wanted to ask you if things have really been that bad."

Nolan turned to look at me. "No, you don't. You want to ask me if she's telling you the truth."

I shrugged. "So what if I am? I'm almost at term here, Nolan. What could possibly be so important that it can't wait a few weeks to let me give birth? With the way I heal, you know I'll be ready for duty by the next morning."

"Look." He sighed heavily. "Some of the stuff that's been swiped, it's not great. We can't have it among the populace any longer than necessary, especially not right now."

"What's so important about right now?"

He pulled a face, moving to take Simon's deserted chair. "Based on what I know about you, time was you'd have been the one bringing this to our attention. Weren't you a part of the changeling underground?"

"Weren't you asleep back then?"

He smiled a little. "Touché. Anyway, what I hear says you used to run with the criminal element in this kingdom."

I bristled. "Those two statements aren't the same thing. Changelings aren't automatically criminals."

"No, but we force them to be, sometimes." He shrugged. "When you can't get a place without either prostrating yourself or violating your morals, it starts to look like your choices are servant or thief. And thief starts looking better and better. You can't ask people to eat shit and pretend it's gourmet cooking forever. You shouldn't even do it once."

I must have looked stunned, because he smiled again, shrugging this time.

"I was a labor man before the elf-shot. Luxury of knowing I would never be king: I had time to worry about what the rest of the kingdom looked like. Changelings weren't thriving even then, and everything I've heard says it's gotten worse. Am I wrong?"

"No," I admitted.

"Arden handles the throne, I try to keep an ear on what's happening that might affect the throne. And the changelings of the Mists are unhappy since the dissolution of Titania's world. I think they saw how bad things could get, and how much of that inequality was rooted in our current system."

"Huh," I said. "No one's said anything to me."

"You've been out of touch, Sir Daye. I doubt anyone was willing to take the risk in coming to you."

I nodded, thoughtfully. He looked at my expression, picked up an egg salad sandwich from the refreshment tray, and rose. "Looks like you've got a lot to think about. I hope you're thinking of how to help Ardy. She's going to need you."

A wave of his hand opened another portal in the air and he stepped through, leaving me alone.

I picked up my own sandwich and nibbled. If the changelings of the kingdom were that unhappy, some of the things Arden had said were missing became even more urgent. One advantage of mortal blood: we're better at handling iron without taking serious damage. And with the fount that dispensed a cure for iron poisoning in the mix, someone who really wanted to stick it to the man—or whatever—could be making iron weapons, swinging them around with abandon, and then healing themselves before permanent injury could set in.

While Arden was trying to be a good queen, she was going against decades of poor treatment, and Titania hadn't helped. Maybe she had even better reasons than I'd thought to be in a rush about this.

I continued nibbling at my sandwich, trying to eat as slowly as I could, so as not to upset my stomach, and was barely a quarter of the way through when someone rapped on the parlor door. I turned toward the sound, but kept chewing rather than saying anything.

The rapping was repeated with a little more confidence when no one yelled at the messenger. The knob turned, and the door creaked open enough to reveal Lowri, the Silene who was the current head of Arden's guard. We'd met while she was still in service to the false Queen, and we were friends, or something like it. She cocked her head to the side, goat-like ears brushing her shoulders.

"You all right in here, Toby?" she asked, stepping into the room.

"Yeah," I said.

"Great. You ready to come and face the court?"

I blinked. "I thought I was going to go last."

"This *is* going last," she said. "Everyone else has given their testimony. Given the false Queen's known and ongoing enmity toward you, and multiple abuses, everyone has agreed that you'll be the last one to speak before her sentencing. Will you come?"

"Of course." I set my plate aside and stood.

I must have looked uncomfortable, because Lowri offered me her arm. I took it gratefully, leaning on her to supplement my balance.

We left the parlor, Lowri folding one hand over mine and keeping me steady as I continued leaning on her arm and let her lead me back toward the main receiving room. She glanced at my swollen stomach, lifting an eyebrow, and asked, "Weren't you planning to wait a little while before you got—?"

"We were," I said. "To be honest, it takes most fae so long to get pregnant that we weren't taking any special precautions. Neither of us expected it to happen this quickly, if it happened at all."

"And what . . . *she* . . . did, it didn't hurt the baby?"

"Thank the root and the branch, no, it didn't," I said. "My own healing powers are strong enough that she couldn't get through them to do any real damage, not without trying so directly that she'd violate her own geas and pull Oberon's wrath down on her head." Not that Oberon had been all that wrath-y since I'd known him. He was mostly a silent, detached, somewhat sullen presence haunting the Luidaeg's apartment, refusing to get involved with the problems and politics around him.

Which would have been fine, if he hadn't been the father of us all and a technical living god. We needed his help, and he was happier sulking in the corners and watching his descendants without letting them know he was there.

It's probably not great for my health to be this pissed off at my own grandfather all the time, especially not when he has the kind of power that can turn continents inside-out, but I've never been all that focused on being good for my own health.

"Do you know yet whether it's a boy or a girl?"

"No," I said. "Honestly, I'm not even sure I won't be having a litter of kittens." I didn't think it was going to be kittens. The baby had been kicking up a storm for the last few weeks, and the impacts felt distinctly like human feet, no claws. One small thing to be thankful for.

"Don't you *want* to know?"

"Not really." I shrugged. "I just want a healthy kid. One I get to stay with, one that Tybalt gets to help me raise. Nothing else matters half as much as that. Plus I haven't been to see any human doctors, and Jin doesn't exactly have an ultrasound machine."

"I guess you can't really involve the humans, can you?" asked Lowri speculatively.

"How's that?"

"I mean, all the prenatal stuff is pretty noninvasive but there's always the risk that the baby wouldn't look human on their scans, and they'd expect you to come back when it was time for the birth, and it would be hard to explain the way you heal in the delivery room." Lowri shook her head. "Better to stick with the court healers and do it all in Faerie."

"Yeah," I said, mind suddenly filled with bloody images of delivery rooms destroyed by my panicking husband when he realized my rapid healing was going to betray the existence of Faerie. "Much better to do it that way."

Lowri laughed and kept leading me down the hall, toward the inevitable chaos of the court.

FIVE

"PLEASE STATE YOUR NAME and title for the official record."

"Sir October Christine Daye, Knight of Lost Words, sworn in service to Duke Sylvester Torquill of Shadowed Hills, wed to King Tybalt of the Court of Dreaming Cats." Technically that last part wasn't in my title, and could have been left out. With what felt like half the population of the Mists staring at me, it seemed like a good idea to remind anyone who might not have my best interests in mind that I had people who not only cared about me, but would have diplomatic immunity if they chose to break the Law.

Oberon's one and only Law: no one is allowed to kill purebloods, not even other purebloods, although changelings are fair game. Due to their somewhat animalistic nature and separate political structure, the Law has never fully applied to the Cait Sidhe. They can, and do, kill each other. Could they get away with killing other fae? I was pretty sure no one here wanted to give Tybalt a reason to find out.

Madden nodded, as did the short woman standing just behind him. She was no taller than an eight-year-old child, with straight brown hair that hung around her face like a curtain and yellow eyes that lacked whites, pupils, or irises: they were just yellow from side to side, nothing like a human's, but also nothing like a cat's.

She was new to Arden's court, and we had yet to be formally introduced—or introduced at all, with the way my family had been conspiring to keep me at home. Still, I'd heard rumors about how Arden had managed to entice an Adhene to join her service, and now here she was, a living lie detector at the formal court that would determine the false queen's sentence.

Not that we didn't all know the false queen was guilty. This was a performance as much as anything else, a way for people to understand just how much she had victimized our Kingdom and its citizens, and I couldn't blame Arden for putting it on. Even if I did need to pee.

Adhene always know when someone is lying. It makes them angry. And while they're small people, they have incredible physical strength. Pissing them off is a bad move.

Madden caught my eye. "And do you have a complaint against the unnamed woman who fraudulently occupied the throne in the Mists following the death of King Gilad Windermere?"

"If I say no, do I get to leave?"

He shook his head. "No. If you say no, I look really disappointed and ask again."

A titter ran through the crowd. It wasn't *that* funny, but they'd been here for a while, and they were looking for anything to break the boredom. I sighed. "Then yes, I have a complaint against her. Several."

"Please detail your complaints. If you state anything untrue, Bahey will interrupt, and I will ask you to reconsider."

Bahey must have been the Adhene. I swallowed the urge to sigh again, and nodded instead. "Understood."

"You may begin."

Madden stepped back, gesturing for me to face Arden. I turned toward the throne, trying not to look at the crowd to either side. It was filled with familiar faces, many of them more than a little bit distracting. The Luidaeg wasn't there. Too bad. If anyone could have demanded I get dismissed on the grounds of "nothing new to say, don't torture the pregnant lady," it was her.

"The false queen's dislike of me began to manifest after I was knighted," I said. "She granted permission for my training, but I guess she thought I'd give up, because she seemed to hold it against me when I went through with it. Any time I had to interact with her she was unpleasant, verging on hostile. She never outright banned me from her court, but she made it quite clear that I was unwelcome among my betters, and that she would prefer it if I kept my distance. After my time in the pond—"

Despite my attempts to tune out the crowd, I saw Simon wince out of the corner of my eye. I understood and shared his discomfort.

The past was the past, but we both hated to be reminded of what he'd done to me, even knowing that it had been done to save my life. I would never have survived Evening's wrath if he'd refused to follow her orders. Neither would he. So instead he'd done his best to seem like her obedient little minion while also letting his daughter live.

It had been a narrow road to walk, and it wasn't one I envied him.

"—when I came back, she started tormenting me more actively," I continued, trying to keep my eyes fixed on Arden. It was better than watching Bahey, who would lose her temper if I dared to say anything that wasn't completely true. No pressure or anything.

Not that I wanted to lie to Arden. I may not be a major fan of the feudal system the way it works in Faerie, but even though I wasn't thrilled about her forcing me back to work, she's not bad as monarchs go. She doesn't go around treating her subjects like trash just because she can, she doesn't belittle changelings or allow goblin fruit to proliferate inside her territory. She could be a lot worse, and that's a relief, since it's largely my fault that she ended up in charge.

"Can you cite examples?" she asked.

"Any time I had to appear before her, she would transform my clothing into something she liked better, even if I'd made an effort to dress appropriately for court. Not illusions, either. Full-on transformations, that I didn't have the capacity to undo. I lost some of my favorite pairs of jeans that way."

Another titter swept through the crowd, and the hint of a smile tugged at the corners of Arden's mouth. "Can you cite a less petty example?"

"I can." I took a deep breath. "She granted me the title of Countess of Goldengreen for my part in the death of Blind Michael, as a part of an intentional bid to strip me from the service of Duke Sylvester Torquill. As a countess of her territories, my fealty shifted to her."

"Most people would disagree with the idea that being ennobled is a torment."

"It is when it's intended to make you vulnerable to attack. She shifted my fealty from Duke Torquill to herself to remove the protections he could offer me, and proceeded to charge me with a violation of Oberon's Law. With no liege to speak for me, I was sentenced to death. She commanded I be taken to the Iron Tree, where I would be bound, blinded, and burned. Prior to my execution, I was locked in an iron-lined cell, and nearly succumbed to the poison before I was rescued by allies who shall go unnamed."

"You were pardoned for the slaying of Blind Michael by High King Sollys, were you not?"

"Yes, but I was imprisoned before the pardon was received. It barely arrived in time to prevent my execution."

Arden hesitated. When she spoke again, she looked as if her own words pained her. "I cannot view a queen, even a pretender, wishing to avoid her subjects murdering one another as an unnecessary cruelty."

"We're allowed to kill in times of declared war," I said. "Blind Michael declared war on the Court of Cats by stealing their children."

"More than just the Court of Cats," drawled the Luidaeg from behind me. I managed, barely, not to turn and look for her in the crowd. "Dozens of people had declared war on my brother over the years. If she'd been looking to keep order in her kingdom, she should either have acknowledged that and left October alone, or accused me of the same thing. After all, I'm the one who gave my niece the tools she needed to kill him. Who's on trial here, anyway? October has been pardoned. The matter is sealed and sorted."

"My apologies, lady sea witch," said Arden. "I am not attempting to accuse Sir Daye of anything, only to understand the ways in which the pretender's overreach harmed a hero of our realm."

"Attempt harder," said the Luidaeg, voice taking on a slight lisp that I knew meant her teeth were no longer strictly human in shape or number.

Arden, looking flustered, returned her attention to me. "Can you cite any other clear incidents?"

"She ordered me exiled from the kingdom for objecting to the presence of goblin fruit in the streets, which led to the deaths of uncounted changelings. She claimed we were her subjects. We deserved better from someone who would call herself our monarch, and she left us to waste away and die. That was when I had to go looking for you. I'd have been thrown out of my home if we hadn't been able to restore the true queen to her throne."

"I do remember that part," said Arden, with a flicker of humor.

"And even stripping her throne from her wasn't enough to make her stop," I continued. "She moved up the coast to the Kingdom of Silences, and when I was sent there on a diplomatic mission, manipulated the puppet king *she* had helped to install into violating the terms of hospitality and taking me captive. She was intending to see me broken and butchered, and said as much in my hearing. I was rescued by my allies, and she was elf-shot, only to be awakened by one of her few remaining allies. Where *is* Dugan, anyway?" The last time I'd seen him, he had been injured and permanently silenced by his attempt to take his own life: the iron knife he'd used to open his throat might not have killed him, but it had damaged his vocal cords so badly that the healers believed he was never going to speak again.

Good. It wasn't like he'd ever had anything useful to say. Still, as far as I knew, he'd been in Arden's custody alongside his mistress when the enchantment had come down and trapped us all.

Arden frowned, a small line appearing between her brows. "Master Harrow was missing from his cell when the real world returned. He has yet to be apprehended."

I managed, barely, to resist the urge to clutch my stomach defensively. "You could have mentioned that sooner."

"It didn't seem relevant."

It was an effort not to snap that she didn't get to decide what was and wasn't relevant to me and the safety of my family. I made it. No matter how impulsive I can sometimes be, I try not to yell at sitting monarchs in the middle of formal court. It's not a great way to stay welcome in their halls, and right now, having the protection of the queen seemed like a good idea.

"The false queen," I said, recovering my poise and resuming my recitation. "After Dugan woke his liege, he helped her abduct my daughter, Gillian Marks-Daye, to use as leverage against me. She was . . . she was human at the time." I swallowed back the wave of grief and guilt that always threatened to overwhelm me when I thought about Gillian's humanity. She had chosen it, she had never wanted to lose it, and now she was more fae than I was. "In the process of getting her back, she was elf-shot. No. That makes it sound too passive, like it just happened. That b—woman we're here to discuss did it on purpose. She stabbed my daughter, my *human* daughter, with an arrow that had been dipped in elf-shot."

"We are informed that the Firstborn of your line was able to save you from elf-shot when you were more human than you stand before us now."

"She was, by changing the balance of my blood. The cost of a cure was a portion of my humanity. I was able to do the same for Gillian the first time she was elf-shot. She was born a thin-blooded changeling, mostly human but partially Dóchas Sidhe. By transforming her into a full human, I was able to burn the poison from her veins. When the false queen assaulted Gillian for the second time, she had nothing left to lose. She had nothing of Faerie left to take away."

I managed to say all that without breaking down. Not a big accomplishment most of the time, maybe, but my feet ached and my baby was kicking and my hormones were completely out of control. The urge to cover my face and cry was stronger than I wanted to admit.

"So when the pretender stabbed your child, she intended that the girl should die?"

"Yes and no," I said. Bahey made a sour face, but didn't object. "The false queen was acting under the assumption that I had the ability to restore things after they'd been removed from someone else's blood. She had been part Siren when she held Your Majesty's throne, compelling and cruel. I was forced to remove her Siren heritage in order to save myself and my allies."

"I was there," said Arden, with a slight nod. "She believed you could give it back?"

"She did, but I couldn't. That's not something I'm capable of." Idly, I wondered whether this line of questioning was intended to make me more of an effective weapon for her kingdom. Anyone who was here now knew for sure that I couldn't give back what I'd taken—verified by the silence of an Adhene. It was a limitation, but a terrifying one.

"As the child was human when this cruelty was committed, the pretender can't be accused of the attempted murder of your daughter, but she still transgressed against you by involving a human to whom you were closely bonded in the affairs of Faerie. The girl survived?"

"The girl has a name," I said, tersely. "Please use it."

"Gillian, then," said Arden. "She lived?"

"The sea witch intervened, binding her to a Selkie skin to save her life," I said. "She has since been further bound at the Convocation of Consequences. She's fully Roane now."

"We cannot apply a retroactive accusation of violating the Law to the pretender's charges," said Arden, with genuine regret. "But your words are heard and held, and will be measured in the setting of her sentence."

"That's all I can ask," I said, and bowed as deeply as my current condition would allow. I teetered when I straightened, feeling my balance shift out of true, and had a moment to consider what it would be like to fall when this far along before there were hands at my shoulder and the small of my back, catching me and pushing me back into an upright position.

"My apologies for the uninvited appearance, Queen Windermere," said Tybalt, with all the politeness his voice could hold. "I intended no offense."

"None is taken," said Arden, and smiled. "You have leave to escort your wife to a place where she can sit and rest. Court is not yet dismissed, but her part in it is finished."

"Your Majesty is kind," said Tybalt, hand tightening on my shoulder. Lips close to my ear, he murmured, "Come with me."

I let him guide me away and down the dais steps. The crowd parted before us, allowing us to pass. I waited until we were approaching the edge of the room, where ranks of chairs lined the walls for those in need, before I turned to face him and scowled.

"That was a little high-handed of you, don't you think?" I asked.

"Would you have preferred I let you fall?"

"I would have *preferred* you let me decide when I was ready to leave."

His expression softened. "Oh, little fish. I'm not trying to take your choices away, only to keep you safe as I can while the need is so very dire. This time is near to done, and soon enough we'll both have better things to worry about."

That was true. I exhaled a laugh, irritation temporarily fading. "Okay, fair," I said. "Just maybe try not to hover so much that you always know when I'm about to trip?"

"I will promise to hover only so much as my nature must demand," he said.

I sat and he sat beside me, angling his body to let me lean against him. He smelled of the comforting musk and pennyroyal signature of his magic. Given his tendency to shift between feline and bipedal forms throughout the night, moving effortlessly from one to the other, he tended to have a stronger scent of magic about him than most of the people I knew.

Magic is the birthright of the fae. It lives in the blood, and it manifests differently in every descendant line. Even the most closely related lines will have distinct abilities. Even beyond that, all fae have a magical signature, and most are olfactory. I can literally smell people's bloodlines and magical abilities when I get close to them. The more magic someone uses, the stronger the scent will be, even if they're not actively casting spells.

As a shapeshifter, Tybalt almost always smelled fairly strongly of his own magic. Even if he'd been in one form for an extended period of time, there was a baseline I could use to identify him. Since every magical signature is different, I'm pretty hard to fool with an impersonator, as long as I knew the person before they were replaced.

"Where did Simon take you?" Tybalt asked, as Arden and her advisors stood on the dais and spoke in low, tight voices. Doing this where the court could watch was theater, but it was effective theater: fae, especially noble fae, tend to get recalcitrant and argumentative when they think they're being deceived. This way, none of them could say the result of today's sentencing had been a foregone conclusion.

"Little parlor where people brought me sandwiches."

"Did you eat them?"

"I did," I affirmed. Even if pregnancy hadn't made me hungry all the time, it would have made me a lot more inclined to slow down and eat, because when I didn't, I started worrying about the baby. "I had a nice talk with Simon, too. Which reminds me—when we get home, we need to discuss something the Luidaeg said to me while you were at the Court of Cats."

"Oh?" he asked, with sudden wariness.

I didn't mention the other thing we had to talk about tonight.

Any anxiety he had over what the Luidaeg was offering would pale in comparison to his reaction to Arden actively trying to put me back to work. "Yeah. We'll talk about it when we get home. We *need* to talk about it when we get home, but it's not immediately pressing, and it's nothing that puts me, you, or the baby in danger."

"Noted," he said, the wariness not leaving his voice.

I sneezed. He sat up straight, looking concerned. I knew he wasn't going to be onboard with Arden's plan for me to get out there and start looking for her missing things. And while I wasn't sure he could stop me, I wouldn't put it past him to follow me the whole time, making it impossible for me to do my job.

"October?" he asked, wariness replaced by anxiety.

"Don't worry, I'm not coming down with anything. I'm not sure I *can* catch a cold these days. It's just the room. Even with the windows open, there's so much magic that it's like trying to breathe next to a department store perfume counter. I wasn't in here long enough before for it to really start getting oppressive." That, and the smell of hors d'oeuvres had flattened me before the magic could start bothering me. "Not everything is an attack. We need to work on getting you to relax before the baby comes."

Tybalt looked chagrined, but I never got to hear what he was going to say next, because the room went silent as if on cue. I lifted my head. On the dais, Arden had finished her deliberations and turned back to face the crowd. She raised her hands in an unnecessary request for silence. No one said a word. It was so quiet I could hear the bubbles popping in glasses of sparkling wine, and the faint buzzing hum of the pixies' wings.

"People in the Mists," she said. "I am Arden Windermere, recognized by High King Sollys as your rightful Queen and regent. It is my duty and honor to protect you. We have gathered on this night to discuss the sentencing of the woman who stole my throne and misled you all for a hundred years. We have established these facts:

"That she lied, stole, and manipulated her way to the throne, but was careful and clever in so doing. She did things any among us must view as unconscionable, unforgivable transgressions against hospitality and custom, but she never broke the Law with her own hands. The only full fae to meet their ends at her order were those who had been convicted of violations of the Law in their own right. At times she manipulated the evidence against them to achieve those convictions, but that still cannot be considered murder, although it should be.

"In her efforts to mold the kingdom into her image of Faerie, she persecuted and mistreated our changeling citizens, encouraging the puppet King of Silences to do the same. We cannot make clear count of the deaths caused by her allowing goblin fruit to flow freely through our streets. There is no proper restitution, only the hope that we can be better as we move forward with our lives, those of us still fortunate enough to have them."

Arden stopped there, taking a deep breath. "I was here in the Mists, hiding from my father's throne, hiding from what I had lost, while she did these things to my people. She is my shame and my shadow, and I apologize to each of you, unequivocally, for allowing her to take such deep root in our shared soil. I should have been here. I was not."

Now there was a sound: a sharp intake of breath from at least half the room. I sneezed again, grateful for the gasping to cover the sound. Tybalt shot me another look, less concerned than confused, as I rubbed my nose.

Sorry, I mouthed. We turned our attention back to Arden. A queen apologizing to her kingdom was unusual enough that no one had spoken after that initial gasp. They were all just staring at her, waiting to hear what she was going to say next. We were drifting into uncharted waters here. I couldn't blame them for being wary. Me, I just wished I had some popcorn.

"For her crimes, we have decided the pretender will be elf-shot a third time," she continued, her mouth pulled downward in a moue of disappointment, like she couldn't believe the woman had the audacity to keep waking up when we clearly didn't want her to. "This time, rather than holding her here, where it's clear we cannot keep her so subdued, she will be given into the custody of the sea witch, who will transport her to a place her allies cannot reach nor interfere with. She will sleep a full hundred years, and when she awakens, she will be elf-shot again, to sleep another century away. At the end of that time, when her offense is not so fresh and bright in memory, we will discuss further discipline, should her surviving victims feel it necessary."

"We're just going to elf-shoot her and put her in storage so we can forget about her" felt anticlimactic, but that was no less than I'd expected. Pureblooded fae generally think in decades, not days. For Arden, this was a good punishment. To me, it was a slap on the wrist. No therapy, no time working to change or make up for her behavior, just sleep. So much sleep.

I sneezed again. This time, Arden noticed. She glanced in my direction and frowned. "As her trial and sentencing were the only matters of direct import to be discussed tonight, those of you who have other obligations are free to go. Bring forth the prisoner!"

Nolan rose from his throne, hand sketching a circle in the air. The smell of sap and blackberries cut through the rest of the magic hanging around us as he stepped through the portal. He reappeared next to the furiously scowling figure of the false Queen, grabbing her by her arm and pulling her toward the dais. Then he stopped, a perplexed expression crossing his face.

"Sir Daye?" he called, voice gone tight with the effort to keep it level. "May I request your momentary attendance?"

I blinked, then began to rise, moving with the speed and grace which had become my hallmark since entering the third trimester of my pregnancy—which was to say, absolutely none to speak of. Tybalt offered his arm and I took it gladly, letting him pull me to my feet. He folded his hand meaningfully over mine, and I sighed.

"Right," I said, keeping my hands where they were rather than pulling away. He led me toward Nolan and the false Queen.

The whole room was staring at us now, and the feeling of that many eyes on me was less unsettling than I would have wanted it to be. I never intended to go into a profession where public speaking would be required. Sadly, heroes don't always get a choice.

"What's up?" I asked, once we were close enough that I wouldn't need to raise my voice.

"I know this is an odd request, but can you please sniff the prisoner?"

Right away, I caught what he was asking of me. "I can, but it won't tell me anything," I cautioned. "If you're asking me to check her magic, she hasn't been casting spells, and there's so much ambient magic in the air already that just sniffing her isn't going to do me any good."

"Obviously we can't allow her to begin casting spells," he said, sounding affronted.

"No, we can't," I agreed. Turning to Tybalt, I asked, "Can I borrow a claw?"

The false Queen's eyes widened, and for the first time, she began struggling against Nolan's grasp. Tybalt removed one hand from my arm, expression grave, and extended his index finger's claw.

Carefully—normal people don't heal the way I do—I guided his hand to the false Queen's arm. "Gentle," I said.

"Always," he replied, and drew his claw along the inside of her arm until it broke the skin and a few bright beads of blood came to the surface.

"Sorry for the intrusion," I said, with brittle chipperness. I lifted her arm to my mouth.

Her blood was sweet and tart and tasted of black clove and panther lilies. I paused mid-swallow, trying to make sense of the flavor. I'd encountered this before, I knew I had, but not—

Not in the false Queen's halls. As if to reinforce the point, memory blossomed behind my eyes as I saw a woman screaming and running away from an unfamiliar Redcap. He swung a sword in her direction. One of her most trusted guards was on the ground, blood dripping from a wound that had blackened around the edges, as if he had been badly burned. She wanted to go back for him. She wanted to save him. She knew she couldn't, and so she ran.

I dropped her arm and swallowed again, this time trying to get the taste of blood out of my mouth. "This isn't the pretender Queen," I said. "This is Dame Eloise Altair. Where is the prisoner?"

A panicky rumble ran through the crowd around us, causing both Nolan and Tybalt to step closer to me, like they were ready to pull me out of harm's way if necessary. I didn't bristle, but returned my attention to the disguised Dame Altair. If I squinted, I could see the haze of illusion around her like a web of threads spun from salt. They were thinner than cobwebs or silk, thin as cotton candy made into an enveloping cocoon. It would be so easy to start snapping them, and the taste of her blood still lingered on the back of my tongue like the memory it had given me . . .

My strength is in blood, whether it's mine or someone else's. I was strictly forbidden to bleed myself when not strictly necessary—Jin had strong feelings about the use of blood magic during pregnancy, and if I was going to insist on doing it, she wanted me using someone *else's* blood whenever possible—but even a few drops were enough to give me the power I needed to do something like reach out and snap a few thin, trailing threads.

If the threads had been literal, breaking a few wouldn't have been enough to tear apart the whole cocoon. If the illusion had been woven by someone stronger, or with more experience, it wouldn't have been that easy to break them. As it was, the threads broke easily, and when they did, they began to unspool, the entire spell collapsing into a cloying mixture of cinnamon and green cardamom. I sneezed.

The illusion shattered, revealing a furious Dame Altair wearing the false Queen's rowan muzzle and shackles. Nolan blanched and hurried to unfasten them, removing the muzzle first. That may have been a mistake, as she immediately began to swear with a degree of creative enthusiasm that would have been impressive as hell, had we not been standing ten feet away from the queen.

"I didn't take enough blood to get any real answers, but I didn't pick up on anything that implied guilt," I said, raising my voice enough to be heard above the swearing. This came with the convenient advantage of letting the people directly around us hear me, meaning the information would spread quickly through the hall. "I think she was a victim here."

"Damn *right* I was a victim," snapped Dame Altair, glaring at me. "I should have known better when I saw that slimy, conniving asshole on my doorstep, but oh no, everyone says he's changed, I'm sure everything is going to be just fine."

Nolan finished removing the manacles from her wrists.

"I'm sorry," I said. "Who do you mean?"

Dame Altair raised one hand and pointed directly at Simon.

Oak and ash, not this again.

SIX

ONCE AGAIN, THE ROOM erupted with whispers as people realized who Dame Altair was pointing at. The false Queen was missing: they had expected to see justice done, if a nap can be called justice, and now they were denied. They wanted their metaphorical pound of flesh, and if it had to come from Simon, that was fine by them. He'd been a villain in the eyes of the Mists too long for anyone to be completely comfortable with him now that he was supposedly redeemed.

I stumbled backward, away from Dame Altair, trying to position myself between her accusing finger and Simon. I glanced over my shoulder at him. He had gone so pale his scarce freckles stood out against his skin like ink blotches on a sheet of parchment. He was shaking. I wasn't too happy to see Dame Altair myself, considering our last encounter had been in Titania's Faerie, where she'd tried to kill me, but I wasn't the target of her malice this time.

Turning my attention back to Dame Altair, I said, "You must be mistaken. The spell I unwound from you didn't match his magic. Cinnamon and cardamom are not the same as mulled cider, even if they're both components."

"I smelled cinnamon," she shot back. "I've mulled my own wine. I know the Baron Torquill's magic."

"There's no such man as the Baron Torquill, not any longer," said the Luidaeg, strolling toward us with a liquid predator's grace that would have seemed almost feline if not for the man I'd married. "Are you truly claiming the ducal consort of Saltmist traveled to the surface solely to enchant you?"

I'll give Dame Altair this: she looked the sea witch in the eyes and she didn't flinch. "I know what I saw," she said.

"An illusionist came to your door and bound you in chains of image and idea, tight enough that until you were unbound, you even stood like the woman you seemed to be, and you can't accept that the illusionist may also have worn an illusion?" The Luidaeg looked past Dame Altair to Arden. "She can't prove she saw whatever she says she saw, and to raise hand against Consort Lorden is to risk the wrath of the Undersea. You know this."

Arden blanched but didn't flinch away. "To allow the citizens of the Undersea to transgress against the citizens of the Mists without recourse is to declare ourselves a vassal state and put my people at the mercy of the waters. You know this as well."

The Luidaeg nodded.

I frowned, looking between the two of them. "So what? The false Queen is missing, and we're just going to stand here talking about what we already know instead of trying to figure out where she is? I'm not always the best detective around, but I know enough to say this seems like a really bad way to actually, you know, *find her.*"

"I know what I saw, and what I smelled," snapped Dame Altair. "I am telling you that Simon Torquill attacked me, and intended me to take the punishment intended for his mistress."

"She was never his mistress," I countered. "He served the Rose of Winter, and has been duly punished for his actions in her name, but he never served her puppet queen." Oh, I hoped I was right about that. Not because serving the false Queen would have somehow been worse than serving Evening, who was a literal nightmare wrapped in a glossy candy shell, but because I didn't want to make things worse by lying. Especially not in front of an Adhene.

Bahey was clutching the side of her head, brow furrowed. Arden looked to her.

"What say you, Lie-Catcher?" Her tone was stiff, her phrasing intentionally archaic. We were trending into areas of court politics and tradition that I wasn't entirely familiar with, and definitely didn't deal with on a regular basis.

Bahey lowered her hand, wincing as she straightened and focused herself on Arden. "None of the speakers have uttered anything untrue, Your Highness," she said. "They speak the truth as they know and understand it."

"That is the burden of the Adhene," said the Luidaeg, all but glaring at the smaller woman. "They know a lie when they hear it, but if the liar believes themself to be telling the truth, there is no lie to hear. An assumed truth is as valid as a true one."

"Okay, you're talking in a circle," I said. "I don't think we need two people in this argument with headaches." The eyes of the court were an almost physical weight against the back of my neck, pressing down on me like they were trying to bear me to the floor. I adjusted my stance, wishing I could lock my knees the way I would if I weren't so damned pregnant. I was excited to meet the child Tybalt and I had created together, but I was also so accustomed to my body taking whatever abuse I needed it to absorb that dealing with my own limitations was becoming more and more difficult.

Two more weeks. That was all I had to endure. Two more weeks and keeping my legal father out of prison, which just meant it would be a more normal two weeks than the last eight and a half months had managed to be.

Bahey looked at me with pained amusement. "Truth," she said. She had a pleasant voice, with a faint Midwestern accent that made me wonder what had brought her to the Mists in the first place. Pureblood fae, especially the useful ones, don't tend to move unless they haven't got a choice in the matter. They're insufficiently fond of change.

Not that I'm a huge fan of change either, but at least being part human has left me capable of adapting quickly when I have to. It's a surprisingly underrated skill, even in the human world. In Faerie, it's virtually unheard of.

"How about this," I said, holding up my hands like I was trying to ward off a pack of wolves. From the way Dame Altair was glaring at me, that wasn't too far off from the situation. "I'll ask Simon for a few drops of his blood, and I'll read the truth in what he remembers."

Tybalt hissed through his teeth, unhappy about me doing blood magic twice in one day. His caution was appreciated but unnecessary. There was no way any child of mine wouldn't be able to handle some light blood-work performed in their proximity, and I would have been able to feel it if anything had gone wrong.

"Consort Lorden, do you consent?" asked Arden.

"I do," said Simon, his first words since Dame Altair's accusation. His voice shook, but not enough for someone who didn't know him to realize how tightly controlled it was, or how close he was to panic. I turned to face him. His eyes were huge in his whey-pale face, more golden than ever when contrasted against the white. He looked at me like a drowning man unsure whether a buoy will be enough to support him through the storm, but his shoulders were straight and his chin was high.

Simon Lorden was a man well-accustomed to being accused of things he hadn't done. Just as accustomed as he was to being accused of things he *had* done. His reputation as someone who might abduct an innocent woman and wrap her in the guise of a known criminal had been well-earned, at the hands of the woman who had controlled his life for so very long.

Well. She didn't control him anymore. I held out my hand, beckoning him closer. Dame Altair made a disapproving sound. I didn't even look at her.

"You're not going to make the pregnant lady walk all the way over there, are you?"

"Sir Daye, it's ten feet of level floor," said Arden, sounding almost amused.

"Yeah, and I need to pee," I said. "The longer we stand around debating this, the longer the traitor has to get away from us. You all understand that, right?"

"I do," said Simon, and walked over to slide his hand into mine. I folded my fingers around his, holding him in place, and started to reach for the knife at my hip, pausing when I remembered that it wasn't there. As a hero of the realm, I'm technically allowed to enter the presence of the Queen armed. As a woman eight months into her second pregnancy, none of my waist sheaths fit, and I hadn't wanted to cut my dress to strap something to my thigh. Not that I would have been able to draw any knife I sheathed there without stabbing myself in the stomach.

"Didn't make choices that could result in stabbing the baby." Oh, yeah. I'm going to win mother of the year.

I paused, trying to figure out how to draw blood without asking

Tybalt for help again when he was already unhappy about me doing blood magic. I was still thinking when the Luidaeg walked over to me, extending one empty hand like a magician preparing to do a trick. She closed her fingers, then opened them to reveal a razor-thin piece of shell. It was curved and colored as if it had been sliced from the outside edge of an abalone, filled with misty, clouded rainbows.

"Here," she said. "You're looking slightly unarmed."

"Er," I said, and gingerly reached over to take the shell. "That looks sharp."

"It is," she said. "It won't scar, and any wound it makes won't become infected. Makes it convenient for bleeding the accused."

"Ah." I looked more closely at the sliver of shell. There was a strip of pebbled brownish gray along one edge, probably from the shell's original exterior. The rest of it looked like it could be used to slice the waves and shave the wind. "It looks . . . *really* sharp?"

"Handle with care," said the Luidaeg. Her eyes flicked to Simon. "Don't break the failure. He's done the best he could, and he's on the verge of changing his title to something less insulting. I'd rather you left him alive when you're done with him."

"I will," I promised, and turned back to Simon, holding up the shell blade. "If I may?"

"You may," he agreed.

I nodded, turning his hand sideways until I could see the large vein running along his wrist. Dame Altair leaned forward, looking almost disturbingly eager. I frowned at her before delicately pressing the sharpened edge of the shell into Simon's skin, careful not to cut too deep.

Blood welled up, bright red and well-oxygenated, smelling of smoke and mulled cider. The notes of cinnamon and cardamom were there, sweet, but mixed with crushed apples and cloves and allspice and star anise. It seemed like a more complicated perfume than many magical scents, but really, it just wore its complexity openly, not buried under veils of detail and disguise.

I met Simon's eyes and waited for him to nod approval. When he did, I raised his wrist to my mouth and pressed my lips against the wound.

The world went away, replaced by red. It was jarring and natural at once, like slipping into sleep after a hard day. In the last instant of thinking as myself and not as the man who called himself my father, I realized this was my first true act of blood magic since escaping Titania's enchantment. That didn't seem right. I'd worked so long to make myself comfortable with my magic that it seemed impossible I should have voluntarily set it aside like that.

But then the red closed around me, and the blood was all.

I wake alone. My chest feels like an empty hallway, a passage for ghosts to wander. I have to return to the land tonight. The Queen—my queen, Arden Windermere in the Mists—has requested my presence, and even dwelling below the waves as I now prefer, her word commands me. If she desires my attendance, I haven't a choice.

I rise, slow and silent, and gather my clothing from the floor where I discarded it at dawn. Helmi will not approve of my wearing it to break my fast, but they have left me alone, and even after months returned to my true existence, I fear their absence. I hurry down the hall to the evening room where they go to dine.

Both turn when I enter, smiling at my presence. Patrick, as always, smiles like I am the moon reborn, like he has never seen so beautiful a sight. Dianda is more reserved, but she smiles with honest affection that is, I believe, beginning to ripen and blossom into genuine love. We didn't love when we were wed, but we were willing to try, and oh, we have been trying. All three of us. Her waistline is a testament to that.

"So you've come to join us, sleepyhead," said Dianda. "Anceline stands ready to see you to the surface when you're prepared."

"Then she'll never see me there, as I may never be prepared," I said. "I'll go, but I won't be prepared."

"You can see your brother," said Patrick. "And October. August says she's been asking after you."

The scene began to thin and fray around the edges, flashes of reality showing through the red. The desire to take another mouthful and continue to watch Simon with his spouses was stronger than I would have expected. I exhaled through my nose, lips still against his skin, and let the magic go.

The red wisped away and I was October again, entirely myself and not lost in anyone else's memory. I straightened and the Luidaeg was there, offering a carved brown sheath that looked to have been made from the outside of the shell, perfectly sized to keep it safe and prevent me from gutting myself by mistake. I took it with a nod, wiping the shell's edge clean on my sleeve before sliding it into the sheath.

"No debts," I said. "I asked for nothing."

"No, you didn't," she agreed. "Call it a gift to my favorite niece, and a courtesy to my dearest failure."

I didn't know what to say to that. I tucked the little shell sheath into the front of my bodice, seating it firmly between my breasts, before I turned to face Arden. "Blood magic is imprecise, but blood doesn't lie," I said, focusing on her, rather than the silently fuming Dame Altair. "Consort Lorden has not set foot on the land since the breaking of Titania's enchantment—which, you may remember, he was instrumental in undoing. Without him, we might still be living in her gilded fantasy. There's no way he could have been responsible for abducting and obscuring Dame Altair."

Bahey nodded as I spoke, verifying my words.

Simon had produced a handkerchief from inside his vest and was busily wrapping it around the cut on his wrist. He looked at my handiwork with a small smile, then looked at me.

"There was a time when you would have hacked my arm open like it was a coconut and you had nothing more precise than a machete," he said. "You're learning subtlety. I approve."

"Good to know," I said, focusing on Arden. "My father didn't do this, Your Majesty, and you know it."

"I do," she said, with a sigh.

Dame Altair sputtered. "Your *Majesty*," she said, sounding appalled. "I am *titled nobility*, and you would dismiss my situation with such ease?"

"Your title's no shinier than mine, Eloise," I said, keeping my tone easy and almost dismissive. "A dame is equivalent to a knight. You have a knowe and servants. I have a paid-off house in San Francisco and a court comprised almost entirely of teenagers who don't know how to operate the dishwasher. I'm not really seeing how you get to call yourself 'titled nobility' like it puts you above anyone else. My father's title eclipses us both."

That was pushing it. He'd been an unlanded baron before he set his land-based titles aside to become Dianda's consort, but even in

Faerie's sometimes overly confusing version of the peerage, a duchess outranked a dame. Simon didn't need to share his wife's title to receive many of its benefits, including the precedence that meant he was treated as higher ranking than he technically was.

Isn't the feudal system awesome?

"I understand your discomfort, Dame Altair, but I must agree with Sir Daye that her magic has absolved Consort Lorden of any blame in this matter."

There had to be a better title for a ducal consort. Even "Lord" would have sounded less awkward than continually reminding people about how he was banging Dianda. And Patrick, I presumed, but because they had the same title in their mutual wife's Court, that aspect of his sex life didn't get shoved in my face quite as often.

Dame Altair visibly bristled but didn't argue any further with her queen, just harumphed and turned her back, folding her arms across her chest in a show of petulance. I was suddenly glad Arden wasn't as fond of iron as the false Queen had been. Dame Altair would have needed medical attention if she'd been bound by that much iron for even the duration of the court, much less however far in advance the switch had been made.

"I understand why we got distracted by Dame Altair's obvious plight and clear distress," I said. "But now that we've confirmed my father wasn't responsible for what happened to her, I really think we ought to focus on the more important problem."

"What could *possibly* be more important than my having been abducted and very nearly sentenced to a century of sleep?" demanded Dame Altair.

"How about the fact that the false Queen is *missing*?" I asked. "She's a slippery thing, and she's managed to evade capture and sentencing before. We don't know whether she has another puppet like Rhys lurking around somewhere for her to run to, and Silences is not going to take it very well if we lose her on a permanent basis."

To be fair, Arden looked as upset by the possibilities as I felt. I could almost admire the elegance of her horror. She didn't move quickly or without deliberation. Instead, with gracious slowness, she beckoned her brother to join her at the front of the dais, which he did through a swift transportation portal. Using a cutout to move such a short distance seemed like a waste of magic, but I didn't really know how much doing that took out of them, and if it got him to her more quickly . . .

Nolan reached out and took his sister's hand, holding it tightly, and I paused, remembering that for them, Evening had never been the greatest monster lurking in the Mists. The false Queen was the one who'd ordered Nolan elf-shot in order to keep her illegitimate grasp on Arden's throne; she was the one who had looked at two terrified, grieving children and only wondered how she could make things worse.

"You are correct, Sir Daye," said Arden, visibly composing herself. "The false Queen must be found and brought to heel before anything further can transpire. All my knights will be set toward this goal, and I will send word to those of my vassals not in attendance and ask that they set their own knights the same."

"Right," I said, stomach sinking as I took in the full meaning of her words.

Sylvester had been unable to come to court. He'd been allowed to make his excuses because his testimony wouldn't have been vital; Shadowed Hills was one of the demesnes least impacted by the false Queen's machinations, possibly because it was too rural for her to have cared much about, possibly because the false Queen had answered to Evening, and possibly because Simon had been able to take steps to protect his brother before his mistress could order him to act. It was hard to say which was more likely to be true. It also wasn't that important.

What *was* important was the fact that Arden was going to order her vassals—because even a polite request from a queen is an order when she holds your oaths—to mobilize their knights. And I was still a knight in service to Shadowed Hills.

Which meant I was about to be mobilized.

Tybalt appeared by my elbow so quickly that I wouldn't have been surprised if he'd pulled his version of Nolan's trick and traveled through the shadows to reach me. He took my arm, narrowed eyes on Arden. "My wife will *not* be set toward a dangerous goal."

"Your wife is a hero of the realm," said Arden, without warmth. "If her liege orders her, she must go."

"My *child* is no hero."

Shit. This was exactly the situation I had begged Arden to avoid. I wanted to interrupt, to argue that I could make my own decisions, but I couldn't. Tybalt was right. The baby hadn't agreed to anything I might decide or desire to do. Arden was also right. I was a sworn knight, and my oaths didn't leave any provisions for pregnancy, in part because when I'd taken them, the idea that I might get pregnant again—or be doing any sort of knightly duties active enough to put me in danger—had been laughable. Changelings didn't get knighted. If they somehow did, they certainly didn't get sent out to serve their liege in any sort of non-decorative fashion.

"I'm not ordering her to take up arms," said Arden. "I hope the pretender will be found quickly and with no need for open conflict, but you may speak to the Duke Torquill directly, and see what promises you can coax from him. What he does and does not demand from his household is outside my influence, even as his Queen."

"She'd be welcome in the Undersea," said Simon. "Even if she was ordered to arms, my brother wouldn't fault her for being down so deep that she couldn't join the quest."

"She is *not* going to the bottom of the sea," said Tybalt.

"All right," I said, putting my hands up. "This is a lot of talk about what I am and am not going to do, and I think I get a say here. So: what I'm going to do *right now* is go home, get off my feet, and eat something. May made spaghetti last night, and she has this amazing trick with carrots that keeps it from being too acidic for me to handle."

Arden was looking at me blankly. Good. That was the reaction I'd been hoping for, and was far better than argument or denial.

"What I'm going to do tomorrow is call Shadowed Hills and make sure my liege understands how pregnant I am, so any choices he makes about where I do or do not get asked to go will be made with total understanding of my situation. And after that, I'll do whatever's required of me to fulfill my oaths. But for right now, I'm going home. Is there any issue with that, Your Majesty?"

"None at all," said Arden, wisely enough. I was sure Tybalt was glaring daggers in her direction. "Your attendance has been noted and appreciated, Sir Daye."

"Right back atcha," I said, glancing to Simon. "You'd be welcome if you wanted to swing by the house after you're done here. I'm sure May would love the chance to catch up with you in private." She was supposed to be at court, but I hadn't seen her, and for all I knew, she'd managed to sneak out as soon as they stopped serving the pretrial champagne.

Simon nodded, not committing to anything. I turned to Tybalt.

"Take me to the car?" I asked.

He'd been reluctant to take me on the Shadow Roads for weeks, but I had correctly guessed that his need to protect me would override his desire to keep me safe. He nodded, wrapping his arms around me, then stepped backward into the shadow formed by a cluster of people. I caught and held my breath, and the floor fell away as we both dropped onto the Shadow Roads.

Everything there was darkness and cold, although I liked to think the cold was less deep than it had been the first time I stepped foot there. The Shadow Roads would never love me, but I had traveled them extensively, both with Tybalt and on my own, and their King loved me. Surely that was enough to buy me a little grace?

Tybalt swung me up into his arms with a small oof of effort, then started running. He didn't run as fast as he had before I was pregnant, which I assumed was less about my weight than it was about the desire not to trip and drop me. I wasn't going to argue. On the Shadow Roads, I *couldn't* argue, because I couldn't catch my breath enough to try. I leaned my head against his shoulder and tried to focus on something other than the growing ache in my lungs.

At least we weren't going far. In a matter of seconds, he was stepping out of the shadows, back into the wavery light of the streetlights around the parking lot. He paused long enough to glance around and be sure that we were alone before swinging me to my feet, keeping his hands on my upper arms until I had my footing back.

Only then did he let go and step back, looking at me with the cool superciliousness that I had come to learn meant he was truly uncomfortable. He'd been a King of Cats for so long, watching his back for challenges to the crown, that he no longer felt safe looking truly upset outside of his own home.

"What are you not telling me?" he asked.

I wiped the ice out of my eyelashes, unsticking them enough to let me blink at him. I was stalling for time and we both knew it. "I already said we needed to talk when we get home."

"I might prefer to have the conversation here."

"And I might refuse,'" I replied.

"You're not easing my discomfort." A branch cracked in the trees behind him, and he whipped around, posture going defensive. "We're too exposed here. We'll continue this conversation in the car."

"You're going to stay bipedal in the car? That's weird. Why are you being weird?" Tybalt was born centuries before cars existed, and had never quite become comfortable with motor vehicles. Our compromise when I needed to take the car somewhere was usually him riding in feline form, curled up on the passenger seat with his head down on his paws. It meant he couldn't wear a seatbelt, but I didn't mind. If we got into an accident, a cat would be much more prepared to weather the impact than a human man would have been.

Tybalt hissed through his teeth, holding up one hand to signal me to silence, and kept staring at the point in the woods where the cracking noise had originated. I moved closer to him, wishing I had more than just the shell knife I'd received from the Luidaeg. If something was about to attack us, I'd be practically defenseless—a single blade shorter than my index finger wasn't going to do much to keep me safe.

I mean, I guess I could bleed on whoever it was until they got disgusted and went away, but that didn't seem like the most effective way to protect myself, and Tybalt would probably have a panic attack if I tried it.

There was another crack from the trees, and then a familiar voice called, "Peace, friend. I approach in good faith."

I stepped up even with Tybalt, blinking again. "Simon?" I asked.

"Indeed so," he replied, stepping out of the trees and into the parking lot. "Queen Windermere asked her brother to bring me to the tree line but not beyond, for fear of human backpackers seeing us appear. I didn't want to sneak up on you. I prefer my internal organs on the inside."

Tybalt took a deep breath, visibly calming himself. "Master Lorden," he said, offering Simon a shallow bow. "I apologize for my heightened wariness."

"No need," said Simon, smile small but sincere. "Any apologies for your overprotection are between yourself and October. But when Amy was pregnant, I was terrified. Both times." He paused then, a complicated expression crossing his face. "No, I . . ."

"You remember her being pregnant with me, even though you weren't there in the real world," I said, understandingly. "It's all right, Simon. I still see the echoes, too."

"Ah." He looked relieved. "With August, I knew both she and the baby would likely recover from any trouble they might stumble into, but with October, there were no such guarantees. I begged her to remain in the tower, to let me wait upon her hand and foot like the queen she deserved to be treated as."

"I take it from the fact that you're telling me this that she didn't listen," said Tybalt dryly.

"Not as such," he said. "She continued to go about her business right up until her delivery. To travel and practice blood magic, and to generally behave as herself. And you know what happened?"

"What?" I asked.

"She had two healthy babies, as different as dusk and dawn, but each one perfect." His lips twitched like he was trying to fight back a smile. "It's a good lesson to have learnt, since I'm quite sure that if I were to try the same with Dianda, she would have my hands."

Tybalt blinked. "Your lady wife is expecting?"

"Our family is expecting a child, yes," said Simon. "Dianda's going to be ever so angry at me for letting it slip, but October knows, and there's no sense in seeding secrets where they don't belong. She's as far along as October, but far larger. Given my own birth, I've dared hope the explanation for her size might be twins. We have a court healer at the knowe in Saltmist, but she refuses to say one way or the other. We'll know when Dianda's been delivered."

On the whole, Faerie was a lot less obsessed with things like knowing a baby's gender before they were born—possibly because some combinations of descendant lines meant "how many limbs will the baby have" was a substantially more relevant question. But when you can decorate a nursery with a snap of your fingers, having a sonogram to influence your color choices can seem irrelevant.

Faerie is also a lot slower to adjust to change than the mortal world. For older fae, pink was still the preferred color for little boys, while blue was generally preferred for girls, and all children were likely to be dressed primarily in white until they were either toilet trained or needed to leave the Summerlands for whatever reason.

"So what are you saying?" asked Tybalt.

"I'm saying we've both married women who prefer not to have their choices dictated to them, and who have done a more than reasonable job of keeping themselves alive against the slings and arrows of their stations," said Simon. "All you're going to do by hovering is drive October further from you at a time when you should be drawing her closer."

Tybalt glanced at me. "Is he telling me to relax?"

"I think so," I said, almost cheerfully. "Simon, did you follow us just to lecture Tybalt about not pissing me off? Because it's sweet if you did, but we really need to get home."

"I'm aware." He smiled and held out his hand. "The keys, if you would be so kind."

I blinked. "What?"

"I'm an excellent driver," he said. "My safety record is substantially better than yours, as I've killed fewer cars, and never driven into a single wall. So I'm driving us home."

"Didn't you just finish telling Tybalt he shouldn't try to push me around?"

"Yes."

"So why . . . ?"

"Because I am your father, not your husband. I can afford to have you a little angry with me if it means I see you safely home. Keys, please."

The sheer surrealism of Simon standing in front of me, demanding my keys, was enough that I dug them out of my dress's side pocket and dropped them into his extended hand. He closed his fingers around them, beaming at me.

"I always appreciated your willingness to see sense," he said. "Where's the car?"

Muir Woods officially closes at sundown, and that includes the parking lots. Which doesn't stop mortals with more longing for the woods than fear of the law, but does mean the authorities will ticket and tow any cars that have been left visible. I indicated a seemingly empty space.

"Over here," I said.

The three of us walked until the faint, lingering traces of my magic told us we had reached our ride. I inhaled and let go of the don't-look-here covering the car, releasing the scent of freshly cut grass and copper into the air. The copper was bloodier than it had been when I was more human. The grass was changing as well, coming more and more clearly into focus. A few more changes to the balance of my blood and I'd be able to identify the *type* of grass. I had to admit I was curious.

Simon walked around to the driver's side and unlocked the doors with the press of a button, getting behind the wheel as I checked the backseat for intruders. Paranoid? Maybe. But someone tried to kill me that way once, and I have a long memory when it comes to assassination attempts. I don't enjoy them, and I didn't want to add one to the confusing mess this night had already been.

Simon watched quizzically until I got into the passenger seat, leaving the door open as I situated myself and fastened my seatbelt. I looked over at Tybalt, who was standing outside the car looking like he didn't know what he was supposed to do with himself, and smiled.

"You coming?"

Understanding washed over his expression like the dawn. He folded inward and was gone, replaced by a large brown tabby. The scent of musk and pennyroyal swirled through the air as he changed, and he stood on four legs, stretching languidly. Then, tail held high, he leapt up into what remained of my lap, curling himself into a ball with paws tucked under and tail wrapped around his body.

I ran a hand along the curve of his back, smiling fondly. "I love you, even if you are being an overprotective jerk right now."

Tybalt looked up at me through half-closed green eyes, a purr rumbling in his throat. I sighed and leaned over to close the car door.

"All right, Simon, you can drive now," I said.

He started the car and pulled smoothly out of the parking space, easily turning us around and heading for the road. It wasn't the most impressive bit of driving I'd ever seen, but he did it without hesitation or confusion. I relaxed, shoulders unkinking as I realized he was as good a driver as he claimed to be.

I should have known. He'd been fond of flashy sports cars before my disappearance solidified him as a villain in the eyes of his brother and drove him largely into hiding; no one spent that much money on a car they didn't know how to drive.

I leaned back in my seat, the events of the evening running wild through my thoughts. So much had happened. After months of idleness, I wasn't used to that sort of thing anymore. But Tybalt was purring, and the baby wasn't currently using my bladder as a soccer ball, and the car was warm and I had a safe driver at the wheel and . . .

Is it really any wonder I fell asleep?

SEVEN

A HAND SETTLED ON my shoulder, squeezing just hard enough to catch my attention without hurting me, and shook.

"October. It's time to wake up now."

"Mrgh," I said, intelligently, and opened my eyes.

I was facing the kitchen window of my house, complete with May's riotous windowsill herb garden and the mismatched spectrum of suncatchers and prisms Jazz had hung from the frame. I blinked to clear my vision, then sighed.

"Did I sleep the *whole* way home?" I asked, turning toward the owner of the hand.

Simon nodded. "I'm afraid so. We considered waking you to take a detour through the McDonalds drive through, but you seemed so peaceful that it wasn't a good enough idea to act upon."

"What?" I glanced at my empty lap, then back to Simon. "How did you and Tybalt discuss anything? I doubt he turned human again during the drive."

"He didn't," Simon agreed. "I proposed the stop, he hissed at me, I took that for negation, apologized, and drove us the rest of the way home."

The car windows were down. Tybalt must have jumped out as soon as we were home. "Hope he had his keys," I said, unfastening my belt.

Simon got quickly out of the car and moved around to open my door. "Here, let me help you," he said, offering his arm. I took it, letting him pull me to my feet. He smiled at me as I rose, then stepped back, leaving me with a clear path to the kitchen door.

I grabbed his hand before he could go any farther. "How were you planning to get back to the shore?" I asked.

"I *did* live in this city for many years," he said. "I intended to walk to the train station and flag down a cab. Most drivers can be convinced to take a man to the sea for a healthy enough tip. And if that should fail me, it's only a two-mile walk to Crane Cove Park. The water is easily accessible from there."

"Yeah, no. I don't care how comfortable you are with the idea, but I'm not letting you wander off alone in the middle of the night to chuck yourself off a pier."

"Dianda has assured me—"

"I know you have ways of coming and going, but no," I said. "Quentin and Dean should be home soon, and I know Dean was planning to spend the night at Goldengreen. He always comes in before he goes home, so he can have a cup of hot cocoa and some of May's cookies. You can hitch a ride with him and go back to Saltmist from the cove there. Much safer. Much less likely to give me anxiety."

Still Simon hesitated, trying to tug his hand out of mine. "I'm not sure whether I'll be welcome within your walls."

"Why wouldn't—oh." I caught myself. My own healing had been sped so much by our time under Titania's enchantment that I sometimes forgot not everyone had been there. Not everyone had received the benefits of a lifetime of false memories.

If it seems a little weird for me to be calling having my existence rewritten by an ancient, borderline-all-powerful bigot a "benefit," well. I can't make it not have happened, so I need to find a way to live with the fact that it did. Accepting that my having a different set of memories around some people has improved our relationships and made them easier is really the smallest adjustment I could make.

The kitchen door opened, revealing Tybalt standing there framed in light. "She's not in the kitchen at the moment," he said. "You can at least come in for a cup of tea."

The corner of Simon's mouth tugged upward. "You can take the man out of England," he said, almost wistfully. "I think I would like that."

"I'll go upstairs and talk to her," I said, letting Simon go ahead of me into the house. "Maybe she'll be okay with it. And if she's not, maybe she'll be willing to stay in her room until you're gone. She stays in her room most of the time as it is."

"I don't want to make her uncomfortable in her own home," said Simon, but stepped into the kitchen all the same, moving quickly out of the doorway so I could follow.

After the cool dark of the San Francisco night, stepping into the bright, sugar-scented confines of my kitchen was like entering another world. It wasn't the biggest kitchen I'd ever seen in a residential home, but May had worked a series of charms on the cabinets that expanded their available space tenfold, meaning she could shop for our six permanent residents along with our rotating assortment of teenagers without taking up all the available room. A few mismatched cloches sat on the counters, protecting the latest assortment of baked goods from going stale.

Not that it was much of a risk with the swarm of teens that swept through periodically: nothing ever went stale in this house. A small table was shoved into the dining nook, mostly clear of papers and clutter; those things dominated the dining room, but this was May's domain.

I paused to lean in and plant a kiss on Tybalt's cheek. "You take care of getting drinks for you and Simon—I'd like a glass of rosemary lemonade if we still have it—and I'll go check on Raysel. Back in a few minutes."

"Of course," said Tybalt, clearly much more relaxed now that we were back in the house, where most of Faerie's dangers would have trouble reaching us without ploughing through my wards.

Titania had ripped our original wards down when she came, shredding them like tissue paper and leaving the house defenseless. It had taken the better part of a month to reset them to a level I was comfortable with after her enchantment shattered, and now the wards, rather than being tied solely to me, contained contributions from almost everyone who lived here. Most people would be hard-pressed to get through uninvited.

Knowing that made it easier to sleep at day, since I didn't feel like my enemies were going to come crashing through the window at any moment. I started pulling myself up the stairs one step at a time, keeping my hand on the bannister for balance. There's no such thing as a good fall when you're eight months pregnant.

Sweet Maeve, I was going to be glad when this pregnancy was

finished. I was excited to meet the baby, and I didn't regret it, but I'm used to being able to jump off roofs without fear of lasting consequences. Until the kid was out of me and we could tell whether they healed like me or like their father, I had to be more careful than I had been in years. I didn't like it. Behaving like I was breakable was so *limiting*.

I was halfway up the steps when I heard a rattle. I looked up to see Spike sitting on the landing, watching me curiously. I shot it a smile and kept moving.

Our resident rose goblin had been roughly the size of a cat when I first brought it home. Shaped like a cat, too, if cats came in pink and green, covered with thorns that clicked together like the beans inside a maraca whenever Spike shook itself. It was still shaped like a cat. But rose goblins didn't exactly come with care and feeding instructions, and it turned out that when you fed and watered them, they grew.

Spike was now roughly the size of a basset hound, and smart enough to know that we couldn't both fit on the stairs in my current condition. Instead, it turned vivid yellow eyes in my direction and rattled its thorns at me.

"Hi, Spike," I said. "How's Raysel doing?"

We'd been worried, when we first orchestrated Raysel coming home with us to recover, that she would find the presence of a rose goblin upsetting. They came from her mother's garden, after all, and getting away from her mother was a large part of why she needed to be here. To everyone's surprise, her reaction had been the exact opposite.

Spike now slept in her room at day, either with her in the bed or on the floor in front of the door, where it could rattle its thorns menacingly at anyone who tried to enter while Raysel was asleep. It followed her around the house when she left her room, providing a form of constant companionship. And Raysel adored it. She brushed its thorns and trimmed the ones that had gotten too long, making it easier for the spiky little creature to move around the house without getting stuck to things.

It continued to watch me as I made it to the top of the stairs and paused to catch my breath. "Is Raysel in her room?" I asked.

It rattled its thorns at me in what I hoped was the affirmative.

"Good goblin," I said, bending to run a hand over its head. As long as I stroked with the grain of the thorns, it didn't draw blood.

This essential errand accomplished, I continued down the hall to Raysel's closed bedroom door room and rapped gently.

"Hello?" she called after a moment.

"It's Toby," I replied. "Can I come in?"

The door inched open, wide enough for Raysel to peer out at me. "It's your house," she said. "You don't have to ask."

"It's your room; I do," I countered.

We'd had this exchange dozens of times, both reciting our lines with conviction. Me knowing what I was supposed to say plainly reassured her, and she pulled the door wider open, letting me inside.

Before Raysel had come to live with us, May had taken it upon herself to prepare our former guest room for a longer-term stay. I would never have thought of that. I wanted Raysel to be comfortable, but I'm bad enough at taking care of my own needs that setting up a whole room for her would just not have occurred to me. The walls were white, the furniture basic and sparse, but the shelves were increasingly cluttered with the things she'd been collecting since she came home. Shells and books and interesting trinkets. Everything but rocks.

She didn't collect rocks anymore.

Raysel closed the door behind me and moved to sit on the edge of the bed, leaving the desk chair open. I sat down, putting myself on her level. "Hey," I said.

She looked at me warily, with a heartbreaking resignation in her eyes. "Is it time for me to go so you can have my room for the baby?" she asked. "I can't go back to Shadowed Hills yet. Do you think Queen Windermere would claim offense against me? I don't think Duchess Lorden would want me in her halls, not after what I did to her sons . . ."

"What? *No.* I told you, Raysel, we're not throwing you out. We're not that tight on space, and the baby's going to be rooming with me and Tybalt for at least the first six months. We can talk about rooming arrangements after that. Worst-case scenario, we can convert the dining room downstairs into a bedroom until we figure out an expansion spell that lets us add a whole additional room. This is your *home*."

"I only have four months left on my offense. Is it really worth the effort?"

"You're worth *every* effort, Raysel. I promise. We're not going to get tired of you, and we're not going to send you back to Shadowed Hills until and unless you say you're ready to go. When your term of offense ends we'll figure something else out. I won't allow your parents to force you to go someplace you don't want to be."

"But my majority—"

"Is not that far away. I will fight to let you stay here until they have no more say over where you go. By the root and the branch, I promise you that."

Raysel blinked, golden eyes welling with tears. No matter how many times we told her she was wanted, she never seemed able to quite believe it. I guess it made sense, given how much trouble she'd caused before she recovered from the conflict between her mammalian and vegetable heritages; it was natural for her to assume we were holding grudges. And to be fair, Dean wasn't her biggest fan. But the rest of us had forgiven her, to one degree or another.

"If you're not here to throw me out, why did you come all the way upstairs?"

"*My* room is upstairs, too, you goof," I said. "But I came upstairs because we have a guest, and I wanted to make sure you were okay with him being here. He says he'll leave if you don't want him in the house."

Raysel sat up straighter, tears replaced by alarm. "Is my *father* here?" she squeaked.

"No, no," I said, holding up my hands like that could ward her panic away. "Your father isn't here. I haven't actually seen him tonight. He wasn't at the court."

"Oh," she said, concern fading. In a much calmer tone, she asked, "Is *your* father here?"

"Yes," I admitted. "He drove me home, in my car, because I was tired and he was concerned about me."

"That was nice of him." She looked down at the hem of her sweater, picking at it with her fingers. "I appreciate you letting me know that he's here, but it doesn't matter."

"It does matter, Raysel, because again, this is your home. If you don't want him here, I can ask him to leave, and he'll go. He already said he'd go if it would help you feel safer."

"I don't *want* him here, but I don't *mind* if he *is* here," said Raysel, emphasizing her words with careful precision. "Does that make sense? I'm not worried about him trying to take me away the way I am when we're talking about my father. He can stay as long as you want him to."

My heart ached for her. Sylvester loved her, I knew he did, but he didn't know how to show it, or how to talk to her now that she was a grown woman with psychological issues and not the child she'd been before she was abducted. Sylvester loved *me*, or at least I thought he did, but he was equally baffled when it came to repairing the damage he had done to our relationship over the years. He knew things were broken. He just didn't know how to fix them. He was failing us both in different ways, and I didn't know how to tell him that.

How horrible was it when we were both more comfortable with the man who'd destroyed our lives than with the man we'd once trusted above all others?

"All right," I said. I levered myself back out of the chair I'd only just sunken into. "I'll be downstairs if you want to join us. We'll all understand if you don't. I don't think your uncle is expecting you."

Raysel nodded, offering a fragile smile as I walked to the door and cracked it open. Spike was waiting just outside. It rattled its thorns at me as it slipped into the room, trotting over to jump onto the bed.

The last thing I saw before closing the door was Raysel moving to curl up next to Spike, her fox fur–red hair falling to cover her face. Then I was alone in the hall, unsupervised for the first time since leaving the house for Arden's court.

When did things get so *complicated*? It didn't feel like all that long ago I'd been alone in the world, depressed and despairing, unable to believe things were ever going to get truly better. It was difficult to look back on that woman and see myself in her, but I knew she was me. I'd lived through every step on the road between us, and there was no reality in which I would have chosen to go back to being her. She was a ghost, a phantom of my past, and while I never wanted her to be exorcised, this wasn't her life anymore. It was mine.

I was halfway down the stairs when I heard low voices coming from the kitchen, Tybalt and Simon taking a moment to talk before I came back. I paused where I was, holding tight to the bannister, and tried to give them the time to finish. They had plenty to talk about.

Simon had actually been with Amandine when August was born; he'd been through all the trials and triumphs of a successful pregnancy and childbirth. Moreover, he remembered being there when I was born, and even if all that had been an illusion, it was a useful one; it was a lie that told him certain essential truths.

I had been pregnant before, and Gillian was proof that I'd been able to do it successfully enough for us both to come through it breathing. Tybalt, though... Tybalt's first wife, Anne, had been fully human. Pregnancy had been hard on her. Childbirth had killed both her and the baby. Maybe Simon reminding him that my bloodline made me all but impossible to kill in the same fashion would help to reassure him, at least a little.

The kitchen door swung open, and Simon stuck his head out, scanning the hall until he found me standing on the stairs. "You can come in now, if you'd like," he said, not unkindly. "Tybalt and I just needed to have a few words in private, father to father."

"Should I be nervous?" I asked, finishing my descent.

"Never, but especially not in this instance. I only hope I've said enough to perhaps make the conversation the two of you are about to have somewhat less painful," said Simon.

I smiled at him. "Thanks, F—Simon."

He nodded, not seeming to catch my false start. "I owe you no less," he said. "How is Rayseline?"

"Relieved that you're not Sylvester," I replied. "She's fine with you sticking around for a bit. I don't think she's going to come down while you're here, but she's not upset about having you in the house."

Something in my tone must have tipped him off to the fact that there was more to the story. He gave me a hard look, then sighed. "But she would object to my brother's presence, would she not?"

I nodded. "She's not ready to see her father just yet. Sylvester's . . . she sees him siding with her mother the way he does as a betrayal."

"She's not the only one, is she?"

I didn't have an answer for that, and so I just shrugged, forced a smile, and said, "Baby wants lemonade. Let's go get baby some lemonade."

Simon was kind enough not to comment, merely nod and step aside so I could return to the warm, uncomplicated brightness of the kitchen. Tybalt was sitting in the breakfast nook with a mug of tea—his—and a tall glass of lemonade—mine. I walked over and took it, smiling my appreciation.

"I still don't understand how this stuff tastes so damned good," I said, taking a quick drink.

"Almost anything would have to taste better than the tarry swill you used to drink."

"Bite your lip." The more fae I become, the less chemical substances impact me—including caffeine. I gave up coffee when it stopped working. Maybe that was petty of me, but I was so angry not to get the results I wanted that I couldn't stomach the stuff any longer.

Tybalt gave me a half-smug look, but didn't comment any further.

Right. No time like the present to start an uncomfortable conversation. I decided to begin with the less uncomfortable part, and Simon might as well hear too. It wasn't like it was going to be a secret for long. "Have you ever heard of the fae having godparents?"

"Yes," Tybalt said, sounding faintly surprised. "It was a common practice when I was younger and there were more frequent wars. It fell out of favor as we scattered ourselves across the mortal world, and conflicts became less common. It has nothing to do with human religion, despite the stolen name."

"Fae steal everything," I said.

He nodded. "It is our way," he agreed. "We stole the name and social meaning, but not the root of it. A godparent has nothing of god in them, only the promise to parent should the birth parents be unavailable for some reason. As the purebloods of the Divided Courts denied death more and more completely, godparentage became less common, and fosterage rose in its stead."

"So godparents are good things for people who live lives like we do," I said, not quite a question, not quite a full statement.

"I should think so, if you could find them," said Tybalt. "Why? Did someone offer?"

"Yeah," I said, hesitantly.

"Who among us is old enough to remember the traditions, and have made you such a costly proposition?" Tybalt's eyes widened, pupils contracting to slits. "By Malvic, you don't mean to say . . ."

"Yes, I do," I said. "The Luidaeg asked if I would be willing to let her stand as godmother to our child. She says we're both in dangerous lines of work, and she knows better than to count on us surviving all the way to their majority."

"Perhaps blunter than I would have been, but not so inaccurate as to become offensive," said Simon. "They have more use for godparents in the Undersea, where the wars continue with more regularity and brutality. It's a fine way to unite households, more reliable than betrothals, since no one gets to change their mind about who their godparents are, and even the cruelest try to avoid killing their own godchildren. It's a banner of safety."

"Oh?" said Tybalt. "Will you be asking someone to stand godparent to your expected child?"

"We already have," said Simon. "Captain Pete will stand for the babe, and has already been more involved in Dianda's pregnancy than is perhaps the norm. What a gift, to have the blessing of your own Firstborn."

"Not all Firstborn," I said sourly.

"Well, no. Neither one of us would want our Firsts anywhere near an innocent child. Or an evil child, or an evil adult. Or us."

"What a fun club we belong to," I said, and turned back to Tybalt, who looked like he was deliberating the advantages of passing out over throwing up. "The Luidaeg offered, and I told her I'd have to talk to you first, since it was such a big decision. Do we let her?"

"To refuse would be to court offense from the sea witch," he said. "In addition to being unwise in the extreme. Any child protected by the Luidaeg's decree would walk the world veiled in security. Of course we'll let her stand as godmother, if she so desires."

"I'll call and tell her," I said. "I'm sure she'll be thrilled." I paused. "Okay, maybe not thrilled so much as 'smug because she knew I was going to say yes,' even though she swears she can't See anything to do with me."

"Why not?" asked Simon.

"Too much Oberon in the atmosphere," I said. "The big asshole distorts the ability of Seers to know what's coming."

"At least that means she's not foreseen our deaths," said Tybalt.

I wisely didn't comment, remembering the sheer number of times she'd predicted my own demise, and the fact that when it came, it was meant to be at her hands. She didn't seem to *want* to kill me. But she kept saying she was going to, and the Luidaeg never lied.

I sipped my lemonade again, looking around the kitchen. "The boys should be back soon," I said. "May and Jazz, too."

"How did May and Jazz get to Muir Woods?" asked Simon, politely.

"Not sure," I said. "They may have hitched a ride with Quentin and Dean, or maybe they called Etienne and got him to portal them there." Sylvester hadn't been in attendance, but that didn't mean my Fetch was above asking his Captain of the Guard to play taxi.

"You were away far longer than it takes to ask if you'll allow the sea witch to stand godmother to our child," said Tybalt, pupils returning to their normal shape and size as he narrowed his eyes at me. "What have you not yet told me, little fish?"

No point in putting it off any longer if he was already asking questions. "Arden wants me back at work," I said.

Tybalt stiffened, pupils widening until they had all but consumed the banded green of his eyes. I held up a hand to ward off the explosion I knew was coming.

"Apparently some people took advantage of Titania's enchantment to loot the royal vaults," I said. "A lot of really dangerous stuff is missing. She wants me to get started on finding it."

"It's close to the birth of our child," said Tybalt. "Your life isn't the only one you'd be endangering."

I glanced to Simon, who shook his head. "I agree with the cat," he said. "I'm not so overprotective as he is, but I wouldn't recommend a treasure hunt in your current condition, and I find it difficult to believe that Arden would."

"Well, she did," I said. "I think she feels like this is important enough to risk irritating the both of you, and making me walk around for extended periods of time."

"*Irritating* us? The risk to your safety is the only thing she should be concerning herself with. What could *possibly* be missing that carries such importance?" Tybalt's voice was harsh, but still tightly controlled. He knew better than to yell at me.

I turned to look at him levelly. "The hope chest, among other things," I said. "We have to find it before someone starts using it."

"Forgive me, my dear, but what harm could be done with a hope chest?" asked Simon delicately. "It allows nothing more than your own magic does."

"Yeah, but my magic has a mind behind it," I said. "A hope chest is a tool, and like any tool, it can be used in a lot of different ways. But hope chests don't care about consent. They don't care if you're screaming no, no, no, and trying to fight back. They're not intelligent; they just do what the person holding them orders them to do. And it *hurts*. Being the subject of a hope chest hurts like your blood is made of fire and acid at the same time. It hurts, and it can take from you, whether or not you want to allow it." The first time I'd touched a hope chest, I'd truly believed that they were a bedtime story intended for naughty changeling children. And that hadn't mattered, because the chest had shifted my blood further away from human even without my wanting it to.

In a way, it had just been putting things back the way they were supposed to have been from the beginning. Amandine hadn't wanted me to be fae at all, and had spent a portion of my childhood trying to sap my fae heritage away, leaving me entirely human. That first hope chest had been returning some of what my mother stole.

Didn't change the fact that I hadn't agreed to anything. "If someone who hates changelings has a hope chest, they can shove them out of Faerie forever. I can't give back a bloodline that's been removed. Or they could turn their targets fully fae. It's *isolating* to lose your humanity. Gillian still hasn't recovered, and she has the largest support network anyone could have asked for. A changeling who becomes a pureblood without warning loses everything. Their friends, their mortal family, their jobs, whatever life they've built for themselves, it's all gone."

Tybalt was looking at me with sympathetic, sorrowful eyes, like he knew I was thinking about the life I'd been building with Cliff and Gillian, back before everything went wrong and I fell into Faerie forever. I liked the life I had now, I truly did, but it still stung to know that I hadn't been given a choice.

"And then there are the people like January, or like Rayseline used to be," said Simon, with dawning horror. "Some of them are torn apart by the clashes between their own bloodlines, but others have found a form of balance. If someone were to disrupt that, they could find themselves plunged into chaos, blood battling blood, magic turning unstable."

It made me uncomfortable to hear him describe it that way, at least in part because that was exactly what I'd done to the pretender. I'd stolen one of her lines of descent without her permission, leaving her body to fight itself in the search for a new normal. Had she struggled? Was she still struggling? Could her being a villain be enough to excuse me for not being overly concerned? She certainly wouldn't have worried about me.

"That's not all that's missing," I said. "The fount that lets you treat iron poisoning without an alchemist to tailor the counteragent is gone, too, and a scabbard that transforms any metal into iron. Apparently whoever has it has already started using it. They attacked Dame Altair's men. At least one of them died."

"Dame Altair, you say?" asked Tybalt.

"Yeah. Which makes the fact that she was grabbed to masquerade as the false Queen interesting. There may be more here than meets the eye. I'll ask Danny to drive me over to her place tomorrow so I can talk to her."

"Absolutely not," said Tybalt, without hesitation.

I turned slowly to stare at him, not otherwise moving, while Simon straightened, pushing away from the bit of counter he'd been leaning against. "As we've established that my presence is not going to cause Rayseline distress, I think I'm going to go and wash my hands without fear of encountering and terrifying her," he said. "I believe I'll rest in the living room after that. Come find me, should you need me." And then he was gone, sensibly fleeing the coming explosion.

Tybalt didn't blink as he said, "You are not going off into danger simply because a few trinkets have disappeared."

"They're not trinkets, Tybalt, and you seem to forget that I may not have a choice. It's better if I go voluntarily, before Sylvester orders me to do my duty." I caught my breath, then asked the question that really mattered: "Or are you planning to keep me prisoner here against my will?"

"You always have a choice," said Tybalt. "Even if Sylvester did elect to make such a foolish decision, would you really endanger our child on his command?"

"I am a hero of the realm, and a grown woman, and you don't get to tell me that I'm not allowed to do my job when my Queen or my liege call upon me," I said, voice going cold. "I have been doing my absolute best to indulge your need to know where I am at all times, and I'm not going looking for danger, but you knew who I was when you married me. Pregnancy doesn't turn me into a different person."

"No, it doesn't," he said, and his own voice was tight. "It does, however, mean that when you risk yourself, you are not the only one taking these risks. You say a hope chest doesn't ask for consent from the people it changes. Right now, I don't see how Arden and Sylvester are any different. They're not asking consent of our child, and neither are you, because you can't. I'm only trying to keep you both safe."

"I know you are," I said. "But caring doesn't mean you get to protect me so much that you suffocate me. I'm not planning to do anything reckless or that could hurt the baby, but it's important that I do my job, and *this*"—I couldn't stop myself from hitting the last word hard enough to make it obvious, because of course it wasn't just this, it was everything since we'd come home from Titania's enchantment—"makes me feel like you don't trust my judgment."

"It has never been my intention to make you feel that way," he said, with obvious care, "and it isn't that I don't trust your judgment." He paused, and I could tell that he was weighing out his words. "But you must see that you rarely plan the things that put you into danger. They seek you out, hero that you are, and then you feel obligated to see them through. Can we be honest about that much?"

"All right, so it's honesty time. I am honestly going out of my mind being locked up like this. I *need* to work. The timing's crap, but I can't take much more sitting and staring at the same four walls. So I repeat: you knew who I was when you married me, and the Luidaeg is right when she says our lives aren't safe ones. I know we'll have to make some adjustments, and we've already discussed so many of them, but do you really think I'm never going to do my job again?"

"Of course not. Just not until you have the baby—"

"There will *always* be a baby!" I half-shouted. "From this point forward, there will always be a baby, or a child I might abandon *again*, the way I did Gillian. She lost me because I did my job. *I* lost *her*. And if you think I won't rearrange the stars to stop that from happening again, I don't understand how you ever thought you knew me."

Tybalt's pupils narrowed. "So you admit that terrible things can happen if you leave our home?"

"I do. I also admit that Blind Michael came to *your* Court before I was even involved, and Titania was masquerading as my best friend from childhood. Nothing I did or didn't do invoked them. My job is not the only thing that puts me in danger. That puts us in danger. Our baby is going to be in danger. That's what being a part of Faerie means. But they're going to have the biggest bad-ass in the realm for a father, and a hero for a mother, and they're going to be okay. No matter what else happens, they're going to be okay. Now please. You have to stop acting like Amandine. She wanted to lock me away from anything that might hurt me."

He went still, pupils narrowing even further, until they were barely slits. "Do not compare me to that woman," he said.

"So don't give me reason to," I countered.

He opened his mouth, then closed it and turned his face away. After a moment of silence, I reached over and put my hand on his shoulder.

"I'm just so *frightened* all the time," he said, voice gone dull and dead. "It was Anne at first, and the thought of you lying dead amidst the bedclothes, as she did, not even a baby's cry to break the silence. But that thought faded quickly. When I dared to fall in love again, I loved an unbreakable woman for a reason. Whatever happens, you will survive. But October . . . when Titania took you from me, took our child from me, I feared I wouldn't survive. I know you can endure whatever Faerie throws at you. I no longer trust myself to do the same. I haven't for a very long time."

"Oh, sweetheart..." I tightened my fingers on his shoulder, not letting go. The kind thing to do would have been to say I could endure the remainder of my pregnancy in semi-confinement, to agree that Arden could wait to be ready for me to come back out into the world. Unfortunately, that type of kindness isn't always an option. And even if it had been, I was realizing that it was no longer the best option for us, if it ever had been to begin with.

"I know how hard this is." He turned to look at me again and I dropped my hand, steeling myself against the entreaty in his eyes. "But I still need you to trust me when I say I can protect our child, and accept that you can't come with me to Dame Altair's because I won't be able to get the answers I need if she's too hostile—which is the same reason I can't take a squad of royal guards with me. Arden offered, but I refused—"

He snorted before saying dryly, "Of course you did."

"Just like you knew I would. Because you have to let me be myself, or you're trying to change me just as much as Amandine did, and I can't bear that. Not from her, not from you, not from anyone."

He was silent for an uncomfortably long moment. "I don't like it," he said at last, and I could hear the anger and terror and resignation in his voice. "I *can't* like it. But you're right that I didn't marry you to be your jailer. I don't agree with this decision. It is still your right to make it, and I will try to accept it with such grace as I can."

"And I will always, *always* come home to you. I've made it through Firstborn and monsters, curses and the Summer Queen. I know it's hard to trust me when I say things like this, but just try. Try to believe I'm telling you the truth."

He sighed. "I'm trying, little fish. For all of us, I'm trying."

I knew how much he was. The trauma of his past losses aside, sometimes it can be easy for me to forget how much he's the product of a different time and culture. Even if that weren't the case, sitting back and letting their loved ones rush into danger unprotected is not in the nature of the Cait Sidhe.

"That's all I can really ask you for. That, and please just let me do my job."

"I have said I will do my best."

"I love you, anxious nerd." I leaned over and kissed his temple. "So like I was saying, I'll get Danny to drive me to Dame Altair's place tomorrow, so I can talk to her."

"I can't go with you, but I can't endure the idea of you going alone," he said.

I blinked. I hadn't expected him to capitulate on letting me go without him quite so quickly. "Do you know why you can't come?" I asked.

"Dame Altair is a staunch traditionalist who considers shapeshifters barely more than animals," he said.

"I wouldn't have said 'staunch,' and I wouldn't normally allow her the courtesy of thinking she's right, but she's already spun up and primed to attack. I can't take you with me," I said. "I can take Quentin, though; she'll respect him, even without a known title. And Danny will be there if anything happens. And whatever we find, I promise I won't go off on my own without letting you know, and I'll take backup. I won't leave you a widower."

Tybalt nodded. "I suppose Quentin won't allow you the flavor of foolishness you sometimes seem to prize," he said, reaching over to take my face in his hands. "Only promise me in turn that if I restrain myself like this, if I can resist the urge to follow and protect you, that you'll do your best to keep yourself from harm in my absence."

"What, sir, are you asking me to be careful?" I asked, with exaggerated courtesy.

Tybalt snorted again. "I would never be so foolish. I'm asking you to remember that I am but a man, and not put too much strain on my poor heart by running into danger without concern for your own wellbeing."

"My wellbeing is pretty difficult to damage," I said. "But I promise I'll remember that I'm not rushing in alone, and be as careful as I can, for the baby's sake."

Simon cleared his throat. "I'll witness that promise."

I turned to look over my shoulder at him. "Forgive me if I'm intruding," he said, "but the two of you had grown quiet, and I was hopeful that meant my rejoining you would not be inappropriate." He was smiling approvingly. The expression was more for Tybalt than me; he was clearly proud of him for managing to listen and hold back while I went about my business.

I appreciated it, even as I wished it hadn't been necessary for my kinda-dad to lecture my husband about being chill. It seemed like a shift in our relationship.

But then, our relationship had already shifted, hadn't it? Simon's and mine. It had always been shifting. First he'd been my liege's brother, one more snooty pureblood who looked down his nose at me and would never truly accept me as a member of the court. Then he'd been the villain in my story, the man who condemned me to lose everything. Then he'd been a victim in his own story, a captive whose mind and magic had been bent to the service of a woman who had never seen a beautiful thing she didn't attempt to corrupt. And when that was done, he'd been my mother's estranged husband and the father of my sister, whose existence had been a baffling surprise.

If things had stopped there, they could have been simple between us. I could have gone about my life, letting him be one more shadowy figure in the vast crowd of my background, unwanted and ignored. But then he'd gone and married two of my closest allies, and turned my squire's boyfriend into my stepbrother in one swift, confusing act.

And then, Titania.

That was really the crux of it, wasn't it? Because I *knew* Simon was the man who'd transformed me into a fish and left me to lose everything, and I knew he'd done it to save my life, and even more, I knew he was the man who'd raised me. I knew how he told a bedtime story, and I knew how much he'd loved me. How much he still loved me.

Titania's spell may have been a lie, but the people she'd tangled inside it were real. The feelings had been real. The choices we made had been real ones. If they hadn't been, we would never have been able to break free. And now those feelings, those choices, were bleeding over into the real world. Things had changed, and we couldn't change them back.

"Simon—" I began, barely swallowing the now-ingrained desire to begin my sentence with "Father." He looked toward me, almost hopefully.

Before I could go any further, the kitchen door banged open and Quentin ambled inside, still dressed in his court finery, although he had undone his doublet and the laces on his shirt, and his hair was ruffled so that it stuck out in all directions, making him look somewhat like he'd been dragged backward through a hedge. Dean, who entered directly behind him, was in a similar state. The hedge wasn't out of the question.

I looked at them with amusement as they came to a stop, utterly unashamed but visibly somewhat embarrassed to have this many adults witnessing the aftermath of what must have been a fairly epic make-out session.

"I think they had the right idea," I said, looking toward Tybalt.

He smirked.

"Hello, Dean," said Simon.

"Hi, uh, Simon," said Dean. He paused nervously. "Am I in trouble?"

Simon sighed. "You're a man grown, and the Count of your own demesne. If you had done something dire enough to put you into your mother's bad books, I'm not the executioner she would have sent to deliver the news. I drove October home after she left the Queen's court. She looked tired, and I feared the consequences of allowing her to drive herself."

"I'm right here, you know," I said.

"He's right," said Tybalt.

Quentin's cheeks reddened. "I'm sorry I didn't realize. I could have given you a ride if I'd known."

"And left your car at Muir Woods overnight?" I raised an eyebrow. "Not the world's best plan. The don't-look-here would drop at dawn, and the local chop shop would have your engine in pieces an hour later."

Quentin had been even more shaken up by Titania's distorted version of reality than I had, in part because his reflection had shown him the worst possible version of himself. Cruel, bigoted, and self-absorbed, the kind of man my generally kind and thoughtful squire didn't want to believe he could have become in our reality if things had gone differently. In our collective desire to help him recover, we'd basically all written to his parents to tell them what happened. The end result had been an awkward if excusable weekend visit from the High King and Queen of the Westlands—excusable because we'd just experienced a collective traumatizing event, and not necessarily proof that they were visiting the Crown Prince in blind fosterage.

We all kept pretending no one knew who Quentin really was, even though it became less believable by the year, especially since Quentin looked more and more like his father all the time. It was sort of nice to know what my squire was likely to wind up looking like. Didn't hurt that, like all Daoine Sidhe, the High King was unreasonably attractive.

Anyway, the end result of their visit had been Quentin becoming the proud owner of a newer, nicer car than mine, opening up the entire Bay Area for his enjoyment. Fortunately for my nerves, his enjoyment pretty much consisted of driving from the house to Goldengreen to hang out with Dean, or to Shadowed Hills for sword fighting lessons with Etienne. I would have been getting into so much more trouble at his age.

But then, he'd had access to Chelsea for a while now, and a teenage teleporter with no real impulse control was even better than a shiny new car.

"We could have taken my car and left yours," he offered.

"Over my dead body," I countered.

He blinked. "A fair offer, but Tybalt would object."

"I absolutely would," said Tybalt. "Pray remember that I am yet a King of Cats, and as such, my relationship to Oberon's Law is more negotiable than most people's. Even if they wished to accuse me, they would never find your body. The Shadow Roads have many uses."

Quentin actually paled.

I elbowed Tybalt lightly. "No threatening my squire, please. I was the one who brought up dying, not Quentin."

Simon cleared his throat, pulling the focus of the room back to himself. "Dean, may I get a ride back to Goldengreen with you?" he asked. "I need to return to the Undersea before morning, unless you're truly eager to see your mother again, and October pointed out how much easier it would be for me to depart from the cove inside the knowe."

"You have someone coming to get you?" asked Dean.

Simon nodded. "I have my water-breathing potion, and summoning shells to drop into the sea when I'm ready to go home. Anceline is waiting in the nearby waters to pull me down to the depths."

Living in the Undersea as an air-breathing person without specific aquatic adaptations meant Simon had to work harder to come and go than someone who'd been born to the deeps would have. Dean had the same problem; while his mother was Merrow and hence water-breathing, he didn't inherit those specific traits from her. He was as landbound as the rest of us, which was a large part of why he'd been willing to accept a County in the Mists, rather than staying below where he'd never have been able to freely move through his mother's domain.

Simon and Dean had both had to give up things they cared about in order to live in their preferred environments, but they handled it well, and they'd at least been given the freedom to choose.

"I didn't drive myself here," said Dean. "Are you okay with taking the bus?"

"I lived in this city for longer than you've been alive," said Simon. "Buses hold no terrors for me."

Quentin frowned, focusing on me again. "You were missing for like, half the court proceedings," he said. "What's going on?"

Everyone in this room was someone I trusted to have my back. With the singular exception of Dean, they were also people I knew would follow me into Hell if they were given half the chance. Dean wouldn't necessarily come with me if I went, but he'd have hot cocoa and cookies waiting when I got back. These were my people.

"While the Kingdom was wrapped up in Titania's bullshit, somebody looted the royal treasury," I said. "Apparently, everything you wouldn't want to have go missing is missing, including a hope chest and a scabbard that turns any metal it touches into pure iron. I'm the only hero of the realm Arden has right now, and she wants me to go find her stuff."

Quentin blinked, glancing to Tybalt before returning his attention to me. "She's noticed that you're like, super pregnant right now, hasn't she?"

"Good job, Quentin," I said. "There were at least half a dozen more tactless ways you could have put that, and you managed to avoid them. Yes, she knows I'm pregnant, but pregnancy doesn't excuse me from acts of pointless heroism, and leaving all those things loose in the Kingdom is bad enough for a large enough swath of the population that it's really not something she can wait on. Maternity leave, not so much a thing in this situation. And that's *before* we were also missing a pretender to the throne." I paused, then sighed, making no effort to hide my frustration. "I wish to hell we knew her name. It's annoying to always have to talk around who she is."

"If my mother's stories are accurate, the pretender wishes she knew her own name just as much," said Dean.

We all turned our attention on him, even Simon, who looked uncommonly interested, like this was new information.

"What do you mean?" I asked.

"Sirens and Sea Wights are both found in the Undersea," said Dean. "I don't know who her parents were, or how she wound up with three descendant lines—whoever bore her, they've vanished into the tide, and they don't seem to have any interest in coming forward to claim her. But before she was deposed, whenever Mom talked about the Mists, she'd scoff and say she'd demand the false Queen come down to Saltmist to stand trial for the damage she'd done to relations between the land and sea if she could. Under Gilad, the two realms were as close to united as such things come. Under the pretender, they deteriorated beyond our greatest fears."

"Huh," I said. I'd never considered that two of the pretender's descendant lines were from the Undersea. If she'd been able to breathe water, she might not be able to anymore—I didn't know the abilities of Sirens well enough to say one way or the other. Now that she was balanced between Banshee and Sea Wight, she might be stuck on the land.

Still, that was an angle I hadn't thought of for trying to figure out where she'd come from before she decided to become our problem.

"Are you all right with this?" asked Quentin, returning his attention to Tybalt.

Tybalt lifted an eyebrow. "Not precisely, but October and I have come to an understanding."

"Yes, we have," I said, shooting Quentin a quick, sharp look. "And the rest of us are going to do whatever we can to not make things harder on you."

"I appreciate it," he said.

I yawned, only half-exaggeratedly. "And on that note, the super pregnant lady is going to bed. I know it's only the middle of the night, but I'd rather be asleep when the sun comes up. Tomorrow's going to be busy, especially compared to what I've been doing lately. Dean, you'll get Simon home?"

"I don't want my mother to murder me, so yeah, I'll get him home," said Dean.

"Great. Quentin, will you be up for a while?"

He nodded. "I'll let May know that you're okay, just sleeping."

"Great," I repeated. It was a handy word to use when thanks weren't allowed. I pushed myself to my feet, wobbling before I caught my balance, then moved to hug Simon. I've never been the most huggy of people, but I knew he'd appreciate it, and it was a small enough price to pay to thank him for driving us home.

Indeed, as I had expected, he was smiling and suspiciously bright-eyed when I let him go and stepped back, stopping as my shoulder bumped against Tybalt's chest. "I'll see you soon," I said. "Give my regards to Patrick and Dianda."

"I will," he said, as solemnly as if he were accepting a quest to be discharged before the crown. He even offered me a shallow half-bow.

I answered it with a wave before turning and sliding my arm into Tybalt's. "Walk me upstairs?" I asked.

"Of course, little fish," he said, pressing a kiss against my temple before leading me out of the room, leaving the rest of the evening behind.

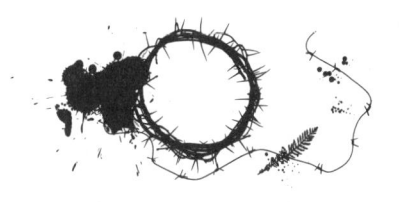

EIGHT

DAME ALTAIR'S KNOWE WAS linked to her personal home, a beautifully maintained Victorian house in the area locals referred to as "postcard row," a neighborhood so packed with ornate Victorians that it probably increased the property values of the entire city by several percentage points. Almost all the houses were whimsically painted in a variety of rainbow and pastel shades, making them the frequent target of visiting tourists and their ever-ready cameras.

Dame Altair's house was on a corner, the tiny front yard filled with a tangled riot of native and invasive flowers, culminating in the white and pink climbing rose that encircled the porch rail and was still blooming even an hour past sunset. The faint scent of black clove and panther lily confirmed my assumption that the roses had been enchanted in some way, just a little tweak to keep them sweet and healthy and flowering for their planter's pleasure.

Titania is the Lady of Flowers, after all, and while the Daoine Sidhe have never been great masters of horticulture, their innate flower magic is strong enough that some of them can figure out a few tricks. I carefully grasped the porch rail between loops of thorny stem.

On the step behind me, Quentin shifted his weight. I could almost hear him deliberating whether I'd yell at him if he tried to help me the rest of the way up the stairs. When he cleared his throat, I knew the question was coming.

I lifted the hand that wasn't holding on to the rail, signaling for him to stay quiet. "No," I said, voice firm and surprisingly calm. "You can't help me. I need to look like a professional here, not an invalid."

"But—"

"Quentin, I know I'm the first pregnant person you've really had to deal with, and I apologize for the inconvenience, but I promise you, I'm not that fragile. I'm here to do my job. Dame Altair's men were attacked by whoever it is that has the missing scabbard, and she was snatched by whoever's helping the false queen. That means talking to her is priority one, and if I want her to take me seriously, I have to show her that I can handle myself. I promise to ask for a chair as soon as we're inside, all right?"

"All right," he agreed.

He was still hovering a little closer than I liked, but he wasn't touching me or saying anything, which was probably the best I could hope for at the moment.

At least Danny had been kind enough to stay in the car. I was trying to seem harmless and deferential. Showing up with a humanoid brick wall at my back wouldn't do anything to encourage that impression.

"Chin up," I said. "We're almost there." I was finally at the top of the stairs. I moved to position myself in front of the door,

Like the houses around it, Dame Altair's home was painted a variety of bright colors. Unlike most of the other houses, hers was done up in the shades of the Mists: blue and silver and a sandy gold. The gold wasn't a new affectation, but it was one I hadn't seen often since Arden's ascension. She favored the blue and silver, with occasional strikes of blackberry purple. It was a nice way for her to put her own spin on the royal theming, even if she couldn't change it completely.

Nothing about the house indicated that it was a fae place. I only knew I was at the right house because I'd been here before—but never inside, oh no, never once inside; Dame Altair might not be as bigoted as some of her cousins, but she was a purebloooded Daoine Sidhe, and they had been encouraged to look down on changelings since the beginning of their line. She could accept that I was a knight. She could accept that I was a hero. That didn't necessarily mean she could accept that I was sufficiently domesticated to trust on her carpet.

She clearly didn't have any sort of proximity wards set on the door. Some noble households liked using those to tell them when they had company; they made it possible for their seneschals and chatelaines to open doors before anyone knocked, thus seeming prescient and all-knowing. Since that hadn't happened here, Dame Altair was either less concerned about appearances or—more likely—simply hadn't thought of it.

I leaned forward and rang the bell before sinking back into a neutral position to wait. I allowed my left hand to rest atop the swell of my stomach. It was a calculated decision, however natural it might feel; pureblood fertility rates are so low that many of them are fascinated by pregnancy, seeing it as something unattainable and thus infinitely desirable. She hadn't shown any signs of that particular fixation during Arden's court, but that could just have been the situation. If I could convince her to treat me well because it would grant her a rare and exclusive proximity to pregnancy, that wouldn't be the worst thing I could possibly do.

Quentin fell into place behind me, standing with a precision and rigid posture that I had never been able to master. Etienne used to despair of me ever serving as a proper knight when he'd been training me, at least in part because he'd failed to beat the importance of standing at attention through my thick head. Well, that was all right. I still couldn't manage it, but at least now Quentin could do it for me.

Footsteps approached the door, loud and echoing enough that I knew they had to be intentional. There had to be some sort of charm in play, something to amplify the sound of someone coming. That impression was only reinforced as the footsteps slowed, the person on the other side of the door clearly taking their own sweet time about getting to me.

Under normal circumstances, I would have been more than content to wait. But here and now, I wasn't in the mood. The baby was using my bladder as a soccer ball. I placed my free hand at the small of my back and pressed, forcing myself to straighten slightly. Even that only did so much to take the pressure off my aching knees.

Quentin shot me a quick, anxious look. "I'm just saying, it's not too late for us to go home and tell the queen you're not up for it. I could come back later with Danny, or we could ask Etienne, or—"

The footsteps were almost to the door. "It's too late now," I said, with exaggerated good cheer. "I'm not fast enough to play ding-dong dash with the nobility. We'd be caught before we made it halfway down the stairs."

The door swung open, revealing a Bridge Troll in a formal footman's uniform, Dame Altair's arms stitched above his right breast. He looked down his nose at us, expression unreadable.

"May I help you?" he asked.

I managed, barely, to control my flinch of recognition. I had never actually been inside Dame Altair's household, didn't know most of her staff—or if I did, didn't realize they worked for her—but I recognized that voice all the same, even if I didn't know the owner's name. This was the Bridge Troll who had been with Dame Altair and the unlamented Kyle in an alley in Titania's San Francisco. The three of them had attacked me, thinking a defenseless changeling would make an easy target for their evening's amusement. Kyle had been the one to actually stab me, and had received my knife to the throat as payment for his efforts, but this Bridge Troll had been the one to hold me in place while Kyle drove his own knife home.

Bridge Trolls are one of the larger descendant lines found on land. While there are types of fae in the Undersea who can grow to truly titanic proportions, the land has always been a little more conservative when it comes to how big the fae can get. This one stood roughly eight feet tall, with shoulders at least three feet wide and arms like Christmas hams. He looked like he could have easily snapped me in half over his knee, and not really noticed that he'd done it.

His skin was a craggy basalt gray, looking for all the world like flexible stone; it crinkled around the edges of his eyes as they narrowed, and he frowned at me. He didn't have any hair, not even eyelashes or brows, and his eyes were that curious shade of pink that sometimes appears in granite cliff faces.

I swallowed, hard. Yes, the last time I'd seen him, he'd been threatening me, but that had been another world, and we'd both been different people there.

"Sir Daye on the business of the Queen," I said, and was pleased when my voice came out level and steady. "My squire, Quentin, accompanies me. I am here to speak with your mistress, Dame Altair, on the matter of her recent abduction, and further, on the subject of the attacks upon her household."

The massive Bridge Troll took another half-step forward, and it was difficult not to interpret that as a threat. I was beginning to regret leaving Danny in the car. It would have been nice to have my own living wall to hide behind. Not that it would have necessarily done all that much good—this man was larger than Danny in every direction, and while size isn't the only indicator of a Bridge Troll's strength, the last thing I wanted to do was get my friends hurt.

"Did my mistress invite you?" asked the man, and his voice was the deep rumble of tectonic plates moving in the darkness, long-buried and cold.

"As stated, I am here on the business of the queen," I said. "I require no invitation when I act in the name of Arden Windermere. Please allow us access."

The man didn't move again, but remained where he was as he looked at me with coldly measuring eyes. Finally, in that same deep, cold voice, he said, "I remember you."

Crap. "I believe this is our first meeting, sir."

"In the better world spun for us by our Lady of the Flowers, I found you by night in an alleyway where you had no business being, and you lifted a weapon against your betters. Kyle died because you could not know your place."

"That world was a lie created by a woman who had just murdered her own child in cold blood," spat Quentin, before I could say anything. He stepped forward, like he was going to put himself between me and the massive footman. "That enchantment was ended by the eldest daughter of Oberon, because it was unjust. How dare you call it the 'better world'? To view a deceit as such is to stand in opposition to all that is right and just in Faerie."

"No one said Faerie was fair, little boy," said the footman. "It was a world where people like myself weren't expected to bow down to our inferiors. I would have expected you to see things as clearly as I do."

Quentin didn't say anything, just glared at him with his mouth set into a hard line, chin jutting forward like a challenge or a target. I reached over and put a hand on his arm.

"I remember our encounter," I said, as calmly as I could. "I remember your Kyle stabbing me before I slit his throat. He thought to kill me first, and I acted in self-defense. Our Queen has absolved me of all blame in that encounter, and the memories of my blood have been viewed by her blood-workers to verify that I spoke truly when I told her what had happened. I am here on royal business. Please, let us pass."

The man took another step forward, filling the doorway like an animate stone wall. The enchantments on the roses that circled the porch were beginning to make more sense; he should have been fully visible from the street, but he wasn't making any effort to disguise or hide himself. Seeing me being loomed at by a Bridge Troll should have brought Danny rushing up the stairs to defend me, but he hadn't come to my defense as yet. The roses were somehow protecting us from view. A don't-look-here worked into the roots, most likely, something too deeply seated to be destroyed by dawn.

It was a clever way to spare her servants from needing to be disguised, and I would have been impressed if I hadn't been working so hard not to get pissed off. The situation was ludicrous. Whether he liked me or not, this man couldn't deny that I was a hero of the realm, making my claim to be here on the Queen's behalf utterly believable. Even aside from that, there had been two attacks on his mistress in the very recent past. I would have expected him to be eager to get answers for her, if only because someone coming at his employer with iron weapons would put him in danger.

I narrowed my own eyes, keeping my hand on Quentin's arm.

"Perhaps you don't understand," I said. "I'm here—we're here—because Queen Arden Windermere in the Mists wants us to be. She wants me to speak with your mistress, and I'm not leaving until I fulfill what my queen has asked of me. Now, I'm sure you don't want to explain to the queen, or to my husband, the local King of Cats, why you left a pregnant knight standing on the front porch while you exercised your petty authority to make things harder for her, hmm?"

Bridge Trolls have such rough-hewn features that they're not famed for the subtlety of their expressions. They can smile and they can snarl, but the little moods are difficult to read. This man was no different. I thought his lips tightened slightly, but it was hard for me to tell.

"I will tell my mistress you have arrived," he said, and stepped backward, slamming the door rather than inviting us inside.

Quentin turned to me, visibly fuming. "He's violating every rule of hospitality I can name, and probably a few that I've either forgotten or never had cause to learn. You don't leave the representative of a friendly monarch standing outside in the cold, and you certainly don't leave a pregnant woman outside the protection of a knowe when you have the ability to welcome her past the wards."

"Changeling," I said, gesturing to myself with one hand. "Remember, the rules are different for me sometimes." Somehow that didn't sting as much as it would have once upon a time. Spending a few months living in a reality where I'd been treated as so far below the people around me that I'd had no hope of ever dealing with them as an equal had pointed out both how far I'd come in my real life, and how bone-deep *stupid* the lingering prejudices of Faerie really were. Stupid things can still do harm, but it's harder to take them seriously.

Quentin glowered. "Even if you want to take that position, which you shouldn't, because it's a terrible position and I hate it, I'm your squire, and I'm not a changeling. My presence should be enough to make him let us inside."

"But it wasn't. I'm not saying we stand out here all night. Just that we give Dame Altair a few minutes to realize how badly her man is fucking up before we start making a fuss." I turned back to the door, smiling almost serenely. "She's a smart lady. I'm sure she'll be able to figure out that pissing off the queen she has to live under isn't a great way for her to keep enjoying the relative autonomy that Arden extends to her trusted vassals."

Faerie's hierarchy is imprecise and incredibly nepotistic, but there are monarchs who are far more unpleasant and aggressive about enforcing "the right way of things" than Arden has ever been inclined to be. I was reasonably sure that Dame Altair was in no real hurry to find out how unpleasant an oppressive queen could really be.

As if on cue, footsteps approached the door. These ones were softer and quicker than the Bridge Troll's had been, not quite quick enough for their owner to be rushing, but definitely quick enough that there was no question of whether or not they were dawdling. I straightened again, trying to look utterly relaxed and not at all as if my knees were hurting.

The person on the other side of the door paused. I tensed, resisting the urge to grumble. All this waiting around was starting to really wear on my nerves.

The door swung slowly open, and I plastered the pleasant smile back across my face as Dame Altair appeared.

Like many among the Daoine Sidhe, she seemed to have taken all her camouflage tips from a macaw rather than a human. Her hair was a deep shade of purple-blue that clearly hadn't come from a bottle, based on the way the color extended from roots to tips, unfaded and layered with natural highlights. Her eyes were the vivid orange of panther lilies, echoing the scent of the magic swirling around her. Unlike most Daoine Sidhe, she wasn't particularly pale, but had a deep natural tan that almost matched the unpainted wood of the doorframe. It was a nice change from the near-universal pallor of her line.

Given that the fae steal surnames from our human ancestors, her complexion was probably a gift from some long-dead mortal whose blood had been purged via hope chest as soon as it became possible, leaving nothing but coloration and a name behind.

She was wearing a long pseudo-medieval gown in steel gray velvet, and she looked me up and down with visible scorn. I managed, barely, not to follow her inspection of me with one of my own: I knew what I looked like, but it was difficult sometimes not to emulate the Daoine Sidhe when they so ostentatiously implied that I was doing something even slightly wrong. My maternity pants and once-oversized sweater were clean and unstained, and that would have to be enough for her. Even if I'd wanted to run home and change into something more formal, all my normal clothing was too small for me right now. I hadn't seen much point in buying a bunch of new maternity gear when I almost never left the house, and I was *not* going to dignify Dame Altair's scorn with one of my nicer court dresses. She could choke on whatever she wanted to say to me.

"Dame Altair," I said, hoping that none of my irritation would show in either my face or my tone. "A pleasure to see you again. I appreciate your taking the time."

"Ehren informs me that you have some cockamamie story about being here on behalf of Queen Windermere," she said, voice tight and sharp. "I know he can't be correct about that. Surely even you wouldn't make such a ludicrous claim."

"Not if it weren't true," I said. "Sorry to disappoint, but I'm here as a hero of the realm to try and figure out why you're being targeted. Which means that yes, Queen Windermere sent me, I'm here on official business, and while I'll try not to waste your time, I would very much appreciate it if you'd allow me and my squire to come inside. I find standing uncomfortable at the moment."

Admitting to weakness was a calculated risk. It was also apparently the right thing to do, judging by the way her expression momentarily softened before she collected herself and straightened again, looking down her nose at me.

"Well, then, I suppose you'd best have a chair," she said. "I'll be sending a letter to the Queen to chide her for her choice of champions. She should send her best to help a valued member of her vassalage, not whatever it is you're meant to represent."

I didn't rise to the obvious bait, only nodded and said, "My lady is kind," before stepping through the open door and into the knowe proper.

As almost always happened when I crossed from the mortal world into the slice of Summerlands contained within a private knowe, the world spun around me, a dizzying whirl of up becoming down, down becoming up, and right and left inverting. I stopped to catch my breath and try to convince my stomach that it didn't want to lose what little breakfast I'd managed to force myself to eat before I left the house. Acid rose in the back of my throat, searing and hot. I swallowed. Then I swallowed again for good measure.

It had been a while since the transition hit me that hard; the more fae I become, the easier it is to slip between worlds. It doesn't seem fair. There should be a few advantages to surviving Faerie as a changeling. The acid receded, and my stomach calmed. Only then did I straighten and look to Dame Altair, who was watching me with a smug sort of satisfaction, like she'd known it was going to hurt me to make the crossing, and hadn't warned me because she'd wanted to see me suffer.

I'd never considered her much of an antagonist before—she'd even hired me to do a few jobs, including the monster hunt that ended with Danny taking possession of his beloved Barghests—but the way she was looking at me now made me think I might need to reconsider how much she disliked me. She was looking at me like I was defiling her knowe just by standing inside it.

I've seen that look on plenty of purebloods. Somehow, it never gets less offensive.

Well, if she was going to look at me like I was doing something wrong by doing nothing at all, I was going to show her the respect that she so clearly deserved. I looked slowly around the room, not making any effort to acknowledge her or the expression on her face.

Dame Altair's décor was clearly intended to compliment the mortal exterior of the knowe. Everything was Victorian, fussy and precise as a BBC documentary. Tybalt would have been able to point out every anachronism and out-of-period knickknack. Knowing that made me feel a little better about the oppressive propriety of my surroundings. She might think she was perfect, but Tybalt would know that she wasn't with just a glance. He'd have some fairly scathing things to say if he were here, I was sure of that.

The carpet was the same blue and silver as the house exterior, woven into a complex pattern of silver birch and strikingly blue lilies. Flowers like that probably grew somewhere in deeper Faerie. That didn't mean she'd ever seen them, but it meant her rugmaker might have been working from life. They were impressively realistic for something we were meant to walk on.

Quentin stopped immediately behind me, where he could easily catch me if I happened to stumble. It was nice to know he was there, even if I was getting well and truly tired of the continual babysitting. I turned to flash him a quick smile, then returned my attention to Dame Altair.

"You have a lovely home," I said politely.

"I have a lovely demesne," she corrected, voice as stiff as her posture.

"I know you're titled," I said, not mentioning that a dame was of the same rank as a knight, and knights don't normally get land. "I was unaware that this was a formal holding. My apologies, my lady. May I know the name of these lands?"

The tips of her sharply pointed ears reddened as she shifted her weight from one foot to the other. Interesting. "It's not a formal holding," she said. "But when I was granted my title—by King Windermere, well before your time—I was able to open a knowe here, with the aid of my brother and his liege, and the king agreed to let me claim all of Postcard Row as my own. My domain has never been properly named. I would need a baroness's rank to call my own before that would be a safe decision."

"I don't understand," I said, frowning. "How would naming the place change anything?"

"A named domain is generally a barony or greater," said Dame Altair. "If I declared my lands a barony, I would be inviting any unlanded baron in the Westlands—including that misfit father of yours—to come and claim my demesne as their own. I refuse to have my hard work stolen out from underneath me by some wastrel who couldn't find their own lands."

"Oh." It was a paranoid way to live, and I suddenly wondered whether King Gilad had done her any favors by allowing her to open a knowe and claim lands she couldn't control. But then, there were precedents for lands belonging to people without the titles to hold them. Amandine's tower was an example. No one questioned her right to hold it, but she didn't name it, and maybe that made all the difference in the world.

True, Amandine was Firstborn where Dame Eloise Altair most distinctly was not, but no one had known that for a long, long time. She had her tower, and when Simon had lived there with her, he had remained an unlanded baron.

"It is as it is," said Dame Altair, shrugging elegantly. "Now. You wanted to speak with me?"

"I did, and I do, but first I want to sit down," I said. "Pregnant people need to sit and stand up a lot, or our joints start to hurt. All our connective tissue loosens and gets softer than it would normally be, to help make it easier for us to push the baby out when the time comes."

Dame Altair paled, looking like she was considering losing her own breakfast. I really hoped she wouldn't. If she threw up, I would *definitely* throw up, and with both of us barfing, Quentin might wind up joining in, and then we'd be dealing with a crisis I was distinctly not equipped to handle. Better for all of us if we could keep our evening meals on the inside where they belonged.

"Forgive me," she said, visibly swallowing. "I forget how fleshy and—animalistic reproduction is."

I frowned. "Forgiven," I said. "I take it you have no children of your own?"

"No," she said, with evident horror. "Should I feel the need to get myself an heir, my brother would be much better suited to the production of such than I have ever been. With no hereditary title to my name, I have less to worry about in that regard."

"Ah," I said.

"Given that *you* have no hereditary title, and to my understanding, titles within the Court of Cats aren't passed along bloodlines, I don't understand why you would go to all the trouble."

I blinked. "Um," I said.

Dame Altair shrugged, turning to walk down a short hall to an adjoining room. She didn't gesture for us to follow, but under the circumstances, it would have been rude not to. So Quentin and I pursued her down the hall and through a door into what proved to be a sparsely appointed parlor that would have made more sense in a hunting lodge than in her Victorian fantasy. There were two large armchairs and an actual fainting couch, which I made a beeline for, sinking gratefully into the leather cushions.

"Were you going to enlighten me?"

I blinked again, looking at Dame Altair. She was watching me with a pleasantly composed expression of unruffled curiosity, lowering herself into one of the armchairs with the sort of graceful muscular control that spoke to years of practicing her etiquette. No one realizes how much core strength it takes for our courtiers to carry themselves with such elegant precision. They'd be a lot more frightened of women in watered-silk gowns if they knew.

"Enlighten you as to what?"

"Why you would bother with all the mess and trouble when you don't have a crown to protect or a throne to pass along." She waved one elegant hand, indicating the overall shape of me. "It seems like it can't help but interfere with your ability to do your job, and I've always understood that you prided yourself on your position."

There was an insult buried somewhere in all of that, but I wasn't going to give her the satisfaction of trying to find it. Instead, I rested one hand atop my stomach and shrugged. "It seemed like a good way to pass the next few decades. We weren't *trying*, but I wasn't on any sort of birth control."

Of the two of us, me and Tybalt, I was the one who would have needed to take steps if I truly didn't want to have a child just yet. Fae have notoriously low fertility rates. Being partially human, it was always going to be easier for me to get pregnant than it would have been for Dame Altair.

There are other factors in play, naturally, but with me and Tybalt it had been—it was—easy.

"Interesting," said Dame Altair. "And you're sure it's safe for someone in your . . . position . . . to stand as guardian to a child?"

"I won't be standing as guardian," I said. "I'm going to be a mother. It's not the same thing at all."

Dame Altair made a noncommittal noise. I decided I was done with this line of conversation. No matter how much I was trying to make nice with the woman, she was one crossed line away from Quentin stealing my phone and calling Tybalt, and that would end with blood on the walls and nothing of any real use accomplished.

"I came here to ask you about your abduction," I said, shifting awkwardly on the fainting couch in an effort to look slightly less like one of the elephant seals that lounged down on the pier.

Dame Altair's expression iced over, turning cold and hard. "You mean when your father snatched me from my own knowe?" she asked sharply.

"His own blood absolved him," I said.

"As if any daughter wouldn't lie for her father's sake," she scoffed.

"I haven't been his daughter long enough to feel that kind of loyalty," I said. "But even if I had, I doubt any amount of dutiful daughtering would have been enough to convince Bahey to let me get away with a blatant lie in front of her. Unless you're questioning the honor of the queen's Adhene?"

"Not at all," said Dame Altair. "But they should have allowed another blood-worker to validate your claims, if you wanted them to carry weight. It seems improper to allow a man's claimed child and potential heir to be the one who absolves him of blame in a crime as heinous as kidnapping."

"There's nothing in the Law about kidnapping," I said. "Besides, you clearly know Simon well enough to point the finger in his direction, but not enough to know how he used his magic when he was actively pursuing villainy. If he'd abducted you, you wouldn't be a biped now. You'd be a tree somewhere on the verge of Golden Gate Park, if you were lucky. If you were unlucky, you'd be swimming with the koi in the Tea Garden, and Oberon help you find a way free of that enchantment."

"*You* did."

"We aren't of the same descendant line," I replied, as coolly as I could manage.

"No, I suppose we're not," she said. "You're something new, but you rebuked your Firstborn in an open forum. However will you learn to serve Faerie as you were intended?"

I didn't have an answer for that, so for a moment, I allowed myself the simple luxury of glaring at her. My sullen silence probably confirmed half of her unthinkingly bigoted attitudes about changelings, but it made me feel better enough that I didn't actually care. I just glared.

Dame Altair pursed her lips and leaned over, picking up a small silver and enamel bell from the table next to her seat. "My, did I hit a nerve?" she asked, and gave the bell a delicate shake. It didn't make a sound, but the air felt briefly electric, like we were sitting in the eye of an approaching storm. She set the bell down again. "I assure you that it wasn't my intention. I just find myself *ever* so curious about how things work for you. You're our only exemplar of so many unique things, however do you stand it?"

"I have a good support system," I said, through gritted teeth. Her genteel hostility was beyond grating. "Can we just agree that the evidence says Simon didn't abduct you, and move on to discussing who might have done so? Would you be willing to bleed for me? A sample of your blood could tell us a great deal about what actually happened."

She actually recoiled, shying away from me until her shoulders hit the back of her chair. It would have been insulting if it hadn't been so bizarrely complimentary. It was like she thought I could call the blood through her skin without reaching for a knife.

"I won't be doing that," she said, tone going icy and brittle. "You can't compel me to bleed."

I couldn't, but Arden could. Looking at the sheer terror on her face, I decided not to mention that. "It was only a request," I said. "If we can both agree that Simon didn't abduct you, I needn't bring it up again."

"I still say I smelled cinnamon," she said sullenly.

"Simon's magic smells of mulled apple cider, which means mulling spices," I said. "It's a complicated magical signature, and cinnamon features in the mixture, but it's not sufficiently dominant to have been the only thing you smelled if he had been behind your abduction."

She made a small sound of disagreement, mouth forming a down-turned moue of disapproval.

"If Simon didn't snatch you, which he didn't, someone else must have done so," I said, ignoring her displeasure as firmly as I could. If she wanted to be a pouty little noblewoman about this, I could just steamroll her until I got what I wanted. She wasn't playing nicely with me. I felt no requirement to play nicely with her. "Did you see the false Queen at all before you were pressed into her place?"

"No," said Dame Altair, still sullen. "I was walking home from an evening outing—"

"To where?"

She stopped and frowned at me, clearly annoyed by my interjection. "I beg your pardon?"

"Where did you go that you were walking home and vulnerable? Did you have any of your guards with you?"

"My guard has been reluctant to accompany me on city streets since Ehren's brother, Helge, stopped his dancing."

Meaning she'd been employing at least two Bridge Trolls. That was interesting in its own right. Bridge Trolls form very tight family bonds. Even if they don't have born siblings, they'll go out and find siblings they can claim as their own. Danny, who was presumably still sitting outside in his cab, lived with his sister, and I neither knew nor cared whether they were related. For Dame Altair to have employed a

Bridge Troll who'd died in her service and then retained his brother was . . . well.

Ehren suddenly moved to the top of my list of people whose magical signatures I needed to document for similarities to the smell of cinnamon. Getting a Bridge Troll's brother killed was an absolutely viable motivation for abducting someone, although it didn't answer why he would want to free the false Queen—and that had to be a part of the motivation behind the whole mess. That woman was so unpleasant that no one with any sense would have let her out.

"I see," I said, as neutrally as I could manage. "So you went out alone shortly after the death of a member of your staff?"

"Yes," said Dame Altair. She was starting to look anxious, although she was trying to hide it behind a veneer of arrogant serenity. It wasn't going to work, but I had to admire the effort. "I needed to take some air, so I went for a walk, and to visit a friend of mine. Lady Pilar, who keeps her court at Buena Vista Park."

I made a noncommittal noise, nodding.

Lady Pilar was a Silene, titled during her brief marriage to a Daoine Sidhe Count who had long since left the kingdom for greener pastures that didn't include his ex-wife. She'd been fairly active in local society when I was a child, but had withdrawn to her knowe at Buena Vista Park after she remarried. Her second husband, a Tangie man I'd never met, didn't care as much for the social whirl or the needs of etiquette, and had convinced her to stay home with him. I'd never considered that she might still have friends. I certainly hadn't thought Dame Altair might be one of them.

She frowned. "You think I'm lying," she accused.

"What I think is less important than finding out what really happened," I said. "You went to visit Lady Pilar and her husband at Buena Vista Park, walked home alone, and were abducted by someone whose magic smelled of cinnamon. Do you remember anything else about them?"

"I never said I went to visit Pilar's husband," she shot back. "Eanraig is no friend of mine, and I no friend of his. He tolerates my presence for her sake, but only because he doesn't have a choice in the matter."

The parlor door swung open and a narrow-faced Candela appeared. She was dressed in a variation of a Victorian maid's uniform, down to the little white hat pinned atop her ashen hair, and her Merry Dancers circled her in an endless swirling dance, their skins glowing a pale slate blue. She was carrying a silver tray, and she stopped just past the threshold.

Dame Altair turned toward her, but didn't smile. "I rang for refreshments some time ago; where have you been?" she asked, and while her tone was mild, there was a venom there I couldn't fully understand.

There are times when I wonder why anyone in Faerie chooses to serve the noble houses. Hearth fae like my friend Kerry can feel compelled to stick near kitchens and bathhouses; they serve because their magic makes it easy and satisfying in a way that none of the rest of us can truly understand. But they don't make up the majority of the servant class. Silene and Candela, Glastig and Tuatha de Dannan are all found in noble halls with reasonable frequency, and none of them *have* to be there. They stay of their own free will.

In Titania's world, I was raised to consider myself fortunate to serve my betters, and I didn't have a choice in whether I stayed or went. But this wasn't Titania's world, and I couldn't imagine what the woman in the doorway was getting out of her service to Dame Altair that was worth the way the lady was looking at her now, like she was lower than the scum the rest of us scraped off our shoes.

"Pardon, ma'am, but I didn't know how many I was meant to be preparing for until I found Ehren in the hall," said the Candela, her Merry Dancers dimming as the tide of words spilled out of her mouth. Candela are famously terse. To have her babbling like that was almost alarming. "I brought the drinks you rang for. Forgive me?"

"Unlikely," sniffed Dame Altair, and gestured broadly toward the small table at the center of our little seating area. The Candela hurried forward, setting her tray down at the center of the table. Seen more closely, it contained a silver teapot, three cups, and smaller pots for cream and sugar.

Dame Altair watched this, then nodded sharply, and the Candela woman picked up the teapot, carefully filling each of the cups two-thirds of the way with liquid. Mine came out pink, Quentin's yellow, and Dame Altair's brown. I raised an eyebrow.

"No caffeine for pregnant women, but blackcurrant juice is safe and even beneficial, thanks to the vitamin C," she said, mildly, as she began adding cream and sugar to her tea. "Squires are by definition children, and lemonade is the appropriate drink to serve children in polite company. No trickery here, simply hospitality in its most basic form. Please, drink."

She picked up her teacup and took a careful sip, tasting the balance she'd created. This done, she turned to the Candela and inclined her head. "Barely acceptable. Not a total failure. You may go."

The Candela turned and fled the room as quickly as propriety allowed. Interestingly, she did it on foot. Candela are short-range teleporters, capable of accessing the fringes of the Shadow Roads. They aren't usually talkative, and they aren't inclined to walk when they could be flitting through space like it doesn't actually mean anything of any importance.

I picked up my teacup. It was light and delicate in my hand, more like it had been crafted from rose petals than any sort of ceramic or stone. I sniffed the liquid inside, finding it sweet and fruity. *Blackcurrant*, confirmed the part of my brain responsible for cataloging scents and identifying them in people's magic. This wasn't magical, but it was distinct, and I would remember it if I encountered it again.

I glanced at Quentin. He had his own cup, and was emulating Dame Altair, sipping politely. I gave my cup another look.

Dame Altair was watching me. I met her eyes and smiled politely, then took my first careful sip. Sweetness flooded my mouth, with a sour undernote that tasted almost like palatable decay. There wasn't any other way of describing it. I swallowed, barely managing not to cough.

"That's . . . interesting," I said, setting my cup aside. "Now, you visited the Lady Pilar alone? No escort or guard of any sort?"

"Mine all refused to accompany me," she said, pursing her lips unhappily. "Pilar offered two of her own men to see me safely home. You may want to speak with her next. I'm not sure whether they made it back to her after I was taken. I only got home from the court a few hours before your arrival, and I haven't had the time to go and check. She doesn't have anything as modern as a telephone."

Maybe not, but Dame Altair had a Candela; sending a message should have been as easy as deciding to send a message, and not something she needed to spend time thinking about. I was starting to get more and more uneasy about the way things worked in this household.

"Where was I—ah, yes. Roughly halfway between her home and my own, the air around us began to chill too swiftly and too sharply to be a simple shift in the weather. I moved closer to the guards, positioning myself so they would be able to defend me from whatever was about to happen, and the smell of cinnamon was suddenly everywhere, thick enough to be cloying. I staggered away, trying to breathe despite the weight of that perfume, and my vision began to blur around the edges. Have you ever been so overwhelmed by someone else's magic that it stole your sight away?"

"Sight, no, but consciousness, yes, and ability to breathe, yes." I took another sip of my fruity drink, frowning a little at the contradiction between this version of her story and the one she'd given at the court.

Dame Altair nodded. "Then you surely understand why I don't have many details. The world spun, the air smelled of cinnamon, and at some point, I was too overcome to endure and my awareness simply slipped away. When I awoke, I was bound in rowan and dressed in a gown I remembered from the former Queen's wardrobe. There were no mirrors in the room where I was prisoned. I didn't realize what I looked like until I was taken before the court."

Something about the way she was ordering her words seemed wrong, the contradictions mounting. I frowned deeper and put my cup aside, as carefully as I could. Not carefully enough, somehow; it sloshed as it landed on the tray, spilling its contents over the silver. That was odd. I was usually better than that at controlling my motions.

"I'm so sorry for the mess," I said—or tried to say, anyway. What actually came out was a garbled moan, syllables blending together and melting into a singular guttural mass.

Dame Altair smiled. "Yes, well, I thought that might be the case. You're rather famously difficult to incapacitate, Sir Daye. I'd heard the rumors, but I honestly thought they'd been exaggerated. With your allies, well. You can't blame me for believing they'd go out of their way to talk you up as a bigger threat than you are."

She put her own cup down and leaned forward to tap my nose with the tip of one finger.

"Boop," she said.

I tried to smack her hand away. Like my apology, the action was a failure. My arm refused to move, no matter how hard I ordered it to do so.

Her smile grew. "You can fight all you like, but even your infamous recovery time isn't going to get you past this that quickly."

The edges of my vision were beginning to go gray, charring like a burning piece of paper before they dropped away to reveal only an endless, aching nothingness. I tried to turn toward Quentin. By forcing myself as hard as I could, I could move my head just enough to see him slumped over in his chair, eyes closed and mouth slightly open. A bead of drool was collecting in the corner of his lips. That seemed impossibly important. It shouldn't have been, but it did.

"Don't worry," said Dame Altair. "I'm not going to kill you. You're far too valuable for that. You, and everything you carry."

The threat in her words was clear, for all that it was unspoken. If I'd been capable of it, I would have lunged for her then. Instead, I rolled my eyes, and the char continued to advance, and the nothingness consumed me.

NINE

I KNEW I WAS still inside Dame Altair's knowe as soon as I woke up. It wasn't the lingering scent of her magic in the air, although that was a factor—it was the fact that I'd been stowed in a bedroom as Victorian and fussy as the rooms I'd seen downstairs. I'll give her this: when she found a decorating scheme she liked, she committed to it completely.

Consciousness returned in a trickle, drop by drop, until my skull was so full that it overflowed and I woke up, head pounding, eyes blurred, but otherwise fully present. I tried to sit up. The chains holding my hands above my head and my legs in a spread-eagled position stopped me. I frowned, craning my neck to get a better view of my bonds.

Padded manacles made from yarrow braided with silver clasped my wrists and ankles, keeping me on my back. Cute. They looked fragile, but I knew from their design that I wouldn't be able to break them if I spent a hundred years pulling as hard as I could. This was Coblynau crafting, and it contained far more metal than it seemed.

Yarrow dampens the magic of the rare descendant lines who aren't bothered by iron. Enough silver to enhance that effect, and yarrow can be used to dampen *anyone's* magic, including my own. I tried again to sit up, testing the limits of my bonds. The cuffs around my wrists prevented me from using my hands, while the ones around my ankles were tight enough to keep me from really moving my legs.

The only reason I didn't immediately spiral into panic was that I could tell I was still pregnant. The baby wasn't currently moving around, which was a little worrying, since there weren't any outward signs to tell me what my own injuries had been. The trouble with healing like it's my job is that any injuries I might have incurred while I was knocked out were already gone, my body undoing any damage with effortless speed.

I exhaled, relaxing more than I probably should have—I was also still captive, bound in one of Dame Altair's guest chambers for no reason I could guess.

I fumed, glaring at the room around me like it was somehow personally responsible for my situation. The walls didn't offer me any apologies, which was honestly a little rude of them. The air was cool if not quite cold, and my captors hadn't given me a blanket, although there was a pillow under my head, probably to add one more limiting factor to my movement. Bit by bit, the blurry edges of my vision turned crisp, although the aching in my head remained. Headaches aren't always strictly physical for me. They can also mean I've done too much magic, or had too much magic done to me, and that sort of thing doesn't heal as quickly as everything else.

I didn't remember doing that much magic, but anything was possible. She'd dosed me with something strong enough to put me under, and that sort of thing isn't supposed to be possible anymore. I froze, the implications of that sinking in. She'd dosed me with something so powerful that it could get past my healing to hurt me.

The baby.

I bit my own lip, trying to focus on what the blood had to tell me despite the humming interference of the yarrow and silver, like white noise injected into what should have been a private conversation. The static it created was severe enough that I had to bite myself twice more to get enough blood to understand what my body was saying.

The baby was fine. The baby had been knocked out alongside me, but had woken up, and there were no traces of whatever poison or potion she'd used remaining in either one of us.

That answered a question I hadn't been actively asking, since I'd been trying to let myself be surprised by this pregnancy as much as I could. While the baby and I currently shared a circulatory system, it seemed increasingly likely that they had inherited at least some degree of my ridiculous healing speed. That was a good thing—in my line of work, having an indestructible kid is far from the worst possible complaint—but it was also a bad thing. No human school for this kiddo. No trips to the public park until they were old enough to avoid skinned knees and split lips.

Children pay attention, and human children are much more willing to believe impossible things than their parents are. We would need to keep our kid away from places where recovering too fast for Band-Aids might endanger our ability to keep Faerie hidden.

Of course, before we had to worry about playgrounds and playdates, I needed to worry about getting out of this alive. I tugged on my bonds again, uselessly, then slumped into the bed, trying to figure out how I was supposed to navigate my current shitty situation. Normally I would either dislocate a joint or find something sharp to saw my bonds against; no such luck this time. My cuffs were padded, I didn't have a knife, and I didn't have anything hard enough to throw myself against that I could reliably dislocate my shoulder.

My magic is pretty great when it comes to tracking people down or shredding spells, but it's not so useful when I'm trying to get out of situations like this one. I didn't get any of the big flashy tricks. No teleportation or voluntary transformations here.

I paused. I didn't have either of those things, but my husband did. Tybalt had to have noticed by now that Quentin and I had been gone for too long. Even if he'd gone feline and somehow lost all track of time—not likely, when I was out in the field and he couldn't directly keep an eye on me—Danny would have noticed our failure to return. The cavalry was coming. All I needed to do was wait it out.

Just wait.

There were no clocks in the room, and while there was a window, it looked out on the eternal twilight of a Summerlands sky, giving me nothing I could use to hang the passage of time upon. I tried to focus on my breathing, the beating of my heart, and the occasional, comforting movements of the baby as they rolled inside of me, flailing against their increasingly limited living space.

This pregnancy was so much easier and so much harder than my pregnancy with Gillian. I had different fears now, bigger fears than just "will I drop the baby" and "if the baby has pointed ears, will Cliff break up with me?" Now I had "will my estranged mother show up to abduct her grandchild and reassert her ownership over her descendant line" and "will I have to die to save Faerie before the kid is grown?" I'd already been an absentee mother once. I didn't want to do it again.

And still no one came.

My shoulders began to ache from being held in a slightly elevated position, and my bladder began to ache from being unable to get myself to a restroom, and no one came to either rescue or reposition me. The baby's kicks were becoming less reassuring and more concerning, since they were inevitably going to culminate in something deeply embarrassing.

I squirmed, trying to find a more comfortable position on the bed. All I managed to do was make my shoulders ache even more. I slumped.

"Well, fuck," I said.

Those were the first words I'd uttered since waking up tied to a bed. Maybe it shouldn't have been a surprise when the door creaked open only a few seconds later, but it somehow was. I turned to stare for a moment before letting my head flop back down into the pillow that had been mercifully placed beneath it.

"How long have you been out there waiting for a sign that I was awake?" I demanded.

"Long enough to worry that the mistress had given you too much tincture of cinnabar when she put you under," said the Candela from the parlor, stepping fully into the room. She crossed to the bed, where she began to check that my cuffs were secure.

"You could let me go," I suggested, trying not to sound like I was whining. "I promise not to tell anyone."

"But you wouldn't need to," she said. "My mistress would know it must have been me, and she would make me pay for my insolence. Is there anything I can do to make you more comfortable?"

"Unfasten these cuffs."

"No."

"I'm extremely pregnant, I'm unarmed, and I really need to pee."

"And at least two of those conditions will remain unchanged, no matter what I do," she said, continuing in her inspection of my bonds. "I can bring you a chamber pot, if you'll cooperate with me in getting it beneath you."

The thought of pissing into a bucket while she stood there and watched to make sure I didn't have magical acid urine or something else that might make it possible for me to get away was a repulsive one. I didn't want to do that. I also didn't want to wet the bed when I was pretty clearly going to be here for a while, and the longer she spent in the room, the more chance there was that I'd be able to trick her into revealing more than she'd intended to. Not needing to feign shame in the least, I dropped my gaze to the swell of my own stomach and said, in a meek voice, "I'll cooperate."

"Good." She sounded a lot more pleased than I would have been if I'd been in her position. She leaned up and gave my pillow a quick, efficient plumping, then stepped away again, moving far enough back that I could see her smile at me. It was a distressingly maternal expression, combined with utterly empty eyes. She looked like she wasn't seeing me at all, but was looking at someone else altogether.

"I'll get that chamber pot," she said, and turned to leave the room. I watched her go. There wasn't anything else I could really do in that moment.

As soon as the door was closed I began testing my bonds again, in case she'd accidentally loosened something when she checked them before. There was no change. Every attempt to pull or break free just rattled the chains—which shouldn't have been metal enough to rattle—against the bedframe.

I had just finished my check when the door opened and the Candela bustled back into the room, a ceramic chamber pot in her hands. "Here we are, dearie," she said. "You'll feel all better soon."

"Great," I said, and watched her approach the bed, only to stop and look at me expectantly.

It was difficult not to start laughing when I realized she was waiting for permission to unfasten my maternity jeans. They were comfortable poisoning and restraining me, holding me against my will, but she drew the line at pulling my pants down so I could pee? I guess it was nice to know I was being held by people who had *some* standards, even if I wished they'd drawn the line substantially further back than they had.

"Please," I said. "I don't want to pee on my clothes."

She nodded and moved to tug my stretch jeans down over my

hips, before manually shifting me into position, first hiking my hips off the bed, then sliding the chamber pot beneath me.

I squirmed a little, adjusting my position over the pot. "Can you step back and look at the wall?" I asked. "I still have *some* pride."

"Of course, dearie," she said, and stepped away from the bed, turning ostentatiously away from me. I managed, barely, not to sigh.

"Do you have a name?" I asked, talking to mask the sound of urine hitting ceramic. I really *had* needed to pee, more badly than I had realized before it became possible; my kidneys are very efficient things, and my body contained a lot of toxins it needed to filter out and dispose of. Once again, I silently resolved to kick Dame Altair in the head as soon as I had the opportunity to do so.

"Halcyon, ma'am," said the Candela woman—said Halcyon. "It's a pleasure to meet you."

"I can't quite say the same, Halcyon," I said. My back was starting to ache from the effort of holding myself sufficiently above the chamber pot that I wasn't overly peeing on either myself or the bed. The sound was tapering off. She'd be able to take it away in a moment. "Do you know why your mistress has decided I need to be an involuntary guest in her knowe? Because my husband's going to be pretty pissed when he realizes what's going on."

"You mean the cat-king, yes?" she asked, turning back around and moving to remove the chamber pot from beneath me. "Pardon my boldness, ma'am, but I'm not sure he *can* be your husband. There were rules against good, proper fae laying down with beasts when I was younger. The shame of it all. Your Firstborn must be rolling in her grave."

"My . . . Amandine isn't dead."

She frowned as she straightened. "Standards have fallen even further than I believed, if you don't know your own First's name. Eira Rosynhwyr begat your line."

"No, she really didn't," I said. "I'm not Daoine Sidhe. My Firstborn is Amandine the Liar, Last Among the First, and bearer of the Dóchas Sidhe."

"Oh, my." She crossed the room to set the chamber pot delicately down on a side table, then returned to ease my pants back over my hips. She neither offered nor attempted to clean me up. Under the circumstances, the discomfort this was going to cause was probably better than the thought of her touching me. "I've never heard the claim."

"It's been all the news in the Mists since she was revealed as her father's daughter," I said, watching her carefully. "Have you really not heard?"

"Oh, I don't get out much," she said. "My lady needs me here to manage her household and see to her needs. I have plenty to keep me busy inside the knowe, and I've not heard anything of a new Firstborn or descendant line."

"Well, you should get out more. And I assure you, Tybalt is *definitely* my husband. We were wed by the sea witch, in full view and with the approval of the High King. He couldn't be any more my husband if Oberon himself had chosen to bind us."

"Even so, he won't be a bother here."

I frowned. "Why not?"

"My lady decided long ago that she didn't like intrusions without her consent, and barricaded the Shadow Roads. No one here dances those paths. Your cat-king won't be able to reach you even if he tries."

"You might be surprised." Dame Altair being able to seal the shadows against ordinary use was surprising, but not outside the realm of believability. Her being able to seal them against an enraged King of Cats trying to reach his wife and child? That was a little harder to accept.

"We shall see," said Halcyon. She picked up the chamber pot and started for the door.

"Wait!" I said, and cringed from the desperation in my own voice.

She looked back toward me. "Yes?"

"Do you know why I'm being held here? I didn't offer any insult or threat to Dame Altair. I came here to find out why she'd been attacked, and hopefully help her to receive justice."

Halcyon made a noncommittal sound and continued toward the door.

"I didn't do anything that would justify this! Please, you have to know there will be consequences for abducting a hero of the realm!"

"Only if you're unwilling to leave the realm in question," said Halcyon mildly. She left the room then, and I was alone.

For a moment, I considered the virtues of screaming. It would have been so satisfying. Then, deciding that wouldn't do me any good, I turned my thoughts to my situation.

I was bound to a bed by both wrists and both ankles, with enough give to shift slightly, and not enough to let me majorly change position. The give was actually part of the problem—if I'd been bound more tightly, it would have been easier to start using the cuffs on my wrists to cut myself and get access to the blood my magic needed. Tension is as good as a knife under the right set of circumstances.

Wait. I paused. Dame Altair poisoning me had confirmed something we'd all been too cautious to test: the baby healed at least partially the way that I did, meaning I probably couldn't do them any serious damage without doing something I couldn't personally recover from. Since I'd come back from the dead several times, I didn't think I *could* do something I couldn't recover from. Before, I'd been approaching my situation from the perspective that I couldn't try anything that might harm the baby. If harming the baby was less of a consideration, my options were a lot more open.

I looked thoughtfully to my left. The bed was standing in the middle of the room, with a wall behind the frame but open space to either side. I'm right-hand dominant, meaning that if I rolled as far to the left as I could, I'd be yanking my right arm out of the socket—and possibly dislocating a hip. That wasn't the worst possible outcome. What I needed to figure out was which arm I wanted to have available when I started trying to move.

The right. I took a deep breath, said a silent apology, and rolled hard to the left, wincing as the motion pulled my hips from the mattress. The cuff on my right wrist snapped taut, stopping me before I could roll onto my front.

With the right-hand cuff holding tight, I forced myself to roll just a little further, a little closer to the bed's edge. The rowan and silver bit into my wrist, forming a solid surface harder than it should have been. The padding mostly blunted the braided cuff, but what of it did make contact with my skin should have felt like wicker, like solid macrame, like something other than a hard cuff. That's magic for you, I guess.

My shoulder ached, not quite wrenched out of the socket, but close enough that I could feel the individual muscles straining not to tear. I did my best to ignore the pain and began twisting my wrist back and forth, pulling as I did, until the padding ripped and the cuff bit into my skin, ripping and tearing with the friction. Blood started to trickle down my arm. I yanked hard, taking advantage of the lubrication the blood provided, and was rewarded with half an inch or so of give. It was accompanied by a bolt of searing pain that traveled all the way down my arm to my spine, and from there to my hips.

I was suddenly *very* grateful that I'd been able to access a chamber pot as recently as I had. I bit my lip, hard enough that it also started to bleed. The taste was revitalizing. I swallowed, flickers of my own memory exploding behind my eyes, and began to twist and yank again, trying to get just a little more give from the cuff. Silver and yarrow tore at my skin, and as the blood cascaded down my arm, I was able to pull my hand another half inch downward.

My thumb folded inward toward my palm with a sickening cracking sound that I felt as much as heard, like a rotten tooth had suddenly become embedded in the meat of my hand. I bit my lip harder and arched my neck, tension lighting my spine like a burning brand as I continued to pull.

There was another, louder crack, and my hand was free, thumb folded so far that the nail had slid into the meat of my palm. I rolled onto my back, panting, and brought my throbbing right hand around to my left, using my working fingers to dig my thumbnail loose and shove my thumb back into its normal position.

In that regard, the cuffs were doing me a favor. Yarrow and silver can't completely suppress magic that's turned inward, onto the caster, rather than outward to the world. I was still healing. I was just healing minutely more slowly than I would have done normally, allowing me the time to get my bones back where they belonged before they healed crooked and forced me to break them again.

The pain when I snapped my thumb back into position was briefly dizzying, making the world flash white. I inhaled sharply through my nose, waited for the throbbing to stop, and then reached down with my now-free hand to begin tugging at the other cuff.

Like many cuffs designed to be "inescapable," this one was reasonably simple from the outside, with a wrapped latch system that surrounded a locked hasp. I folded my thumb toward my palm and forced it as hard as I could with my free hand, until the fingers dislocated and I could pull my hand loose. The cuff dropped away and I immediately reached up with my left hand to shove my right shoulder physically back into its socket. There was a sickening popping sound, and I collapsed into the mattress for several seconds, breathing hard, while I waited for the flare of dizziness to pass.

Once it did, I sat up on the now-bloody sheets and reached as far down as I could manage, trying to get to my ankles. Normally, that would have been the easy part: I had two free, fully working hands, and a comfortable bed to bleed on. This was where I should have broken free and gone racing for the next trouble I could throw myself into.

Unfortunately, the situation wasn't normal. I reached for my feet, and I failed to touch them. My stomach was making it too hard for me to bend forward without moving my legs into a more accessible position, and the cuffs on my ankles were making it impossible for me to move them in any meaningful way. I pulled as hard as I could. Nothing budged.

There was a chance that if I repeated the "throwing myself to the side" trick, I could break one of my ankles. But without being able to reach my ankles and with my shoes on, I didn't have the flexibility in my feet to dislocate them and yank them loose the way I had my hands. I stopped pulling and started trying to kick instead, with no better results. My legs were tied too far apart, and the cuffs were too secure. I couldn't even try reaching for whatever spells might have been braided into them; with the silver and the yarrow so close together, I'd never be able to get up the strength to hook and snap the threads.

What I *could* do was move my hands and arms with ease. I reached behind me and grabbed the center of the bedframe, using the leverage it provided to pull myself further toward the top of the bed. This drew the cuffs even tighter, my legs going straight as the conflicting forces of cuffs and hands met and fought with one another.

When I was sure that I was as upright as I could possibly get, that there was no further give in the chains holding my feet in place, I gripped the bedframe even tighter and closed my eyes, bracing myself against what I was about to do. Anticipation only made it worse.

Unable to stand the waiting any longer, I threw myself hard to the side, letting momentum carry me over the edge.

There was a sickening crunch and my head hit the floor, and everything became darkness and bright, flashing pain.

Way to go, Daye.

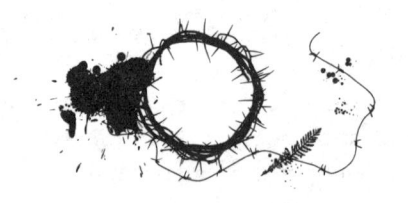

TEN

FORTUNATELY, IT WAS JUST a minor skull fracture, and it didn't knock me out for long; I'm not sure I even lost consciousness. My head was the farthest point of me from the silver and yarrow cuffs on my ankles, and when it cleared, my hip and ankle were still on fire, telling me that any bones I'd broken or dislocated were still busted. That shouldn't have been a good thing, but under the circumstances, it was the best I could have hoped for.

Cautiously, I tried to move my left leg. The hip was almost certainly dislocated on that side, and *might* be broken. If it was broken—or if I'd managed to injure my spine—my leg wouldn't move. If it was just dislocated, it would hurt, but should still work. To my immense delight and relief, my leg moved, a little jerkily, a lot painfully, but obeying my commands. I twisted my hips as far to the right as they would go, and focused on trying to shake my leg until my broken ankle lay at an angle that might allow me to pull it out of the cuff.

My damned sensible shoe made it even harder than it should have been—and I'm saying this as someone who had just intentionally dislocated her hip in the pursuit of getting loose—but in the end, I was able to kick, shake, and contort my foot until it was pointed virtually flat, like I was emulating the world's most broken ballerina. Grasping the bottom of the bedframe for leverage, I pulled as hard as I could.

A white-hot sheet of pain cascaded over me, wiping everything else away, and I felt my heel start to slip out of my shoe and through the cuff. I stopped, panting, and clenched my fingers around the bedframe, hard, like I thought I could just claw my way to freedom. The immediacy of the pain retreated, leaving only the sharp throb of broken and dislocated bones behind. That was a pain I could cope with. I braced myself and pulled again.

This time I *definitely* felt my heel slipping free. I bent my abused knee as far as it would go, and with an anticlimactic pop, my left foot came out of both my shoe and the cuff that held it.

I immediately rolled onto my back, grasping my left thigh with both hands and pulling it upward and inward, until I felt my thigh bone snap back into my hip socket. The pain accompanying the adjustment was intense enough that I had to bite my lip to stop myself from screaming. My teeth clacked as they met through my tongue, piercing cleanly through the center, and I gasped, inhaling a salty mouthful of blood.

The taste soothed me, even as it kicked my healing into a higher gear. It seems wrong that my own blood should be enough to fuel my magic the way it does—somewhat self-cannibalistic, like I'm going to consume myself in the pursuit of a perfect equilibrium that doesn't exist—but it works, and I'm not going to argue.

With my hip handled, I bent my leg toward myself until I could reach down and grasp my ankle, snapping the bones back into position. They went easily enough, but I could feel the small tears in the surrounding tissue; they'd already started to heal. Breaking bones is awful. Rebreaking them because they healed wrong is one of my least favorite ways to abuse my body, which already puts up with enough of my bullshit.

Now that I had both wrists and one ankle free, it was relatively easy to haul myself back onto the bed and reach down to remove my right shoe. Once this was done, I grasped my right foot and snapped it sharply to the side, breaking the ankle and allowing me to yank my foot out of the cuff. With this finished I sat up, legs dangling over the edge of the bed, and stretched extravagantly. Things were about to get a lot less pleasant than a few hours chained to a bed trying not to wet myself.

As if in answer to the thought, the baby rolled over and kicked me in the kidneys. I winced.

"Chill, kiddo," I said. "We need to find a weapon."

The room didn't have a lot of options. The bedframe was metal, but so well-assembled that I wasn't going to get a piece of it without a screwdriver—something I most distinctly didn't have. Still, no one had shown up when I started thrashing and banging around, and there was no way that hadn't been audible from the hall. I had a little time.

I stood cautiously, testing my abused legs. They twinged as I put my full weight on them, but even with the cuffs blunting my magic, they had healed enough to hold my weight, and I hobbled toward the table where Halcyon had placed the chamber pot before taking it away. The table was sturdy mahogany. I tipped it up onto two legs, looking critically at the joins. Then, with a bit more effort than I would have preferred, I flipped it over and sent both it and the chamber pot crashing to the floor.

"Oopsie," I said, and began viciously kicking the spot where one of the legs joined with the body of the table. Every kick hurt like hell, but I kept going. On the third kick, it cracked. On the fourth, it began to tilt dangerously over. On the fifth, it listed to the side with an almighty snapping sound, and I grabbed it, putting as much of my weight as I dared onto it until it broke off entirely, leaving me with a hefty wooden club. The jagged splinters making up the larger end were just a bonus.

It was no sword, but I started my career in heroics with a baseball bat, and there was something nice about returning to my roots. I gave it a practice swing, testing the way it felt in my hands, then turned speculatively toward the closed door to the hall.

No time like the present.

The door wasn't locked. That made a certain amount of sense—why bother locking the door when there's no way for your captive to escape—but it was still incredibly stupid of the people who were holding me here. I guess Dame Altair wasn't a frequent flyer in the "taking local heroes captive" club. I eased the door open, granting myself a view of the hall, or at least, a narrow slice of the hall.

The décor continued here, with plain white wallpaper, an intricately patterned runner rug, and multiple small decorative chandeliers hanging from the ceiling. They were lit by balls of lambent witch light, not pixies, and for once, I was almost sorry to see a pureblood not abusing our smallest kin as household accessories. I felt guilty for the thought as soon as it formed, but still. It would have been incredibly useful to be able to call for help by smashing a few glass balls, and it would have made such a satisfying sound.

Bouquets of panther lilies and ginger cardamom flowers dotted the small tables that appeared periodically along the length of the hall, their blooms perfectly open, unbruised and perfuming the air with a sweet, compelling mix. It wasn't a combination I would have considered, but they worked well together. I stepped out of the room, table leg in hand, and looked around again, scanning for threats.

No one moved. There were three doors I could see along the length of the hall, as well as the one I'd just emerged from, and doors at either end. Those were the most likely to either lead to the way out or to Dame Altair's private quarters. They could wait.

That left me with three possibilities for finding Quentin. If I'd been trying to take the two of us captive and had only one hallway where I could reasonably imprison people I had no business abducting—which was, alone, a major assumption—I would have wanted to keep the knight and her squire as far apart as possible. With this in mind, I crossed the hall and went to the door farthest down from my own.

It wasn't locked either. If I hadn't already hated these people, I would have felt the need to lecture them on operational security.

Easing the door open, I looked carefully inside. There was another bed like the one I'd been bound to, and Quentin was there, tied to the four corners of the bed and clearly pissed off about it. He was glaring at the ceiling, jaw set in a stubborn line, hands balled into fists.

"I'm not telling you *anything*," he spat. "You can go and tell your mistress that she's made the biggest mistake of her life, and I'm not telling her *anything*."

"That's cool," I said, easing the door shut again behind me. "I don't think I want to hear anything you haven't told me already, since you're a grown-up now and the only thing we *really* don't talk about is your sex life. Whatever it is you and Dean get up to, I would really prefer not to know, if that's all right with you."

His eyes widened as the first words left my mouth, and he whipped his head around, staring at me instead of the ceiling over his head. "Toby?" he squeaked. "Promise?"

"Hang on," I said, and bit my lip, swallowing the blood and closing my eyes. The smell of my magic rose around me. Quentin was good enough at reading magical signatures that smelling me in the process of spellcasting should be easily sufficient to confirm my identity . . . if this was Quentin, of course.

Pulling the blood toward the part of me that burned it for power, I looked at the bed without using my eyes, studying the shape of the person inside it. There were no cotton candy threads of magic wrapped around his outline; this was either Quentin or a true shapeshifter, not someone wearing a disguise.

True shapeshifters are mercifully rare, and after my last encounter with a community of Doppelgangers, I don't think they'd mess with me by impersonating my squire, even if someone offered to pay. I opened my eyes and smiled wearily at Quentin.

"Promise," I said. "You satisfied?"

"Freshly cut grass and copper that's halfway to becoming blood," he said. "Yeah, it's you. Do you think it's going to go all the way to blood?"

"Maybe eventually," I said. "How are you feeling?"

"Like someone's been using my head as a punching bag," he said. "That creepy Candela who works for Altair brought me some sort of antidote. It tasted even worse than the things the Luidaeg comes up with. I can still feel it coating my molars. But I stopped throwing up after that."

That explained the faint smell that lingered in the air, sick and sweet at the same time. I grimaced.

"I didn't get an antidote; I guess they figured I wouldn't need it," I said. "I think I might be glad to have been the somewhat neglected prisoner."

Quentin's eyes widened in alarm. "You didn't—the baby."

"Is fine," I assured him. "Looks like they found a way to test whether or not the kiddo would heal the way I do, and it looks like we have a winner in the 'whose magic is going to come out dominant' competition. Baby and I are both fine."

"You can't *know* that."

"I can know it well enough to keep standing, and to get myself free," I said, slapping the chair leg against my palm to punctuate my words. "Do you want me to let you up, or do you want to keep trying to upset me when I'm already having a lousy night?"

"Up, please," said Quentin immediately.

I crossed the room to study the cuffs on his wrists. They were of a different composition than mine had been, less yarrow, more silver. I wondered, briefly, what the balance meant. I'd never studied the interactions of the Sacred Woods closely enough to know what shifting the proportions would do. That was more of an alchemist thing. Silently, I vowed to ask Walther what the way the cuffs had been woven meant. It was a good promise to make to myself.

Among other things, it meant I was promising to get out of here without actually making the mistake of thinking the words. It can be dangerous to tempt fate that way.

The cuffs were locked, and I scowled, casting around for anything I could use as a pick. There wasn't much—this room was as barren as mine had been—and I was about to go back for the flowers I'd seen in the hall when I shifted positions and something dug into the side of my breast, hard enough to hurt. I yelped and stuck my hand down my shirt.

Quentin blinked at me. "Uh, Toby?" he asked. "You okay over there?"

"I'm fine, I just—" I pulled my hand out of my shirt, clutching the little shell knife in its little shell sheath. I blinked at it. "Where the hell did you come from?"

The knife didn't answer.

"What is it?"

"The Luidaeg gave me a knife. I guess I wanted it more when I needed to get you loose than when I was trying to free myself." I'd think about that one later. Or maybe never. Never might be the way to go.

Pulling the small knife out of its sheath, I turned to picking the locks. They weren't complex. The magic of the cuffs, combined with the way they were used, was supposed to supply most of the security. It only took me a minute or so to free Quentin. He sat up, rubbing his wrists as he tried to ease the circulation back into his hands, and watched me unfasten the cuffs on his ankles. "You're *covered* in blood," he said.

"Unavoidable side effect of getting myself loose," I said. "If Dame Altair employs a Bannick, we can ask them to clean me up before Tybalt sees."

"Why isn't he here yet? I don't know how long we were out, but I feel like he should have freaked out and come looking for us *ages* ago."

"Halcyon—the creepy Candela—told me Dame Altair had sealed the knowe against the Shadow Roads. Candela usually teleport through their edges, so them being sealed would explain why she's going everywhere on foot, and it would definitely keep Tybalt out."

"It would stop him from coming in without an invitation, but what stops him from ringing the doorbell?"

That was a good question. I paused, frowning.

The location of Dame Altair's knowe was well-known throughout San Francisco, if not the entire kingdom, and Tybalt was still King of Cats, with a virtual army of feline spies answering to his call. Quentin and I had gone out and not come back again, and it had been long enough for even Quentin to wake up on his own. What was there to stop Tybalt from getting tired of waiting and marching down to the house to find out where we were?

The two remaining closed doors suddenly seemed much more concerning.

"See if you can get your own table leg," I recommended. "There are two more doors in this hallway. I'm going to go see what's behind them."

"Or you could wait three minutes and we could go together," said Quentin, sounding exasperated. He didn't move to stop me as I turned back toward the door, though, only slid off of the bed and moved to knock his own side table to the floor.

Maybe we were going to get out of this with no further trouble.

The first room I checked was empty. The second stopped me in my tracks, because there was a man inside, bound to the bed as both Quentin and I had been.

He was tall, skinny to the point of being scrawny, and while he was bipedal, the outline of his body wasn't entirely human. From the thigh down, he had the legs of the largest goat that had ever lived, complete with scraggly brown fur and black cloven hooves. His ears were equally goat-like, dangling well past the line of his jaw. Unlike a Satyr, he didn't have any horns, only a smooth brow and a receding hairline that was mostly notable in relation to how hairy the rest of him was. His clothing was worn and threadbare, combining shorts that stopped just below the knee with a T-shirt that would have been vintage if it hadn't been barely better than a rag, the marijuana leaf printed on the front so faded that it looked more like the pawprint of some unknown creature.

His face was turned toward the wall, but he was awake: I could tell from the tension in his neck, the way his jaw was clenched. He knew he wasn't alone.

For a moment, I considered turning around and going back into the hall. If Bucer O'Malley was here, we probably knew who'd been stealing all Arden's things, and there was very little Dame Altair could do to him that he wouldn't inevitably deserve. Only for a moment, though.

I didn't like the man. That didn't mean he deserved to be left captive to a woman who thought nothing of poisoning her guests, violating half a dozen rules of hospitality in the process. There was no Law against it if the poisoning wasn't fatal, but Faerie doesn't operate on law most of the time. It operates on customs, traditions, and rules, and all the rules about hospitality said that once Quentin and I had been welcomed into the knowe, we should have been untouchable until we either offered some offense or a certain amount of time had passed. Unless Dame Altair's knowe was one of the kind where an hour was a day, we hadn't been there remotely long enough to have worn out our welcome.

There's no specific time frame for hospitality unless it's stated during the offer or acceptance of same. Even so, poisoning your guests is generally frowned upon, even when they *aren't* there on behalf of the local regent, and letting Dame Altair hang on to her other victims didn't suit my sense of justice.

I started toward the bed. "I can let you go, but you have to promise not to attack me or try to use your stupid persuasion magic on me," I said. "I'm really not in the mood to be charmed. If you can promise me that you won't, I can release you."

Bucer's head whipped around so fast that he hit himself in the face with one of his own ears, eyes wide as he stared at me. I lifted an eyebrow and looked impassively back. Unusual eyes are nothing strange in Faerie, odd as that statement may seem: enough of us have animal attributes that pupils can come in all shapes and sizes, and many descendant lines seem to view sclera as entirely optional. Even so, Bucer's horizontally slit pupils were always a little unsettling to look at. All the more so because I wasn't seeing him on a regular basis anymore, and hadn't since we'd both left Home.

"October?" he managed, finally. His voice was as squeaky and thin as it had always been, his tone that of a man who'd been born to cringe and grovel his way through life. Hearing it was like someone running their fingernails along a chalkboard.

I ground my teeth, not letting him see how much I didn't want to be in this room.

"It's still Toby, Bucer," I said. I used to hit people to reinforce how much I didn't want to be called by my full name. But that was a long time ago, and I didn't do that anymore. Bucer had been out of my life for a while. He might not realize that I'd learned some basic self-control, and I wasn't going to inform him.

"Toby," he echoed, not a question this time, but with dawning belief, like he was coming to accept that I was really here. His eyes flicked down to my bloodied belly for a moment, then back to my face. "You got . . ."

"Careful how you go," I said.

". . . really fat," he finished. "Never thought I'd see the day."

"And you got caught," I said. "I always knew I'd see the day, but I thought when it finally arrived, you'd be smart enough to not antagonize the person who might be able to release you."

"How do you know I'm not here because I want to be?"

"Oh, are you? My mistake." I began to turn away.

"Wait!" he yelped.

I looked back to Bucer. "Yes?"

"I'm not here because I want to be."

"I didn't assume you were," I said, and started toward the bed. "What happened? Why *are* you here?"

He shrugged as much as his bonds would allow, expression turning shifty. "It's not important."

"Oh, but I think it is, especially if you don't want to tell me." I leaned a little closer. "Come on, Bucer. Spill. Why were you in the Mists? Last time I saw you, you were returning to the Kingdom of

Angels. The time before that, you were in the process of fleeing the kingdom. For good reasons, too, if I recall correctly."

"I went back to Angels after the death of King Antonio, yeah, but I didn't stay there," he said, watching me warily. "His widow wasn't as forgiving as he was when it came to certain . . . little errors I had made in my past, and then the kingdom was adapting to life under a new king, with a regent who wasn't as willing to ignore what was going on under her nose. I was still trying to hold out when I heard a rumor that you and the King of Cats were coming there on your honeymoon, and then I figured it was time for me to get the hell out of Dodge. Congratulations for that, by the way."

"For which part?"

"Convincing the kitty-cat to marry you. I never thought I'd see the day when that old tomcat would settle down." He attempted an expression that I thought was meant to be a leer. It made him look more constipated than anything else.

I looked impassively back at him. Tybalt had never had a reputation as a heartbreaker, except for possibly in the literal sense; he'd always been a beautiful man, but I'd never heard any rumors about him being particularly promiscuous. Interesting that that was what Bucer was trying to needle me with.

And he *was* trying to needle me. I'd known him long enough to recognize a barb when it was aimed in my direction, and even as he tried to leer, I could see the familiar tension around the corners of his eyes. He wanted to provoke me. But why?

Part of it may have been the fact that not all that long ago, he'd been an accessory to Raysel abducting my daughter, Gillian, who had been mostly human at the time, and should have been able to live her life free from the machinations of Faerie. Bucer never touched Gillian himself. That hadn't mattered then, and it didn't really matter now.

"You know, when I told you to get the hell out of this kingdom, I also told you I'd never be charged with breaking the Law, because no one would ever find your body." I gave his lanky, chained body a slow up-and-down look, slapping the chair leg against my palm as I did, just to punctuate my point. "Maybe you thought that because I didn't kill you at the conclave, I'd forgotten my promises, but no. I was working then. I'm not working now. I've been poisoned and taken captive, and you don't want to know how many bones I had to break to get myself loose. So if you're going to keep making snide comments and implying things you know aren't true, maybe I should just hit the bricks. No one else knows that I've seen you."

"No," he said. "No-no-no. You need to let me loose. I know we've had our differences in the past—"

"You helped Raysel *abduct* my *child*," I snarled. "That's not having differences. That's inviting me to murder you."

"Fine, fair, but still," he said. "You can't just walk away and leave me here. You're a hero now, but I remember when we were delinquents together. We made promises then, too. There's no way you've forgotten." He paused, and added, in a calculated tone that told me he didn't really understand what he was saying, "Stacy wouldn't want you to be the kind of person who forgets."

I went still as white-hot rage flashed through me, moving so fast that it left not even embers in its wake, just a cold resignation that burned in its own terrible way. "Bucer," I said, forcing my voice to stay level, "what do you know about Stacy?"

"Stacy Brown. Left Home to marry that Mitch guy, just because he was tall and built like a brick wall with opinions about interior decorating. I still say I could've taken him in a fair fight, if he'd ever been willing to stop hiding behind being big and strong and handsome."

I snorted and finally moved to begin using my shell knife to unlock the cuffs at his ankles. Bucer watched with wide eyes, not moving, like he was afraid that even the slightest twitch would remind me of who he was and make me realize what I was doing.

"Yeah, that's Stacy," I said.

Bucer wasn't finished. He'd apparently decided that talking about my best friend was the key to my good regard, or at least the key to getting the hell out of here. "Five kids. Which is a little excessive if you ask me, but then, I've never been a stud goat. No little Glastig for me. I haven't heard much about Stacy recently. What's she been up to?"

It was almost nice to hear him say that. It meant the reality of her ending hadn't completely wiped away the story of her life. People might still remember her fondly, as Stacy, the woman who fixed my eyeliner and never learned how to cook bacon on the stove without burning the edges, who forced herself onto a diurnal schedule for PTA meetings and bake sales. Who loved me. In all the years we'd known each other, that was one of the only things I had never seen the cause to question. Stacy had loved me. From the very beginning to the very end, she'd loved me.

I moved to the head of the bed, reaching for the first of Bucer's wrist cuffs. Then I paused, pulling back.

"Hey, what are you doing? Let me out."

"Just wondering, Bucer. What are you doing here? Like I said, last I heard, you were still down in Angels. What changed?"

"Oh, yeah. I guess we got sort of off topic, didn't we? I heard you were coming to town for your honeymoon, thought you might finally remember that little promise of vengeance you'd made, and hit the bricks. Wound up on the Golden Shore. They're nice folks there, if kind of gullible, and they believed me when I told them I'd been turfed out for having hooves and smelling like wet goat when I got caught in the sprinklers. They set me up pretty sweet as one of the palace courtiers, and I managed to keep my hands to myself for a while, if you can believe it."

I made a noncommittal sound, and reached for the first wrist cuff.

"I'd still be there, but the world went all funky and wrong, and everything changed. All of a sudden, Queen Windermere and her brother were living there, and had lived there all along." He watched avidly as I unhooked the first cuff. "I didn't know what was wrong when it happened, just that I needed to be in the Mists. So I came home."

"Uh-huh." There were large parts of his story that were either missing or didn't add up. Glastig had been as caught by Titania's enchantment as the rest of us; he wouldn't have known that anything had changed when it happened, just that the world was the way it had always been meant to be. And for a changeling to seek the Mists during the spell Titania had so carefully crafted was... wrong. Something about it was *wrong*.

I unhooked the second cuff and let it drop away from his wrist, then stepped back as I watched to see what he would do. Bucer sat up on the bed, alternately rubbing his wrists with one hand or the other, and looked at me with wide, earnest eyes.

"Gosh, Toby, you didn't have to let me go, and we both know that," he said. "You would have been within your rights to just leave me here to rot. I'd thank you if I could do it without insulting you. Instead, I guess I'll just say I appreciate how well Devin taught you to pick a lock."

"These were barely worthy of the name," I said. "Come on. I still need to know how you wound up here, and why they had you tied to a bed, but Quentin's been waiting long enough for me to come back, and he's *my* squire, meaning he'll be here any minute. Kid does not do idleness well."

"You're still kicking around with the crown prince?" Bucer scoffed. "I'd have ransomed that kid back to his parents ages ago. You know, royalty pays pretty damn well for their children, but not necessarily for their adult claimants to the throne. Your window's closing."

I whipped around as fast as my perpetually unsteady balance would allow, pointing the jagged end of my table leg at his throat.

"What did you just say?" I hissed.

He put his hands up and swallowed hard, and didn't say anything at all.

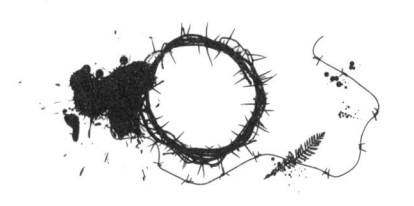

ELEVEN

SECONDS TICKED BY AS our standoff stretched from a reaction into a decision. Bucer continued to stare at me, and the smell of pine and damp linen pervaded the room, making me wonder how long I'd been distracted enough not to notice that he was trying to influence me. Not just trying but succeeding, if the fact that I'd uncuffed him even while I was considering the holes in his story was anything to go by.

I hate the fae whose magic bends toward mental manipulation. There aren't many of them, but too many of the ones that exist use their magic to bypass common sense and consent. They can make people do things they would never do under normal circumstances . . . like untie an enemy who shouldn't even be in the kingdom.

Bucer broke first, of course. "I'm sorry," he said. "I wasn't threatening the kid, and I won't tell anyone. If this is about me influencing you, I didn't mean to. You don't have to want to heal, do you? Well, if I'm in enough danger—or under enough stress—I don't entirely have to want to make people see things my way. My magic just tweaks things so people see things the way that's best for me. It's why I tell people I'm not a thief, because I'm really not. When I look desperate enough, most people will just give me things."

"It's still stealing if you cloud their minds first," I snapped.

"Is it?" He took a half-step forward, reaching for my table leg, and for a moment, I almost let him have it.

Then I realized how strong the smell of pine and linen had become, and bit down hard on the inside of my cheek, filling my mouth with blood. The taste washed everything else away, including Bucer's reaching magic, and I raised the table leg, pointing it more firmly at the center of his throat.

"Back the *hell* off, Bucer," I said.

I couldn't leave him loose without keeping an eye on him, and I couldn't trust him behind me. That didn't leave a lot of options, but I've always been pretty good at improvisation. Still glaring at him and pointing the table leg like it was a sword, I inched around him to the foot of the bed, where I grabbed the yarrow and silver chain they'd used to hold him in place. They'd been less concerned about him deciding to break an ankle in his pursuit of freedom: his cuffs had been connected to a chain threaded through a single metal ring welded underneath the bed.

One quick pull and the whole thing was loose. I wrapped it loosely around my hand and walked back over to Bucer. "Turn around," I commanded.

He shot me a wounded look, like he couldn't possibly believe that I was doing this. "Toby, there's no need—"

"Turn *around*."

Either my tone or my expression got through to him, because he stopped protesting and turned meekly around, letting me wrap the chain tight around his wrists. I kept looping until I had a secure tangle, then experimentally pulled on one of his arms, trying to see if the chain would budge. It didn't.

"You didn't have to tie it so *tight*," said Bucer sullenly, shooting an unhappy look over his shoulder.

"Tell it to whoever didn't teach you to control your magic," I suggested, planting a hand between his shoulder blades and shoving him toward the door.

He stumbled, but went willingly enough, if someone who's been tied up with a magic-dampening chain can be said to do anything willingly. Really, I wanted to feel bad for being so rough with him. I just couldn't find it in me. My history with Bucer was a tangled, unpleasant one, and while there had been flashes of friendship when we were much younger, they were so vastly outweighed by what he'd done to Gillian that it was a miracle I wasn't already beating him to a pulp.

Not all my impulses are noble ones. I just do my best to make the noble choice when the nasty impulses make their presence known.

The hall was still empty; the entire exchange had taken only a few minutes. That was something of a relief. The rug was thick enough to muffle the sound of Bucer's hooves, which was an even bigger relief. The trouble with the various breeds of hooved fae is that they're shit at stealth. I pushed him along in front of me until we reached the door to Quentin's room, then knocked very lightly, barely a whisper of my knuckles against the wood.

Bucer scoffed and began to open his mouth. I shook my head, motioning for him to stay silent. He clammed up, watching me warily.

The door eased slowly open, revealing no one on the other side. That was clever. Hide behind the door and be prepared to ambush anyone who means to do you harm. I shifted my grasp to the front of Bucer's shirt and stepped into the room, pulling him along behind me. If Quentin had any big ideas about assaulting whoever came to check up on him, I could absorb the damage better than Bucer could. That didn't mean I'd changed my mind about trusting the man, just that I knew which one of us could shake off a concussion like it was no big deal and which would become whining, useless dead weight if Quentin cracked his goaty skull.

No attacks were forthcoming. I kept pulling Bucer until we were both clear of the door, then turned to look behind it. Sure enough, Quentin was crouching there, a broken-off table leg in his hands and a deeply relieved expression on his face. I made a shushing motion with my free hand. He nodded, then eased the door carefully closed again.

Once the door was shut and we had a modicum of privacy, he turned back to me. "You're all right! And there's no blood on you now that wasn't there before you left."

"You don't have so sound so surprised about that," I grumbled.

He turned his attention to Bucer. "I remember you from the conclave about whether or not we'd be releasing the elf-shot cure. You're from Angels, aren't you?"

"Bucer O'Malley, originally of the Mists, now apparently of the Mists again," said Bucer. "I'd bow, but your knight has my wrists, and I think she'd hurt me if I moved in a way she didn't like."

"Probably," said Quentin. "What did you do?"

"Pardon?"

"Toby doesn't take people captive unless they've done something to deserve it." He shrugged. "I trust her, I don't know you. So what did you do to make Toby tie you up?"

"I . . . gave information to Rayseline Torquill that led her to the location of Toby's changeling daughter," admitted Bucer. "And I stole the crown jewels of Angels, and there may have been a little recreational theft when I made my way back up to the Mists, but I didn't take anything from anybody who was going to miss it, I swear."

Quentin, whose eyes had been getting bigger and bigger as Bucer spoke, turned to me. "So he's who cleaned out the treasury, right?"

"What?" squeaked Bucer.

"That's what I'm assuming too," I said. "Known thief who's successfully stolen from royalty before shows up back in the Mists just as we discover that the kingdom's vaults have been cleaned out? That's not a coincidence, that's a contrivance . . . unless he did it."

"How could you—" Bucer caught himself mid-sentence and sighed, heavily. "Okay, so if you're so smart, why am I tied up like the two of you? Wouldn't I be in cahoots with somebody?"

"If you stole all that stuff for Dame Altair, and didn't tell her everything you had, you could have been doing a little fencing on the side," I said, watching his expression carefully. One of his ears twitched, telling me I was on the right track. "So you go in, get everything she's said she wants, and grab a few extras. But she doesn't necessarily know about the extras, so you see them as a bonus—free money, free power. Only when they get into the hands of people who are willing to use them against her, she figures out that you must have double-crossed her. Am I in the right neighborhood here, Bucer?"

He ducked his head. "I never thought you'd be the one to turn into a lapdog for the nobility."

"And I never thought you'd be the one who could keep worming your way into their courts, but here we are," I said. "Why were you stealing for Dame Altair?"

"She heard a rumor about a hope chest in the vault," he said. "Not much that's worth more than a hope chest, you know. Get your hands on one of those, you can have a kingdom named after you. She wanted it, and by that point I'd already wandered up from the Golden Shore, and someone told her I was the changeling who could steal anything. So she sent her boys to find me, and once they did, she offered me a deal."

I nodded as I listened. Based on the timing of when the things had gone missing, this must have happened while Titania's enchantment was still in place. That made the question of guilt more difficult, since we literally hadn't been ourselves under the spell.

But we'd all remembered our enchanted actions once the spell was broken, meaning Dame Altair would have known what she'd paid Bucer to do as soon as we were all restored to ourselves. And that was months ago. Had she been waiting all this time for someone to show up looking for Arden's missing treasures? Had this been a setup from the start?

"The hope chest," I said. "Did you find it?"

"No," said Bucer. "I searched the whole vault, but it wasn't there."

Quentin frowned. "How did you know where to look?"

"What?"

"If this happened while we were all enchanted to think we were other people, then the knowe at Muir Woods would have been sealed. So how did you know where to go looking for the vault?"

"Kid, I just went where Dame Altair pointed me. Thought it was weird at first that she had me squirming through this wormy, root-filled tunnel to nowhere, but once I got inside, it was a thief's paradise and I stopped asking questions. I don't know how she knew where to send me, but she set the job, and I fulfilled it. All except for that damn hope chest."

"And since you started your little side deals and got caught at it, Altair decided you must have been lying about the hope chest, didn't she?"

Bucer nodded, so vigorously his ears flapped. "She said there was no way I could have resisted such a big score, I must have stolen it for myself, and even when I offered her blood to test against my word, she just said I wouldn't offer if I hadn't found a way to manipulate what it would show her. But I never found that hope chest. It wasn't in the vault, and even after the spell broke and I realized who I'd actually been robbing . . . the Queen and her brother and most of the court were missing. I went back while everything was still in chaos, just in case I'd missed something."

He stopped then, and it was clear he was waiting for one of us to ask. I glanced at Quentin, who was watching Bucer with a steady, unblinking gaze. I decided to do something similar, and focused on picking the blood out from under my fingernails. There was an unsurprising amount of it caught there, dried brown and flaky.

Seconds passed. Bucer finally scowled and said, "I found a plinth I hadn't seen before, about the size of a shoebox—or a hope chest, if the descriptions I've heard of them are correct. I don't know how I could have missed it, with as thoroughly as I searched the place."

"Secondary spell," I said. "Something designed to keep the hope chest hidden from people who weren't meant to know that it was there. It probably came down in the shockwave from shattering a kingdom-wide enchantment. Really, it's impressive that it held as long as it did. I'll have to ask Queen Windermere who did her warding."

Bucer paled. "You can't tell the queen. She'll have me elf-shot. She'll get one of her magicians to turn me into an entire goat and sell me to a petting zoo. I don't want to eat grass pellets and stand on haybales for the next twenty years!"

I raised an eyebrow. "Maybe you should have thought of that before you went and cleaned out a royal vault?"

"I don't see any reason why I would have," he countered. "I didn't know it was a royal vault at the time. I thought it was just a smuggler's cache that Dame Altair had been lucky enough to find. I thought those things were lost treasure. I didn't know I was risking the wrath of a seated queen."

"Speaking of seated monarchs, we've been standing around long enough," I said. "Tybalt's going to tear this place down brick by brick if we don't get out of here and let him know that we're all right. Quentin, you're going to take the rear. Bucer, you're going to walk very carefully, because if you trip, you won't be able to catch yourself."

His eyes widened. "Hey, you can't seriously intend to leave my hands tied!"

"You're my captive now, and I have a lot more questions," I said. "You don't have any weapons, and if I remember correctly, your best move in an unarmed fight was always headbutting someone and running away. You can still headbutt anyone who tries to stop us."

"I hate this," muttered Bucer.

"I'm pregnant and covered in blood, and my husband is probably going to lock me in my room for the next year," I said. "I'm not a big fan myself. Move."

Together, the three of us eased open the bedroom door and crept out into the empty hallway. The doors at either end were still closed. I looked to Bucer.

"Which way?" I asked, voice low.

"That way's the stairs, the other way should be Dame Altair's parlor," he said, accompanying each description with a quick jerk of his head to make sure I knew which door he meant. "Stairs will lead us down to the front room."

"Stairs it is," I said. I started toward the relevant door, Bucer behind me, Quentin behind him. Together, we crept along the hall, moving as quietly as we could. I paused at the door and sniffed the air, looking for the scent of magic.

Panther lily. Black clove. Fig. Honey. Cinnamon.

I froze, holding up one hand for silence as I began to frantically review everything Dame Altair had said to me since my arrival. She'd been able to open this knowe with her brother's help. Her brother. I'd never heard of her having a brother before, but either she had one or she lied with an offhanded ease that she'd never demonstrated before. No, her lies were the more methodical kind, formed by the space between what she said and what she implied. She'd accused Simon, said she should have expected it after he'd shown up on her doorstep, but she'd never given any evidence that it had actually been him, had she? Nothing beyond the smell of cinnamon.

Simon's mulled apple cider–scented magic included cinnamon, yes, but it was Ceylon cinnamon, light and aromatic and inextricably mingled with the rest of his magical signature. This, though—this was cassia, sharper, stronger, and more aggressive. The difference was strikingly obvious, at least to me.

It would also have been obvious to someone whose brother had magic that smelt of cassia. Dame Altair would have known the magic she smelled wasn't Simon's, but that didn't mean she couldn't make an accusation, carefully threaded through the fact that most people couldn't smell magic with enough precision to tell cinnamon from cassia. They were different plants entirely. Both used the name "cinnamon." Calling cassia cinnamon wasn't a lie.

She had set up a situation that would allow her to accuse Simon, all without telling a single actual lie. He was a redeemed villain in the eyes of many, but that didn't mean he'd been forgiven in the eyes of all. He was a soft target for a wild accusation. It wasn't that long ago that I would have believed her without hesitation. I couldn't feel bad about that—I'd had good reasons at the time—but that didn't mean I was going to sit back and let people keep acting like nothing he'd done to atone for his past was ever going to make a difference.

"Toby?" Quentin's voice sounded like it was coming from someplace very far away. "Is everything okay?"

I wrenched myself out of the tangle of magical signatures with a physical effort, turning to offer Quentin a strained smile. "I'm fine," I said. "We have a lot to talk about, but we can discuss it when we're out of here. All right?"

"All right," said Quentin.

"Are you taking me home with you?" asked Bucer.

"Unfortunately, yes," I replied. "If I hand you over to Arden, I may not get you back, and right now, I need you. Come on."

I turned back to the door, exhaled to clear the last of the magic from my nose, and turned the knob.

And came face to face with Dugan, who was standing on the stairs in the process of reaching for the doorknob.

I really should have guessed it would be him.

He raised an eyebrow and simply looked at me, expression caught between challenge and stoic disdain. His throat was a ruin of uneven scar tissue, ropey and thick and never quite fully healed. That's what slitting your own throat with an iron knife will do for you.

He was still a devastatingly handsome man for all of that—blame the fact that he was Daoine Sidhe, and they're pretty much all upsettingly attractive—with sharp, symmetrical features and dark green hair that curled around the lines of his chin, cupping his jawline without doing anything to soften the wreckage of his throat.

He narrowed his eyes as he saw me staring at him, then smiled slyly and tapped the scar tissue on his throat with the fingers of one hand before hooking both hands through the air and pulling toward himself. The air promptly turned hot, smelling of cinnamon and cardamom.

Whatever he was casting, it was big, and probably not any good for the three of us. I had only a few seconds to react. I would have had even less than that, but he couldn't speak, and that was slowing him down. Words shape and focus magic, making it easier to convince it to do as the caster orders.

I brought my chair leg up and then down on his wrist, hitting hard enough that I heard bone crack. He hissed through his teeth and stumbled back a step, face going white with the pain. I lifted the chair leg again, ready to hit him a second time. Dugan bared his teeth at us, producing a small vial from inside his shirt. He smashed it on the ground and was gone, slipping through a teleportation circle to somewhere else.

I'd seen him perform that trick before, and it may have partially explained where Dame Altair had gotten the idea of blaming Simon for her brother's actions. Simon had been the one to bottle many of the borrowed-blood tokens I knew of, creating them at the order of his former mistress. Someone who really worked at picking apart the captive magic would find his signature in the mix, blended and buried but still present. They could run around leaving traces of Simon's magic, and for most people, that would be as good as a confession.

Sometimes I hate Faerie. Being surrounded by immortals means being surrounded by people who can never, ever let anything go. Something someone did centuries ago can be a completely acceptable reason for attacking them today. No wonder Oberon thought "hey, don't murder each other" was the only command important enough to codify into Law.

"Come on," I said, starting down the now-empty stairs as fast as my awkward balance would allow. "Dugan's gone."

"How the hell is Dugan still *alive*?" asked Quentin.

"We knew he survived cutting his own throat. Arden had him taken into captivity. I guess he got out when everything went to hell."

"That *sucks*," said Quentin, with surprising fervor. I glanced at him. He was scowling.

"I miss something?"

"I just really hate that guy, is all," he said petulantly. "I've had real trouble finding Daoine Sidhe who could train me in illusions the right way. His illusions are ridiculously strong. Why'd he have to go and be an asshole? I can't learn illusion magic from an asshole."

Under any other circumstances, I would have laughed. Instead, I nodded gravely and kept walking down the stairs.

"We can look harder to find you a tutor," I offered. I had learned many useful things from assholes, but that didn't make them my first choice in every situation. "Maybe Garm? He's not Daoine Sidhe, but the principles should be the same."

Quentin hesitated, then nodded in turn. "That might be a good thing."

In Titania's version of Faerie, it wasn't just that the purebloods were better than the changelings; the Daoine Sidhe were better than all the rest of the fae. Quentin probably didn't want to insist on teachers of his own species, because it would edge up too closely upon the values of that other world. Even gone, Titania was making our choices for us.

I really hated that woman. And not only because she'd killed my best friend. Titania would have insisted that she'd done no such thing, that Stacy had never been real and was thus impossible for her to have killed, but I knew the truth. A story you told loudly and clearly enough for long enough could take on a life of its own.

The stairs ended in a narrow, virtually featureless hallway. I blinked, then kept going, recognizing this as a servant's corridor, something meant to go unseen by the main occupants of the house. There was probably another set of stairs that I'd missed, some more respectable route that led to the floor where we'd been held. It didn't really matter in the moment. What mattered was getting out.

We passed a kitchen, a dining room, and what was pretty clearly a cellar door, marked with a small wooden sign graven with potatoes and onions. At the end of the hall was a door taller and nicer than the others. I motioned for Quentin and Bucer to stay where they were, then crept forward, feeling about as stealthy as a draft horse as I approached the door.

Still, it didn't open, and no one appeared to accuse me of criminal activity, so I took that for a good sign. Shifting the table leg to my other hand, I reached out and tried the door. Locked. I leaned back against the wall, letting my fingertips rest against the brass doorknob.

"Your mistress drugged and captured us," I said, voice pitched low. "It wasn't very kind, and I'm afraid we've damaged some of your furniture getting ourselves loose. I know it wasn't your fault. You didn't do anything wrong. It would be a real help if you could let us out. At the very least, it would probably go a long way toward our allies not being angry with you over us having been held here. None of this should reflect back on you. Your mistress and her brother helped to bring you into the world, but now that you're here, you should be allowed to make your own choices. What do you think? Can you help us?"

Quentin sighed, muttering, "I hate it when she does this."

"What is she doing?" asked Bucer.

"She thinks knowes are alive. I think she's probably right, because this works almost every time. She's trying to suck up to the knowe so it will let us leave." Quentin sounded more frustrated than I would have expected. "It's just weird."

"Nothing's weird if it works, kid," said Bucer. "Hey, nice knowe, it'd be really swell if you could let us out. We don't want to be here any longer. And we're not really the kind of people your lady likes hanging around with most of the time. If you let us out, we'll leave, and she won't have to worry about us being here any longer."

I don't know whether it was my request or Bucer's that got through, but I heard a very soft click, and when I tried the knob again, it turned easily under my hand. I pushed inward. The door swung gently open, revealing a Victorian-themed foyer. I exhaled, relieved, and stepped through, Bucer and Quentin close behind.

"You are a wonderful knowe," I said, stroking the wall once I was on the other side of the door. The knowe didn't respond, but I felt better about convincing it to go against its owner's will. Addressing the knowes with respect is so often a self-serving act, intended to get me out of bad situations, and I always worry a little about getting them in trouble with the people who have actual control over them.

Quentin eased the door closed behind him as he entered the foyer. I looked carefully around, then started in the direction I judged most likely to lead to the exit. Knowes have a tendency to shift their layout around when no one's looking, and most of them seem to take rearranging the rooms on guests—willing or unwilling—as a funny way to do things.

Nothing moved, and the next room after the foyer was a short hall I recognized from our arrival. There was no one between us and the door. I walked faster, and the knob turned easily under my hand, swinging open to reveal the porch.

Cautiously, I stuck my table leg through the open door, swinging it around in a short spiral. Nothing happened. Bracing myself against whatever traps Dame Altair might have set to keep her captives contained, I extended my free arm through the opening as well. Again, nothing happened. I relaxed. Yeah, it looked silly for me to test the opening so thoroughly, but better silly than suddenly turned into a frog or whatever.

Dame Altair had never struck me as particularly dangerous in this reality. In the other reality, when she'd threatened me, she'd run as soon as it looked like there might be consequences. Now, though, I was rethinking things, especially since Dugan was her brother. Dugan was no more or less dangerous than most Daoine Sidhe, but he was a fanatic who was willing to do anything for the false queen of the Mists. With him added to the mix, her escape suddenly made far too much sense.

I turned to Bucer. "Looks like it's safe," I said. "You go first."

"You're not afraid I'll run?"

"I'll be right behind you," I said, a thin line of danger in my tone.

He paled but nodded, swallowing hard.

Maybe it wasn't very heroic of me to allow someone else to walk through the doorway first and trigger any lingering traps, but my baby couldn't consent to me going through the door first, and if it wasn't going to be me, it wasn't going to be Quentin, either.

Still pale, Bucer squared his shoulders and stepped through the doorway. Nothing happened, and so I followed him, taking hold of his arm, while Quentin followed me, closing the door behind him. We were out.

So was the sun. Based on the light, it was sometime in the early afternoon, meaning we'd been held captive for somewhere between four and six hours. Tybalt was going to kill me, once he got through checking me over to be sure that I was all right.

Still holding Bucer's arm, I started down the porch steps, using him for balance until we got to the bottom. Once there, I started to let go, then hesitated. I was forgetting something. What was I—?

The sunlight glinted off the soft hairs on Bucer's ear, and my breath caught in my throat. Disguises. I had been so distracted with the need to get out of the knowe, to get *away*, that I had forgotten about human disguises. Quentin and I might be able to get away with it—there was nothing blatantly inhuman about us except for our ears, which could be hidden in our hair or passed off as something from a *Lord of the Rings* costume party. Bucer, though . . .

Even if his ears had been some sort of headband and his eyes had been really expensive contacts, his legs were anatomically impossible. There was no amount of costuming skill that could make the bones of a human being bend that way. I moved so I was standing between Bucer and the street, blocking his body with my own as much as possible.

"Quentin," I hissed.

He stopped in the process of coming down the stairs to frown at us. Then his eyes widened, and I knew he'd reached the same realization I had.

With the chain wrapped around his wrists, Bucer couldn't exactly disguise himself. He didn't flinch as Quentin raised his hands and chanted something under his breath—probably a verse to some old maritime song, if I knew my squire. The smell of heather and steel rose around us, wreathing us both in ropes of perfumed air. Then the spell burst, leaving illusion in its wake.

Bucer suddenly looked like a skinny, sleazy human man. His clothing hadn't changed, except for the addition of clompy boots with hard plastic soles, which would help to explain the way he sounded when he walked. My ears itched, which told me that Quentin had decided to disguise me at the same time.

Most people enchant me, I get annoyed. My squire does it, I take it as him helping me conserve my magic for what I'm actually good at. I looked at my hand. I could still feel the table leg clutched there, but it was no longer visible; instead, I appeared to be holding a cellular phone. Raising an eyebrow, I looked back to Quentin, who shrugged.

"You needed to be holding something to explain the way your fingers were bent, and this seemed better than a popsicle or something," he said.

"Fair enough," I allowed. "Weird, but fair."

Danny's car was gone. We were close enough to the center of San Francisco that almost all the available parking was occupied, although there were three open slots in front of Dame Altair's house—honestly, a bigger indicator of the presence of Faerie than all the pointed ears in the world. Street parking doesn't just linger in San Francisco, a city made of hills and narrow side streets where people have been shot for a decent spot.

Quentin was also wrapped in a human illusion, looking like a sporty young man in his early twenties, clean cut and mundane. I offered him a smile, which he returned in earnest.

"Let's go home, kiddo," I said.

Quentin sighed. "I guess they took your actual phone, too?"

"They took everything I had on me."

"Oh, Tybalt's going to love that," he muttered. "I wish there was a spell to summon a cab."

"Come on, it's not that far." I wasn't thrilled about the hills between here and home, but I was still upsettingly glad to be out of the house—especially since I knew this brief brush with freedom was going to end soon.

"What about me?" asked Bucer.

"We're taking you with us until we can figure out what else we can get out of you," I said, silently adding, *and until I can find out what you know about Quentin.* "Behave and I won't tell Tybalt you're partially responsible for me getting poisoned. He tends to take that sort of thing personally."

Bucer swallowed hard and didn't say anything else as he fell into step beside me.

San Francisco is a big city in the sense that it looms huge in the cultural landscape. In the mortal world, it's a trendsetter for art and technology, reshaping their reality around its ideas and discoveries. In the fae world, it's the center of the Kingdom in the Mists, which may not be the largest kingdom in the Westlands, but is certainly the source of more chaos than any other location we have. But geographically, San Francisco is tiny. Dame Altair's house was less than two miles from mine, with winding streets and steep hills between them, but still, not all that much distance.

We started walking. Our progress wasn't fast; every time we hit an incline, I had to slow down, dragging myself up and staggering downward, unsteady on my feet, which I couldn't even see half the time. The whole way, Quentin was there, stabilizing me, offering his arm and keeping me from toppling over. I leaned on him more heavily than I was entirely comfortable doing, periodically checking his face to be sure I wasn't hurting him. He kept smiling the whole time.

"Gosh, kid, suck up a little harder, why don't you?" asked Bucer.

"You try having Toby for a knight," Quentin countered. "There's almost nothing I can do for her that she can't do for herself. She has to protect me during fights, because if I take a really solid hit, I'll go down and not get up again. Meanwhile, she's out there recovering from everything short of a decapitation. I can't even carry her stuff, because Tybalt always gets there first. It's nice to be able to feel like I'm keeping up my part of the bargain."

I blinked at him. "I didn't know you felt that way."

Quentin shrugged, looking away from me and down at the sidewalk. "Yeah, well, 'I wish you'd need me more' isn't the sort of thing a guy wants to say to his knight," he said.

"Still, I want you to be happy."

"I know. The fact that you want that is why I didn't say anything before."

I frowned. "You're not worried about things changing, are you?"

"Worried? No. Excited? I'm really excited. It's been a while since I got to be a big brother." He slanted a fragile smile in my direction. "I haven't seen my baby sister since I came to Shadowed Hills."

"I always forget you have a baby sister."

"I do, and she used to be my very favorite person in the whole world. On good nights, I think she probably still is. On the bad nights, I realize I don't know her anymore. I haven't seen her in eight years. A lot can change about a person in eight years. I'm not the same as I was when I left home. What if she doesn't like me when we get back into the same place? What if I don't like her?"

His voice broke on the last word. I sighed. "No one can tell you the answer to that. We can't see the future. But maybe it's time I write your parents and ask if they've considered bringing her home."

Quentin looked alarmed. "I don't want to go home. I'm happy here, and I haven't been knighted yet. I'm not leaving until you think I'm good enough to bear my own, *earned* title."

Because of course he would have a title whether he attained his knighthood or not. Quentin was going to be High King of the Westlands one day, and the crown wouldn't care whether he'd earned his laurels. He was only studying with me because tradition said he should try, as the heir to the throne.

The sky above us was clear and bright with the deepening afternoon sunlight. Soon enough, twilight would come, and then the star-starved San Francisco sky, flattened and rendered empty by the light pollution from below, which could drown out all but the very largest, brightest celestial bodies. Some stars would still shine, of course, and the moon, which never went away, but the glorious noise of the sky would be swallowed whole by the electric lights below.

There was probably some great message in that, but whatever it was, I couldn't see it at the moment. I kept walking, leaning on Quentin when I had to, pulling Bucer along with me when he slowed, and bit by bit, we closed the distance between Dame Altair's house and my own.

My car was in the driveway, as was Quentin's. Danny's was nowhere to be seen. I would have to go and check on him after we'd checked in at home. If Dame Altair had done anything to him, I was going to . . .

Well, I didn't know what I was going to do. But whatever it was, it would be painful, and she wasn't going to like it.

My feet were throbbing, my knees ached, and I needed to pee so badly it was almost all I could think of by the time we reached the front door. I climbed the front steps laboriously, trying to pretend I didn't know Quentin was following closely so he could catch me if I fell, and only paused when I reached the top and automatically checked my pockets.

No keys.

"She took my keys," I complained.

"You already knew that," said Quentin. "You said she took everything."

"Yeah, but . . . my *keys*."

"She probably thought you were going to use them as a weapon," said Quentin.

"Because I would absolutely have used them as a weapon," I said, sourly. "So she got that much right."

"Are you really mad at her for taking a weapon away?" asked Bucer.

"Given that I hadn't done anything to provoke her or give her a good reason to take me prisoner, yeah, I'm a little pissed," I said. "She poisoned me, tied me to a bed, and stole my phone and my housekeys. I think I'm justified in being ticked off."

All this said, I reached up and rang the doorbell, feeling the warning tingle of the wards against my skin. Then I stepped back to wait.

My house wards won't keep me out—that would be silly. But they aren't so strong that having them meant we could leave the doors unlocked all the time. I leaned against the porch rail to take some of the pressure off my knees, feeling increasingly put-upon as I waited for someone to come and let us in.

Finally, footsteps. I straightened, catching a glance of blonde-streaked brown hair passing the edge of the window. The color was enough to set my teeth on edge. I took a step backward, putting myself between Quentin and the door.

The knob turned. The door swung open. And the pregnant woman with my face looked impassively out at the three of us. She was wearing the same outfit I was, bar the sheer quantity of blood that had soaked into my clothing, which thankfully was being covered by Quentin's illusions. She raised an eyebrow anyway, apparently seeing something out of order about my attire.

"We're not looking for a new religion, thanks," she said, in my voice, and began to swing the door closed again.

"How about buying some cookies?" I asked.

She smirked. "Funny," she said, and slammed the door.

"We should go," said Bucer, voice low and urgent. "She could come back, and if she sees through these illusions, we're going to have a problem that I don't think we're prepared for."

He was making good sense, and the house was already effectively conquered ground. I stood there for a few seconds, trying to figure out why I wasn't more upset, before I turned to Quentin. "You got your keys?"

"No," he said, and blinked hard. "How are you so calm?"

"Dugan's a champion illusionist, so we can assume Dame Altair is too. May's indestructible, Tybalt's a nightmare when he wants to be, I'm a little worried about Raysel and Jazz, but I trust our people to take care of them. For right now, I say we steal my car and head someplace where we can regroup and figure out our next moves. If anything, knowing that Tybalt isn't going to freak out and come looking for us means we have a little more flexibility."

Quentin frowned, stopping where he was for a beat. He blinked several times, eyes going slightly unfocused, then jabbed a finger at me as I started down the porch steps. "You're enjoying this," he accused.

"Maybe a little." I shrugged. "Look. My hormones are all over the place. Yesterday I burnt a piece of toast and I started crying because what if I'd hurt the bread's feelings. So I don't think I can be entirely blamed if my reactions to things aren't exactly what you'd expect them to be. And I've been locked inside the house for *months*. I understand why, I know the reasons behind it, but that doesn't mean I've enjoyed it, at all. Now I'm finally doing my job, and I'm not actually worried about our people, because they can handle themselves. Let these assholes think they got one over on us. Hopefully it takes them a while to figure out that we escaped."

Bucer looked at me flatly. "You *knocked* on the *door*."

"Yeah, because I didn't set the wards to just let me in, whether the door was locked or not, and we're all disguised, and they have no reason to think I'd let you loose if I found you. So there's a chance they're not onto us."

Reaching the bottom of the steps, I started for the corner of the house, pausing only to let the two of them catch up. "Hey, Bucer, remember when Devin taught us about boosting cars?"

"I remember you hated it," said Bucer. "I remember you used to let me take care of it whenever you possibly could."

"Accurate memory," I said, with far more cheer than was probably appropriate to the situation. As we entered the driveway area I stopped again, trying to bend enough to flip a large flat rock at the edge of May's herb garden. To my deep annoyance, I couldn't get more than halfway there without the risk of toppling over, so I sighed and straightened.

"Quentin, look under that rock," I said.

"Why?" he asked, even as he was flipping the rock to reveal a long metal toolbox pressed into the soft ground beneath. He shot me a sharp look, pulling the box free. "This what you were looking for?"

"It was," I said, and moved to unbind Bucer's hands. "Don't get any smart ideas about running away or trying to fuck me over. I'm tying you up again as soon as this is finished."

"Of course you are," said Bucer, alternately rubbing and shaking his wrists. He held one hand out toward Quentin. "Box, please."

Quentin frowned. "Toby?"

"Give him the box," I confirmed. "He can use what's inside to break into my car."

"Why your car? I have better insurance than you do."

"Because your car is too new to be easy to hotwire," I said. "And because this way I get to drive."

Quentin huffed and handed Bucer the box. I moved to stand next to him, keeping one eye on the kitchen window in case someone went in there. There wasn't any motion: for the moment, it seemed we were in the clear.

Opening the box, Bucer removed the slim jim and moved to the driver's side window on my car, working the tool through the seal between the door and the window. He'd clearly been practicing since we'd studied together: the slim jim went in smoothly, and he had the lock popped in a matter of seconds.

"How come you haven't taught me how to do that?" asked Quentin.

"I taught you to pick locks. That's a lot more relevant in your daily life," I said. "Plus I don't know how to steal anything newer than the late 1990s, and that's not going to help you all that much."

He huffed again and settled back to watch as Bucer opened the door and slid into the driver's seat. A few more seconds of work and the engine rumbled on, the car coming alive around him. I promptly moved to grab the open door and smile sunnily at Bucer.

"Out," I said.

"But—"

"We're going to Goldengreen," I said. "You can argue with me there. For now, get in the back. Quentin, tie his hands as soon as he's in the car."

Bucer was at least smart enough not to argue again. He got into the backseat, and Quentin waited until his belt was fastened before leaning in and looping the yarrow and silver chain around his wrists.

Quentin got into the front passenger seat, and I slammed the driver's side door before pulling out of the driveway, leaving my compromised home behind.

TWELVE

THE COUNTY OF GOLDENGREEN is seated in the knowe of the same name, which is anchored at the Fine Arts Museum at the Legion of Honor. Being tied to a museum made it easy to explain the strange people coming and going, as long as we showed up during open hours. When the museum was closed, there were other ways to get inside, but as they often involved things like throwing yourself bodily off a cliff, they weren't always advisable. They could attract a lot of mortal attention.

Also, there was the part where sometimes I just didn't feel like throwing myself off a cliff to get inside someone else's knowe. The other outdoor options were normally more pleasant, but as one of them involved a rusty shed and the threat of tetanus, and the other required me to wander around the grounds for an extended period of time, touching sundials and exhausting myself, neither was really on the table.

Fortunately, as I squeezed the car into a parking space near the front of the lot, the sign on the museum door said that we had another twenty minutes before closing. I plucked a sprig of lilac off the bush outside the door as I stepped inside, Quentin and Bucer close behind me.

The guard on duty offered me a professional smile. "How many tickets?" he asked.

"Three, please."

"That will be sixty dollars."

Of course it would be sixty dollars. I put the lilac sprig on the counter between us, reciting quietly, "At the setting of the sun, larks and lilacs have I none, and as the moon comes into view, I gather roses, mint, and rue."

The smell of my magic rose around us, sharp and stinging, and the man's eyes glazed over, gaze going briefly unfocused. He reached for the lilac. "Let me get you your change, ma'am," he said.

"That's all right," I replied. "Come on, boys."

Quentin waited until the bewitched guard was out of earshot before he leaned closer and hissed, "Dean doesn't like us to fox the museum staff."

"I understand, but Dame Altair didn't leave me with any cash," I said.

"Me, neither," he admitted.

We walked onward until we came to the narrow, unmarked door that would let us into the knowe. Anyone without fae blood wouldn't have been able to see it at all. I gestured them both closer and opened the door, revealing the long, dimly lit hall of the knowe. I stepped through, the world spinning and shifting around me, and the mortal world was somewhere else entirely, the Summerlands welcoming us with open arms.

Quentin was the last one through. He closed the door behind him, moving to help support me as I leaned against the wall and gasped for breath. Focusing on my need for air meant that I wasn't focusing quite so hard on my need to toss my cookies all over the hallway floor. Things skittered and shifted in the rafters above us, and I knew that the bogeys who claimed the knowe as their territory were on their way to let someone know that we were here.

That was nice. If the bogeys were already on top of things, I didn't need to move for a few minutes.

Bucer looked at me and frowned. "It always hit her this hard?" he asked, clearly directing his question at Quentin. I glared at him while I continued to focus on my breath.

"Not always," said Quentin. "Sometimes it's better, sometimes it's kinda worse. It really depends on the knowe, and what else she's been doing to herself recently. I'm pretty sure blood loss is a factor, but I'm not certain how, and it's not like I'm going to start bleeding her to figure it out."

"Huh," said Bucer, far too speculatively for my liking.

Footsteps approached, hurrying down the hall. I took another gulp of air and straightened up, turning to see Dean's seneschal,

Marcia, rushing toward us. As usual, she was dressed like she'd just escaped from a 1970s commune, with a loose peasant blouse and a long, layered skirt that fell all the way to her ankles. Her shoes were basic brown brogues, and her stockings were striped red and blue. Her curly blonde hair had been pulled into a braid, dangling over her shoulder, and glittering rings of fairy ointment surrounded her eyes, taking the place of more conventional cosmetics.

Marcia was a thin-blooded changeling, no more than a quarter fae, and without the fairy ointment she wouldn't have been able to perceive the knowe around her. She had too much of mortality in her to see Faerie without assistance.

"Toby!" she exclaimed when she saw me. Then she stopped, blinking, and squinted. "Why are you covered in blood? You're too pregnant to go around covered in blood when you don't have to be, and you shouldn't be getting into situations where you'll have to be. What's going on? Hi, Quentin. Dean's in his office."

"I'm here to make sure Toby avoids any more 'covered in blood' situations; I'll see him when I see him. Toby's here because . . . I'm not actually sure why Toby brought us here." He turned to look at me, assessing. "Toby, why are we here?"

"Because we needed to be somewhere while we regroup, and this is closer than either Shadowed Hills or Muir Woods." I straightened, still leaning against the wall, and mustered a smile for Marcia. "Hi, Marcia. Anything for lunch today?"

"Nothing prepared, but there's fresh bread and we can make sandwiches," she said, agreeably. "What do you mean, regroup?"

"We just got kidnapped, my family is in danger, and the hope chest is missing." It was a blunt way to say things, but I wasn't worried about Marcia spreading the news around, and as a thin-blooded changeling in a position of power, she was likely to be approached if someone decided to start using the hope chest to cash in. Some changelings would pay anything to have the balance of their blood adjusted.

The thought made me feel more than a little guilty. I could do for free what someone was probably going to start charging for, and yet I hadn't started doing it yet. Partially because I didn't like telling people I thought there was something wrong with them—I didn't, and there wasn't. Changelings are just as much a part of Faerie as purebloods are, and we have just as much of a right to exist. We should be able to choose how mortal we want to remain, and having someone imply that there was anything wrong with that wouldn't help people make the decisions they could live with.

And partially because I was finally starting to feel like my life made sense. I was going to be a mother, again, and this time I was going to be able to raise my child, with my husband by my side. In Titania's version of Faerie, Amandine had been open about the fact that our line existed to fill the void left by the loss of most of the hope chests, and she had never been able to rest. Her place in our society had become a constant rush from one place to another, and when she'd tried to stay home with her family, she'd been constantly besieged by requests to get back out there and back to work. I wasn't ready for that.

Maybe it was selfish of me, and if it was, I wasn't sure I actually cared. I wanted to have my own life for a little while before I handed it off to someone else, the way I always seemed to wind up doing.

Marcia blinked several times, very slowly, as she digested what I had just said. I could tell it was sinking in when her eyes widened and her mouth dropped partially open, leaving her gaping at me.

"Yeah," I said.

"How did that *happen*?"

"We don't know," I said. "Arden sent me to ask questions because *someone*, who turned out to be Bucer here"—I indicated Bucer with a sharp jerk of my head—"emptied out most of the royal treasury on Dame Altair's order while we were all enchanted, and only realized after the spell broke that he'd been stealing from the crown. But the hope chest was apparently already gone."

"That's . . . unnerving," said Marcia.

"It is," I agreed.

With no one in Titania's Faerie making fairy ointment, Marcia had been cut off from her supply, and as a consequence, had fallen out of contact with Faerie for the duration of the enchantment. While the rest of us had been struggling through a parallel version of our lives, she had been living comfortably in the mortal world, unaware of what she was missing. When the spell broke, she'd looked around, realized what was missing, and just . . . come home. Dean had found her waiting for him in Goldengreen when he returned, already back at work in the kitchen, welcoming the residents back with an air of amiable cheer that told them everything was going to be all right.

Any maybe for her, it was. Marcia had been one of Lily's subjects, back when the long-lamented Undine had kept her court at the Japanese Tea Gardens in Golden Gate Park. Lily was the first one to see what Marcia was capable of, what her steady, practical presence could bring to a healthy court, but she hadn't been the last. During my brief tenure as Countess of Goldengreen, Marcia had come to work for me, and when I passed the title to Dean, she'd gone with it, becoming a point of stability in an ever-shifting household. He was lucky to have her. I'd been lucky too.

"You have to find it," she said.

I nodded. "I know. But it's worse than just the hope chest. Do you think we could go sit down and have a sandwich, and I'll explain."

"Sure," said Marcia, and turned to head back down the hall.

In remarkably short order, all four of us were seated around one of the kitchen tables, platters of sandwiches in front of us and pixies in the rafters overhead. I didn't know what Marcia's fae heritage was—it had never come up, and it was thin enough that my usual trick of breathing it in and rolling it over my tongue didn't seem to work with her—but I'd be surprised if it wasn't some sort of hearth fae, Brownie or Hob or the like. They have natural talents for cooking and keeping things clean, and the way that woman could put together a tray of sandwiches was nothing short of magical.

I picked up a sandwich, peeling back the bread to check its contents. Ham, cheddar cheese, and sliced nectarine. Next to me, Quentin was munching on a chicken salad sandwich with chunks of apple studded through the mixture. Bucer had a more standard roast beef and cheese with ginger spread.

"So what happened?" prompted Marcia.

"The first part is like I told you," I said. "Dame Altair hired Bucer to empty the royal vaults. I don't know how she found them, or whether she somehow knew they were affiliated with the Windermere family despite Titania reworking reality around us, but she did, and instead of going 'maybe this is something not to touch,' she went looking for a thief."

"Hi," said Bucer.

Marcia gave him a sidelong, noncommittal look.

"She was expecting there to be a hope chest, and when Bucer didn't bring her one, she assumed he must have stolen it."

"Did he?"

"No," said Bucer, sounding stung. "Why would you think that?"

"You worked for Devin," said Marcia, holding up one finger. "He employed you as a pickpocket and petty thief, and you were good enough to graduate from 'kid' to 'associate,' which even our October never managed." A second finger. "Last time we saw you, it was because you'd stolen the crown jewels of Angels, which tells me you're willing to bite the hand that feeds you." A third finger. "You took the job to begin with, when you didn't know who you were stealing from. Could have been the crown, like it turned out to be. Could have been Oberon himself. That shows a certain flexibility of morals that really doesn't make me think you wouldn't fence things out from under your employer's nose. So did you steal the hope chest?"

"No," said Bucer again. He started to stand. Quentin reached across the table and put a hand on his shoulder, pushing him back down into his seat.

"No," echoed Quentin, in a much lighter tone. "We untied you so you could eat something. Don't make me regret that more than I already do."

There was something to be said for having a squire who was large enough to physically control a prisoner. Bucer slumped in his seat, pouting sullenly at Quentin, who ignored him and went back to eating his sandwich.

"M'not a *liar*," said Bucer. "That's the one thing I've never been. I'm a crook and a sneak, and I'd steal from my own mother if she hadn't stopped her dancing after my dad took me into the Summerlands, but I don't *lie* unless there's a profit to be made from it. S'why I get caught so damned often. Can't keep a secret if you won't tell a lie."

"Huh," I said, and took another bite of my sandwich. "I met someone you might like recently. Her name's Bahey, and she's an Adhene."

"There's an Adhene in the Kingdom?" Bucer sat up straighter, ears twitching.

I raised an eyebrow. "Nervous?"

"Delighted! If we can get me in front of an Adhene, Dame Altair will *have* to believe me when I say I didn't steal the hope chest and fence it on the side. She'll let me come back to her household."

I lowered my sandwich, turning to fully stare at him. Bucer blinked.

"What?"

"Why are you so excited about going back to the household of a woman who poisoned me, tied you up, and left you in a room you couldn't escape from on your own?"

Bucer shrugged. "I don't really have anyplace else to go," he said. "Home's gone, and since Lily passed, there's not a real independent demesne in Golden Gate Park. No one's managed to force open a new knowe. The people who *are* there are just trying to stay alive. They don't have anyone to champion them, not really. We need someone who's willing to look out for the independents."

"And you think Dame Altair is going to be that someone?"

Bucer snorted. "Hell, no. She hates changelings, she thinks fae who don't serve a noble household are filthy and beneath her, and she'd pave the whole park for a dollar. But she has a position. She has power. And if I could worm my way deep enough into her household, I might be able to change her mind."

Meaning if he could use his compulsion magic on her long enough, he might be able to bring her away to his way of thinking. It was underhanded and wrong, and it might be the only chance some of the people trying to survive in Golden Gate Park without a champion had. Faerie can be a cruel mistress.

"Would her *brother* ever let that happen?" asked Quentin. "We can't all sit here and pretend that we didn't see Dugan while we were making his escape."

Marcia gaped at him, and then at me. "Harrow?" she squeaked. "Dugan *Harrow* is back in the Mists?"

"He is, and it seems he's Dame Altair's brother," I said. "Which somehow no one ever bothered to mention to me before."

She slumped in her seat. "Everyone in Faerie is related one way or another if you're willing to go back far enough. There are only so many Firstborn, and their kids married each other, or at least dallied, enough that it's less a family tree and more a family thorn briar. Why do we value some family connections and not others?"

Her question was a fair one. I'd never known Marcia to say anything about her family, either fae or human. I didn't know how old she was, or how long she'd been in Faerie—time can get a little squishy in the Summerlands. She looked like she was somewhere in her twenties, but she looked like that before Simon turned me into a fish, back in the mid-nineties. She could be a hundred years old. She could be older.

And she was looking at me like the question I couldn't answer was breaking her heart. I sighed.

"I guess some of the purebloods modeled their ideas of family so closely after the humans that they latched on to the thought that brothers and sisters matter more than cousins, and spread it through Faerie," I said, hesitantly. "Like blood only matters up until a certain degree of removal."

"I hate it," Marcia said, more sharply than I would have expected. "It's stupid and it's wrong and I hate it. Dugan's her brother? Let me guess, she's sheltering him."

"Him and, I suspect, the false Queen," I said grimly.

"*What?*"

"We know his illusions are remarkably strong, and he has some of her supply of borrowed magic from back when she was in power and he was one of her favorites—the kind of little tricks Simon used to make for his owner, the ones that use a little bit of someone else's blood to make their powers temporarily accessible. So we don't actually know what Dugan is capable of, just that he's in the Kingdom right now, and maybe in my house."

"What," said Marcia again. It wasn't a question this time. She looked right at me, squinting a little.

"After we broke out of Dame Altair's, we went back to my place to regroup and tell Tybalt what had happened," I said. "But when we got there, we were already inside. Someone who looked just like me opened the door. So I'm assuming it's the two of them under illusion spells."

"And you just . . . left?"

I blinked at her. "Yeah?"

"And you didn't think anything was strange about that? About you being willing to just . . . leave?"

"May's indestructible, and Tybalt can take care of himself," I said.

"And are May and Tybalt the only people in the house?"

"No," I admitted, more slowly. "Raysel's in there, and Spike. And my cats."

"Uh-huh." Marcia nodded exaggeratedly, like she was trying to make a small child understand her point. "And don't you think you should have been worried about them, not just left them there with dangerous people?"

"Maybe." I took another bite of my sandwich. It was a good sandwich. Marcia always made good sandwiches. I'd have to ask her sometime how she could do that so effortlessly. In her hands, ingredients even I would have thought couldn't possibly go together could somehow be combined into a coherent, delicious whole.

"I don't think 'maybe' is good enough here, Toby." She turned her attention to Bucer. "You want to cut this shit out before I summon my liege and make you face *him*? Because Dean's originally from the Undersea, and he doesn't have a lot of tolerance for this sort of thing."

Quentin frowned. "What are you talking about?"

"I know you squires are always eager to graduate and become knights in your own right, but believe me when I say that one of the best parts of being a squire is that none of this is your problem: Toby's the one who gets to deal with it. You get to sit back and eat your sandwich and be decorative. Play to your strengths."

Quentin wrinkled his nose at her. "Why do I feel vaguely like I've just been insulted?"

"Because you're smarter than you're acting right now," said Marcia kindly. She turned her attention back to me. "Toby. *Think*. Why did you leave your people to take care of themselves when you were right there to try and help them?"

I couldn't think of a good reason. I also couldn't think of a good reason why I wouldn't have done that. I just blinked at her.

Marcia heaved a heavy sigh and stood. "Wait right there," she said. "All three of you. Bucer, you are *not* allowed to get up and run away while my back is turned, and if you try, Toby will have the clarity to stop you. Do you understand me? This is not your opportunity to escape."

"Yes, ma'am," said Bucer, sounding baffled.

Marcia walked across the kitchen to open a cupboard and produce a heavy glass mug. She opened another cupboard and started pouring things from it *into* the mug. None of the liquids were purple, but somehow combining them resulted in a mixture the color of blooming larkspur, streaked with blue and white. It was so vivid it was difficult to look at directly.

Marcia sniffed the contents of the mug speculatively, then made a sour face and picked up a paring knife. Before I could react, she nicked the side of her index finger and added several drops of blood to the liquid. It shifted shades, going the deep purple of forest violets, and she nodded, walking over to put the mug in front of me.

"Drink this," she said, in an authoritative tone that didn't leave any real room for argument. I blinked at her and picked up the mug.

Its contents *smelled* like violets, those sticky-sweet candied violets that used to flavor old-fashioned hard candies. There was a layer of chalkiness underneath, echoing the impression of old-fashioned candies, and a hint of vanilla and peppermint. No blood at all. It should have been the strongest scent in the mixture, but I couldn't smell a drop. I lifted my head and blinked at Marcia.

"You can't serve the courts as a thin-blooded changeling as long as I have without learning a few tricks," she said. "It's all hedge magic and marshwater charms, but it does me well enough. Please drink it."

The mug was halfway to my mouth before I thought better of it, and once I'd gone that far, it seemed only reasonable to finish the motion.

The first sip was overwhelming in its sweetness. The second was like taking a mouthful of swamp water, murky and dense with muck and green waterweeds. Somehow the change, unpleasant as it was, made me want to keep drinking: it was like the potion she'd mixed was a riddle, and now that I had heard its opening words, I desperately wanted to untangle the full complexity of it.

I took a third mouthful, this one filled with fruits, cherries and quinces, peaches and strawberries, rosehips and raspberries. They formed an impenetrable wall of sweetness that I was still trying to puzzle through when I felt the mug plucked from my hands. I swallowed, raising my head to blink at Marcia, who was standing on the other side of the table, the half-filled mug in her hands.

"That should be enough for right now," she said. "Too much deeper and you'll drown. Now, October, why did you leave your home and your allies to your enemies?"

I blinked. Then I blinked again, and frowned so hard that it hurt my mouth. "I . . . I don't know," I said. I turned to Quentin. He was still eating his sandwich, apparently unbothered. "Quentin, why did we leave the house?"

"I mean, technically, we never went *into* the house, so we couldn't *leave* the house," he said, sounding as unconcerned as he looked.

My frown deepened. "We went there, our people were there, Altair and, presumably, Harrow were there, and we just walked away. We *left*. Why did we do that?"

"I dunno." He swallowed. "It just seemed like a good idea, I guess."

My head felt light and almost fuzzy, the way it used to back before alcohol had stopped having an effect on me, on days after I'd been drinking. I slowly turned to look at Bucer, who looked away. "And why would it seem like a good idea?"

"Hey," he said. "Hey, you can't blame me for wanting to stay alive. I didn't—you told me not to use my magic to force you to do anything, and I didn't. If staying around me for too long meant that you got more open to suggestion, that's not my fault. I can't help it."

I frowned. "What do you mean?"

"He means Glastig can be intentionally convincing when they want to, but even if they're not trying, people who spend a lot of time around them will get gradually more and more pliant," said Marcia, sounding annoyed. "It's the difference between taking a hit off a joint or breathing in a room where other people are smoking. You'll get drugged either way. What changes is how fast, and how big of a dose you get. I thought your control would be better by now, little goat. Haven't you been around long enough to learn how not to leak?"

Bucer almost visibly bristled. "It's better for me if I'm just a little sloppy. Keeps people from taking advantage of me."

"But October found you tied to a bed." Marcia handed me back the mug of purple liquid. "Here, drink a little more of this—but only a little. You need to clear your head."

When I took another sip of the juice, it had a completely indefinable flavor, which was confusing in its own way. I'm not a supertaster or anything, but thanks to my magic, I'm better at picking out and separating individual ingredients than most people. This didn't taste like anything specific. It was just sweetness and a distant hint of something strange and spicy, like ginger or some sort of pepper.

The more I drank the more my head began to clear. I took a second sip, and swallowed. It trickled down my throat and my confusion and calm were entirely gone, replaced by a cold rage. I lowered the mug, setting it gently on the table.

"Bucer," I said.

He actually cringed, shying away like he thought I was about to stab him with one of the knives I wasn't carrying. He didn't get up from the table, probably because Quentin, while still disinterested, was right there to stop him if he tried.

"I'm just trying to survive here," Bucer whined. "You'd do the same thing in my position! I didn't do anything *wrong*."

"You used your powers to make me walk away and leave the father of my child with a woman who'd already tried to poison me," I spat. "That's pretty damn wrong, if you're asking me."

"I wasn't?"

"Too bad. Might have gone easier for you if you had been." I leaned closer to him. "Hey, Marcia, you want to go find something you need to sweep? Bucer and I are going to have a little conversation."

"That sounds like a great excuse to go and borrow the Count's phone so you can call home and warn your people before you start committing acts of unspeakable violence in my kitchen," agreed Marcia easily. "Quentin, you want to come with me?"

"Sure," he said, agreeably, and rose, sandwich still in hand, to follow her out of the kitchen.

Bucer and I were alone.

I turned to fully face him, very slowly. He met my eyes, barely managing not to cringe again.

Once I was sure I had his full attention, I did the only thing I could think of that would make him understand how serious I was without actually attacking him.

I smiled.

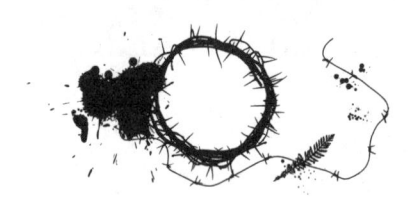

THIRTEEN

THERE WAS A TIME when I thought a smile was an inherently positive expression. That was before I spent some time working as a shelf stocker at Safeway, and more importantly, before I started spending my time with the sea witch. The Luidaeg had been hurt deeply enough and frequently enough that her smiles had transformed over the course of centuries, becoming endless passages full of knives.

I was nowhere near her league, but when I wanted to smile in a threatening way, I could absolutely manage it. Bucer recoiled, making a small, unhappy noise that was more like a bleat than any human sound. I kept smiling as I walked toward him.

"Come on, Bucer, is that any way to behave toward an old friend?" I asked. "After I cut you free and got you to a sanctuary? I haven't done anything to hurt you, not once today, but you've tricked me without raising a finger, and you may have put the people I care about in danger. You may have put my liege's daughter in danger. She's defenseless. That was a bad decision on your part."

"I didn't decide anything," protested Bucer. "If you break a bone, you heal whether you want to or not. If I'm scared and need to get to safety, I'll put that into the air whether I intend to or not. I didn't manipulate you on purpose."

"But you knew it was happening." I stopped smiling. "You knew as soon as I agreed to turn and walk away from my own front door that it was happening, and you let me walk away. That's where you really fucked up, Bucer. That's where you should have said 'hey, Toby, maybe my magic is making you make bad choices.'"

"Would rushing Dame Altair have been a good choice?" asked

Bucer, desperately. "I let you have a good reason to protect yourself, and to protect your baby."

"Don't pretend you were thinking about the baby."

"I was, really. Because if I let you get hurt badly enough to hurt that baby, you'd kill me."

I stopped for a moment, his words echoing in my ears. No matter why I'd turned away from that door, no matter how out of character it had been for me, it had been exactly what Tybalt would have wanted me to do if he'd been able to influence my decision. He'd tried to keep me safe not because he thought I could be hurt—he knew better than that—but because he wanted to protect our child.

All his smothering, borderline obsessive attempts to keep me home and safe had been aimed at my innocent passenger, who would be out in the world soon enough, but was still my responsibility now.

And that didn't matter one damn bit, because he was my husband and May was my sister and Raysel was my cousin and responsibility, and this asshole had been willing to let me walk away from them all. He'd been willing to leave them in danger for the sake of his own skin. All the self-serving bullshit about keeping my baby safe was exactly that: bullshit. He'd been more interested in protecting himself than he'd been in anything else.

"Who says I'm not going to kill you anyway?" I asked, and somehow the question came out both perfectly reasonable and utterly threatening.

Bucer paled. "You're a hero! Heroes can't just go around killing people!"

"I'm a hero with the Queen in the Mists on speed dial," I said. "I call Arden, I tell her what you did, and she'll have her guard here in the snap of her fingers. Literally. She'll portal them in, and you'll go into her custody. It'll be much harder for you to escape than Dame Altair was ever going to be."

"Wait!" He threw his hands up, borderline frantic. "Please, you can't do that to me. We were at Home together. That has to mean something."

I paused, tilting my head to the side as I studied him. "Maybe it does."

He perked up, expression going hopeful. "Really?"

"Really," I said. I smiled again. "It means I know, for a fact, that you can control yourself better than you're trying to pretend. Devin would have had your hooves and horns if you'd been a walking consent violation when you were around people he considered his possessions. But I'm not going to hand you over to Arden just yet."

"Really?"

"Really." I shrugged. "You're too upset by the idea, which tells me you don't want to meet her new Adhene, no matter what you were saying earlier. She'd know you were lying immediately. I need to know what you're lying about."

"How are you planning to find that out? Drink my blood?"

"No. When I drink someone's blood, I get their memories and their magic, and I don't want to risk making it easier for you to influence me, if your magic reinforces itself. You could make this so much simpler, for the both of us. You could tell me what you're lying about, and we could call it square."

"You'd let me go?"

"Not at this point. You made me complicit in leaving my family in danger, and that's not something I can forgive that easily." I looked over my shoulder at the kitchen door, which Marcia had politely closed when she left with Quentin. There were no pixies or bogeys I could see. "Get up."

"What?"

"Get *up*." I closed the distance between me and the kitchen table in three long steps, regretting the motion almost as soon as it ended. My pregnant body was neither made nor inclined to move that fast. I grabbed the untied chain from the table where it had been placed during our meal, shaking it at Bucer.

He swallowed hard and stood, hooves clattering against the stone floor. "Toby . . ."

"Shut up and turn around."

He started to object, then caught himself and sagged, turning around and putting his hands behind his back without being ordered to do so. Clever boy.

I began wrapping the chain tight around his wrists and forearms, going all the way up to the elbow. Bucer made a soft hissing sound, teeth bared.

"I don't heal like you do," he said. "I need a little blood circulation to my hands."

"Maybe you should have thought of that before." I grabbed the chain, yanking it toward me so that he stumbled. "I'd tie your hands in front of you to make this easier on myself, but I don't want you to be able to catch yourself if you fall trying to get away from me. Here's how this is going to work. You're not going to influence me again. Or Quentin, or Tybalt, or any other member of my family. You're not going to try to do it to Marcia, either, or Dean, or anyone else inside this knowe. You're going to be a good little criminal, and let me haul you around the city until I'm finished with you. Got it?"

"Got it," said Bucer, meekly.

"Good." I wrapped the remaining chain around my own hand and stormed toward the door, hauling him along with me. He did stumble, hooves finding little traction on the well-washed floor, but caught himself before he could slam into me.

I kept pulling as I walked, dragging him out of the kitchen and down the hall beyond, heading for the central courtyard where Dean seemed to spend the bulk of his time in the knowe. If not there, he'd be down in the cove, and Bucer would get the chance to experience stairs with his hands tied. Not the most fun thing, but at least the sand would soften his fall at the bottom of the stairs.

Maybe I was being uncharitable in the way I was thinking about him. Maybe not. He was the one who'd decided to put the whammy on me and on Quentin, and make us think that leaving our people behind was a good idea. He was lucky I hadn't hit him until he passed out and started dragging his unconscious body around the knowe—and that I was pregnant enough that even the idea of trying to haul that much dead weight made my back hurt.

The courtyard was set up in concentric circles, each one brimming with trees and bushes, all thriving despite the fact that we were indoors. That was courtesy of the Goldengreen residents who had once belonged to Lily's court in Golden Gate Park: she had been a safe place for multiple Dryads and Hamadryads to make their homes, and now they lived here, their ambient magic making sunlight unnecessary for the plants around them. Some of them were resting in and around their trees, outlines of faces etched in the bark or brown-streaked bodies curled in the interwoven roots of the captive forest.

Dean was in the center of the room, standing on the cobbled central zone, Quentin and Marcia nearby. Quentin was standing so close that their shoulders were almost brushing, and he was the first to look around at the sound of Bucer's hooves against the floor.

He looked incredibly relieved when he saw the pair of us approaching. The question of why was answered half a beat later when he said, "Toby. You didn't kill him."

"Killing him would be absolutely justified in the Undersea," grumbled Dean. "Manipulating someone else's mind is considered a declaration of war on a personal level, and murder is always acceptable during wartime."

"Sometimes it really amazes me how much effort the Undersea put into finding ways to be allowed to kill each other," said Marcia, with a small shake of her head. "Maybe we don't need to go around finding more excuses for stopping someone's dancing?"

"I don't like it when people control my boyfriend's mind," said Dean. "I didn't like it when Simon did it, I don't like it when this asshole does it."

"At least your mom isn't likely to marry this guy," said Quentin.

Dean grimaced. "Oh, don't even joke," he said. "Two dads are more than enough."

"You seem like yourself again," I said, focusing on Quentin.

"Your line is susceptible to transformation, and that includes transformation of thought," said Marcia. "I just needed to get him out of the room for a few minutes in order for his head to clear. I tried calling your house, but no one's picking up." She said the last part like she was worried I would start yelling immediately. When I didn't, she untensed and continued: "Do you have a plan for what to do from here?"

"Working on it," I said. "Dean, can I borrow your phone, please?"

"Of course," he said. He was already reaching into his doublet pocket, and he held his mobile out to me even as he asked, "Who are you going to call first?"

"Backup," I said. I thrust the chain at Quentin, who unwound it from around my wrist and wrapped it tight around his own. I nodded my thanks and retreated to the other side of the courtyard, punching all the numbers on the keypad in reverse order.

When I held the phone up to my ear, it sounded like the sea.

I waited, trying not to let myself think about the reasons why Tybalt or May hadn't answered the phone. Raysel wouldn't have answered it. Tybalt generally ignored it, but I wasn't home, and he should have been worried. Seconds ticked by, and the waves crashed against the shore. A seagull screamed somewhere in the distance. Even as I started to get impatient, I had to admire the Luidaeg's dedication to the bit.

Finally, the phone started ringing. It was a distant, almost tinny sound, like something that had been traveling along the lines for a hundred years or more. There was a click, followed by an all-consuming silence that was finally shattered by the Luidaeg's voice demanding, *"What?"*

There was a time when that voice speaking in that tone had filled me with more dread than I could properly express, when it had been enough to make me feel small and vulnerable and in danger. Now, it sounded almost like coming home. What a difference a few years can make. "Hey, Luidaeg," I said, my own tone calm and mild. "Got a minute?"

"Right now, for you? I do. I'm not doing anything. I will be soon, I think—Poppy's seen a few changelings sniffing around the neighborhood, and that usually means they're trying to work up the nerve to come and talk to me. But they're not here yet, and until they are, I'm free." Her feigned irritation faded as she spoke, becoming easy and relaxed. I smiled to myself.

The Luidaeg can't lie, but she can still deceive. She uses illusions and misdirection to shape the world as she wants it to be, and sounding angry when she's not is one of those techniques. She's almost always got something to be genuinely pissed off about, thanks to the web of geasa and enchantments that control her life. Her being able to relax around me was a victory beyond words.

"Okay, so, did Arden tell you about the thefts?"

"Thefts?" Her voice sharpened.

"Guessing not. Someone cleaned out the royal vaults while we were all under Titania's spell, and our charming queen asked me to find her missing stuff. With me so far?"

"Yes..."

"After the nonsense at Court last night with the pretender queen disappearing, I went to have a word with Dame Altair about why she'd been targeted—twice. Once to put her in the false queen's place, and once in an attack on her household, using a stolen scabbard that turns anything metal it touches into iron."

The Luidaeg made a disgusted scoffing sound. "My brother Hugleikr created that thing. It's basically indestructible. We all thought he was an asshole for making it, just because *his* descendant line was immune to iron, but I won't deny that it came in handy when Titania's kids were hunting us through the fens. Being able to make weapons they couldn't stand against out of rust and shrapnel saved a lot of lives."

"It's not saving lives now. Dame Altair's footman was killed with iron, according to Arden."

"May he rest in the comfort of the root and the branch," said the Luidaeg gravely.

"Yeah," I agreed. "Anyway. Went to Dame Altair's knowe, and she invited me and Quentin inside to make polite conversation while she poisoned us. I woke up tied to a bed without my weapons, keys, or phone."

"That explains the unfamiliar number, I guess."

"Can't call you from a phone I don't have. I borrowed Dean's."

"So you got away."

"We did. It hurt like hell, and I've definitely ruined this shirt, but I got loose, freed Quentin, and then found Dame Altair's accomplice. Bucer O'Malley."

"That Glastig kid from Home?" She sounded faintly offended, like she couldn't believe Dame Altair would stoop so low.

"Yeah. Also turns out Dame Altair is Dugan Harrow's sister. Did you know?"

"I did," admitted the Luidaeg. "I'm sorry. You didn't ask, and I couldn't volunteer the information."

"I don't actually expect transparency from you anymore. I wish I could, but I know why you can't provide it, and I don't see any point in making us both miserable by requesting something impossible all the damn time. Okay, so you knew. What's the story there? Can you tell me?"

"It's not protected information, and no one's asked me to keep the secret," she said, voice going thoughtful. "She poisoned you *after* I offered to stand godmother to your child, which can be seen as a slight against me and my ability to protect the pair of you . . . yeah, I can spin this as selfishness. So." She paused to take a deep breath. "Dame Altair was born Eloise Harrow, younger sister of Dugan. She married an unlanded second son in Londinium, and the pair of them struck out for America in hopes of being able to move upward in the nobility. She made the crossing, her husband didn't. Once she got to the Mists, she threw off her widow's weeds inside of a season, called her brother over to join her, and opened that little knowe she's so proud of. He stayed there with her until Gilad died, and then appeared in the pretender's court inside of the year. I don't think they intentionally hid their relationship, so much as it just didn't matter for their respective ambitions, whatever those happened to be."

"So Dugan could have been feeding her information about what was in the vaults the whole time the pretender was on the throne." It made a horrible sort of sense. "And for some reason Titania let her keep that information when she spelled us all. Why would she do that?"

"Easy enough to mask dreams of treasure as just that—dreams. Wrap them up in veils and turn them into children's stories, so Altair didn't know what she was really sending her little thief after. People have done more for less. How did she find O'Malley?"

"He was already on his way back up the coast when everything got weird. He came back to the Mists, she recruited him. Only it turns out he's still a shitty little thief at heart, and while he was stealing *for* her, he was also stealing *from* her—skimming off the things she didn't specifically ask him to get, which means anything she didn't know about may be out in the wild. She caught on, and had him tied up, too."

The Luidaeg sighed heavily. "You released him, didn't you?"

"He could have useful information about where things are, and why Dame Altair felt the need to poison me, although I didn't know about Dugan when I released him, and her being the sister of someone who's tried to hurt my family before probably has something to do with it. We got out of her knowe, and on the way, we saw Dugan. He used another of those borrowed blood charms to teleport away—and how long do those things last, anyway? Doesn't stolen magic have a shelf life?"

"Fae flesh doesn't rot, fae blood doesn't curdle, and charms made from either will stay fresh for centuries if that's what their use requires."

"Great," I said sourly. "Anyway, we fled the knowe and went back to my house, which is where I get really homicidal."

"What happened?"

"We got there to find Altair and Harrow were already in the house, disguised as me and Quentin. And when I realized what had happened, I turned around and walked away."

"Glastig got you, huh?"

"Yeah," I admitted. "Marcia realized I wasn't acting right and mixed me some sort of weird concoction that knocked me out of it, and Quentin's fine now too, but I don't know whether Bucer's going to be stupid enough to try something like that again. He seems awfully worried about his own skin."

"What does Altair think he stole?"

"The hope chest."

The Luidaeg breathed in sharply, the world's smallest sound of surprise. I held my tongue, giving her a second to recover her wits.

That second passed. More followed, a cascade of seconds rolling down the slope of her silence, until I couldn't wait any longer: "Luidaeg?"

"You couldn't have started by telling me that Goldengreen was missing?"

For a dizzy moment, I thought she was talking about the knowe. Then I remembered that the hope chests all had proper names, once upon a time, and the one that had been in the kingdom vaults was Goldengreen, the namesake for the county where we now stood. Its importance was such that Evening had named her county after it, to brag about the fact that it was in her care. Now, even with the hope chest gone, the name endured.

"I wanted you to understand the whole situation," I said. "She turned on Bucer when it wasn't there."

"But it really wasn't there?"

"Not when he broke into the vaults, or so he says. I haven't been able to check the truth of what he's been telling us quite yet."

"Uh-huh." Glass clattered in the background, the sound heavy and somehow threatening, like it was a portent of something much larger. "Out of everything that could go missing, you don't think it's strange that the thing Altair is most concerned about getting her hands on would be the hope chest?"

"No. It's not strange."

"Explain." Her voice had turned icy.

"The false queen still thinks she can recover the Siren blood I took away from her. Dugan is her man, and Altair is his sister. If Dame Altair somehow remembered the vault, she may have also remembered that the hope chest was important to elevating her family standing in some way. After the enchantment broke, retrieving the hope chest for her brother and helping the false queen escape would have seemed like a perfect opportunity to get in the good books of someone their family is already connected to. They have her, I'm sure of it. Everything Altair said about her attacker's magic could also be true of Dugan's, and nothing she said was a lie. She was just describing her brother while she pointed at Simon."

And she was going to pay for that, just as soon as I had the opportunity to hand her the bill. I was still getting used to the idea of having Simon in my life on a permanent basis. I didn't need some assholes taking him away from me.

"All right, so why are you calling me?"

"I need your help."

"Help how? You know I need specifics, Toby, or I can't do anything."

I took a deep breath. "Luidaeg, can you please come to Goldengreen and bind Bucer's magic so he can't influence us again? I need to take Quentin back to the house and get Altair and her trashy brother the hell out of there before somebody gets hurt. I'll call Arden, too, to get more backup on the ground, but I can't risk leaving Bucer here to hurt Marcia and Dean, and I can't take him anywhere with me if he can change my mind without my noticing."

"That passes outside the scope of selfishness. Hold on."

There was a clunking sound, followed by silence. I frowned at the phone, looking over my shoulder to where the others waited for me to finish. Quentin gave me a quizzical look. I shrugged. He turned back to Dean.

"Hello?" I tried. "Luidaeg, are you there?"

"This would have been so much more impressive if you'd been patient for another ten seconds, you know," said the Luidaeg, walking into the courtyard. She was back in her customary overalls and heavy boots, with strips of electric tape holding her hair in twinned ponytails over her shoulders. She looked more human than anyone else in the room, even Marcia, and she was carrying a canvas shopping bag over one shoulder. She nodded to the others as she walked over to me. "Dean. Quentin. Marcia." When she got to Bucer she paused, then smiled, showing a full mouthful of razor-sharp shark teeth. "Bucer. I thought you were well quit of this kingdom. Maybe you should have been."

He paled, taking a half-step back. The Luidaeg snapped her teeth at him with an audible clicking noise, laughing at his expression of sheer terror.

"I didn't know you were coming," I said.

She finally focused on me. "I don't have to tell you everything I'm doing," she said. "This was just easier if I could do it in person. Give me your wrist."

I hung up Dean's phone and stuck it in my pocket before holding out my right arm, wrist tilted toward the ceiling. She nodded approvingly, taking hold of my hand and tilting it a little further toward her.

"You asked for a way to protect yourself and those around you from the Glastig's magic," she said. "You fear for the safety of your family, and so you bargain with the sea witch. Is this true?"

I nodded, meeting her eyes, which had gone as white and wild as seafoam. There was no trace of a pupil, but I knew she was still watching me. It was evident in the small motions of her head, the corrections of her gaze. She knew exactly where I was. Still, she didn't say anything, evidently waiting for me to say something.

"It's true," I said.

"How much will you pay?"

"Whatever you require, as long as it offers no harm to my child," I said.

She smiled. "Good girl," she said, sounding incredibly pleased with my reply. "The first price my geas offered me would have had the baby in my arms rather than yours, and we could both have grappled with that nightmare for the rest of your life. Instead, I can offer you another option. I'll give you what you ask of me, and you'll give me blood—"

I'd done that before. I smiled, starting to agree, and she cut me off.

"—and bone," she finished. "I'll lay you down and slice you open, and I'll have your ribs for my own, taken one by one from the willing. Do you agree?"

I'd lost bits of bone before, and they'd always grown back. But the process was excruciatingly painful, and I wasn't going to pretend to be excited about the idea. Still, I forced myself to nod.

"I agree," I said. "Blood, and bone, both given freely to you, to be used as you see fit—but not until *after* the baby is born."

"I can throw in a small freebie," she said. "They won't be used against you or your blood, either by me or by any who come seeking them. I'll use what you give me in ways that won't harm your family."

I sighed, relieved. "That's ... good to hear," I admitted.

"Wait before you say that," she said, and drove her suddenly taloned forefinger into the space between the bones of my wrist, splitting flesh and skin in the same gesture. It ached like acid. When she pulled her talon from the wound, the skin was blackened around the edges, and didn't start to heal for several seconds, giving the blood plenty of time to well up and spill over.

The Luidaeg took a step back. "All our distinctions are artificial ones," she said, voice calm. "Water magic and blood magic are the same thing, because blood is nothing more than an isolated ocean. We prison the tides in our veins and pretend to be independent islands. We *are* water."

She raised her bloody hand, and the blood dripping from my injured wrist rose with it, floating off the floor and away from my skin as it danced like ribbons in the air between us. My skin was finally knitting back together, whatever she'd done to slow my recovery fading. She apparently had enough blood for her purposes, because she didn't cut me again, just twisted her hand back and forth like she was trying to wind yarn around her fingers.

The blood responded to her motions, swirling closer and resolving into four discrete ribbons, each one about an inch wide and several feet long. They stayed bright red and arterial, not drying or browning.

"Bucer, I need you," she said, sounding bored.

"Uh, no, I'm good over here," said Bucer.

The Luidaeg turned to face him. Her eyes, white only a moment before, were suddenly as black as the depths of the sea, captive slices of void surrounded by skin. She pursed her lips, visibly unhappy.

"I will ask one more time," she said, in a voice like ice breaking on a frozen river. "Bucer O'Malley, come here."

He swallowed hard and walked toward her on unsteady legs, hooves clacking against the floor. As he drew closer, she held her hand out and waited for him to offer her his arm. Bucer shrugged and turned to show her that his arms were bound behind him, making it impossible for him to do as she was asking.

"Sorry, ma'am. I'm a prisoner," he said. "I can't accommodate your request."

The Luidaeg scoffed and snapped her fingers. The chains on his arms fell away in an instant, wood and silver both transmuted into saltwater.

I scowled. The Luidaeg raised an eyebrow and offered him a slow smile, then beckoned him forward again.

"We needed him tied up," I said.

"This will be better," said the Luidaeg. "Trust me."

And I did. Oberon help me, I did.

Bucer shot me a look, clearly miserable, and took the last few steps to reach her before he held his arm out as she was asking.

"I'm not—you know I won't—Toby's different from the rest of us," he babbled. "I can't heal like she does."

"I know," said the Luidaeg. She didn't stab him like she'd stabbed me, only grasped his wrist and pulled him toward her before using the edge of her thumbnail to lay the skin of his wrist open. She didn't cut him as deeply as she'd stabbed me, and while he certainly bled, it was slower, more controlled. She waited until she judged he'd bled enough, then reached over and pinched off an inch or so from one of the ribbons she'd crafted from my blood, laying it across his wound.

Adding blood to blood only makes things bloodier, and for a moment, I couldn't see what she'd done. Then she rubbed her thumb across the site of the injury, and there was nothing there but skin. She let Bucer go, stepping back.

"You're done for now," she said.

He nodded and fled, hurrying back to the others like he thought they were the last source of safety in his world. He even ducked halfway behind Quentin, using my squire as a shield.

The Luidaeg raised both hands, and Bucer's blood rose from the floor, becoming a broad, flat ribbon before splitting in two. She spread her arms, fingers splayed, and the ribbons of blood danced through the air around her, becoming three-strand braids, his blood and mine tangling tight together until the weave was done.

"Hold out your arms," said the Luidaeg. "You, too, Quentin, if you want to be included in the protections."

I did as she bid, as did Quentin. Bucer kept his arms firmly by his side until she glared at him again, then raised them up.

Dean also raised his arms. Marcia didn't. I shot her a confused look, and she shook her head.

"Seeking protection implies that you'll need to be protected from something," she said. "I'm going to stay right here inside Goldengreen, and I'm not going to need to be protected from anything within these walls. I'm good. Don't waste your magic on me."

"All right," said the Luidaeg. She looked at the four of us. "Eight it is."

Turning back to her two floating braids of blood, she brought her hands together in front of her, making a scissoring motion with the first two fingers of each hand. The ribbons split into four equal parts each, and a flick of her fingers sent them floating over to us. They wrapped around our wrists, unsettlingly warm against our skin, drew themselves tight enough to be snug but not tight enough to be uncomfortable, and popped like soap bubbles. The blood fell away in a red haze, leaving bracelets of willow wood behind.

I raised my hand, blinking at the bracelet circling my wrist. "This is your protection?" I asked.

"Mm-hmm." She nodded, looking pleased with herself. "It's been a while since I've tried to blood-bind a Glastig, but this is good work, and it'll hold. Bucer, as long as you're wearing those bracelets, your magic will be sluggish, slow to respond. It will still rise if you call it, but it won't be swift or easy. You'll have to work for it. Most importantly, you won't be able to use the excuse so common with your kind, that you didn't know what you were doing. The world will be free to continue as it likes, uncontrolled by your desires."

Bucer gaped at her, then began to sputter. She snorted. "Would you prefer I had stripped your powers from you completely? Because I could still do that, if that works better for you. It would please me enough to count as a selfish action, and I wouldn't even have to charge you."

Bucer stopped sputtering and looked sullenly away.

"What else do they do?" I asked, raising one hand to the level of my chin to make sure she saw the bracelet clearly.

"Good question," said the Luidaeg. "They're going to slow your magic, too—try to avoid mortal wounds while you have these on. I don't think you remember how to be hurt the way the rest of us do. But they'll also grant a measure of extra resistance against magic that might change or control your mind. Glastig, Siren, any of the manipulators will be held at bay for so long as you wear those. You have two each; they can be separated without voiding the protection. But if any of you removes both bracelets they'll return to the blood that bound them, and be lost. Share, but not to the point of risking your own safety."

I nodded. "Understood." I understood that she'd given us more than she charged us for, probably in part by winding the cost up in selfishness. We couldn't give our protection away, but we could share half of it without risk to ourselves, which made it twice as valuable. I'd be able to keep Tybalt safe.

"Good." The Luidaeg looked at the spotless floor. There wasn't a speck of blood anywhere around us. "Blood and water are the same, and flowers thrive on both. Remember that the divisions between us are as false as they are true. They always have been. Now if we're done here, I have some hungry petitioners on their way to my lair, and I still have a job to do in Faerie."

"All right," I said.

"You'll call me when you know where everything is, won't you?" It was barely a request.

I frowned. "Luidaeg, do you want Goldengreen returned to you? I think I'm obligated to give it to Arden if she asks, but a Firstborn outranks a queen."

"I do, only because I think the hope chests should be back in the hands that were intended to hold them," said the Luidaeg. "They hold no temptation for my siblings and me, or they shouldn't, which is sometimes the same thing. But no, in this case, I just want to know where the hope chest is, and where it's been. As to the other matter between us, we'll finish that in private."

I swallowed. "Yes, we will," I agreed.

Tybalt had already said that she could stand as godmother to our child, but announcing it in a room full of people—a room including *Bucer* of all people—felt fundamentally wrong.

The Luidaeg nodded, turning to Dean before she bowed ceremonially. "Count Lorden," she said. "Please continue to keep your domain in peace and pleasure, and I'll see you when next the tides command me here."

She turned, walking out of the bloodless courtyard. Whispers erupted from the trees around us, and I remembered for the first time since her arrival that we were not and had never been alone there: many members of Dean's court had watched the whole scene play out. I turned to look at them, and they stared at me, wide-eyed and pale.

The sea witch is a fact of life in the Mists. She chose to settle here long ago, and she's one of the only Firstborn whose situation didn't allow her the luxury of disappearing into obscurity. Most of the others could hide. She was compelled to tell the truth and share her power, no matter what else she chose to do, and so she could only go so far underground.

Everyone who lived in the Mists knew she existed, but most of the time we could dismiss her as the fae equivalent of an urban legend, someone whose reality would never truly impact us. Having her appear in front of them in their home and perform acts of strange, near-impossible magic had to be disorienting as hell for people who weren't normally confronted by her in such a direct, immediate way.

"Er," I said. "Sorry, everyone. We'll get out of your hair now. Quentin?"

Quentin, who had been looking at the bracelets on his wrists like he'd never seen anything like them before, raised his head. "Toby? Are you going home to make sure everyone is okay now?"

"Yeah, we are," I said. "The bracelets are going to be a big help, since Bucer turns out to be an environmental contaminant when he's stressed out. Today's been pretty damn stressful, and I doubt it's going to get better from here. He won't be able to do that anymore. That should make things easier on the rest of us."

I walked back over to Quentin and the others, scrolling through Dean's phone as I walked. Unsurprisingly, he didn't have Danny's number saved. Why would he? The two of them had never spoken in my presence. I didn't know if they'd ever even met.

I offered the phone back to him. "Appreciate the loan," I said. "I should have things from here."

"Do you have a *plan*," asked Marcia, "or is this going to be one of those fun 'Toby rushes in and tries not to get herself killed' situations? We should at least call Arden."

"Little bit of column A, little bit of column B," I said, sounding much calmer about the situation than I actually felt. We were going to get two Daoine Sidhe out of my house, where the wards were keyed to me, and where I knew how to find all the weapons. They had illusions and blood magic. That wasn't enough to truly threaten the people they were—what? Holding hostage? Deceiving? I didn't have the vocabulary to truly explain what they were doing. "As for calling Arden, no. I'm sorry, but not while Altair and her brother have our people. If the two of us go in quietly, we can potentially get them back while they don't expect us. If we come in with a whole army, they're going to see us, and they're going to react badly. We don't know what kind of magic or weapons—or magic weapons—they have, and them reacting badly could get Tybalt and Raysel hurt." May too, technically, but May can't really *be* hurt for very long. She's even more indestructible than I am.

Under normal circumstances, anyway. I glanced down at myself, thinking of the small shell knife that was currently my only weapon. "Hey, Dean, you got any weapons I can borrow?"

He sighed. "I was wondering whether you were going to remember the importance of self-defense," he said. "Yes, we have some weapons you can borrow. Quentin, are you sure you don't want to stay here while your knight runs off into certain doom?"

"I'm sure," he said, sounding almost regretful. "I'm supposed to stay with her when she's in danger, and back her up, and let her teach me how to survive in a bad situation."

"How's that working out so far?"

Quentin shrugged. "Well, I'm not dead yet, so it must be working pretty well so far," he said.

I laughed. After a moment, the rest of them joined in—all except for Bucer, who crossed his braceleted arms and watched us with wary dismay, clearly not excited about whatever was going to happen next. Which, to be fair, I wouldn't have been excited about either, if I'd been in his place. I wasn't exactly excited myself, especially about the chance of getting into a fight while this pregnant—which I was going to avoid if at all possible—but I was going to do whatever I had to in order to get my family back.

We were all going to be okay. I wasn't going to accept anything less.

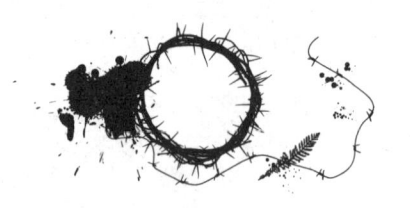

FOURTEEN

GOLDENGREEN WASN'T A MARTIAL county, and as far as I was aware, had never been involved with a war, declared or otherwise. And for all of that, it was a county controlled by our first landed noble from the Undersea, whose domains were traditionally submerged. Faerie wasn't as bloodthirsty as it was said to be in the histories and old stories, but the threat of violence was always there, and Dean had grown up in the depths. He knew what it meant to defend his home, and he was always prepared to do so.

All of which went to explain why Goldengreen, a relatively small holding, had an armory almost as large as the one in Shadowed Hills. Racks of polearms and longswords stood alongside hanging bows and veritable piles of short swords, knives, and other weaponry. I could have fit out an army from that room. After a few moments to stand there and contemplate the amount of damage the armory's contents could do, I'd grabbed a baldrick large enough to be worn by a centaur and strapped it on, drawing it tight enough to stay on without pinching me, and filled the sheath on either side with knives taken from the seemingly limitless pile.

After another moment's contemplation, I'd added a short sword to my haul and stepped back, secure in my conviction that I could defend myself if necessary.

Quentin had been quicker. He'd skipped the knives entirely, going straight for the short swords and strapping one to his hip with the quick, efficient motions of someone who was getting all too accustomed to the need to arm himself in a hurry.

I had even allowed Bucer a weapon, a short staff that would hurt like hell if he rapped someone in the knuckles with it, but wasn't going to turn the tide of battle on its own. He seemed to feel better with *some* sort of weapon in his hands, and since he was coming with us, that made things easier on me.

I ducked off to the bathroom once we were all armed, to pee and clean myself up after my unpleasant chamber pot experience back at Dame Altair's knowe. Marcia met us at the exit with a bag of additional sandwiches and we were off, our illusions refreshed to conceal the number of weapons we were now carrying. Quentin had even remembered to tell Dean about my foxing the museum staffer, and gotten an assurance that the registers would balance at the end of the day.

Sometimes it's good to be friends with the people in charge. We walked through the empty, silent museum, unnoticed by the motion sensors and bathed in the moonlight through the windows, out the seemingly locked doors which opened easily at our approach, and into the parking lot, where my car was parked.

Crickets chirped from the grass around the parking lot as I unlocked the car and bent to peer inside, verifying that no one had broken into the backseat while we were busy inside. Bucer scoffed but didn't try to interrupt me, while Quentin checked the other side of the car. I opened my door.

"Bucer, you get in the back," I said.

"Aren't you afraid I'll bop you with my stick?" he asked.

"Should I be? Because if you think I should be, then the correct answer is probably taking the stick away." I managed to sound more exhausted than annoyed. That was a nice trick.

I wedged myself into the driver's seat and rubbed my stomach where it pressed against the steering wheel, trying to reassure myself that everything was all right, and this was going to be over soon. "You okay in there, kiddo?" I asked, bending my head slightly to make it obvious to Bucer and Quentin that I wasn't talking to them.

Although it would have been weird for me to call Bucer "kiddo," since I was a year younger than he was, and Quentin was so used to it that he wouldn't bat an eye at the address.

Indeed, Quentin slid into the passenger seat, slamming the door so hard it shook the whole car. "Dibs on the radio," he said.

"You can't dibs the radio," I said.

"Sure can. Just did. Want me to do it again?"

I rolled my eyes and twisted the wires to start the engine, pulling out of the lot while Quentin flicked through the radio stations, seeking his beloved Canadian folk music. April had arranged satellite radio for the car on his most recent birthday, and despite the fact that we didn't have a subscription for anything of the kind, it worked.

Settling on a station, Quentin relaxed into his seat and stole a glance over at me.

"They're going to be just fine," he said.

"I know. But I still feel terrible for leaving them the way we did, even if it wasn't entirely our choice."

In the rearview mirror, I saw Bucer wince and shoot an apologetic look in my direction.

"That would work better if I actually thought you were sorry, Bucer," I said.

"I *am* sorry," he protested.

"Sorry you did it, or sorry you got caught?"

He didn't have an answer to that one. I snorted.

"Yeah, about what I thought," I said.

"You have to understand, Toby, not all of us are heroes here," he said. "Some of us are just trying to do whatever we can to keep body and spirit together, and we're not here to play chicken with certain doom."

"Neither am I," I said sourly. "Hero, yes, trying to get myself killed, no. I've been out of commission for months, and I wasn't planning to go back into the field now. I wouldn't be here if the queen hadn't made it difficult for me to refuse."

"We both learned a lot about taking orders from Devin," said Bucer. "I learned how much I hate it, you learned to look for someone else to hold the leash."

"Hey!" snapped Quentin. "You don't get to talk to her like that."

"It's okay, Quentin. Let him sulk because I grew up and he didn't. He's just pissed off that he decided it was better to steal and run than to find a way to stand within Faerie's hierarchy."

"You *hate* Faerie's hierarchy."

"Yes, and Bucer is a great example of the reason I choose to be a part of it anyway. Him, and the people like him, who decided that hating it meant they didn't need to do anything to try making it better. I may not be able to change the way the whole world works, but I can change enough to make things a little bit better for people like me. And some days, that's enough. Some nights, that's everything."

It was late enough that the first part of our drive had been smooth and relatively quick, but we were approaching the part of the city where "late enough" only existed between three a.m. and sunrise. Cars began to crowd the streets, and red lights blinked menacingly from atop the traffic cameras, alerting wary drivers to the presence of traffic cameras.

I took one hand off the wheel and slapped the roof of the car, chanting, "Give me roses red, my lovely, give me lilies fair, give to me a darling girl with violets in her hair."

The smell of cut grass and copper rose to fill the cab, stronger than it would have been even a year before, if still tinged inexorably with my mortality. The spell built and then burst. I tested it by hitting the gas a little harder and cutting off the mortal driver in the next lane, sliding in front of him without using blinker or brake lights to signal my intentions.

The driver didn't react, just kept on going as if that hadn't happened, and I smiled. My don't-look-here was good enough to get us where we were going.

Bucer, on the other hand, yelped. "What are you *doing*?" he demanded.

"You know defensive driving?"

"Yes..."

"The opposite of that."

The spell I'd cast would make it difficult for other drivers to notice or care about my car, without removing it entirely from their awareness: they knew *someone* was on the road with them, just not any details about the other car. If I ran a red light, the resulting picture would come out blurry and without any identifying marks the police could use to track me down. The technology would probably advance beyond such simple spells eventually, but until it did, this would be enough to get me where I was going.

I pressed the gas pedal down as far as it would go, the car leaping forward with a snarl and a shake, the wheel shuddering in my hands as I pushed the machine to the absolute limits of its endurance. We were going fast enough that every cop in San Francisco should have been on my tail.

We screeched up the driveway of the house fast enough that I risked losing control of the car. I killed the engine when I saw the kitchen lights on, a knot letting go in my stomach. They weren't answering the phone but someone was home, even if it wasn't necessarily someone I wanted to deal with.

"Toby, wait—" began Quentin, but I was already out of the car, moving with a speed I was under no illusions of being able to sustain. In that moment, I didn't care.

I released the illusion on myself as I stormed up the back steps to the kitchen door, glad that I'd recast my own human disguise before leaving Goldengreen. The door was closed and, naturally, locked. I hammered my fist against it, paused to listen for footsteps, and then hammered again as no one moved anywhere beyond the door.

I was on my third round of hammering, and giving serious thought to having a proper panic attack, when I heard someone approaching. I stopped and stepped back, hand on the hilt of my borrowed sword. If I was going to get into a fight, I was going in armed this time.

The lock clicked. The door eased open, just a crack, and Rayseline's pale, worried face appeared, golden eyes bright with tears and filled with wary trepidation.

"Prove it," she said, not pausing to ask who I was or let me offer any excuses.

Dame Altair had dropped the charade at some point, then, enough to frighten Raysel into this sort of reaction—but not enough to stop her from opening the door. That was probably a good sign, given the things she could have done.

"Your magic has always been built on a base of heated wax, probably inherited from your maternal grandmother, but after I changed your blood, the secondary note went from mustard flower to crushed blackthorn fruit," I said hurriedly. "You consented to be changed even though you were asleep, because I came to you in a dream and asked if I could. *You* asked *me* if I'd be willing to claim offense against you, because you needed to get out of Shadowed Hills for a little while—"

That was apparently enough. With a choked-off, hiccupping sound, she threw the door open and flung herself at me, locking her arms around my neck. I took my hand off the sword, leaving it sheathed, and caught myself on the metal porch rail with both hands, letting her sob against my neck.

"Guessing things haven't been going well, huh?" I asked.

She didn't reply in words, only an incoherent babble of sounds that all blended together into something like the cry of the wild parrots that flocked on Telegraph Hill. I brought one hand up and began to pat her back, trying to be soothing.

"Uh, Ray? What's with the waterworks?" asked Quentin, standing behind me on the porch stairs.

Raysel lifted her head, still sniffling, but at least no longer babbling, and wiped her eyes with one hand. "Um. Hi, Quentin," she said.

I was pretty sure she had a crush on him. I wasn't worried about either of them doing anything about it. My squire was growing up to be an attractive young man, but he was in a pretty serious relationship with Dean, who had a complicated past with Raysel. She wasn't going to risk her place in our household by getting between Dean and his boyfriend, and Quentin wasn't going to endanger his existing relationship to mess around with his liege's daughter. I was his knight, but Sylvester held his fosterage, and Sylvester wasn't always rational where Raysel was concerned.

And yeah, I was enough of a hypocrite to not want Quentin and Raysel goofing around under my roof. I couldn't stop them—I wasn't actually sure I'd try if I caught them. Both of them were over eighteen, which mattered more in the mortal world than it did in the fae one, but my human-influenced sensibilities told me that if they wanted to get naked, they absolutely could. I just didn't want to know about it.

"Hey, Ray," said Quentin. "Why are you crying?"

"Because I thought you were—there were—" She pulled back enough to look at my face, then burst into tears again, sobbing loudly and messily.

Raysel was Daoine Sidhe, but she couldn't cry pretty, despite all the ethereal beauty she was heir to. Her eyes got red, and snot bubbles formed on her nostrils. Under other circumstances, and if she hadn't been so clearly distraught, I might have been pleased by the reminder that being a pureblood didn't guarantee that you would always look perfect. In the moment, spending more than a fleeting thought on anything other than her obvious distress would have been utterly cruel.

"Raysel." I gripped her upper arms, turning her so that she was fully facing me. "Where are May and Tybalt? Are you alone?"

She nodded vigorously at the second question, strands of fox-red hair clinging to the tears on her cheeks and making her seem disheveled and impossibly fragile. "They wuh-were here," she sobbed. "*You* were here too, but it wasn't you, and Spike kept rattling all angry, so I didn't come down to the kitchen, I stayed upstairs in my room until there was this big thud, and then I came to the top of the stairs and I saw—I saw—"

Her words dissolved into sobs once more, hysteria overwhelming whatever she was trying to say. I began to let go of her arms and straighten and she immediately reached up, clamping her hands over mine and holding me where I was.

"Don't . . . don't let me go," she managed. "I feel like I'm falling, all the time, forever. Please don't let me go."

"Okay, Raysel," I said. "What did you see?"

"The people who looked like you and Quentin were dragging Tybalt and Aunt May out the front door. They looked—" She stopped again, this time not because she was crying, but because she'd just realized that maybe she was about to say something that could be dangerous while I was standing that close to her.

"That was Dame Altair and her brother, Dugan, wearing disguises to look like us," I said, as patiently as I could manage. I gave Raysel's arms a squeeze, then let her go, and this time she let me. "They like poisons. I'm sure May and Tybalt are just knocked out."

May was effectively unkillable—even closer to truly immortal than I was. I'd once seen her grow back the bulk of her internal organs after they'd been shattered by a tree branch. As for Tybalt . . .

The reason I wasn't going to let myself give in to panic was simple: Quentin and Bucer had both been poisoned without my healing abilities to help them recover, and they'd both woken up just fine.

Whatever Altair had dosed Tybalt with, he'd wake up, and he'd be fine. *Furious*, I was sure, but fine. And I had to believe that with all my heart, or I was going to turn around and kill Bucer where he stood.

Bucer. Oh, hell. I whipped around, and found him standing in the driveway next to the car, a downcast expression on his face and his hands dangling by his hips. "The bracelets don't come off," he said. "In case you were wondering. When I try to pull them off, it's like they grow thorns all over the inside, and they dig into my skin, and they don't come off. So that's definitely awesome and not at all going to be a horrible thing for me later, when I have to try leaving here with my magic bound."

"I know the Luidaeg well enough to say that they'll probably come off if I'm the one pulling on them," I said. "But no, I'm not going to test that until we're done with you. You leave when I say you leave, and if you have a problem with that, I can remind you that right now, you're in the best position you're ever likely to be in again."

"What's that?" asked Bucer.

"You're on my side," I said, voice cold, and turned back to Raysel. "You must have come downstairs after that. Did you try calling anyone?"

"No," she said, in a very small voice. "I don't have a lot of phone numbers written down, and I don't have my own phone yet, and I didn't want to call anyone at Shadowed Hills because if I called there wailing about you poisoning Tybalt and dragging him away, I know my father would come, and just make everything even worse. Also, I wasn't sure it was really you."

"Why not? Poisoning Tybalt—which is something we both know I'd never do—aside."

"She wasn't moving like she was pregnant. She was moving like she had a pillow stuffed under her shirt, like she was pretending she was pregnant, but not like she had a baby in there. I've been watching you move for months. You don't step lightly anymore." She had the grace to look embarrassed as she said that, looking down at her feet. "You sort of . . . not stomp, but you plod around, and you look uncomfortable all the time. This lady wasn't doing any of that, and she was dragging Tybalt by his wrists and snapping at the man who looked like Quentin. And he didn't say *anything*. He just followed her without saying anything."

"Where would they take them?" asked Quentin.

I focused on Raysel again. "Okay, Raysel, I need you to think very carefully: was either one of them bleeding? Was there any blood at all, anywhere?"

"I don't know," she said, sniffling again.

"All right. How long ago was this?"

"Maybe half an hour? I don't *know*."

She was starting to sound mulish, which made me want to shake her, and feel bad for wanting to shake her. None of this was her fault. "All right, sweetheart. You're doing great. Did you hear a car when they were dragged outside?"

"I *always* hear cars. The cars never stop." She scowled. "But... yes. There was a car right after they left the house."

"Good girl. You've been a great help." I stepped around her and into the kitchen, pausing in the doorway to survey the scene. There were four mugs on the table, containing the dregs of what looked like hot chocolate with whipped cream and multicolored marshmallows—one of May's specialties. I had never been particularly impressed with Dame Altair, but if she'd managed to poison May's cocoa in May's own kitchen, she was more subtle than I had ever taken her to be.

Great. Why do the bad guys always have to turn out to be better at their jobs than I want them to be?

Still, if anyone should have realized that she wasn't me, it would have been Tybalt. If even Raysel could see that Dame Altair's faux pregnancy didn't look right, he would certainly have caught some turn of phrase or gesture that didn't synchronize with what he expected from me. He had to have figured out at some point that something was wrong.

I moved to the middle of the kitchen and closed my eyes, breathing deeply. All the usual smells of a well-used room came to my attention, underscored by a faint ribbon of red. May had cut herself here, several times, and she didn't heal like I did; when she broke skin, she bled until her blood could clot. None of the blood smelled fresher than a few days old. That wasn't what I wanted.

I kept walking across the kitchen, heading for the door to the hall, and stopped dead as fresher blood assaulted my nose, rich with the mingled scents of pennyroyal and musk. "Oh, you clever, clever cat," I murmured.

"What did you find?" asked Quentin.

"Tybalt must have felt the poison kicking in, and clawed himself." I couldn't kneel, so I looked down, studying the floor until I found the smallest smear of red against the wooden floor. "He left us a trail."

"How far . . . ?"

"He heals like a normal person, and I doubt Altair or Dugan stopped to bandage him up," I said. "Right. Do you still have the phone from before your last upgrade? Because we need to go after them, *now*."

"I'll get it." Quentin ran for the stairs.

I turned to glare at Bucer. "You're coming with us," I said. "We need to find the things you stole, we need to stop Dame Altair, we need to find my people, and we need to find the missing pretender to the throne."

"That's a lot of finding," he said. "Why do you think I can help with any of this?"

"You have a lot of fingers," I said. "Why do you think you need them all?"

"Okay, okay!" He threw his hands up and walked across the kitchen to stand next to me.

Raysel, who had been watching quietly since I started searching for blood, followed him. "What do you want me to do?" she asked.

That stopped me. I couldn't leave her here by herself, not when Altair and Dugan were on the loose, and she didn't know how to drive. Bringing her with us would be counter to my promise to protect her. Dragging her into danger might be convenient, but that didn't make it good.

Quentin came thudding down the stairs, phone in one hand. He stopped when he saw the expression on my face. "Toby?"

"We need to get Raysel to safety," I said.

He nodded, clearly following my line of thought to the inevitable conclusion that she couldn't stay here alone. "I'll call Chelsea," he said.

Raysel's eyes widened. "I don't want to go to Shadowed Hills," she said, words tumbling over each other in her haste to get them out.

"I'll tell her that, and you can tell her that, too," said Quentin easily. "It's only eight. There's plenty of stuff open downtown. You can go see a movie and get something to eat."

"I . . ." Raysel glanced at me, then visibly composed herself, clearly trying to look braver than she felt. I don't think I'd ever been prouder of her. Sometimes it could be easy to forget that she was barely older than Gillian. Thanks to the way she'd grown up, she was physically mature, with less life experience than a young teen. It could make it difficult to accurately estimate how she was going to react to things. "I think I would like that, if Chelsea's willing. I have some money, even, so I can help pay for things."

"How did you get human money?" asked Quentin, tone all curiosity without accusation.

Raysel shrugged. "Aunt May pays me to help her around the house sometimes. She says a girl should be able to go out and buy a soda if she wants one, and not need to ask people to pay for her all the time."

"Practical," I said, while Quentin brought the phone to his ear, waiting a few seconds before he started talking in hushed tones to the person on the other end. He turned back to flash me a quick thumbs-up, smiling at Raysel, then turned back to his conversation. I shifted my weight from foot to foot, trying to lessen the pressure on my knees. Charging into danger used to come with a lot less in the way of logistics. We didn't have to make sure people were safely out of the way. We just did what needed to be done.

And sure, there was a lot of blood loss in those days, and some exciting near-death experiences that weren't remotely as fun when they were happening as they were in hindsight, but at least everything happened *faster* back then.

Quentin lowered the phone, looking to Raysel. "Are you ready to go?" he asked. "Because she's going to be right—"

A portal opened in the air beside him and Chelsea bounced through, black hair slicked down to hide the points of her ears, and copper-colored eyes muted by tinted glasses. She wasn't wearing a human disguise. Despite the fineness of her features, she didn't need one; as long as she kept her ears covered and her glasses on, she could pass for human. She was wearing jeans and a dark orange sweater, and would have looked perfectly at home lounging around any of San Francisco's many malls.

"Hi," she chirped.

"—here," finished Quentin. He leaned over to punch Chelsea lightly in the arm. "You were supposed to wait a few minutes so I could make sure she was ready for you."

"But I wanted to get moving *now*," said Chelsea. She turned to Raysel, beaming. "There's a showing of *Kung Fu Panda 3* starting in fifteen minutes at the Metreon. We can absolutely make it. There's a good spot at the back of the arcade to pop in where no one will see us, and the box office is on the same floor."

"I have no idea what you just said," said Raysel, sounding befuddled.

"We're gonna have a good time, that's what I said," said Chelsea. "You got any money? It's cool if you don't, my dad has no idea what anything costs, so he gave me two hundred dollars. We can get burgers after." She held her hand out to Raysel, clearly expecting her to take it.

Raysel looked at me, anxiety in her eyes. "This is safe?"

"Safer than staying here alone when we don't know who might show up," I said. "The world isn't safe. But some risks are worth taking. A movie and dinner are pretty low on the ladder of possible dangers. Just go and have a nice time, okay?"

"Okay," said Raysel. She scooped her hands through the air like she was filling them with water, bringing them to her face. The air around her blossomed with the smell of hot wax and lightly crushed blackthorn fruit, and when she lowered her hands again, she looked perfectly human. Still striking, with red hair and vividly hazel eyes, but human. She and Chelsea were going to catch some admiring looks tonight. They looked like movie stars walking among ordinary people.

That was at least within the realm of possibility. I smiled encouragingly at Raysel, and she walked over to Chelsea, taking the offered hand in hers. Chelsea grinned, stepping backward as she sketched an arc with her free hand, and a portal opened to swallow them both. Before it closed I got a glimpse of a darkened room filled with flashing video game consoles. The faint scent of popcorn and floor cleaner wafted through.

Then they were gone, and I was alone with Quentin and Bucer. I exhaled.

"She'll be safer this way," I said.

"She will," verified Quentin. "If anyone tries to mess with them, Chelsea will get them both out of the situation. Even without being able to take Raysel to Shadowed Hills, Chelsea can get them out of harm's way. And she's been wanting to spend more time with Raysel. She feels like they don't know each other very well, what with the whole 'elf-shot followed by voluntary exile' thing on Raysel's part, and their dads are sort of best friends."

"Good," I said. The social web formed by Quentin and his peers was complicated and constantly changing, and I didn't feel like they wanted me intruding on it any more than I'd wanted Melly and the other adults intruding on my time with Kerry and the others when I was his age. Childhood and adulthood are nebulous concepts in Faerie, where some people can hit puberty in their seventies, no one reaches their full majority until thirty years of age, and even after that, they'll be considered young and dismissible until they're at least a century old. Chelsea was nineteen, adult by human standards, and Raysel was older, and I still felt like I'd just sent a pair of twelve-year-olds to the mall alone.

Oh, well. There would be time to brood over time and maturity in Faerie later, after we had my husband back. I put two fingers in my mouth and whistled shrilly. A second later, a rattling sound from the hall told me that Spike was trotting in our direction.

"Quentin, do you want to drive?" I asked, lowering my hand.

He shot me a startled look. "Are you sure?"

"My knees hurt, and I'd like to give my feet a rest," I said. "Plus some asshole cracked the central column on my steering wheel, and I'm going to need to get that fixed before I can drive around safely."

Spike entered the kitchen and rattled its thorns at me, then began to prowl around the border of the room, sniffing the floor and rattling angrily.

"You want to come with us, buddy?" I asked. "We're going to find May and Tybalt."

"Jazz," said Quentin, tone horrified.

"What about h—oh, root and bloody *branch*." Jazz was May's

live-in girlfriend and functional fiancée: there hadn't been a formal marriage proposal yet, but she'd agreed to the idea of marriage, and that seemed to be more than enough for my Fetch. She should have been home at some point between my poisoning and now. "Can you call her store?"

"On it." Jazz owned a small antique store in the unaffiliated part of Berkeley. They would be closed by now, but she had a habit of picking up the phone even outside of business hours.

Several seconds ticked by. Quentin lowered his phone. "Voicemail," he said grimly.

I shuddered. I have a special aversion for voicemail and answering machines. Nothing good is ever recorded on them.

"Okay," I said. "That doesn't mean anything bad has happened to her. Raysel would have said something if she'd seen them dragging Jazz out of the house too. For right now, we need to focus on the people we know are in danger. May will be able to tell us if we're wrong about that, but for her to say anything, we need to save her first."

"All right," said Quentin reluctantly.

I turned my attention back to the single drop of blood I'd been able to locate, breathing in the scent of it and biting the inside of my cheek at the same time. The familiar, almost comforting taste of my own blood flooded my tongue, trying to drag me into memories. I shunted them hard to the side, pulling on the power of the blood rather than the images it contained.

The drop of blood on the floor lit up like a beacon, becoming the brightest thing in the room. Dots of brilliance surrounded it, tiny flecks of blood that had splattered when the main drop hit the floor. I forced myself to focus on the largest brightness, refusing to get distracted, and followed the little glittering flecks out of the kitchen to the hall.

There was considerably more blood there, although not enough for anyone else to have noticed; you'd get more of a mess from the average bloody nose. Still, there were brilliantly gleaming drops all along the length of the hall, and out the front door to the porch and steps beyond. I paused to throw up a human illusion before following the trail onward.

They wouldn't have bothered to drag the bodies out of the house if they were just going to teleport. I clung to that belief as I followed the blood down the steps to the sidewalk, where it stopped about ten feet further down the street. "This is where they got into the car," I said. Spike was standing next to me on the sidewalk. I turned to it. "Hey, buddy. I know you can use the Rose Roads. Is there any chance you could follow the blood trail through the roses to Tybalt?"

It looked at me and chirped, rattling its thorns. I sighed. "Thought not, but it was worth asking."

I turned back to the porch, eyeing the steps unhappily. Quentin and Bucer were standing on the porch, watching me. "Lock the door and come down?" I suggested. "We can go around the house to get in the car."

"Fine by me," said Quentin, coming down the stairs to stop beside me. Bucer followed. Even the appearance of human feet couldn't stop his steps from sounding like hoofbeats. Spike looked at him and hissed, clearly unhappy with the man's presence. I couldn't blame it for that one. We needed someone who was familiar with Dame Altair's home and defenses, but that didn't mean I liked having him here.

Bucer looked back at the rose goblin and shook his head, putting his hands up defensively. "Nice, er, horticulture," he said. "Be good."

"It knows goats eat rose canes," I said, leaning down to run a hand over Spike's head.

Bucer grimaced, and followed as we began walking toward the driveway, and the cars.

"Pregnant woman gets shotgun," I said, once we reached the corner of the house. Quentin sped up, unlocking the car and checking the backseat for possible attackers. I was never going to get tired of seeing that kid demonstrate basic situational awareness.

Bucer didn't object, only got into the back of Quentin's car, Spike hopping into the backseat beside him with a final ominous rattle of its thorns. The rose goblin curled up, compact as a cat despite its larger size, and tucked its paws under its chest as it closed its eyes.

I lowered myself into the front passenger seat, groaning a little as I sat. "Can you give me your phone? I want to check on Danny," I said.

"I don't have his number."

"Of course you—wait." I paused. Quentin had never been the one to call Danny directly. "Did I really never give you his number?"

"Nope. And I didn't ask. You have lots of friends whose numbers I don't have." He shrugged. "Well, some friends."

"Oak and *fucking* ash," I swore. "When this is over, we're updating your address book."

"Works for me. You know, you're a lot calmer than I thought you'd be," said Quentin.

"I'm not calm," I corrected. "I'm seething. I am furiously angry right now, and the only thing that's keeping me from screaming is the knowledge that I can't do this alone, and we don't have much in the way for available backup."

I couldn't call on Sylvester without compromising Raysel—assuming he would even answer, which was still a large assumption. I was pretty sure Arden would be willing to send guards, but that would take time, and make us all less agile. No. We needed to find out where May and Tybalt had been taken, and we needed to do it as quickly and quietly as possible.

"You thought there wouldn't be any trouble going to talk to Dame Altair on your own," said Quentin. He was smart enough not to verbalize the unspoken "and look what happened that time."

"All right, that's fair enough," I agreed, as he pulled out of the driveway and onto the street. "But there shouldn't have been. She's a minor noble, she's been around as long as I can remember, she's never committed treason against the crown before."

"Temptation gets to everyone eventually," said Bucer. "Maybe the dame just needed to reach the right level of greedy before she was willing to act. And there's her brother. Last I'd heard, he was pretty much banished from the kingdom."

"He was in prison," I corrected. "I'm a little surprised he hadn't been elf-shot by now. I know we have a cure, but it's not like it isn't still a useful way of putting purebloods into storage while we figure out what we're going to do with them."

"I guess Arden's trying to be more reasonable about casting her enemies into eternal slumber," said Bucer.

I sighed. I'm not the biggest fan of elf-shot—never have been. Elf-shot is fatal to changelings in a way it isn't to pure fae. The mortality in us objects to the idea of sleeping forever, and it rips our bodies apart, kicking off an internal war that we can't win, only die of. I've been elf-shot repeatedly. The first time I survived only because Amandine interceded, giving me the Changeling's Choice for a second time and using my answer to let her pull the poison out of my veins.

By the time I was elf-shot again, I was fae enough to survive until the cure could be administered and wake me up. Still, it hurt, and I was in no rush to go through that again, or to subject anyone else to it. But it would have been nice if Dugan had been out of the picture, at least until we were finished dealing with his sister.

Quentin drove quickly and efficiently, paying more attention to traffic laws than I ever had. I relaxed into my seat, pondering our next steps.

Dame Altair and Dugan had taken our people somewhere. They didn't have a lot of options that I could think of. Dugan had never been in possession of his own household as far as I was aware; he'd been a hanger-on of the false queen's, living in her knowe until she was deposed and it was deserted, left to rot and collapse. Titania had been able to call echoes of that knowe out of the void when she spun her false reality, but they'd been unstable even then, and I didn't think he could get back there even if he wanted to. He'd fall through the bottom of the world if he tried.

Knowes are dug out of the barrier between Earth and the Summerlands, anchored to both places but technically hovering between them. They can become unmoored, and they can dissolve. I don't know what would happen to someone who entered that space without the protection of a knowe, a skerry, or a road already forged through the nothingness. So far as I'm aware, only the original Three could walk in that space without dissolving.

Presumably Titania and Oberon still can, since we know where they are at this point. It's not like I was going to ask.

So the most likely place for them to have gone was back to Dame Altair's knowe, which would only make sense if she believed they could be safe there. Without driving to distract me, I was just spiraling through my thoughts. We needed someone who could help us find our people, who could do better than a single drop of blood.

"Quentin, can I have your phone?"

He took a hand off the wheel long enough to extract the phone from his pocket and pass it over. "Should be unlocked," he said.

I tapped the phone's screen to wake it up, dismissing the picture of Quentin and Dean being absolutely adorable with one another, then opened the contacts app, selecting the number I needed from the list. I tended to assume Quentin would have the number of anyone I trusted enough to call for help: there was always the chance he'd be trying to find me and I'd be with one of them, making me easy to locate if he knew where to start. It wasn't always the right assumption, but it worked about as often as not.

The phone rang and I waited until there was a click and a friendly voice said, "Borderlands Café. Madden speaking. How may I help you today?"

I relaxed, sinking deeper into my seat. "Hey, Madden. When do you get done with your shift?"

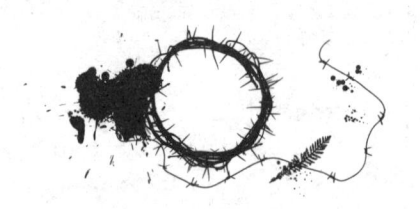

FIFTEEN

MADDEN, IT TRANSPIRED, WOULD be able to meet us in half an hour, since he got off work in fifteen minutes, and as a Cu Sidhe, he had alternative means of getting across the city in a hurry. That meant we'd have time to at least try to get into Dame Altair's knowe while we waited for him, and also that I didn't need to worry about updating Arden on the situation. Involving her seneschal would do that for us.

Quentin pulled up outside Dame Altair's house, turning off the engine. I stayed in my seat, scanning the cars around us for any that I recognized. To my relief, Danny's car wasn't there; she hadn't suborned another of my allies. I unbuckled my seatbelt.

"You good?" asked Quentin, who had noticed my pause.

"I am," I said, and got out of the car, joining Spike and Bucer on the sidewalk.

Bucer looked at the house like it was a giant predator and he was afraid of being swallowed. "We could walk away," he said. "I made a decent amount fencing stuff before I got caught, and there was some money in there too, enough for all three of us to start over somewhere else in the Westlands. We could just disappear. Doesn't that sound good, Toby? Vanishing into the dark?"

"She has my husband," I said, voice flat and cold. "I didn't marry him because I didn't want to keep him. I want him *back*. And even if I didn't, she has my *sister*. May is mine. I don't leave her behind."

"I thought she was your—" Bucer's lips began to form an f sound, but he caught himself, taking a half-step back. "Right. Okay. We go in, I guess."

May wasn't technically my sister by birth, for all that we both acted like she was; she was my Fetch, a death omen summoned by the universe before my first brush with elf-shot. Before she became May and mine, she'd been a night-haunt named Mai, and the last memories she'd consumed had belonged to a changeling girl named Dare who died to save me. Becoming my Fetch had added my memories to the ones Mai already had, creating a whole new person, with her own preferences and feelings. And she was my sister in every way that counted. We didn't hide the fact that she was originally my Fetch—how could we?—but that didn't mean Bucer got to act like it made her less worth saving.

The smart thing to do would be to find a back entrance. With most knowes, that was exactly what we would have tried to do. Getting into a knowe can be like solving a riddle written by a drunkard, but it's usually possible if you have time. The location of Dame Altair's knowe made that approach impractical. The physical house that anchored her knowe was sandwiched between two other houses, without even a walkway between them. There was a small backyard, I was sure, but we had no way to access it without trespassing or breaking into someone else's property.

I'm not innately opposed to a little light breaking and entering, although I prefer not to do it when profoundly pregnant, but breaking into an expensive house without preparation or the proper tools is a fool's game that I wasn't particularly in the mood to play. Not unless we had absolutely no choice, and I already knew of one method for getting into the knowe.

We just had to go in through the front door.

"Everyone stay close together," I said, and started for the porch steps.

Bucer and Quentin followed me. We were almost to the top when the climbing rose that was wrapped around the porch trellis turned one massive blossom toward us. The flower opened into a fanged mouth and snarled, displaying a fine array of thorn-sharp teeth.

"Shit," I said. "Get behind me."

Quentin managed to oblige before the rose vines began whipping out of the foliage and slapping at us, thorns driving deep with every hit. Bucer wasn't so quick. He bleated as the whipping vines struck him, staggering and dropping to his knees on the porch stairs.

I hissed between my teeth at the impacts, reaching up to grab the largest of the vines as it pulled back for another strike. The rose paused, apparently confused by this action. I squeezed harder, driving the thorns into my own palm and embedding them there, keeping the wounds open. Blood began to drip down my hand to my wrist.

"Back *off*," I said, trying to use the magic to put the force of a command behind the words. I had no reason to think it would work, and nice as it would have been to unlock a new tool for controlling possessed flora, nothing happened.

Behind me, something started to growl. That word doesn't do the sound justice: it was like listening to someone revving a chainsaw, undulating and primal and sliding up and down a register of notes that my throat wouldn't have been capable of matching. The vine I was holding tried to pull away, and this time I let go, allowing it to work its thorns loose and withdraw.

The sound got louder, coming closer, and I glanced down. Spike was standing next to my right leg, eyes fixed on the roses that had been attacking us, thorns bristling out in all directions, for all the world like a furiously angry cat.

Which, in a way, was exactly what it was. But it was also a cutting from one of the world's few Blodynbryd, the Dryads of the roses. Rose goblins are technically a descendant line of Acacia, the Mother of Trees: she's the mother of Blodynbryd, too, and when they walk in the world, they leave rose goblins behind.

I don't know how the hierarchy of flowers works, but I know that when Spike snarled at that enchanted rose, it backed down, even going so far as to unwind from the trellis and retreat all the way from the porch. I glanced at the exposed wood this left behind, wondering whether the illusion that shrouded fae activity from mortal eyes had gone with the roses. We were all wearing illusions, but I'd been counting on the illusion to make us just that much harder to see while I was picking the lock on the door.

"Bucer, stand behind me," I said, climbing the last few steps to the porch.

"I'm bleeding everywhere!" he protested, the hint of a bleat still distorting his words.

I turned to look at him. There were scratches on his arms and face, and I had little doubt that his ears were equally shredded. None of them looked as deep as the punctures on my arms had been, but even a shallow rose scratch can sting like nobody's business.

"I'm sorry about that," I said. "I didn't expect Dame Altair's security system to be based around a rabid attack rose. Maybe we can find a first aid kit inside?"

"We better," muttered Quentin. "I just got this car. I don't want to ruin the upholstery until I've had it for at least a year."

"My little optimist," I said warmly. "Bucer, can you walk?"

"I can," he admitted, in a grudging tone.

"Great, then you can come and stand behind me."

Slowly, clearly pained, he moved to do precisely that. I reached for my lockpicks—which of course weren't there, having been taken away along with everything else when Dame Altair poisoned and imprisoned me. I made a frustrated sound and beside me, Spike rattled. I turned to look down at the rose goblin, which met my eyes and rattled its thorns again, pushing its head against my thigh.

My knee threatened to buckle. "Okay, buddy, okay," I said. "You have to be gentle with me right now, or I'm going to fall down, and it's going to be really hard to get me back on my feet if that happens."

Spike made a frustrated sound and nudged me with its head again. I frowned, taking a closer look at it. Some of the thorns growing along the central crest of its skull were almost as long as my index finger. I reached down and touched one of them. "Is this what you're trying to tell me?"

In response, Spike shoved its head into my hand with more force than it usually used, driving several thorns into my palm. When it pulled its head away again, the thorns remained behind, detaching like a porcupine's quills.

"That was a very violent way to offer me an alternative to using the Luidaeg's shell knife again," I said, plucking the thorns out of my palm. There were four in total, all several inches long and flexible enough to get the job done. "But I still appreciate it. You are an excellent rose goblin, Spike. I'll get you a bag of fertilizer when this is all over."

It chirped, sounding self-satisfied, and slunk away to stand behind Bucer, blocking off any chance that he was going to cut and run.

I returned my attention to the lock. It was pretty standard, and didn't look like it had been upgraded since the 1970s. I slid the first thorn into the lock, trying to feel the internal pins. I twisted; they shifted; the thorn broke. Swearing, I pulled the broken portion out of the lock.

Quentin looked over his shoulder at me. "Everything okay?"

"Everything is fine," I said. "Just need to try again."

The second thorn didn't fare any better than the first had. On the third thorn there was a click, and the door swung silently inward by a few inches, revealing a slice of the darkened hallway. I straightened, sliding the remaining thorn into my jacket pocket before bracing my hands at the small of my back as I tried to catch my balance.

"I'm fine," I said, before Quentin could ask. "Just sore. My body's been through a lot today, and it's still busy building another person, after all."

"Given the way you heal, couldn't your body do things faster?" he asked. "I hate seeing how much this is hurting you."

The question came with a whole series of gruesome, unwanted images. I shook them away, shuddering. "Let's just be glad my body didn't think of that. Stay behind me and keep your voice down."

I bit the inside of my cheek and squinted at the darkness in the doorway, looking for ward spells or anything that might sound an alarm. I didn't find them. There were no threads stretched across the doorframe, no enchantments lurking in wait for us to come back to the scene of the crime. I hadn't checked the wards when I arrived; I couldn't tell whether they had never been there in the first place, or whether Dame Altair had allowed them to collapse.

Either way, what wasn't there couldn't hurt us. I took one last quick glance around for witnesses, then stepped into the house, making the transition into the knowe at the same time.

The room spun and wove around me, and I was standing in the hall. It was identical to its appearance in the mortal world, save for the light. From the porch, the hall had seemed completely dark, filled with shadows that omitted even moonlight. In the Summerlands, twilight pooled in the corners of the hall, coming in through high windows set against the line of the ceiling and refracted by prismatic crystals hung from the chandeliers. I wondered, somewhat uselessly, whether the mortal side of Dame Altair's home had any furnishings at all. If I could wiggle through a window or come in through the back door, would I find myself in an empty house, set up entirely for show? It seemed likely.

Quentin and Bucer came in behind me, Spike rattling at their heels with every step. The rose goblin sniffed the floor and rattled again, making any attempt at stealth even more pointless than it had seemed before.

"I don't think anyone is here," I said, voice low.

"Neither do I," said Quentin. He made a scooping gesture with one hand, like he was collecting a handful of bubbles from a bubble bath. It turned into a tossing gesture as he finished the initial motion, and he threw a ball of lambent witch light into the air, where it hung and bobbed and cast a pale white illumination over everything around it.

I nodded approvingly. Fae have excellent night vision, but even excellent night vision isn't great when it comes to looking for clues in a room filled with shifting, irregular shadows.

"Bucer, you were here for a while before you decided to bite the hand that paid you," I said. "Any idea where she would go to conduct business or plot evil?"

"Her study," said Bucer. "I can lead you there."

"Good. I was hoping you'd volunteer. So much simpler than my needing to twist your arm until you understand the value of cooperation."

"I'm cooperating!" he protested.

"For now," said Quentin darkly.

Bucer shot him an irritated look and started walking deeper into the knowe, Spike close on his heels. The rattling would make the pair of them easy to track, even if the rugs muffled Bucer's hoofbeats.

Quentin and I exchanged a look and went after them, working our way down the hall and through a palatial parlor—not the one where we'd been poisoned; there seemed to be a plethora of parlors—and into a receiving room, which gave way to another hall. It was difficult to say how much of this was the original floor plan, and how much of it was the knowe showing off how many rooms it had for company. I got the sense that Dame Altair didn't have a lot of visitors, and the ones she had probably weren't overly interested in admiring the architecture.

I ran a hand along the wall as we walked, fingertips trailing against the wallpaper and skimming over the decorative flourishes in the architecture. Very quietly, I said, "It feels like she's abandoned you, and I'm sorry. But please. We're looking for my husband and my sister. If she brought them here, can you turn on a light for me? Just one little light. I'll find them if you tell me to start looking. Otherwise, I don't think there's anyone here but us."

Nothing changed. The air around me seemed to grow heavier, like I had the knowe's attention, but no lights came on, and nothing else happened. I sighed, then turned as I felt a hand on my arm.

Quentin was looking at me with concern. "We'll find them," he said. "I know we will. Once Madden gets here, we'll know if they were ever here, and we'll find them."

"I know," I said. "I just hate everything about this."

Bucer at least seemed to know where he was going. As we got deeper and deeper into the knowe without hearing any voices or seeing any lights apart from Quentin's witchlights, my belief that we were alone got steadily stronger.

"Here," said Bucer.

He opened another door, and behind it was a parlor, decorated entirely in leather and dark woods, with bookshelves swallowing one wall entirely and a large desk dominating the whole space, sitting in front of the only window. It, too, was empty.

"Madden should be here soon," said Quentin, following me and Bucer into the parlor.

"We left so much blood on the porch, he's not going to have any trouble finding us," I said. "Can you toss one of those lights over here? I want to go through the desk."

Quentin obliged, tossing another ball of lambent white over to hang above the desk. I allowed myself to collapse heavily into the large leather chair between the desk and the window and tried the top drawer. It was locked. Pulling the last thorn out of my pocket, I got back to work.

Altair didn't invest any more heavily in desk locks than she did in door locks, and it wasn't long before I heard the click that meant the lock was open. I removed the thorn and eased the drawer gingerly open, watching for traps. Not well enough, it seemed, as a needle flashed abruptly out from the drawer's edge, biting into the side of my hand.

I swore, dropping the drawer onto the desk and yanking the needle out. It burned with the specific sickening wrongness of cold iron, and I dropped it in turn, recoiling. Leave it to someone who would willingly ally with the pretender queen to think that iron was a reasonable reaction to someone invading her privacy.

The needle wasn't hollow: it hadn't been delivering poison, only itself. I rubbed the side of my hand, watching the skin around the puncture grow rapidly red and inflamed, then turned my attention back to the drawer. The damage, such as it was, had been done, and that little iron wasn't going to be enough to hurt me *or* the baby; I needed to just get on with things.

"Don't touch that," I snapped, and reached for the drawer.

There were no further traps, and after all that, it contained nothing but a black leather ledger. I pulled it carefully out, wary of further traps, and flipped it gingerly open. "Maybe she left us something useful," I said.

The pages were blank. I sniffed the air. Traces of black clove and cardamom lingered around the ledger—Dame Altair's magic and Dugan's. They were both Daoine Sidhe. I bit my lip, looking for the threads of an enchantment. I found them this time, a faded mass of orange and brick red, but when I reached for them, there was nothing there. It wasn't a spell I could easily untangle, especially if I couldn't get my hands on it.

"Toby?" asked Quentin. "What is it?"

"She's spelled this ledger somehow," I said. "But it's faded out and distant, like it's barely here. Like it's—" I paused, sudden thoughts of Marcia flashing to the front of my mind. I frowned. "Like it's a marshwater charm of some sort," I concluded. "I can't catch hold of it because the magic is too far removed from my own. It's weak enough that it's like I'm trying to pick up a grape with a steam shovel. I can't *aim* that small."

"That's a weird problem to have," said Bucer.

"It is," I agreed. Dame Altair and her brother were both Daoine

Sidhe, meaning almost anything they did would be rooted in blood magic. That was their natural comfort zone. That was also the basis for all Simon's magic-borrowing charms. Blood was the common link.

I looked speculatively at the thorn I'd used to pick the desk lock. It had been dulled by the process, but it was still more than sharp enough to draw blood if I really needed it to.

"Quentin, start searching the room for anything out of place," I said, still looking at the thorn. "I'm going to try something with this ledger, but we don't want to miss something just because I decided to focus on the most obvious clue."

"All right," he said reluctantly, stepping away from the desk.

"No one leaves this room," I said, perhaps needlessly. It's always better to make clear statements than it is to count on common sense. I speak from experience as much as anything else.

While Quentin moved to start checking the bookshelves on the other side of the room, I jabbed myself in the index finger with the thorn, pushing down until I broke skin. A bead of blood formed on my fingertip, gleaming and perfect.

Carefully, I reached down and streaked the blood across the page, trying to focus on how much I *didn't* want an illusion to stop me from seeing what was written there. It wasn't a normal application of my magic, but if this was a blood-based marshwater charm—and from the smell of it, that was a reasonable guess at what I was dealing with—I might be able to overload it and wipe it away.

My blood didn't soak into the paper. Instead, it beaded up and rolled down the page, illuminating cramped black writing as it went. I couldn't read anything that was written there—there wasn't enough blood for that—but I could see that the page had been filled out completely before it was concealed. When the blood reached the bottom of the paper, it rolled off to splatter uselessly against the desk. I tapped it with a clean fingertip and brought it to my lips, tasting red salt and nothingness. The magic my blood normally contained was gone, soaked into the paper and dissolved from the world.

Interesting. I jabbed my finger again and repeated the process at a different point on the page, illuminating more text. It took ten jabs before the whole page had been bled across, the blood rolling and beading away each time, leaving the text revealed in its place.

It was a ledger. Items and names, written in a tightly controlled hand, followed by figures. Some of the figures had checkmarks after them, presumably signaling that the item in question had been delivered; others were still open. A few were crossed out. I squinted at those. Whether it had been Dugan or his sister keeping the ledger, they'd been smart enough not to write things out in full: that would have been an easy conviction, erasing plausible deniability. Still, I could make reasonable guesses.

One of the crossed-out lines read "S.S., any—T.W." If I read that correctly, it had been an order for a Selkie skin or skins, probably placed by my old semi-friend, Tracy Wilson. Tracy had been at Home with Bucer and me, and her daughter, Jocelyn, had been responsible for the last time my daughter had been attacked. I rubbed my stomach with one hand, only half-aware of the gesture. A Selkie skin would have allowed Tracy to become fully fae, or to make her daughter fully fae, but there were virtually no Selkie skins left in the world, and the ones that remained were under such tight guard that trying to steal one would be a creative form of committing suicide.

I tapped that line with my finger. "Bucer, can you come over here?"

He turned away from the bookshelf and trotted back over to the desk, leaning down to look where I was pointing. He nodded. "Yeah, she asked me for a Selkie skin. I couldn't get it."

"Did you *try*?"

"I told her I tried." At my withering expression he took a step back and raised his hands defensively. "Hey, she was my employer! She wanted it, I said I'd go for it, I went down to Half Moon Bay and kicked around for an afternoon, then came back and said I couldn't manage it. I got some really nice ice cream. I'd do it again."

"But you didn't mess with the Selkies?"

"She asked for that before the enchantment collapsed. I thought she was requesting something that didn't actually exist anymore, since the Selkies had been gone for centuries. But I dug around in some secondhand stores, looked at this place that sold weird taxidermy, and didn't find any pelts with magic associated with them. Then the enchantment collapsed, and I just didn't remind her that there might be skins available again in a world where the Undersea still existed."

I eyed him warily. "If the Undersea was lost, how did Tracy know to ask for a skin?"

"She was flailing around looking for ways to turn her daughter fully fae before she was executed," said Bucer. "Jocelyn was being held by the nameless Queen for crimes against pureblood society—didn't know her place, didn't bow her head, pushed too hard and too far—and she was going to be killed after Moving Day. Tracy thought if she could make her pureblooded, she'd be pardoned. Selkie skins and Swanmay cloaks were at the top of her list. I couldn't find one of those, either, don't worry."

"Are Swanmay cloaks valuable?"

"Moreso than Raven bands. There's not as many of them, and most people who think turning into a bird would be cool would rather be a giant bad-ass steroid duck than a flappy goth pigeon."

I frowned. I had never considered the price of essential pieces of people's connection to Faerie. "Did you steal any of those?"

"A couple," he said, waving it away like it was nothing. "Dame Altair had orders. Never did manage to get one for Jocelyn, though. Poor Tracy was still looking for an answer when the world fell down, and then we got back into reality, and she wasn't interested in trying hard enough to meet the going price."

"Why not?"

He shrugged. "Arden's not going to execute Jocelyn for being a twit and abducting her college roommate. Even if that college roommate was your daughter, that shouldn't be a dying offense."

Much as I wanted to object, I couldn't. Gillian being my child didn't mean upsetting her should be punishable by death. Sure, what Jocelyn had done had resulted in more than upsetting Gilly—it had cost her the last of her humanity, invalidating the choice she'd made the first time she'd been elf-shot. I resented that. Even knowing my daughter would be with me forever now, I still resented it.

"Has anyone checked Arden's dungeons to see if Jocelyn's still there?"

Bucer snorted. "Tracy said she was when she came and made another bid for a Selkie skin. Altair told her to fuck off. Said we don't do second tries for impossible things."

"Okay..." I turned back to the ledger. Tracy might still be someone we needed to talk to as part of the investigation Arden had tasked me with, but not until we had our people back. Maybe there would be something in these lists of sale that would tell us where Altair and her brother had taken them.

The fear was starting to bubble up in my gut, making me nauseous and uneasy. Tybalt wasn't indestructible, not like May. He could be in real trouble. He could be hurt, or worse. This ledger proved that Altair wasn't above dealing in fae bodies as if they were commodities. No one had to die to steal a Selkie's skin or a Swanmay's cloak, but for the person who lost them, being left suddenly mortal and cut off from Faerie might as well have been a form of dying.

There were other things written down there, most of them unfamiliar. I didn't know what the abbreviations meant, although she had helpfully labeled some of the items as "pers.", which I assumed meant "personal." Most of those were checked off, which didn't make me feel any better. The second most common entry was "M.M."

I did feel a tiny spark of satisfaction when I reached the line that read "H.C., vault—pers." and saw that it was neither checked off nor crossed out. She didn't have the thing she'd wanted most. There were no items listed after that: that was when she'd lost faith in her thief.

"Who's M.M., Bucer?" I asked.

He shrugged. "I don't know. That was Dame Altair's mystery buyer. She never let me know who it was, but they paid with some pretty weird shit. Old money, jewels, alchemical supplies, plants—whoever it is, they're pretty well-connected."

"Because *that's* not ominous or anything," I muttered.

"What?" asked Quentin, turning away from the bookshelf.

"Nothing. You find anything we can use?"

"Not really," he said. "Lots of old books. Some of them are in languages I can't read. Some jars of seeds and stuff. Not alchemical supplies—they're not prepared or anything. They're just in glass jars, like someone's going to start a garden."

"What languages *do* you read?"

He shrugged. "English, French, some Breton, and Welsh."

"Huh." That was three more languages than I could read. I closed the ledger, tucking it under my arm as I moved to stand. "Can you tell what kind of seeds they are?"

"Apple seeds," said Bucer. He picked up two small jars that had been tucked back into the shadows of the shelf, carrying them toward me. When he was close enough he held the jars out to let me see their contents.

They were indeed apple seeds, dozens of them in each jar, tiny brown teardrop shapes piled upon themselves and preserved behind glass. That wasn't the strange part. The strange part was the way they glowed, pale silver in one jar, pale gold in the other.

"How—?"

"Sun-apple and moon-apple seeds," said Bucer. "I told you that one client liked to pay in weird shit. These are worth their weight in diamonds in the mortal world, and priceless in Faerie. Even the Golden Shore doesn't have these in their orchards."

"Huh," I said. Something about that made my brain itch, but the thoughts weren't quite connecting, much as I wanted them to. I started to reach for the silvered jar.

I pulled my hand back as claws scraped on the floor out in the hall. That was our only real warning before a large white dog with bloodred ears and paws came racing into the room, equally red tail waving like a banner behind him. He saw Quentin and performed an enthusiastic play bow, paws straight out in front of himself while he stuck his backside in the air and let his tongue loll in the canine version of a hello.

Spike hissed and rattled its thorns at the dog like the cat it resembled, leaping up onto Altair's desk with a sound like a dozen maracas rolling down a flight of stairs. It continued to rattle and snarl, crouching safely out of the dog's reach.

Turning, the dog came bounding over to the desk and stood up on his hind legs. Somehow, midway through this gesture, he was a virtually human-seeming man rather than a canine, complete with sharp canines and bloody streaks in his otherwise platinum hair. He was wearing archaic, almost medieval clothing, which would have made sense if he'd come straight from court, but he'd come from work, which was much more modern. I raised an eyebrow.

"Sorry," said Madden, sounding halfway abashed. "I was supposed to meet up with Charles after work. When I called to let him know my boss needed me for something, he dropped off my backpack at the coffee shop. I changed in the stockroom before I went dog and ran out the back door."

"Ah," I said. Charles was well-accustomed to unusual hours and strange wardrobe choices. Claiming to work for a drag queen was a pretty solid cover, as such things went.

"I didn't go home to change because I know you said it was important. But what's important?" He looked around the dark room like he was seeing it for the first time—which maybe he was. Dame Altair had never been a social butterfly, and the invites I knew of had never extended to the shapeshifters. "Why are we here?"

"Dame Altair is responsible for most of the disappearances from the royal treasury," I said. "I just learned that Dugan Harrow is her brother, and she was paying Bucer here to steal artifacts for her and a list of clients. She was trying to frame Simon for the false queen's escape, when it was Dugan all along. And when I came here to talk to her about what happened at court last night, she poisoned my drink, knocked me and Quentin both out, and tied us to beds upstairs with silver and yarrow chains."

Madden blinked, several times, looking thoroughly nonplussed by the information I had just piled on him. Then he growled, lips drawing back from his teeth in a distinctly inhuman way. "Why haven't you involved the crown yet?" he asked.

"Because while she had me captive, Dame Altair disguised herself as me and went to my house, where she was able to subdue and abduct Tybalt and May," I said. "We're here because we're trying to figure out where she may have taken them. Tybalt managed to cut himself before he lost consciousness entirely, and left a blood trail. I didn't want to call Arden and mobilize her guard until I'd tried to get my people back with less of a production."

Madden looked dubious. "Productions produce results," he said.

"Yeah, and those results are all too frequently blood and screaming," I countered. "Right now, we're dealing with two assholes holding two captives. If we can sneak in and free them without a confrontation, we might be able to get out of this without hurting anyone else."

"Small groups are better for stealth missions," Quentin agreed.

"And pregnant women are bad for stealth missions," said Madden.

"So we're running neutral, and I'm running out of patience," I said. "Do you smell Tybalt or May anywhere around here?"

"Hold on." Madden dropped to all fours, unfolding into a dog. It was a transition so seamless that it wasn't really a transformation or a morph: he was one and then he was the other, like our eyes had been deceiving us when he seemed to have thumbs and a biped's spine. He was supposed to be sniffing the floor, ears cocked forward and tail waving. He moved closer to me, head cocked like he was asking for permission. I nodded, and he shoved his snout in my crotch just like a real dog before stepping off and moving to do the same to Quentin and Bucer.

"Get off," Bucer objected.

"He's just eliminating our scents from the search," said Quentin. "He knows what Tybalt smells like, but his nose can get confused, because it doesn't have the smarts a person's brain would have."

"That doesn't make any sense."

I shrugged. A Cu Sidhe's sense of smell is magical as much as it's physical; I assume it's similar to whatever quirk of my own magic that allows me to identify magical signatures with such impossible precision. Madden sniffed until he reached the door, then turned and trotted back over to me, shifting back to his humanoid form in the process.

He didn't stand up this time, but remained crouched on the floor, almost like he was offering me some sort of fealty. I knew he wasn't, but the position was still jarring.

"He wasn't in this room," said Madden. "Lots of other things were here that shouldn't have been. Not Tybalt, though. But someone with his blood on them was, and it wasn't you. I can smell the blood on you—so *much* blood, how do you lose that much blood and not just topple over?"

"Marcia gave me a sandwich," I said.

He looked at me sadly, and I flushed red, feeling oddly like I'd just been scolded. "You need to eat more, or bleed less, or maybe both," he said. "But someone—I'm not sure who, I'd need to smell them to know for certain—was here, and they had blood on them too, and it was Tybalt's. I can't follow the blood from here. I can follow the person."

"Now that you have the trail, can you follow it from a moving car?" I asked.

Madden nodded.

"All right, then: let's go for a ride."

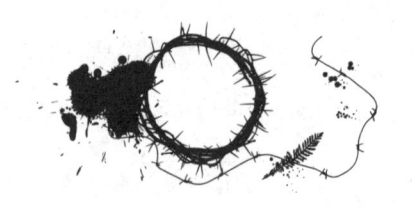

SIXTEEN

TRACKING THE SCENT TRAIL from the car required two concessions: first, that Madden had to ride in his canine form, since his human nose was so much less sensitive that he'd never be able to find the trail, much less keep hold of it. Second, he had to ride in the front seat. Since he couldn't speak, he needed to be as close to Quentin to possible to make sure that his signals got through. Said signals were simple: he'd bark if he was losing the trail, allowing Quentin to back up and try another route, and he'd wag his tail as long as were heading in the right direction.

As I folded myself into the backseat, I was intensely grateful that I'd asked Quentin to drive. My car was great, but it wasn't as large, and I had a tendency to treat it like a rolling trash can sometimes. The back was full of food wrappers and unwanted mail. There was no way I'd have been able to fit comfortably.

I still wasn't *comfortable*, but at least I had enough legroom. Spike settled in the middle seat, curling so its thorns were pressed flat against my leg rather than impaling me every time it twitched. I appreciated that. It looked at me with sleepy eyes before putting its head down on its paws.

Bucer climbed into the remaining backseat and smirked.

"Both of us get to ride second-class this time, eh, Daye?"

"I could punch you in the throat, you know."

Spike raised its head, rattling ominously. Bucer ignored it.

"Ah, you're enjoying our reunion or you'd have turned me over to that shiny new Queen of yours already. We both know you missed me."

"I didn't, Bucer." I leaned back, resting one hand atop my stomach and the other on Spike's back. "I really, truly didn't."

Quentin got into the driver's seat after holding it open to let Madden leap in and across the car to the passenger side. "Sorry about this," he said, concern making his Canadian accent broader than usual, so that for a moment he sounded like he was setting himself up for a joke about pronunciation. "You all right back there, Toby?"

"I'm fine," I said. "Go ahead and drive, and we'll get this taken care of."

"Got it." He closed the car door, turned the engine on, and touched the roof with one hand, humming several bars of an old sea shanty. The smell of heather and steel rose around us, and he dropped his hand, looking pleased with himself as he pulled away from the curb.

"Don't-look-here?" I asked.

"Big one," he replied. "Can't have a dog this good-looking hanging out the car window without people noticing us."

Madden had put his own mortal disguise back on, and now looked like a golden retriever rather than an inexplicably red and white dog out of a fairy tale. He barked once, agreeing with Quentin, then stuck his head out the open window, plumed tail waving wildly to signal that the trail was still in range.

Oh, I hoped he could stop wagging if he needed to. He said he could, but I didn't like gambling my ability to find my husband on a dog's ability to stop wagging his tail.

Still. Quentin was driving, my hand ached where I had stabbed it on the iron needle, and I was exhausted. Maybe Tybalt had the right idea, encouraging me to stay home for months after Titania's spell was broken. Being out in the field was a lot harder on the body than I remembered, even without excessive blood loss—and if I'm in the field, there's going to be excessive blood loss. That's sort of inescapable. I know my weaknesses. Fortunately, bleeding is one of my strengths.

Keeping my eyes open in the back of a car as it's being driven through the darkness is not one of my strengths. They slipped slowly closed, and the world slipped away with them as I fell into a mercifully natural sleep, dozing as the car turned, sped, and hit the inescapable bumps left behind by the California highway system.

It was the deceleration that woke me. I opened my eyes, shifting to sit back up from the slight slump I'd developed while sleeping, and wiped the drool from my chin before looking around. We were driving down an urban street I vaguely recognized, brick buildings and glass storefronts. It wasn't San Francisco. I could tell that much.

"Where are we?" I asked.

"Berkeley," said Bucer. There was genuine fear in his voice. I turned. He was sitting rigidly in his seat, one hand on the handle above the door, gripping so tightly that his knuckles had gone white. If not for the human illusion covering him, I was sure his ears would have been pressed flat against the sides of his head. Much like Madden's tail, a lot of the part-animal fae have trouble keeping their bodies from visibly betraying them.

"Berkeley?" I asked. I rubbed my eyes, trying to clear the sleep away. I could have done with another hour or three. And a bed. A bed would have been absolutely amazing. And a bathroom. I winced, suddenly realizing how much I really needed to pee. "Hey, Quentin, can you be careful of the potholes?"

"Sure, Toby. Sorry, Toby." I saw his grimace in the rearview mirror. He knew as well as I did that I was asking him to help me not pee in his car.

"It's okay. I'll hold on."

Madden shimmered and was a man, awkwardly folded into the front of the car. "The trail's been getting stronger for a while," he said. "We should park."

I looked around. "We're near the campus," I said. "This late at night, the student lots should be fairly open, and if you leave the don't-look-here up, we won't get ticketed."

Quentin nodded. "And Walther may be at his office, which means you won't have to pee in a bush."

Did I like the idea of pausing our search so I could use an actual bathroom? I did not, and I didn't think Tybalt would do it if our positions were reversed. But I also didn't love the thought of trying to squat in a bush while I was so unwieldy, or figuring out if Quentin had anything in his car that could be used for toilet paper, and not having to do that seemed worth taking ten minutes out of the quest at hand. There was also the possibility that Walter might somehow be able to help us now, as he so often had on other occasions.

Quentin pulled off the road and into the student parking lot closest to the science buildings, driving toward the hall where Walther's office was located. There were only a few cars this late at night, and I was pleased when I saw Walther's beaten-up old sedan in the faculty rows.

"There," I said, with increasing urgency. Quentin pulled into the spot I was indicating, turning off the engine.

I had my seatbelt off by the time the car stopped running, and was already halfway out the seat. Madden was still substantially faster. He looped around the car to offer me his arm and help me to my feet, then began to hustle toward the chemistry building. Quentin followed behind, all but dragging Bucer by one arm.

The door was locked. Naturally; it was after midnight. I was thinking miserably of the effort needed to get another thorn from Spike and pick the lock when Madden brushed the keyhole with his fingers and muttered something under his breath.

There was a clicking sound and the door swung open. I lifted both eyebrows, blinking at him.

"I don't have thumbs half the time," he said. "I had to have *some* way of getting through closed doors. I can do that when I'm a dog, too."

"You're gay and I'm married, or I'd kiss you," I said, and pushed through the unlocked door, into the cool, lemon-scented hall beyond. The floor was slick but not slippery: while the custodians had clearly been through recently, they had only washed, not waxed. I was grateful for that, even as I was focused solely on getting to the bathroom halfway down the hall.

Spike accompanied me, charging into the bathroom ahead of me and rattling its thorns with a degree of menace that would have triggered any ambush in pure self-defense. Nothing stirred in the darkened space. I crashed onward, into the first open stall, and managed to get myself situated in time.

Sagging with relief, I put my hands atop my stomach again. "You are a complication," I informed it. "I'll be really glad when peeing isn't an emergency anymore. But hey, you're getting another adventure with Mom before it's time for diapers and overprotective dads. Congrats, kitten."

The baby, naturally enough, didn't reply.

I finished my business and cleaned myself up, leaving the sink running after I was done so Spike could get a drink. Rose goblins are plants—I think. They don't eat so much as they photosynthesize, but they love a good drink of water.

When Spike dropped back to the floor I turned the faucet off. "Appreciate the help," I said. It rattled its thorns at me. "Ready to go?"

It didn't nod, but it did turn and trot toward the door, waiting there for me to come along. I smiled and followed after it.

There was an open door in the hallway that had been closed before, buttery light spilling out to illuminate the tile. I turned in that direction, hurrying when I heard Walther's voice drifting out, words unintelligible but tone light. Whatever we'd interrupted, it wasn't so important as to be a problem.

Once I reached the office door I looked in. Walther was standing next to his desk, facing Quentin and Bucer. As was often the case late at night, he had a full chemistry set out and in use, distilling various herbs and flower petals into something more esoteric. He taught chemistry to human students, and he did alchemy at night, working his magic in a more solid form. It's a gift that often seems to arise in the Tylwyth Teg, although it isn't limited to them.

"Bucer, show him those apple seeds," I said.

Walther turned toward the sound of my voice. He was wearing a disguise to make himself look human, and he had a pair of slightly tinted glasses on, blunting the unnatural blue of his eyes. No illusion in the world has ever been good enough to make a Tylwyth Teg's eyes look human without a little extra assistance.

"Apple seeds?" he asked.

"He knows what I'm talking about." I focused on Bucer, raising one eyebrow. "Come on. I know you pocketed those jars."

Bucer scowled at me, reaching into his pockets and pulling out the jars, one from either side. "Show, not give?" he asked.

"For now. Those aren't yours."

"They aren't yours either!"

"I'm a hero of the realm, and they were received in exchange for stolen goods," I said. "I think I can make more of an argument for a claim than you can, don't you?"

Walther, meanwhile, was staring at the jars of seeds like he was seeing the face of Maeve herself. He stepped toward Bucer, hands already reaching out. "Are those . . . ?" he breathed.

"Sun- and moon-apple seeds," said Bucer. He sounded a little smug, like he had somehow been responsible for growing or harvesting the seeds in question. "Fresh, even. Dame Altair germinated a few of them to prove that they could grow."

Again, something about the seeds nagged at me. Both sun- and moon-apples were fruits from deep Faerie, originally from Avalon, and all the trees had died centuries ago, either consumed by pests and plagues or crossbreeding with mortal apple strains until they disappeared, creating the equivalent of changeling fruit. But I had seen them not all that long before. I knew I'd seen them.

Bucer surrendered one of the jars to Walther, who gazed at it with open awe.

"Give him the other jar," I said, through numb lips. "We need to go."

"What?" Bucer jerked like I'd pricked him with a pin, while Quentin and Madden just turned to look at me with confused concern.

"We need to go," I repeated. "We're almost there." I turned then, walking out of the room, Spike at my heels.

As I had hoped, the boys followed, even Walther, who was still holding the jar of apple seeds. I glanced at him.

"They tell you what's going on?" I asked tightly.

He nodded. "Tybalt and May are missing. You know we could make things a lot easier if we just tagged everyone in your household with tracking devices."

I snorted. "It's a fun thought, but I doubt they'd let me."

"Come on, you know it's a good idea. You lose your people like Cinderella loses her shoes. Things would be so much more straightforward if you could just pull out your tracker and head straight for their current location."

"Isn't that what Madden is for?" I asked.

"I resemble that remark," said Madden mildly.

"But seriously, Walther, you don't have to come with us," I said. "This could get dangerous."

"Says the pregnant woman to the alchemist," said Walther. "If anyone is sitting this out because it could get dangerous, it should be you. But I don't see you sitting down and letting someone else handle things."

"It's my husband and sister," I protested.

"It's my friends," said Walther. "See, we can both play this game."

The campus wasn't as dark as I would have expected. As a student safety measure, there were lights everywhere, making the walkways easy to follow. We did exactly that, following them to the edge of campus and out onto the sidewalk, where Madden sniffed the air before excusing himself to step behind a bush.

The golden retriever came bounding out to join us only a second later, pressing his nose to the pavement and starting off down the road. The feeling of déjà vu was becoming overwhelming. I hadn't just seen those apples before, I'd taken this exact walk through Berkeley before, following Madden toward an inevitable destination.

And indeed, he stopped at a blank brick wall. Too blank: there was no graffiti, no posters advertising local events or student shows. Only brick, smooth and untouched as the day it had been installed. He looked back at me. I nodded.

"I know where we are, Madden," I said. "Go on through."

He turned back to the wall, then ran forward, vanishing into the brick, which trembled for a moment, like it was a pattern somehow painted on a soap bubble and he had just stepped through without popping it.

Spike was the next one through, trotting calmly into the brick without looking back at me. I grabbed Bucer's arm, motioning for Quentin to go through ahead of us.

"If you know anything about this, now would be the time to say something," I said pleasantly to Bucer, while he looked at me with wide, overly rounded eyes.

"I have no idea what's going on," he said.

"Well, then, this is going to be educational," I said, and pulled him through the brick, into the impossible courtyard on the other side.

The courtyard was dark, which made sense: I didn't think its owner ever came here at night, and since we were still technically in the human world, anything that might have attracted attention was probably not the best idea. The sky above us remained exactly the same, true night, clouds streaked over single moon and distant, glittering stars.

The lack of light didn't really matter for fae purposes. The trees, herbs, and flowers that grew in wild profusion all around us were limned in starlight, and might as well have been fully lit from the way Walther was staring. He wasn't moving, wasn't trying to take it all in: he was just staring at one of the moon-apple trees like it was a miracle, like he had never seen anything so beautiful in his life.

"Moon-apples were used in beauty potions and tinctures to reshape the body for centuries," he said, voice low and intense. "With a bushel of these, I could help every trans changeling in the Kingdom. I could stabilize some of the temporary health fixes for ailments that purebloods don't suffer from, the ones we've been treating as if they were as good as it was possible to get. And this is just *here*?"

"It's not ours," I said. "It belongs to my grandmother."

"Your . . . *grandmother*?"

"It's a long story. Madden, where does the trail go from here?"

He looked at me and didn't bark, only tipped his nose back to the ground and started walking toward the back of the courtyard.

There was a half-collapsed house taking up the entire rear wall—but as it hadn't changed since our last visit, I was beginning to think its decay and disrepair were as much a matter of presentation as the "brick wall" we'd walked through to get here. Someone was deeply invested in this house looking like it was about to collapse. There was a nest about five feet across in front of it, made from woven branches, vines, and mismatched fabric strips.

Crouched in the middle of the nest was what looked like a children's playhouse with feathery chicken legs. It shifted positions as we approached, looking at us with its glassy windows. I didn't know whether they were eyes or whether they were some sort of distracting coloration surrounding and concealing the real eyes. I wasn't sure it mattered either way, since the end result was the same: a small house was looking at us.

"I think it's harmless if we don't mess with it," I said. "Just keep going."

Madden reached the porch of the collapsing house and looked back at us before bounding up the stairs. We continued to follow. He brushed his nose against the front door and it swung open. More of that dog magic of his, convenient mostly because it meant we didn't need to slow down. We continued to follow.

When we reached the front room of the house, Madden was human again, and there was no one else there. He turned to look at us, clearly uncomfortable.

"I don't like this," he said.

"I don't either," I agreed. "This is the second time we've followed a blood trail to this courtyard. At least we know who owns it now."

I had been inside this house before, and nothing had changed since the last time. The door opened straight onto the front room, which was small and spotless, with rose-patterned wallpaper and a polished wood floor. Everything looked like it had been dusted recently; it gleamed. The air smelled of Lemon Pledge rather than any identifiable magical signature.

From the front room, I could access the stairway to the second floor, the kitchen, or the hallway which led to the other downstairs rooms. I hadn't bothered checking most of them the last time I'd been here, and I really didn't have time to waste searching them all now.

"Yeah, and that doesn't make it better," said Madden. He dropped back onto all fours, seeking the comfort of a fur coat and sharp teeth. I couldn't blame him. If I'd been able to remove myself from the conversation by turning into something else, I would almost certainly have done it.

"Cheater," I muttered.

"Not everyone knows," said Walther, giving me a hard look. "You want to let me know who's been hiding a Firstborn's ransom in rare alchemical materials less than a mile from my office? Because I'd really like to have a few words with them about the good of Faerie. I'm willing to pay."

"I don't think money is much of an object here, I'm afraid," I said. "And I already told you who owns this place. My grandmother."

"Okay, and your grandmother would be . . . ?"

"Me," said a voice, and a blonde woman in a long green dress stepped out of the shadows on the other side of the room.

Janet Carter, betrayer of Faerie, breaker of Maeve's last Ride, still looked just as young as she'd been on the day when she walked into the woods of Caughterha to save her lover, who had been earmarked to die for Faerie's sake. It had been centuries, but she truly hadn't aged a day. She looked at me and smiled, slow and cold, and I finally understood just how screwed we really were.

"Hello, October," she said.

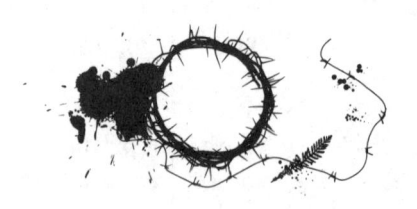

SEVENTEEN

WE ALL STARED, ESPECIALLY Madden, who shifted positions to lean against my leg and whine unhappily.

"Grandmother," I said, doing my best to keep my voice level. "Assuming you are my grandmother, after I chose your daughter's ex-husband in the divorce. I guess legalities don't change blood, as much as we might wish they would. I had no idea you were here."

"You wouldn't," she said. "I know you understand marshwater magic better than most of your kind, October, but what you don't understand is what it's capable of being, when you have the right ingredients. Sunlight obscures things from the fae. Walk in the light of day and you can go unseen forever."

"Quentin, get behind me," I said, voice low.

Quentin blinked at me, mouth opening like he wanted to object, but the habits of obedience that had been ingrained in him by his time as my squire were momentarily stronger than his stubbornness. He stepped behind me. It was a futile gesture, since he was taller than I was and had been for some time now. Still, it made me feel a little better to have something between him and her. Even if that something was my body.

"What are you doing here?" I asked.

She scoffed. "I thought you just admitted that this was my place, deeded to me long ago, and forbidden to all of Faerie. I could be asking you the same question, but with much more authority on my side of things. You shouldn't have come beyond the wall, October. You know better than that."

"I know my husband has been taken, and the blood trail left by his captors led me here."

"Wasn't that your excuse *last* time? That the blood trail left by *my* daughter had led you to my holdings, past the door that was never to be opened, into the air that was never yours to breathe? Either you're lying, or you're no good at holding on to your family, because this is sheer carelessness, to lose so many in such a short time."

I clenched my jaw against all the hurtful, hateful things I wanted to say in response to her. "I thought we were getting along these days," I said, almost desperately. "For Gillian's sake, I thought we were trying."

"I *was* trying," countered my grandmother. "I was trying to let you in, to let you be a part of her life, and to believe that Faerie wasn't here to steal everything away from me one more time. And then she went with you on a trip across the sea, deep into Faerie, and she came back to me no more human than a houseplant. Do you know what that's like? To let someone else walk away with your daughter and get a cheap replacement in her place? No. Of course you wouldn't know. When you had a daughter, you couldn't vanish fast enough. You only came back when all the hard work was done."

"That's not true!" Gillian was the only reason I couldn't fully forgive Simon for what he'd done to me, couldn't fully relax into the idea that my fourteen lost years had eventually been a good thing. Gillian was two years old when I disappeared from her life. Two years old, my little fairy tale, and I had never wanted to leave her, and I would still have given up everything to have her back again, to be returned to the life that had been stolen from me.

But time doesn't run backward, not even in Faerie, and Gillian had grown up believing I was a deadbeat who'd deserted her, calling another woman "Mom"—calling *Janet* "Mom"—and turning to her when she was lost or lonely. We'd been rebuilding a relationship. It was never going to be the one we should have had.

"You promised me you wouldn't take her away, that you weren't here to steal her, and yet the first chance you had, you swept her into your world with no way back to me." She shook her head, expression one of pure disgust. "You ruined her. *Faerie* ruined her, even as it ruined you. Gone for months without a word. She still won't tell me where she was, only says she didn't have a choice and changes the subject."

"... oh, no." Titania's enchantment had caused most humans to forget anything related to Faerie that had ever touched on their lives.

Bridget's renters had disappeared for the spell's duration, and while I was sure they'd had issues returning to their lives once things were returned to normal, they hadn't noticed the gap. But Janet wasn't an ordinary mortal anymore. Maeve had cursed her after she broke the Ride, freezing her in place in a way that humans weren't meant to be held. She could probably still die—she was still mortal—but she didn't age, and Faerie's tricks rarely worked on her.

One Queen had cursed her, and the other had swept her adopted daughter away. Could the second's spells supersede the first's? I had been assuming yes, if I thought about her at all. And maybe I'd been wrong.

Janet nodded, looking quietly smug. "You thought I wouldn't notice that she was gone for four months? That you were nowhere to be found for the same amount of time? You promised you weren't here to turn her against me, and God forgive me, I stood by while you dragged her an inch at a time into Faerie."

"Blame me if you need to, but Tybalt and May didn't do anything wrong," I said. "Give them back."

"Why do you assume I have them?"

"Because the people you've been paying to rob the kingdom while no one was looking brought them here to you," I said. "I don't know why you've been doing that, but I want my family back."

Because this garden was where I'd seen the sun-apples before, where they still grew in the mortal world. And her initials, in her current mortal identity, were M.M., for Miranda Marks. The woman who'd married Gillian's father in order to take my place. I should have made the connection sooner.

Janet smiled, bitterly. "Funny," she said. "That's all I ever wanted, too. Maybe we're more similar than I thought we were, granddaughter. Faerie's stolen so much from me, I can't possibly steal from Faerie. I'm just taking payment with interest for what I never agreed to give."

"Give me back my family."

"Or what?" She tilted her head to the side, still smiling. "You'll stab me with that sword you're carrying? You'll let your replacement child stab me? I don't think that can kill me, but you're welcome to try. Prove that the fae are monsters. Attack your own flesh and blood. Do it."

"I could handle her for you," said Walther, quietly. "She's not *my* flesh and blood. I could take care of things without proving anything about monsters."

"That's a very kind offer," I said. "But no. We're not going to fight her. Bucer?"

"Yeah?"

"Remember the Luidaeg said no more passive effects; you'd have to try?" I grasped the bracelet on my left wrist with my right hand, twisting it until I worked it over past my thumb, then pulled it entirely off. I reached around and offered it to Walther.

Quentin, catching my line of thought, removed one of his own bracelets and handed it to Madden.

"Put those on," I said, voice low and urgent. Walther blinked and slid the bracelet on without objection. Madden held his bracelet in his jaws like it was a chew toy.

Bucer looked at me, apparently confused, then nodded and turned to Janet. "I don't think you're thinking this through," he said. The air around us began to swim with the faint smell of pine and damp linen. It was thinner than it should have been, like it was being filtered through a screen, but it was distinctly there. Without the Luidaeg's bracelets muffling his magic, I had little doubt the compulsion to go along with whatever he said would have been enough to knock me on my ass.

"No?" asked Janet.

"You were hiring my boss to steal things for you, weren't you? Dame Eloise Altair? How did you find her?"

Bucer couldn't command, only influence and convince: Janet wouldn't do anything under his control that she couldn't have been convinced to do on her own. Which made me feel even worse about being convinced to leave Tybalt and May in danger before, because it meant that was something I could have been talked into all along. I didn't want to think of myself as that kind of person. And yet I knew where the root of the urge had come from.

Months of confinement dropped on top of memories of an entire lifetime of being kept locked away from the world for my "own good." They'd been trying to protect me, and I'd let them, because I'd known that they were right, even as I'd hated every single moment.

Apparently, my hatred had gone even deeper than I thought it had, if I'd been so willing to grasp an excuse to walk away.

Janet looked at Bucer, her smile melting into an expression of confusion. "I know who all the landed gentry in the Mists are. It's a matter of self-preservation. I can't keep my eyes open for your kind if I don't know who the players are. Dame Altair has always been . . . flexible when it comes to things like artifacts or information. Slip her a few seeds or a jar of jam and she'll do almost anything I ask. Are you one of her contractors?"

"I guess you could say that. She hired me to clean out the vaults. Why now? Why did you decide this was the time to act?"

"My daughter was missing. I knew Faerie had to be responsible. I started looking, and discovered my granddaughter was also gone, meaning they must have disappeared together, just like they promised me they were never going to do. None of the nobles I was accustomed to avoiding were in their places, and I saw an opportunity. I contacted Dame Altair. She seemed to have forgotten me, but she was willing to establish a new iteration of our existing relationship all the same. I always knew she subcontracted her retrievals. You're not special."

"Never wanted to be," said Bucer. "Why did you want all those things?"

I realized what he was doing. Janet was very old and, for all her hatred of Faerie, was so tightly entangled with us that she couldn't tell her story to most people. She wanted to talk. He was just convincing her that talking was a good idea.

Villain monologues are a cliché for a reason. Most people who've been sitting on what they consider a great plan are desperate to share it with *someone*. Give them an excuse when they think they've already won, and they'll tell you more than they ever intended.

"Faerie has stolen from me for the last time," she said. "I needed to be able to defend myself. To have ways to stop them from attacking me, deterrents for my door."

"Why did you attack Dame Altair's people?"

"She didn't get me what I needed most, and she called me a filthy human when I objected to her refusing to return my payment," said Janet calmly. "She needed to learn that being fae didn't make her better than me. Your people live in the human world. This is *our* world, not yours. You need to show some respect for the people you would so gladly abuse."

"So you used iron on her footmen?"

Janet scoffed. "Where I come from, the crimes of a lord fall upon their vassals. They should have made better choices about their service."

She was fully focused on Bucer by this point. I began moving slowly toward the kitchen door, easing my feet down with as much care as possible.

"It still wasn't really a balanced exchange," said Bucer. "Their employer let you down, so you attacked them with the one metal that can devour magic? Death by iron doesn't just hurt fae, it destroys them. Setting them on fire would have been kinder."

"But I don't have a flamethrower," said Janet, almost reasonably. "I have a magic scabbard that turns other metals into purest iron. There was a time when you could have destabilized the economy of a kingdom with that thing, but now, all it does is devalue more precious metals. And help you kill fairies, of course. Sometimes fairies need killing."

Even Bucer looked horrified. "That's—"

"No worse than your kind throws at mine? I know. It's like centuries of being treated like our lives don't matter has left me a little bit bitter. Or are you really going to tell me that Faerie somehow learned to play nicely with the short-lived, magic-free neighbors while I wasn't looking? I didn't listen when my father told me not to go to the woods because he told me not to go anywhere for fear of the fae. 'Don't go by the river, Jenny, the hags will pull you under.' 'Can't take you to the harvest fest, Jan, two maids vanished there last week after they caught the eyes of the Sidhe.' My world has always been hemmed in at the whim of the fae. Is it so wrong that I should try to balance the scales a bit?"

"I would never have stolen those things if I'd known they were being put into the hands of a human," said Bucer.

"Well, then, it's a good thing you didn't know, because I needed them," said Janet. "I still need my hope chest."

"Why? You're not fae. It won't do you any good."

"No, but I'm expecting to come into the custody of a part-fae infant very soon, and when that happens, I want to be ready to make sure it becomes permanent."

She started to turn, as if to look in my direction. Bucer saw it too. He grabbed her arm, snapping her attention back to him. I was still furiously angry with him, but I had never been prouder. Maybe I'd find a way to forgive him after all when this was finished.

"You can't *do* that!" he said, the smell of pine and linen getting even stronger. Almost desperately, he continued, "Hope chests aren't meant to be used before people can—before they make the Choice! They're not supposed to be used to erase Faerie from the places it belongs."

Janet refocused her attention on him, scowling. Meanwhile, I had an open doorway into the kitchen. I stopped there, fighting back the urge to charge at her and make her stop talking—forever if possible. I had no question that she meant my child. She wanted *my* baby, and she was intending to use the hope chest she'd asked Dame Altair to acquire for her to turn that baby fully human before they were old enough to understand what was happening to them.

My own mother had changed the balance of my blood when I was too young to remember. Only the fact that she'd been trying not to do me permanent harm had stopped her from taking it all the way before Sylvester found out what she was doing and intervened. I was still recovering the ground she'd stolen from me. A hope chest wouldn't be able to feel the baby's suffering. It was an object, a tool, and it would do as it was commanded.

Quentin was suddenly beside me, having crossed the room quickly and silently while Bucer had Janet distracted. He put a hand on my shoulder.

"We have to go," he hissed.

"I will kill her," I replied.

"You'll do a better job with Tybalt to help you," he said, voice soft but reasonable.

I turned to meet his eyes. Janet had been closer than she knew when she called him my replacement child. I wasn't his mother, but I was his mom, even as Janet was with Gillian. I'd been the only stable adult in his life for too many years to call myself anything else. I hadn't been trying to put myself in that position. I'd done it anyway, one lesson and adventure at a time.

"Okay," I whispered, and stepped through the doorway.

It was quiet in the kitchen. Too quiet—we should have been able to hear Janet and Bucer talking, even if we couldn't see them anymore. I realized guiltily that Madden had stayed behind rather than sneaking after us as I'd expected, probably realizing that she would be able to hear his claws clicking on the wood if he'd tried to follow. Walther and Spike had also remained behind. Thanks to that strange silence, I no longer believed that I'd be able to hear them if they decided to follow now.

I pulled one of the knives from my belt, using it to lay open the ball of my thumb with a quick slash. The smell of blood overwhelmed the smell of floor cleaner that lingered in the air, and I stuck my thumb into my mouth, sucking as hard as I could to get the most blood possible before the wound sealed over.

"Maybe hurry," said Quentin urgently.

I swallowed, not saying anything, and closed my eyes for a moment, searching for the gleam of blood. The house was so clean that it was even easier to spot than it should have been: a small streak on the doorframe, as if it had been carelessly left by a man slung over someone's shoulder. I took note of its position, the taste of blood still filling my mouth and lighting up the world. It was inside the kitchen. Tybalt had been here.

With this knowledge in mind, I turned to study the kitchen around us with new eyes, still sucking blood off my thumb. It was a crudely infantile gesture, and I didn't give a damn if it helped me find my husband.

The kitchen was as clean as everything else I had seen in this house. The exterior was decrepit, but in here, the walls were straight and strong, with no sign of mold or water damage, and the floor was level, covered in linoleum slightly younger than the rest of the house around it, but still old enough to qualify as vintage, if not antique. Two more doors marked the walls. One had a large window, showing another slice of garden; this place apparently had a backyard of some sort. Quaint.

The other had a drop of blood on the floor in front of it, setting my path. I turned that way, Quentin still following close. I reached for the doorknob.

He touched my shoulder again. I stopped.

"Are you sure?" he asked.

I nodded, biting the inside of my cheek this time. When I inhaled, I could pick up faint traces of magic, left behind by people who had passed through here—panther lily and cinnamon, cotton candy and pennyroyal.

And rowan. Beneath everything else, faint and pale, but present, rowan. I set my jaw and opened the door.

A narrow set of stairs descended into darkness on the other side. Everything about this house felt like it had been constructed without the use of magic, and these stairs were no different. I looked down into the dark and wondered what Janet had been thinking, digging a basement in a seismically active place like Berkeley.

But it didn't matter. I stepped over the threshold, into the dark...

...and nearly fell down the stairs as the world spun wildly around me, the rarely used transition between the human world and the Summerlands smacking me in the head for daring to go where anyone with human blood wasn't welcome. Even the baby kicked, hard enough to be momentarily painful. I grabbed the stair rail, driving splinters into my palm and re-scenting the air with my blood.

That helped. Blood is centering for me, and breathing in the scent of it let me get my balance back, although I still felt as if I might throw up at the slightest additional distress. I took a few steps down the stairs, making room, and mustered a smile as Quentin came through behind me.

There were no visible light sources, not even the open door that should have been behind us, but somehow the space around us was more late twilight than true night: I could still see. He began to move his hand as if to call a ball of witch light, and I grabbed his wrist, shaking my head. He blinked at me, barely visible in the gloom.

"No lights," I whispered.

He paused before lowering his hands. I nodded firmly as I turned to face front once again, then began descending into the dark.

Knowes remain anchored to the mortal world because they're used, as a general rule; it's why the transition is so much more harrowing when it involves an unusual route. They can be sealed and eased into sleep for long periods of time, if the right person does the sealing, but most of them will collapse if not in common usage. Personally, I think they get lonely. No one does well for long in true isolation. If knowes are alive—and knowes are alive, the evidence is overwhelmingly in support of that idea—then they can get lonely when they're left by themselves.

There are other means of digging holes in the barrier between the mortal world and the Summerlands. Shallowings are exactly that—shallow—and frequently share the physical rules of the mortal world to a degree that knowes do not. This didn't feel like a shallowing. It felt more like a den, the habitat of some wild creature, dug as deep as necessary and no deeper. Which meant it wouldn't be very large.

That was something, anyway.

We continued to descend, and the reason for the shadowy nature of the light, rather than true darkness, appeared ahead of us: a torch was set into the wall, burning with a pale gray flame, only a few shades brighter than Quentin's witchlights. As we drew closer to it, I realized that it wasn't putting off any heat; it was a cold light, swallowing warmth from the air around the flame.

No one else was coming down the stairs behind us. I paused to spare a concerned thought for Walther, Spike, and Madden—Bucer could take care of himself—and kept on going. There was no time left to waste.

As if summoned by the thought, the end of the stairs came into view, flanked by two more of those cold torches. I sped up as much as I dared given my current physical condition, putting one hand on the hilt of my sword, gripping it until the metal of the pommel bit into my palm.

Stepping off the stairs into a narrow, stone-walled corridor was so anticlimactic it was almost shocking. The corridor extended in both directions, lined by those cold torches. I looked both ways, trying to pick up on something—anything—that would tell me which way to go. There was nothing.

I bit the inside of my cheek again, grinding down until I drew blood. The Luidaeg's bracelets were slowing my healing enough that it hurt more than it usually would have, my molars slicing through already-bruised tissue. But the blood came, as the blood always did, and I saw more droplets leading off to the left.

I turned, and Quentin followed, and we made our way deeper into the impossible dungeon beneath Janet's equally impossible house.

We had gone about thirty feet when two things happened in quick, terrible succession. There was a soft gasp from behind me, and I turned to find Quentin gone, leaving only empty hallway behind me.

I began to draw my sword, only for something to hit me in the back of the head hard enough that I actually heard the bone crack before my eyes rolled back and I collapsed like a sack of potatoes to the floor. I managed to stay awake long enough to feel myself land on my side, rather than my stomach, and then the darkness was all, and nothing else mattered.

EIGHTEEN

FOR THE SECOND TIME in as many days, I woke up tied to a bed, my arms above my head and my legs spread apart. This time I was tied with stronger stuff than silver and yarrow; these ropes were rose boughs and thin iron wire, cutting and burning my skin at the same time. The remaining bracelet of the pair the Luidaeg had made from my blood was still on my wrist, slowing my magic and making my healing more painful than it would normally have been. Every twitch and tremor burned. I still tried to jerk myself free when I finally opened my eyes and realized the situation I was in.

The burn of the iron threads being pressed against the open wounds created by the rose thorns dissuaded me from trying again. I hissed and sagged back into the bed, which was surprisingly comfortable, smelling of herbs and—from what I could tell—spotlessly clean. The sheets were still cool beneath me, despite the fact that I'd been here long enough for the fracture in my skull to mend, even with the bracelet on my arm.

I was also naked, something I hadn't realized until I started noticing the sheets. I looked down at myself. A top sheet was draped across me, presumably to preserve my modesty, but from the way it had settled, I could tell there was nothing else beneath it. No clothing—and no weapons.

I pulled on the chains again, despite the pain. This wasn't good. Nothing good has ever come of involuntary bondage and nudity. I don't think that's a very controversial position to take.

The iron dug into the wounds opened by the rose thorns, and blood ran down my arms, too far from my face for me to get any proper benefit from it. I strained anyway, trying to reach it, to no avail.

I couldn't repeat the trick I'd used to get away from Dame Altair.

I was tied more tightly, without the slack I needed to roll, and digging iron wires that deeply into my flesh would come with a degree of damage that my body would be hard-pressed to handle, even if my magic hadn't been slowed by the mixed-blessing of a bracelet I was wearing. The bed also felt like it was larger, making it harder to suspend myself in a way that gave me any leverage.

"I learn from my mistakes," said Dame Altair. I jerked my head around. She was standing in a corner of the spare, unadorned room; there was no wallpaper on the stone walls, and while I couldn't see the floor, I had little doubt that it would be equally bare. We were still in the dungeon-like space beneath Janet's house, the rooms that inexplicably burrowed into Faerie. "I'm sorry I tied you incorrectly back at the house. This would all have been so much simpler if you'd stayed where I put you."

"What the hell are you doing, Eloise?" I demanded, using her given name rather than her title. I couldn't sit up, and so I settled for glaring at her. It was a small comfort, but my temper was still my own.

"Fulfilling a client order," she said calmly. "And don't worry about the iron in your bonds. That's just there to keep you from gnawing your own arm off to get away from me. If you stop struggling, you won't get any more of it in your bloodstream, and I have the fount that lets me treat iron poisoning. I'll let you use it before I let you go."

I gaped at her. "Janet didn't attack you for failing her. She attacked you because she was helping you lure me out of the house!"

"Took you long enough to figure that out. But then, you were never smart—just persistent. It's amazing how far that can get you when you're also indestructible. Yes, I arranged the attack, and when Dugan said he needed to get his liege out of Windermere's custody before the sentencing, I agreed to help him. I was never in any danger, and it all went exactly as I had planned. Crafting a narrative of the abduction that would work in front of an Adhene without triggering their tedious need for the truth was the most difficult part." She smiled, slow and languid. "And now here we are."

"You know I'm going to kill you as soon as I get off this bed."

"You realize statements like that are just an incentive for me to make sure that you never leave that bed," she said. "But it won't matter. I'll treat your iron poisoning before I leave you, and my employer has paid me enough that I can go anywhere in the Westlands or Aztalan and fund a comfortable life for myself. I won't break the Law."

"Where are Tybalt and May?" I demanded. "Where is Quentin?"

"Your cat and death omen are in cells of their own," she said. "One of the artifacts Bucer was kind enough to steal for me sets wards against the Shadow Roads so strong that I doubt their First could tunnel through them. The cat-king isn't going anywhere before I'm ready. As to the Fetch, she hasn't even tried to escape since I told her that one of my tasks was gathering as many skinshifting tokens as possible. She worries for her little bird. What *is* it with your line and the shifting kinds?"

I raised an eyebrow. "It's not my whole line. Last time I checked, August wasn't seeing anyone, and Gillian *is* a shapeshifter. She doesn't need to date one to keep up the family tradition." I paused then, and asked the more important question: "Did you hurt Jasmine?"

"No." Janet shook her head. "The bird landed on the roof as we were loading the Fetch into the car, and my brother disguised us well enough that we were able to drive away without her following. Wherever she is now, that isn't down to us. But I may have implied to the Fetch that we would hunt the bird if we released her from our custody. Need to get paid for something."

"And Quentin?"

"The boy? Oh. We may have hit him a trifle harder than intended while we were apprehending you—my brother forgets which of you is the unreasonably fast healer, and which is the pain in my ass. The alchemist is seeing to him now."

"Walther's not a healer! He's not going to be able to fix a cracked skull!"

"Oh. Oh, no." Dame Altair put a finger to the corner of her mouth like she was thinking very hard. "Sounds like you need to get him out of here sooner than later, and that's not going to happen unless you agree not to fight while I take what I've been hired to provide."

Janet's obsession with raising Gillian as a substitute for the child who'd been taken away from her and hidden in Faerie, where she couldn't reach. Dame Altair's questions about my pregnancy when

I'd first come to see her. The search for the only hope chest in the kingdom, and her frustration when it was nowhere to be found—meaning she *knew* it was real, *knew* it would work, and had a specific reason to want it.

If I'd been able to move my arms, I would have been clutching my stomach. As it was, I tried as hard as I could to roll onto my side and shelter it from her with the bulk of my body. All the action did was rock me a few inches to the left and drive the rose thorns deeper into my wrists and ankles, bringing a fresh wave of pain and a fresh cascade of blood.

She sighed. "Oh, don't be so *stupid*, October. I knew you weren't the brightest pixie in the flock, but that doesn't mean you need to behave this way. You have no way out. You're tied and taken, and all you're doing is making it worse for yourself. If you don't stop behaving this way, I'll have to take steps to prevent you from damaging the merchandise."

"My child is not *merchandise*," I spat.

"Maybe not in your eyes," she said, and turned, letting herself out of the room. "Maybe a little time to think about the situation will help." She closed the door when she was gone, making sure that anyone who passed in the hall wouldn't be able to hear me. Not that it would matter: the only people who were likely to be passing in the hall were Dugan and Janet and, for all I knew, the false Queen. No one who would be able or inclined to help me.

Every inch of me was beginning to ache. The burn of the iron at my wrists and ankles was constant and impossible to ignore: the closest human comparison I can come up with is something nuclear, like uranium. It harms the fae through contact alone, and once it gets into our blood, it keeps doing damage.

Radiation poisoning isn't the worst comparison I could make, really. Iron poisoning is remarkably similar. It starts with aches in muscle and bone, progressing to swelling of the joints that can be so painful it becomes incapacitating; sometimes in all of that, hallucinations and dizziness will become a problem. Finally, it makes its victims go rigid, their every muscle locking up and refusing to respond as the iron begins shutting its victim's organs down. It's anybody's guess how painful it is by that stage. No one's really survived to give it a review.

How can we be allergic to iron when iron is found in almost every living thing in the world, including humans? I have no idea. I just know that the purer the iron, the more it hurts. When you reach what we call "cold iron," which is iron unalloyed with anything else and alchemically treated to harden it, you've got something that can kill us with proximity alone. Most fae won't use it, no matter how malicious they are.

But the false Queen of the Mists always favored the stuff. She lined her dungeon in it. I'd always wondered how she could get that much iron, that pure, and now I knew. Hire some Gremlins and Coblynau to do your construction—two of the only types of fae unbothered by iron—and use that damned scabbard to convert the metal you needed, one ingot at a time. It was an elegant solution to an unnecessary problem. She had probably been the one to suggest dipping a spool of copper or aluminum iron in the scabbard, converting it to something cruel and unforgiving.

I did wonder who had woven it with the rose boughs for a moment before my brain caught up with my speculation and reminded me that Janet was still human. Immortal, all but indestructible, but human. How much of my descendant line's strength had been dictated by Maeve's curse on Janet? I knew from the Luidaeg that it had been proximity to Tam Lin's transformations that made us so easy to change: our blood had learned to be protean just because my grandmother had been *next* to Titania's spellwork. What could being born to a cursed woman have done to us?

My wrists and ankles ached. The burn was getting worse, and I no longer dared to struggle, because if I did, I'd just drive the wires deeper and speed up the progress of the poison. If I wanted to walk away from this intact enough to kick every person involved soundly in the head, I needed to minimize my exposure. Did I believe that Dame Altair was going to let me use the fount to cure my iron poisoning when this was all over? I did not.

However fae I've become in the last few years, I'm still part human, and as long as I'm part human, I'm still a changeling. I'd been hanging on to my humanity out of habit and comfort, trying to keep my human father a part of me for as long as possible, even though I'd long since slipped over the line into "mostly fae," meaning there were more downsides than advantages to staying mortal. Well, this was another downside, honestly: as long as I was a changeling, Dame Altair could kill me without fear of breaking the Law. Oberon's Law doesn't cover changelings.

After she sliced my baby out of my body, she could leave me here to die, and it wouldn't matter one little bit.

The door she'd left by creaked open. I turned my head toward it, ready to spit at whoever stepped into the room, and blinked as no one entered at all.

Wait. No: no one entered that I could see. The way I was tied to the bed, only the top half of the door was visible. I blinked, straining to see anything below that, and heard claws clicking on stone a moment before the door slid shut again and Madden's head popped up over the edge of the bed, ears pricked forward in evident concern. He still looked like a Golden retriever.

I managed—barely—not to laugh in relief. "Madden," I said instead. "How did you get here?"

He folded inward on himself, becoming a crouching man. "Janet thought I was Walther's dog. I barked and tried to bite her when they moved like they were going to grab me, and she said they could leave me outside. Bucer didn't tell. He went in with her and Walther, and she didn't grab him, just said come and he came. I don't know whose side he's on by this point. Your rose goblin ran into the bushes and disappeared."

"Bucer is on Bucer's side," I said. "Can you untie me?"

Madden nodded as he turned to look at the ropes around my wrists, then recoiled, eyes going wide. "Toby, that's iron."

"Oh, believe me, I am *exceptionally* aware."

"Doesn't it . . . I know you're a changeling, but doesn't it hurt?"

"It burns," I said, and was almost ashamed of how small my voice became when I spoke. "But I think that was the point. I can't hurt myself to get away when it burns like that. My body wouldn't let me, even if I was desperate enough to try. Please, can you untie me?"

He stood, moving to look at the bedposts. "It looks like the loops are tied here and here," he said, indicating something I couldn't see. "I don't heal the way you do. Even if I wrap my hands in the sheet, if I let you loose, I'm going to burn my hands so bad I won't be able to run after they're paws again."

"I know," I said. "The fount that lets us cure iron poisoning is here somewhere, based on what Dame Altair said, but it's still going to hurt, and I'm sorry."

"I could run and tell Ardy what's happening," he said, reluctantly. It was clear that he didn't want to run away and leave a pregnant woman tied to a bed when there was something he could do to help. "Or I could run and find the cat-queen, tell her what's happening. I bet she'd bring her cats to help if I told her."

Shade, Queen of Berkeley's Cats, was an ally and—according to Tybalt—a much closer one than she'd been before Titania's spell. He'd helped her save her Court when the Cait Sidhe were all held captive on the other side of the Shadow Roads. The idea was briefly tempting.

But not as tempting as not being here any longer. I took a deep breath. "Dame Altair's been trying to lure me out of my house for I don't even know how long," I said. "She agreed to help her brother bust the false queen out of Arden's custody because she knew that was the thing that would get me back into the field."

"Why?"

"Janet wants my baby." Saying the words so bluntly made them feel real in a way they hadn't before. It made sense. She'd been trying to get a child back from Faerie since Amandine was taken away from her.

Trauma moves in cycles. We pass it down, one to another, and there's no time limit on how long that damage can endure. I didn't know who'd been responsible for taking Amandine away from her mother, but whoever it was, they had a lot to answer for. And Faerie being Faerie, they might still be around to give those answers.

Madden looked horrified and immediately reached for the ropes looped over the bedframe.

"Nope," he said. "That is *not* going to be happening today, no, not today, not tomorrow, not any day that I have a part in. We're getting you out of here, even if I have to stay human until someone can treat my hands. Nope and nope."

He hissed between his teeth, and the smell of his blood filled the air, perfumed with Scotch pine and dried lichen. I'd never smelled his magic before. Cait Sidhe smell of their magic when they transform. I turned to blink at him, confused.

"Madden, why don't I smell your magic when you change forms?"

He kept working. "Little busy here, Toby. I want to be careful."

"I identify people by the smell of their magic half the time, and I've never smelled yours before, which means I don't know for sure that you're actually you. Why don't I smell your magic when you transform?"

He sighed, pulling his hands away from the rope. "Is this really important enough to interrupt me in the process of letting you go?"

"Yes," I said, voice blunt.

"Right. Right." He shook his head, flipping his hair out of his eyes. "Cu Sidhe don't change shapes the same as Cait Sidhe do, because we carry our magic differently. They carry theirs in their hands, just the way a Daoine Sidhe does. It's always right there. It's why they're better at being part one shape, part another, while we're either people or dogs, no in-between. When we were first born, our father, Culann, looked at us and saw our noses would be our best advantage, so he took us to the shore and threw all three of his pups into the waves. Two washed back onto the beach, and after that, their magic didn't smell when they changed shapes. They'd been washed in salt and struggle, and the sea granted them the ability to pass without leaving as much of a trail."

"What happened to the third pup?" I asked, half-curious, half-horrified.

"He was a Firstborn's son, and they're hard to kill, so some of us think he didn't drown, just swam off and away to somewhere else, and maybe someday we'll find a descendant line of sea dogs that want to be our friends," said Madden. "Do you believe me now?"

"I want to," I said. "I really do. But I'd never heard that before, and maybe it's true and maybe it's not, but either way, please finish untying me."

Madden nodded. "All right," he said, and started working on the ropes again. "You can ask Ardy when we get out of here."

"I'll ask the Luidaeg." Any story that involved throwing children into the sea would be something she'd know. She wouldn't approve of it—she doesn't like people hurting kids—but she'd know it.

"All right," said Madden again. The rope holding my left wrist slackened, making it possible for me to move my arm into a slightly less strained position.

"Try to keep still."

"Sorry."

The more he worked, the more the ropes loosened, and the harder it became for me to keep still while he untied me. The thorns coupled with the iron made it slow going, and I was starting to worry when the ropes that held my hands finally let go, freeing my arms. I hurried to shake the remaining loops from my hands, revealing raw, red wrists that looked like they'd been the victims of some wild animal, then pushed myself as upright as I could, trying to lean down and help him untie my ankles. I couldn't reach, only watch from a slightly better vantage point as he began undoing the ropes at the foot of the bed.

Madden's hands, when I glimpsed them, were even worse off than my wrists—at least I'd been healing as I hurt myself, body struggling to patch itself despite everything. He didn't have that benefit. His fingertips were burnt and blackened, and there were deep, painful-looking slashes across his palms. I hissed between my teeth.

"Madden, how are you still working?"

"I work in food service," he said. "Sometimes I have to finish out a shift with some pretty nasty burns on my hands. Alan would let me leave if I asked, but I'd rather do my job, clock out, and go to Muir Woods where I can be healed properly and not have a hospital bill or need to miss work on the far end. That, and I do drag with Charles sometimes. After I've been tucked and tied and fitted with stiletto heels, normal pain just doesn't compare."

He was trying to sound light, but I could tell how much he was downplaying his pain. I nodded, deciding not to say anything else, and worked the bracelet off my wrist. It immediately dissolved back into the blood that had been used to create it, and I knew that somewhere, the bracelet on Walther's wrist had done the same. I sent a silent prayer to anyone who might be listening, hoping that he hadn't been relying too heavily on the bracelet in that moment.

As soon as the bracelet dissolved, the remaining cuts and punctures in my hands and wrists started to seal themselves, skin regrowing at a phenomenal rate. Unusually for me, they left scars behind, the skin around them red and angry from to the iron poisoning. I hissed as I looked at them, hesitantly touching one with the tip of a finger. It throbbed. Until I got the iron out of my system, the damage wasn't going to truly heal.

But it would heal enough to let me get out of this room.

Madden pulled the last of the thorn loops off of my ankles, and I sat up all the way, sliding my feet around to touch the floor, while Madden rose, whining as he looked at his hands.

I flinched. He'd hurt himself like that because of me, and while I was grateful, I still hated that he'd had to do it.

Even more, I hated that I had no clothes. I pulled up the bottom of the sheet and ripped off a long strip, tearing it in two before offering it to him.

Madden took it gratefully, winding it tightly around his hands. I stood, draping the sheet carefully around myself. Blood had soaked into the fabric, from the both of us, dappling it red and brown. I could use that. I took a deep breath, reaching out and grasping for my magic, until I felt it snarling around my fingers like rough twine.

It wasn't normally so scratchy or resistant, even when it didn't want to rise. I attributed that to the iron in my system and pulled it toward me.

"Oh the broom, the bonny, bonny broom, the broom of the Cowdenknows. I wish my love were here with me, as long as love allows," I chanted. The smell of copper and bloodied grass rose around me, then burst like a soap bubble, leaving the sheet feeling much tighter around my chest and upper arms.

I looked down at myself. The sheet was gone, replaced by a red and white dress that looked like something out of an overambitious Christmas pageant. I could have been one of the Candy Cane Fairies of Sugarplum Lane. But it was fitted to my current shape, with a high waist that sat just below my breasts and swooped around my stomach, and I wasn't going to be escaping either naked or wearing a bedsheet.

Madden snorted. "You really need to read some fashion magazines if you're going to start designing your own dresses."

"I used to do it all the time, back when the false queen was in charge," I said. "I didn't have much of a wardrobe then, and I think she liked to watch the changelings struggle."

Madden scowled, expression going deeply disapproving. "It's not right," he grumbled, voice halfway to becoming a growl. "Shouldn't pick on changelings just because their magic is less developed, or less focused. It's not right."

"And on that, we agree." I wiped my hands against my new dress to clear away the last lingering threads of magic, then looked toward the door. "You can't shapeshift anymore, right?"

"I *could*, I just wouldn't be able to walk if I *did*," said Madden. He held up his burnt and blistered hands, showing me the wreckage of his palms. The damage was even worse than I'd assumed. I was suddenly glad Dame Altair had stolen my weapons again. At least now I'd only be tempted to break her nose, not stab her in the kidneys. And the shell knife would return when I needed it, I was sure of that. "But I can walk as a man. I have feet still."

"That's good," I said. "We need to go." There was no telling when my jailer would be coming back to take my baby and deliver it to Janet, who must be getting impatient by now.

Madden nodded and crossed to the door. Unable to open it with his currently useless hands, he just stood there, waiting for me to follow him. I did, grasping the handle and pulling to reveal the dark hallway on the other side.

We were still in the dungeon beneath Janet's house, then. I'd suspected as much, and having it confirmed didn't change anything. We crept down the hall in darkness, Madden close behind me, my back to the wall and my hands against the stone as I crept along. It was slow and awkward, but striding didn't seem like the best idea, not when I couldn't see well enough to make out tripping hazards and Madden couldn't catch me if I fell.

We reached a T-junction, the hall continuing ahead of us and off to one side at the same time. Squinting down the side corridor, I saw more doors, and turned in that direction.

Naturally, the first door I reached was locked. "Madden?" I whispered. "Can you still . . . ?"

"I can," he said, and reached out to brush one damaged hand against the knob. The door swung promptly inward, and we slipped into the cell on the other side.

It was identical to the room where I'd been kept, down to the rose thorn and iron ropes securing the prisoner to the bed. Whoever it was, they were holding themselves perfectly still to avoid contact with the thorns. I moved toward the bed, bare feet silent on the stone, and my breath caught in my throat as I saw an older iteration of my own face on the prisoner, crowned with a peacock's crown of dyed hair, blue and green and purple.

I leaned in as close as I dared, and in a soft voice, said, "May, it's me. Do not shriek or shout or anything else that might attract attention. We're going to get you out of here."

"Iron in the ropes," said my Fetch, not opening her eyes. "You're not you, you're a hallucination."

"Then I'm the hallucination that's going to release you," I said. "Just keep still and quiet."

I leaned up, reaching for the ropes that held her left wrist in place. As soon as I touched them—as soon as she felt the tugging, however gentle, brushing the thorns against her wrist—her eyes snapped open and she turned to look at me with terrified hope. *"Toby?"*

"I told you I was," I said, trying to focus on what I was doing. The knots weren't particularly sophisticated, but then, they didn't need to be: not when the rope they were securing was literally toxic. May could never have fought her way free, not without poisoning herself to a degree that her body simply couldn't handle. No, she wouldn't die. But oh, she could spend some time wishing that she would.

I could understand that wish. Every time a thorn drove particularly deep or I brushed against one of the iron wires with an exposed wound, a jolt of sickening wrongness shot through my entire body, like I was biting down on a rotten tooth and inflaming the nerve with a sensation more primal and horrific than pain. I had to pause every few seconds to give my hands a chance to heal. Even without the bracelet that would protect me from Bucer's influence if we saw him again, my wounds were healing more and more slowly as the iron built up in my system. Still, I worked as quickly and unflinchingly as I could, freeing first her hands and then her feet.

May sat up on the bed and stared at me, eyes wide and round and terrified. "Jazz?" she asked, in a whisper.

"They don't have her," I said. "She's hiding somewhere—she flew away before I got back to the house—but she's safe, and once we're all out of here, I'm sure you'll be able to find her and convince her to come home."

May sagged, putting her hands over her face. Her wrists were ringed with strips of ragged red, skin lividly inflamed from the proximity of the iron. She had surprisingly few scratches, but that may have been because the blisters forming there had already swallowed them whole. She needed medical assistance, sooner rather than later.

"They told me they would catch her and pluck her feathers until she turned human, then steal her feather-band so she'd be trapped that way," she said, voice low. "She's a skinshifter, they'd lock her outside of Faerie if they did that."

"It's not going to happen," I said, shaking my hands to try and lessen the sting of my slowly healing skin.

May's eyes flicked from the motion to my face, and finally to Madden. "How bad is this?" she asked.

"They have Tybalt, Quentin, and Walther," I said. "They clearly aren't reluctant to use iron to keep prisoners in their place. Oh, and this was a setup from the start. Dame Altair was trying to lure me out of the house so she could kidnap me for her employer. Who turns out to be Janet, my—"

"*Our* grandmother," May interrupted. "I'm not letting you take the fall for that one alone. I thought she was chilling out these days."

"She was, and then Titania screwed everything up by making Gillian go missing for months, which naturally caused Janet to decide I'd abducted her, since it was the easiest conclusion to reach—it also explained why Cliff didn't remember having a daughter, since in that world, he and I had never met, much less hooked up. So she got it in her head that Faerie was trying to screw her all over again, and decided to strike back as soon as she had an opening."

"What does she want?"

I put a hand on my stomach. "What do you think she wants?"

I wouldn't have believed May's eyes could get any wider, but somehow, they managed it. She stared at me for several silent, heavy seconds before she shook her head and said, "No. I don't care what she thinks Faerie took from her—or what Faerie actually *did* take from her—but we stopped trading in firstborn children a long time ago, and we're not switching over to secondborn out of convenience."

"My thoughts exactly. Can you walk?"

"I think so." May stood, somewhat wobbly. Like me, she had only a sheet to cover herself. Unlike me, she didn't bother with transforming it into something more suitable for a jailbreak, just wrapped it around herself and tied it over one shoulder, forming a rough toga. "Let's go kick Grandma's ass."

I led her to the door, which was still unlocked, thanks to Madden. Careful not to make a sound, I eased it back open and led the way into the hall.

The three of us stayed close together, moving with as much caution as we could manage. Unlike Madden, May wasn't content to let me take the lead; she pushed her way to the front of our little group, shielding me from view as much as possible. I wasn't too proud to pretend that I didn't appreciate it. I healed like nobody's business, but she was literally indestructible, and I was pregnant. This made more sense.

The next door opened on a larger room that was actually lit. Walther stopped moving and stiffened when he heard the door open behind him, his hands stilling in the work they'd been doing. He had some sort of rough alchemical array set up on a low wooden table, and was blending and mashing a variety of fruits and flowers. Some of them I recognized from the courtyard.

"I told you, I'm not a healer," he said, sounding utterly resigned. "I'm doing what I can, but if you want to avoid breaking the Law, the boy needs proper medical help."

"How bad is he?" I asked, voice soft.

Walther whipped around. "Toby!" he exclaimed, almost too loudly.

He realized it, too, because he winced as soon as my name left his mouth, looking warily around for any sign that he'd been overheard.

We waited in tense silence for several seconds before the three of us pushed deeper into the room, heading for Walther's workbench. "Where's Quentin?" I asked.

This room was larger than the ones where May and I had been kept, almost large enough to qualify as a guest chamber, if only it had been a little better decorated . . . or decorated at all. Walther was at least free to move around the room. He saw me looking and shook his head wearily.

"They don't need to tie me up, and they know it," he said. "Quentin's too badly hurt. I won't leave without him, and nothing I can do is going to get him back on his feet in less than a week. Maybe longer."

I remembered the sound of bone cracking after they'd hit me in the head. "Did they forget that he's not *actually* my kid?" I asked.

Walther nodded. "I think Dugan may have. That, or he sees Quentin as a traitor to his descendant line, since he stood with you against their First. Either way, he fractured Quentin's skull. I'm not sure how he's not dead yet."

I looked at the array of ingredients on his workbench. "What have you tried so far?"

"I've dropped his core temperature to stop—or at least slow—the swelling, and I've made some extracts of comfrey and boneset that will help the bones knit, if he makes it long enough for that to matter." He looked at me, openly weary. "I understand why running around with you all the time could make people feel like they're invulnerable, but I need the bad guys to stop aiming for the head. Normal people don't bounce back from a fractured skull like it's no big deal. You don't just damage bone. You bruise and traumatize the brain, and if it starts swelling, there's not a lot of space available. Half the time, it's the pressure that kills people in head injuries."

His voice was hollow, pained: he'd seen this before. I didn't know how or where, but he was very much speaking from experience, and it hurt him to think about it too much.

It hurt *me* to think about it at all. This couldn't be how Quentin died. I wouldn't allow it. "I don't expect you to be able to make a full counteragent, but do you have anything that can reduce the amount of iron poisoning in somebody's bloodstream?"

"I could pull iron out of blood, but not while that blood is inside a body," said Walther. He eyed me warily. "Why?"

I took a deep breath, then forced myself to meet his eyes without flinching away.

"I have an idea," I said.

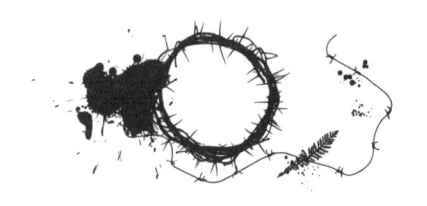

NINETEEN

NEITHER MAY NOR MADDEN tried to tell me we didn't have time for this, despite the urgency of our situation. They took up positions by the door, standing guard. Madden was still in his human form, teeth bared and shoulders tensed as he readied himself to attack anyone who tried to come into the room. May was just in the mood for a fight.

Walther listened to my proposal without saying a word, not blinking or even visibly breathing. When I was done, he gestured to the low bench next to his workstation. "Sit," he said, brusquely.

"Do you think it'll work?" I asked, feeling suddenly unsure. I sat. The relief as I took the pressure off my knees was almost obscene, even though my entire body still ached from the iron in my veins.

"I think we're out of better options," he said, getting a beaker from the array of flasks and vessels, and picking up one of the small knives he'd been using to dice the herbs. "Do I like the idea of bleeding a pregnant woman who already has a mild case of iron poisoning? No. Do I like the thought of what Tybalt is going to do to me when he finds out? Also no. Do I have a better idea? For a third and hopefully final time, no. Give me your wrist."

I offered him my arm, wrist tilted toward the ceiling. Walther leaned over and pressed his knife against the thinnest part of my skin, bearing down until it parted. I hissed between my teeth. Blood welled to the surface, and he drew the blade hard toward him, opening the wound wider until he could get the blood he needed.

Even without the bracelet, I was healing more slowly than I would normally have done. That was the iron in my veins, making my magic sluggish and reluctant to respond. Walther put down the knife, then grasped my wrist and turned it, holding the beaker underneath. Blood began dripping into the glass.

"We don't really have the time for this," I said. "We need to find Tybalt. But saving Quentin still comes first."

"My favorite part of this whole horrible experience is that as long as Quentin doesn't die, no one here's done anything actively *wrong*," said Walther, giving every indication of ignoring my babbling. He let go of my wrist and picked up his knife again, reopening the skin of my wrist to keep the blood flowing. "Kidnapping is an offense, but it's not illegal. We could all complain to the Queen and there'd still be a chance Dame Altair could get away with nothing but a slap on the wrist. I'm not sure Arden *can* do anything to Janet. Do enchanted mortals bound by the missing Queen of Faerie fall under her jurisdiction?"

"I don't know," I said, watching myself bleed. The beaker was more than half full when he finally took it away. I quickly moved my arm so that the last drops of my blood would fall onto my dress. I wasn't going to swallow that much iron on purpose, but I also wasn't leaving these people anything I didn't have to.

Walther took the beaker and swirled its contents, beginning to chant in soft Welsh. The smell of yarrow and ice filled the air, which dropped several degrees in temperature, and the contents of the beaker started to separate, a layer of black forming at the bottom. When the entire bottom of the beaker was black as pitch—or iron—he picked up a pipette and began syphoning off the red from the top.

"There was more iron in your blood than I thought there'd be," he said. "You're moving around better than you should be by this point. I'm going to blame it on your magic. But Toby—magic isn't infinite. You're going to run out sooner or later, and when that happens, with this much iron inside you . . . I don't know what's going to happen, but I'm betting it won't be anything good, for either you *or* the baby."

"So I find that cure sooner than later," I said. "Appreciate the heads-up."

Walther gave me a withering look, then turned to begin mixing my purified blood into a mortar filled with gray-white paste. Adding the blood turned it an odd shade of silvery purple that actually glittered as he spooned it out of the mortar and into something that looked like a pastry bag. He looked first at me, then at Madden and May.

"Well?" he said. "Come on. I don't want us to split up again. It ends poorly."

I rose and followed him through the narrow doorway at the back of the room, into an equally narrow hallway that lasted for only a handful of steps before leading into a room barely big enough to hold a bed.

Quentin was there, stretched out on the thin mattress, arms at his side, not moving. The air was substantially colder than it had been anywhere else in the dungeon—that would be Walther's stasis spell, keeping him from getting any worse. Walther waved a hand and the cold shattered, beginning to dissipate at once. Quentin took a shallow, pained breath, chest clearly struggling to move.

"Toby, I want you with me," said Walther, approaching the bed.

I followed close behind. It was difficult not to see this as a form of punishment, a way of saying "See? See what happens when you let your squire follow you into danger?"

But sadly for all three of us, I'd learned that lesson a long time ago, before Quentin was even officially my squire. I'd learned it in gunfire and weeping, in blood on the floor and deaths that would never be undone. Quentin knew what he was getting into when he signed on to train with me, and maybe more importantly, *I* knew what he was getting into. Seeing him like this hurt. I couldn't pretend it didn't. I also couldn't pretend that we hadn't always known this was a possibility.

He was still breathing shallowly, the skin of his face waxen and unwell. He looked like he'd aged years since we'd entered the house. That was impossible—adult fae don't age—but the appearance was still there.

"Help me roll him onto his side," said Walther.

We were well outside the realm of my limited medical knowledge now, which said that someone with a skull or spinal injury shouldn't be moved unless absolutely necessary, but what he was doing wasn't mortal medicine. I grasped Quentin's hip while Walther grasped his shoulder, and on the count of three we rolled him toward the wall.

I almost let go when I saw the back of his skull. I managed, barely, to hold on, but I couldn't stop the choked-off gasp that rose to my lips, or the rush of bile that filled my mouth until I swallowed it back down. His hair was matted with blood, as was the back of his neck, and the shape of his head was wrong, staved in by the blow that had taken him out. If they hadn't been aiming to kill him, they should have been; they would probably have succeeded.

"Hold him," said Walther curtly, letting go of Quentin's shoulder and leaning in to begin piping the purple paste onto the injury. He didn't rub it in or manipulate it in any way, but it still sank through the hair and into the skin, disappearing without even a hint of color left behind.

When the bag was empty Walther sighed and turned to me. "You can let him back down now," he said. "If I did this correctly, he'll wake up. If I didn't, he won't. I'll freeze him again and try something else."

"We've used my blood to heal people before," I said, looking anxiously at Quentin as I sat on the edge of the bed and eased him back to the mattress. "Usually they have to drink it, though."

"With the amount of iron in your system, drinking your unfiltered blood would probably kill him in his current condition," said Walther bluntly.

I blinked, turning to meet his eyes. "Are you mad at me? Because it sounds like you're mad at me, and I know that can't be the case right now."

Walther scowled. "Damn right I'm mad at you. Root and *branch*, October, Quentin's lying here half-dead with a brain injury because *you* led him into danger. I think I have a right to be a little bit miffed!"

"He's my squire. Following me into danger is part of the job description."

"Did he know that? Did his *parents* know that? Because this is a rather excessive amount of danger."

"You came of your own free will."

Walther froze for a moment. "I didn't know I was walking into this," he said finally.

"None of us did," I said. "We were just trying to find out why Dame Altair kept getting targeted. We didn't realize it was a trap until it was too late."

"Double that one," said May. "I got jumped in my own home, which is also Quentin's home, which means that Toby pretending she didn't need her squire with her wouldn't have been enough to keep him out of harm's way. He'd have been here whether he went with his knight or not. Stop picking on the pregnant lady, Davies, it's a bad look."

Walther turned his scowl on May, who shrugged, unbowed.

"You know I'm right, because I'm always right. I'm older than any of you, and I'm telling you, this is what squires *do*. They walk into danger, and if they're well-trained and lucky, they walk back out on the other side."

On the bed, Quentin made a small mewling noise. Both of us snapped our eyes back to him, and I very nearly laughed out loud when I saw that he was shifting in his sleep, repositioning himself to get more comfortable. I caught myself at the last second, leaning over to gently shake his shoulder instead.

"Hey, sleepyhead," I said softly. "You've got some people here who'd really like to see your eyes again."

Dutifully, he opened his eyes, then yawned, covering his mouth with one hand as he gave me a perplexed look. "Toby?" he said. "Where are we?"

"The dungeon under Janet's house," I said. "I don't know what's up with this place, and I don't care so much. We still need to find Tybalt before we can get the hell out of here."

"What happened?" He pushed himself into a sitting position, looking around himself with bewilderment. He paused when he saw May. "May?"

"You got it, kid," she said, shooting finger guns at him.

"You got your skull cracked by Dame Altair's brother," said Walther. "The pair of them dragged us both in here, and she told me to save your life before they became Lawbreakers. She implied, fairly heavily, that right now they could run without any lasting damage done, just a few untitled ruffians and beasts who might try to claim offense against them, but if you died, they'd have broken the Law, and they'd have nothing left to lose."

Sometimes the convoluted rules and rituals the purebloods live by can work in our favor. My stomach still clenched at the idea that we would all have become expendable as soon as they were officially Lawbreakers.

Quentin gaped at Walther, as stunned as the rest of us. "They wouldn't have done that," he said.

"Maybe not, but Janet would have," I said. "She doesn't know the Law. Or if she does—if she's been around Faerie long enough to have learnt it at this point—she doesn't *care* about the Law. She's outside it. She's been an entity unto herself since Maeve's Ride was broken."

"Maybe she shouldn't be," said Quentin, and there was an uncharacteristically grim note to his tone. I glanced his way. He met my eyes and shrugged. "That hurt. A lot. I could have died. And now you're telling me that if I *had* died, you would all have been murdered, because you can't become more of a Lawbreaker by killing more than one person. That sounds like the sort of idea someone who isn't at risk has and hands to you on a shiny silver platter."

"Maybe so." I stood, offering him my hands. He took them and pulled himself off the bed, and I didn't comment on the bloody mess that was the pillow and the back of his shirt. "But right now, we need to get moving if we're going to get out of here. I'll fill you in on the rest while we find Tybalt."

Telling Quentin about Janet's plans while we were working our way down the hall might be the only way I'd stop an explosion. I no longer thought we needed to be completely silent—and we couldn't be, not with five of us trying to stay together in a dark, narrow hall with unpadded floors—but he had the sense not to start yelling while we were potentially exposed.

He didn't get that from me. With every discovery along this glory road of horrors, I could feel the screams building in the back of my throat. I was just glad we only had Tybalt left to find. If he was still breathing, if he was still in one piece, I would be able to swallow those screams before they gave us away. If anything had happened to him . . .

If he'd been damaged in any lasting way, I was going to rip Bucer apart with my bare hands before moving on to his allies. Even if he wasn't working with them anymore, his service to Dame Altair had put us in the same place, had driven him to use his compulsion magic to dredge up deep desires I would never once have chosen to act upon. Every couple fights. Everyone who's being coddled feels smothered at some point. But if not for Bucer, I would never have walked away and left Tybalt in danger.

It was easier to blame other people, even if the impulse had been partially my own. Given the circumstances, it was probably healthier, too.

Walther only looked back once at his alchemical station, loaded with ingredients he'd probably never seen before and might never see again, before he followed the rest of us to the door. I could see the longing in his expression. It wasn't enough to keep him here.

He still looked annoyed as he turned to face me. I offered him a small nod, and was relieved when he returned it.

Quentin stuck close to me, which seemed a little counterintuitive—it was sticking close to me that had gotten him hurt in the first place. I guess habits are hard to break. For years, I had been seeing him safely through situations as bad or worse than this one, although I couldn't really imagine things getting much worse than they already were. Together, the five of us slipped back into the hall.

Normally I would have been criticizing our captor's prisoner management—leaving us in isolated rooms without guards on duty was nowhere near as secure as they seemed to believe it was—but under the circumstances, I couldn't. I didn't want them to have more people on their side, which criticism would have absolutely implied they should have, and they'd been binding us with iron. That's normally the end of escape attempts. But they hadn't anticipated Madden, and he was making all the difference in the world.

"Madden, I owe you when we get out of this," I said, voice low. "Is there anything I can do to repay you for your help?"

"How good are you at throwing things?"

"Not amazing, but not terrible either."

"Wanna spend a day down on the beach, throwing a stick for me to bring back to you?"

The question was sincerely asked, and I managed, barely, not to laugh. "That would be fine, yes."

Madden looked pleased as he returned his attention to the hallway ahead of us. I looked over at Quentin. "Hey," I said softly.

"Hey," he said.

"You really feeling okay?"

"I am *now*. What did you do?"

"Me? I just bled. It was Walther who did everything that mattered. He mixed the base for the poultice he applied to the back of your head, and he pulled enough of the iron out of my blood to make it safe to use."

Quentin's eyes widened, then narrowed as his expression hardened. "What do you mean, he pulled the iron out of your blood? Toby . . . ?"

I winced. "They had me bound with iron," I said. "May, too. Madden wasn't bound because he wasn't caught, and Walther wasn't bound because he was supposed to be keeping you alive. So they were our wild cards, and now we're out."

We passed more doors as we walked. Each time, Madden would tap the locks with his blistered fingers, then ease the doors open and look inside, searching for more captives. Each time, he would pull back and close the door again, shaking his head.

This complex seemed to go on forever. It didn't feel alive the way most knowes do; it felt more like we were walking through the body of some great beast that had fallen long ago, dying quietly and unremarked in the wilderness. There was no sense that we weren't welcome here, that we didn't belong, only that nothing was meant to be walking here any longer; this was a place for the dead, and we were still terribly, vitally among the living.

"Why?" asked Quentin.

I sighed. "What Janet said in the front room—this was all a trap, Quentin. It was a setup from the very beginning. Dame Altair was trying to get me alone, because the last thing she'd been hired to steal was my baby."

"Janet wants your baby."

"Yes."

"Your *grandmother* wants your baby."

"Yes. I guess she thinks Faerie owes her one at this point—and I can't entirely say that she's in the wrong for believing that. I can't say that she's right, either. Some debts can never be paid. They just get to go on existing, forever."

I rubbed my stomach protectively as I spoke. Janet wasn't going to get anywhere *near* my baby. None of them were. No matter how else this day ended, I knew that part for certain.

We were approaching the end of the hall, and another door. Unlike the others, which had been set into the passage walls, this one was on the dead end, standing alone. I swallowed hard as I looked at it. If he wasn't here, we were going to need to start looking elsewhere— and I wasn't sure how much more walking I had in me. My knees felt like they were on fire. The rest of me wasn't much better.

As Madden approached the door and brushed his fingertips against the lock, I leaned against the wall, trying to take some of the pressure off of my joints, even if it was only for a few seconds. The door swung inward. Madden began to stick his head into the room, then staggered back, swearing more loudly than any of us had dared to be since stepping into the hall.

I jerked upright, staring, as Madden slammed into the wall, clawing uselessly at his face. His hands were too damaged for him to grasp the furious beast that had latched onto his head, spitting and clawing, and even if he'd been able to try, I wouldn't have liked his odds. This wasn't Tybalt as he'd been after my mother kidnapped him, traumatized and lost in the twists and turns of his own mind. This was a King of Cats enraged.

He was fully feline, tail puffed out until it was a visible beacon of his anger, and in his feline form, he was a tabby tomcat that weighed easily twenty pounds. It was easy to think of him as small, because he *was* small in comparison to his human form, but as cats go, he was quite large, and quite capable of doing a *lot* of damage. And he was set on doing all that damage to poor Madden.

I pushed away from the wall and hurried over as quickly as I could. "Tybalt," I said urgently. "Hey, Tybalt, hey. Madden didn't do anything wrong. Stop trying to chew his face off, okay?"

I grabbed for the flailing, furious form of my husband, and winced as he whipped around and drove his teeth into my already-injured hand. Then he stopped, ears coming up from their flattened position and wildness clearing from his eyes. He pulled his claws out of Madden's skin, then took his teeth out of my hand and looked at me.

No matter what shape he wore, his eyes were always green, banded like malachite, and beloved. I raised my other hand and rubbed the top of his head, pressing his ears briefly flat.

"Hey, baby," I said.

Tybalt pushed away from Madden and into my arms, spending a few seconds there, pressed against my chest to let me feel the depth and volume of his purr, before he leapt down to the floor and became a man again, the scent of musk and pennyroyal swirling in the air around him.

"October!" he exclaimed, taking me in his arms and wrapping me in a fierce, almost desperate embrace. "What happened? Did they get you, too? Are you injured? What happened to your hands? Is the baby—"

"Whoa, babe," I said. "Slow down. You can only throw so many questions at me before you stop to breathe, and I have some questions for you. Are you all right? We've been looking for you."

"Dame Altair did something that locked down my access to the Shadow Roads," he said, tone grim. He put his hands to either side of my face, studying me like he hadn't seen me in a hundred years. "Once imprisoned, I couldn't leave. The walls are stone, and the door wood, but she covered the door in garlands of rose thorn and iron thread, like some bitter tapestry. I couldn't touch it. I've been lurking next to the doorway, ready to make my escape at the first opportunity presented to me."

"I just wish that opportunity hadn't been Madden." I looked past Tybalt to where Walther was using a strip torn from his own shirt to dab at Madden's wounds, trying to clear at least some of the blood from his face. "Poor guy didn't deserve that."

"It's okay, Toby," said Madden. "He missed my eyes."

I returned my attention to Tybalt, leaning in to kiss him quickly. "It's good to see you, sweetheart."

"Yes. And both of you are well?"

"We are."

He frowned, deeply. "I know now probably isn't the time to say I wish you'd listened to me about staying safe inside the house—"

"No, it's not. We're here because someone went to a lot of trouble to lure me out, and I was desperate enough to take the bait. That doesn't mean I wanted a jailer instead of a husband. Safety shouldn't feel like something to escape."

Tybalt sighed. "I never wanted you to see me that way."

"We all make mistakes," I said. "But none of this would have happened if I hadn't felt so confined that I was willing to make poor choices for a moment's freedom, and if I hadn't been trying so hard not to upset you. I have to be myself, even when I'm vulnerable, or bad things happen to us."

He blinked, then sighed and drooped, taking his hands away from my face. "I understand."

"Oh, for—this isn't your *fault*, Tybalt. I agreed to stay in lockdown, even when I knew it was making me miserable, and you were just trying to do what was best for our family. If there's anyone to blame here, it's Dame Altair and her damned brother, and my grandmother."

He frowned. "Janet?"

"Janet," I confirmed.

"I'm going to kill her."

"Not if I get to her first. Family privilege."

Everyone else grumbled, until May finally said, "I could claim the same thing."

"Oh, probably," I agreed. I turned back to Tybalt. "Bucer O'Malley is here. He's a Glastig. He's changed sides, and I'm pretty sure he's working with us at this point, but we didn't find him in any of the holding rooms, and he may well be back with Dame Altair."

Tybalt's frown deepened. "The Glastig can convince a person of almost anything."

"They can," I agreed. I half-hoped we wouldn't run into Bucer again; the first time someone had taken control of Tybalt's actions, it had been the false Queen, and that encounter had ended with him ripping my throat out with his claws. It took him ages to get past the horror of that moment, the knowledge of what he had been compelled to do to me. The more recent time he'd been controlled, it had been Titania, and she had again used him as a weapon against me. I wasn't going to let that happen a third time, even if it meant making sure Bucer couldn't use his magic against anyone else, ever again.

I twined my fingers with his as I turned back to the others, holding fast.

"Madden, you all right over there?"

"I should be," said Madden. He sneezed, shaking his head the way a dog would, leading with the nose rather than the chin. Then he sniffed, admitting with embarrassment, "I'm allergic to cats. Not bad allergic, but allergic enough that it's not awesome for me to take one to the face. No offense, Your Majesty."

"None taken," said Tybalt. "I'm sorry I tried to claw your eyes out."

Madden waved off the apology with a flap of his hand, looking to be in far too good of spirits for someone who'd just been mauled by a twenty-pound tomcat.

I looked to Quentin and Walther. "You ready to move along?"

"Where are we going?" asked Walther. "I didn't see an exit."

"If we backtrack to where I was being held, either Madden or I should be able to pick up the trail our captors left when they brought us here," I said. "Blood for me, everything else for him."

Madden whined, the sound distinctly canine. "I still can't walk on all fours," he said. "My hands are too hurt."

"Then I will gladly carry you," said Tybalt gravely. "Consider it a proper apology for my assault."

Madden looked startled, but finally nodded. "All right," he said. "When we get back to where I found Toby . . ."

"I appreciate your willingness to salve my wounded pride," said Tybalt.

We started walking again, back the way we'd come. There were six of us now, fighters and diplomats both, and I began to hope we might be able to get out of here after all. We would get out of this dungeon, back to where Tybalt could reach the Shadow Roads, and then I'd convince him to carry me with him through the cold and dark at least far enough for us to find a phone. I'd call Arden. She'd come, descending with all the fury of a Queen, and this would all be over.

This would all be over.

Tybalt stayed close to me as we walked, his hand in mine, careful not to bump into me, but still close enough that I could feel the heat off of his skin, could hear the soft rhythm of his breathing. I squeezed his hand. He shot me a grateful look. I smiled. And still we continued walking.

When we reached the room where I'd been held, I grabbed Tybalt's arm to keep him from looking inside. "No," I said, voice low. "You don't want to see how much I bled for them."

"I can smell it from here," said Tybalt, sounding half-strangled—but he didn't try to look inside the room, and for that, I was grateful.

He turned to Madden. "Can you follow her trail from here?" he asked.

"Can you actually carry me?" Madden replied.

Tybalt nodded solemnly. "I've carried more for longer. I can carry you wherever you require."

Madden eyed him, then folded inward on himself and disappeared, replaced by the red and white dog that was his second form. He sat back on his haunches, whining as he tried to balance without putting any weight on his injured paws.

Tybalt moved to scoop him off the floor, hoisting him with more ease than I would have expected, given that he didn't spend a lot of time carrying dogs around his Kingdom. He wound up holding him belly-down, Madden virtually reclining across his arms, plumed tail waving joyfully back and forth as he leaned against Tybalt's chest.

"We may continue now," said Tybalt.

He took the lead, Madden sniffing the walls as they moved, indicating the way Tybalt needed to go with jerks of his head and small, almost inaudible noises that never quite rose to the level of barking.

We moved farther and farther from our starting point, my body screaming at the discomfort of it all, my head starting to swim from the need to stop and eat something already. I forced myself to keep going. I needed to get the iron out of my system. As soon as I did that, everything would be fine. My injuries would heal, and my body would get back with the program of tolerating however much abuse I wanted to hurl in its direction.

Then we turned a corner and saw the stairs, stretching upward into the dark like the answer to all our prayers . . . or the final punishment after a long day of tortures. I stopped dead, staring at them with blank, almost unfocused eyes.

I couldn't. Even the thought of beginning the climb made my back ache and my knees want to buckle under me.

May looked at my expression and sighed. "Madden, if this is the way out, can you be a biped again?" she asked.

In a twinkling, Madden was back in his humanoid form, still draped across Tybalt's arms like something out of an old movie. He squirmed, and Tybalt set him on his feet. Madden grinned at him.

"Good carrying," he said. "You should get a dog. If you ever want to, let me know, and I'll take you to the shelter."

"No," said Tybalt simply, brushing the dog hair off his chest with both hands. "But I was more than glad to assist with our escape. I still can't feel the Shadows, so clearly we have farther yet to go."

"That's why I asked Madden to get down," said May. "You need to carry October."

Tybalt turned to look at me, eyebrows raised. "Have you been hiding an injury from me, little fish?"

"Not hiding," I said, indicating my stomach with a sheepish shrug. "And it's not an injury so much as it's a temporary change in ability. I don't think I can manage the stairs."

"She's being coy about how much pain she has to be in by this point," said May. "I remember the last time she was pregnant, with Gillian. She'd have shanked anyone who tried to make her climb stairs after this much walking. She might not have been healing then the way she does now, but she also didn't have iron poisoning then."

"May!" I protested.

Tybalt ignored me, moving to sweep me off my feet and into his arms, getting me into a bridal carry in a matter of seconds. I didn't squawk, but relaxed against him as best as I could while my body got busy trying to repair itself. It was faster without the bracelet, although it was still slower than it should have been, thanks to the iron in my system.

I was mostly just relieved that Tybalt hadn't freaked out over being forced to acknowledge my iron poisoning.

"We are leaving," he said, and started up the stairs. The others followed.

We heard nothing as we made the long climb back up to what should have been Janet's kitchen. When we stepped through the doorway, however, we found not a well-lit room, but a cavernous space that would have made a dragon proud. The walls were rough stone, barely shaped from whatever they had been originally, and lined with shelves that reached up into the darkness until they disappeared into the gloom. That was impressive enough.

But what really made the space breathtaking was the contents of those shelves. They were packed with precious treasures and antiquities, like the back room of a particularly well-funded museum. Among them were bushels of fruit and even potted plants, the air around them gleaming with the stasis spells that held them as they were, keeping them from falling into dust and decay.

Chests and jars of coins and loose jewels were scattered across the floor, as were wooden crates whose lids were only partially askew. I saw a cage large enough to hold an adult Minotaur, and a Wyvern's nest complete with eggs, also glimmering inside a stasis shell.

"We found the treasury," I breathed into the silence.

No one else had anything to say.

TWENTY

TYBALT SET ME VERY gently on my feet, keeping one hand on my waist until I managed to get my balance back. I shot him an appreciative look before moving to sit down atop a nearby crate and turning my attention to the others.

"Find weapons," I said. "Whatever you can."

"There's only three of them," said Walther.

"Yes, and they've already managed to take us all out once. I want us armed," I said. "If anyone can find the fount that cures iron poisoning, that would be a nice bonus."

I wanted the iron out of my system before it could do more damage than it already had. It wasn't good for me, and if it wasn't good for me, it certainly wasn't good for the baby.

The others nodded and moved away, Tybalt staying close by my side. I turned to look at him. With me sitting up on the crate we were very nearly the same height, which made it easier than it might have been. There was a glint of worry in his eyes that I didn't like.

"Still can't touch the Shadow Roads?" I asked, as lightly as I could manage.

He shook his head. "I cannot. October—"

"These are some nasty wards," I said. "Dame Altair said she has an artifact that's setting them for her, something that was probably made to protect against the Court of Cats."

"Such a thing was made, once, but it was lost very long ago, and we believed it had been broken and destroyed forever," said Tybalt. "We would have gone to war against all the Divided Courts to destroy it had we known that it was still loose in the world."

"And I believe you would have won," I said. He was still looking at me, the worry not fading. I blinked. "What is it? Do I look that bad?"

"You have a scratch on your cheek," he said.

"And you almost ripped Madden's face off! Is a scratch really something worth worrying about?"

"Do you think I didn't hear May say that you had been poisoned with iron, or your request that we find a treatment as quickly as we could? I worry because you've had a scratch on your cheek since you opened the door to the room where I was being held." Tybalt reached over to run one fingertip gently down the line of my jaw. "It's just near here. It isn't healing at all. October, precisely how bad is this?"

"It's bad," I admitted. He stiffened, pupils contracting to slits that almost vanished against the green of his eyes. I sighed. "Dame Altair had me bound in ropes of rose and iron, like the stuff she hung on the back of your door. Every time I struggled, I got more exposed. Walther bled me—for good reasons, I promise—and there was so much iron in the flask that it looked like the end of the world. Couple that with how much energy my body's putting into this pregnancy, and I'm guessing it doesn't have the strength left to do much of anything else."

Tybalt snarled, lips pulling back from his teeth in a distinctly feral expression. "We need to get you out of here."

"And that begins with finding weapons," I said. "Go. Find them. I'll stay right here."

He eyed me, clearly reluctant to move. I grabbed his hand and brought it to my lips, kissing his knuckles before I let it go.

"When Dame Altair captured me, she took my knives and my phone," I said. "I don't know if this is where she's been putting everything she steals for Janet, but if it is, I'd bet my dearest grandmother considered them hers. I want them back. Find them for me, please?"

Still reluctant, he nodded, and stepped away. The others followed, all but May, who moved to stand beside me as the four of them moved off among the aisles of stolen treasure and ancient artifacts, skimming through the piles as they searched for things we could use against our captors.

She waited until they were out of earshot before she lowered her voice and asked, softly, "How bad is it really, Toby?"

"It's fine."

"No, it's not. I understand why you wouldn't want to tell Tybalt the full extent of it, but this is me. You're pregnant and you've got a raging case of iron poisoning. How bad is it?"

"I . . ." I stopped, taking a deep breath, and reached inward, trying to feel the state of my own body. It ached and burned, more than it should have after a break this long. I'd been sitting for almost five minutes, and my knees still felt like they were in open rebellion, and like any attempts to stand up would not be met kindly. I exhaled. "It's bad," I admitted.

"How bad?"

"Bad enough that I don't know if I'll be able to walk out of here," I said. "If we can restore Tybalt's access to the Shadow Roads, he can probably carry me home—not that he'll be willing to, under the circumstances. Too much chance of doing further damage. We need to find that fount."

"We do," said May, with obvious concern. "Your magic normally repairs any damage you take, as soon as you take it. But right now, it's not just taking care of you, is it? It's trying to protect that baby. It can't cure iron poisoning—your line isn't *that* powerful, thank Maeve, or you'd be ruling us all inside of the year—but it can spend itself on filtering the iron before it gets to someone smaller than you, with a lower tolerance."

Her eyes dipped to my stomach, then back up to my face. "This is just going to keep getting worse, Toby. If the guys don't find that fount, and soon, we may need to consider—"

"No," I said.

"But—"

"No," I repeated, louder, and wrapped my arms around my stomach for good measure, glaring at her. "The baby isn't ready. It's not time yet."

"You're over eight months along, and you're too calm right now," said May. "Annoyed at me for saying this, but still calm. That means you know something I don't. What do you know?"

She kept watching me, scanning my face for signs that I was holding something back from her. If she'd been anyone else, I would have said she wasn't going to find them. I'm a pretty good liar when I need to be. But May knew all my tricks, all my techniques for bending the truth. I'd been an adult when she was created, and she knew everything I'd known at the moment of her "birth."

"Dame Altair poisoned me to knock me out," I admitted. "But the baby's fine. They managed to clear it all without taking any damage. That means they probably heal the same way I do."

"So a few weeks early isn't going to be a big deal," said May. "The big problem with premature births is their lungs. They're not fully developed yet, so the babies can't breathe, but your baby is close enough to full term that they should be able to breathe just fine—and even if they couldn't, a baby that heals like you do wouldn't have that issue. They'd just grow new lungs if they had to."

I leveled a flat look on her. "Healing isn't painless, May. Regrowing lungs would feel like drowning, over and over and over again. I'm not doing that to my child unless there's no other choice, and right now, there are other choices."

"That won't happen to them, but you may not have another choice for long. Because Tybalt's right. That scratch on your face is still there. I'm not sure your magic can keep trying to protect you *and* protect the baby at the same time. If you don't want to risk dying and leaving your child an orphan, I think you need to be ready for an emergency delivery."

"Go help them find the fount," I said, leaning back on my hands. "I'll stay here and keep this box from floating away."

"But—"

"Go."

May has a lot of my memories, but we're not the same person. She caught the warning in my voice and stepped back, looking at me flatly.

"Just . . . think about it," she said, and turned to vanish into the aisles, following the sound of voices into the distance and leaving me, finally, alone.

I rubbed my stomach with one hand, willing the baby to kick. Just once, just so the sudden fear May's words had woken in me would stop growing so quickly out of control. Because she wasn't wrong, was she? I wasn't supposed to heal this slowly, wasn't supposed to still feel the ache in my knees or the scratch on my cheek.

The wounds on my wrists and hands had sealed over, thin layers of new skin keeping the blood inside, but they weren't *healed*, not all the way down to the bottom like they should have been. They hurt as I flexed my fingers, sending rotten throbs up my arms. Some of them had red streaks around them, implying the onset of infection.

Oak and ash, *that* was something I hadn't needed to worry about for a long damn time. I looked at my hands, then at my stomach, and tried to figure out how I was supposed to get out of this one. It wasn't just the fear of what an early delivery would do to the baby, although that was a big part of it.

It was the fear of what an early delivery would do to *me*. If they didn't have the fount that would clean the iron out of my body, I might not be able to recover from whatever we had to do to get the baby out and into the world—and if they did have the fount, it wouldn't be necessary in the first place. There was no easy answer.

And for once, I really didn't want there to be. Getting the baby out to protect them was the right thing to do if that would work, but it would also make them more vulnerable if Janet wanted to try and snatch them away from us. I sort of wanted to see her try, with Tybalt standing by and anxious from his current inability to access the Shadow Roads. But if she tried while I was busy bleeding to death, he might be too torn as to which of us he needed to protect to react the way he needed to.

There were no good answers here. I rubbed my stomach again, and this time I was rewarded with the smallest of kicks, more like a gentle push, as the baby reacted to the motion. I sighed, relieved. At least one thing hadn't gone wrong yet.

I tried to stand, and fell back to the crate as a wave of dizziness washed over me, the iron making its presence known. We were definitely going to need to talk more about the possibility of an early delivery. It wasn't just about saving the baby, although that was a priority—if we got the baby out, my body could stop spending all its magical reserves trying to protect my pregnancy, and turn them to protecting the rest of me instead. It would still be a race to see if my magic could heal me enough to keep me alive until we found the fount, or were able to get out of here and get me treatment for the iron in my blood, but at least I and the baby would both have a better chance.

I hate iron. Out of all the worlds we could have decided to attach ourselves to, why did it have to be a place with so much *iron*?

Sitting still is a funny thing. It can be a refreshing pause, a chance to take stock and recover. Or it can be a chance for your body to realize just how much hell you've put it through over the last little while and finally decide to start giving up on you. In this specific case, my body seemed to be going with the promises hidden behind door number two. My head didn't stop spinning when I stopped trying to stand up; if anything, it got worse.

I couldn't be angry with my body for the way it was allocating resources. Bodies aren't intelligent. They just try to stay alive, and to protect themselves. Right now, my body still recognized the baby as a part of itself, and it was struggling to keep that part as safe as possible. I knew the placenta played a large part in filtering out toxins, but not enough to know whether that would be sufficient. Would I inevitably start poisoning my baby and killing myself slowly at the same time? And if I did, would it be too late to do anything do about it?

Footsteps in the nearby aisles told me that someone was coming. I tensed, but didn't try to stand again. If it wasn't my people, I might be able to bluff my way into a standoff—assuming I didn't fall down. Once I hit the floor, all bets would be off.

Quentin emerged from the stacks. He had my knives, both the ones I'd been wearing when I went to Dame Altair's and the ones I'd taken from Goldengreen. He also had both our swords, and an arm-mounted shield that looked to be just his size. At least he was thinking about avoiding injury while he could.

"Hey, kiddo," I said wearily. "Where's everybody else?"

"Walther and May are trying to talk Tybalt into letting them do something alarming—May whispered it to Walther, and then they both turned on him. None of them wanted me to hear what it was." He fixed me with a stern eye. "You want to fill me in?"

Not particularly, no. "May thinks I may need to deliver the baby early in order to save us both," I said. "I got the worst dose of the iron out of all of us, because I wouldn't stop fighting against the ropes, and more of the wire got into my wounds than I've been letting on. You should have seen how much iron Walther was able to pull out of a beaker of my blood." The image of the black sludge rose behind my eyes, unbidden and unwanted. It was possibly the most horrific thing I had ever seen extracted from my own body, and I've been impaled on almost everything you care to name.

"How does having the baby help with that?" he asked, coming closer.

"Right now, my magic is mostly focused on trying to keep the baby alive—and that's what it should be doing. When someone gets pregnant, their whole body switches over to building and protecting the baby. It steals calcium from their bones and teeth, it takes nutrients from their blood, it does everything short of steal their wallet and start opening credit cards in their name. That's how babies are *made*. But even though my body is using my magic to protect the baby from all the iron that's in my blood right now, the baby weighs less than a housecat. The amount of iron it takes to do real damage is incredibly small. And with my magic focusing that hard on the baby, there isn't any left for me."

"That's why you're not healing," said Quentin, with slow horror. "There isn't any magic left to let you heal the way you're supposed to."

"I'm healing like a normal person would," I countered. "I *am* healing, just really slowly, because everything else is going to shield the baby from the iron."

"And if you have the baby, things will go back to normal?"

"Maybe," I admitted. "I'm worried that if I have the baby, I'll keep healing too slowly because of the iron, and I'll bleed to death. I don't know that Tybalt's ready to be a single parent."

"That's a good thing," said Quentin.

I raised an eyebrow. "Oh?"

"I mean, not the bleeding to death part. The single parent part. Tybalt would never be a single parent."

"If I'm dead . . . he took a few hundred years to get over the death of his last wife, and they didn't have as long together as we have. I think the baby would be past their majority and moving to the other side of the kingdom before he remarried."

"Who said anything about remarrying?" Quentin shook his head.

"That baby would have so many parents. May and Jazz and August and me—and the sea witch. She'd show up before the night-haunts came for your body and demand to go over the custody agreements she would already have drawn up and ready for him to sign."

The image of the Luidaeg shoving a custody agreement at Tybalt was funny enough to make me snort. "Still. There's not an easy answer here, and the answers I do have, I pretty universally don't like."

More footsteps in the aisles. I held my hands out to Quentin, silently begging, and he smacked a knife into each of them, hilt-first, before gripping his own sword and letting the rest fall to the ground at his feet with a clatter. Thus armed, he turned to face whoever was coming.

Neither of us relaxed until Tybalt, May, and Walther stepped out of the aisle. Walther was pale and pensive-looking. Tybalt was clearly shaken, but doing his best to tamp it down and keep a calm expression on his face.

All three of them were empty-handed. Tybalt walked over to stand behind me, and I leaned back, resting my shoulders against his midsection. I looked up at him.

"Where's Madden?"

"Pursuing a prayer," said Tybalt, looking back into the distant jumble of the storehouse. "He can't move around in his canine form for long, but he swore when he assumed it that he smelled something familiar. He's slowly making his way toward the source, in hopes of finding the solution we need."

"You don't sound too hopeful."

"I am, perhaps, too much the realist, little fish."

I paused before responding, looking at him gravely. "May told you, didn't she?"

"She did."

I turned to Walther. "But you agree that it's dangerous, right?"

"There are enough jarred herbs and salves here that I might be able to cobble together something that would help you," he said. "I don't know that I can do anything about the iron already in your system, not without better ingredients or the fount we've been seeking. But that doesn't make May's suggestion a bad one, only a complicated one. Your body's ability to repair itself is stronger than any

I've ever seen. If we can take off some of the strain, you might be able to recover from the operation and the iron poisoning."

"It's not that bad," I protested.

Walther looked at me levelly. "October, your eyes are bleeding."

"What?" I reached up to touch the corners of my eyes, looking for proof that he was telling the truth. I found a slight dampness, but nothing more than that. Relieved, I lowered my hand.

My fingertips were smeared with red.

"Oh," I said, numbness washing over me.

"It's not catastrophic yet, but it's getting worse," said Walther. "That scratch on your face still isn't healing. You've got a lot more iron in your system than I think is safe for you. May's right. We need to deliver that baby, now."

"I—but—but it's not time." I looked helplessly at Tybalt. "We don't even have a name. And I haven't had a chance to tell the Luidaeg we want her to be the godmother."

Walther blanched, but to his credit, didn't say anything about us trusting the sea witch with our child.

Tybalt stroked my hair back from my face with one hand. "It's all right, little fish. The time is never precisely right for all things, and this is far from ideal, but we can make this work."

"Did they tell you what Janet wants to do?" I demanded, grabbing the front of his shirt with both hands. "Did they tell you why she was setting traps for me? Why she asked Dame Altair to lure me out in the first place?"

"They did." He moved his hand, sliding it down to press flat above my heart. "She doesn't have a hope chest. What she desires cannot come to pass. And if she lays so much as a single finger upon our child, she won't have a hand to hold with. Immortality doesn't mean invincibility. It never has."

I sighed. "How are you so calm?"

"Oh, doubt not that I am in a state of full and genuine panic," he said, with a hint of humor. "But one thing I've learned from my time beside you is this: when we are together, the impossible comes to pass with remarkable frequency and fervor. So let me panic. Let the fates rage. Let the stars tremble in the heavens, should they feel the need, and I will stand by your side, and I will see what cannot be brought to pass with skill, grace, and an utter lack of hesitation. The pain will be yours, my love. The fear will be shared between us, but I know enough of a woman about to face the birthing bed to know that the lion's share will be yours to harbor. I can retain my calm in the face of tempests ahead so that one of us will stand sentry at the gate."

"I'm not sure I understood half of that," I said, and looked to May, feeling obscurely better. "He gets all archaic when he's worked up."

"At least he's not speaking in iambic pentameter yet," said my Fetch, sounding halfway amused. "When he starts that, we need to watch out."

"Heavens defend us from a Shakespearean soliloquy," I agreed. "Do you really think you can do this?"

"You know I remember lives lived before yours," said May delicately. "Other times, other faces. Other professions."

"I do," I said. Most of who May was came from a combination of my memories and the memories of a young changeling girl named Darice Lorimer—Dare. But she had other memories under those, bits and pieces of the various people whose faces she'd worn during her centuries among the night-haunts.

"Among them was a stint working under Gilad's medic, as an assistant and adjutant. What a human doctor would call a nursing aide. I've never been a midwife, but I've assisted in the delivery of my share of babies. And I know where to cut."

Those last words fell ominously between us, heavier than they should have been with all the implications of the idea. Her knowing where to cut made it make a little more sense that she'd been the one to suggest this course of action; she could do whatever was possible to minimize the damage.

Not normally something I needed to worry about very much, but under the circumstances, the concern seemed like a good thing.

"Do you have any of that boneset left?" I asked, turning my attention to Walther.

He shook his head. "I left that whole setup back in the room where they were holding us. But I saw some alchemical equipment in the crates while we were searching for the anti-iron fount. I can probably cobble something together."

"And I found some blankets," said Quentin, clearly desperate to contribute.

"Then let's do this horrible, awful, necessary thing," I said, sagging against Tybalt. I was so damn tired. The exhaustion was sinking into my bones, making it difficult to stay upright. It was like all the concern was giving me permission to be as tired as I actually already was, and now I couldn't fight it off. "May? Do you have a knife?"

"I'll find something," she said, confidently. "Don't worry."

"No. I'm not worried. I just . . ." I lifted my arm with what felt like an impossible effort, reaching into the front of my magically tailored gown, and for the second time, retrieved the shell knife the Luidaeg had given me. I held it out toward May, feeling it slip through my numb fingers, unable to grab it before it clattered to the ground. "Luidaeg's . . . gift . . ."

My limbs felt like they were getting heavier by the second. The iron was singing in my blood, wordless and atonal, jerking the rest of my body's rhythms along in its wake. This wasn't right. This wasn't how I was supposed to die.

At least this was more recognizable as iron poisoning than the slowly growing ache in my joints had been. I knew how to deal with iron singing through me, iron refusing to let me rest. My skin crawled with invisible ants, and I couldn't find the focus to lift my arms and slap at them. I just continued to lean against Tybalt, trying not to whimper in time with the iron-song inside me.

Gentle as he'd been when he rescued me from the false Queen's dungeons, Tybalt scooped me off the crate and into his arms. Quentin must have gone to fetch those blankets he'd mentioned, because when Tybalt lowered me to the ground, there was something soft there to cradle me. Plenty of somethings—the floor was hard stone, like the walls, and yet I felt like I was sinking into a featherbed fit for a queen. I wanted to turn my head and look at it. My body refused to oblige.

Tybalt must have seen the strain, because he leaned close to my ear and murmured, "Take some delight in the fact that we are about to destroy a king's ransom in fine silks and tapestries. Some of them feel woven with old magics, and those may recover, but the rest will be rags when we're done with them. Such riches to welcome our child into the world. Rejoice."

I couldn't reply, but I could close my eyes and smile, the slightest upward quirk of my lips.

There was a clatter as Walther returned and dumped alchemical supplies onto the floor next to me, then began quickly jamming them together. I couldn't see him, but I could hear every sound he made.

"She's starting to go rigid," said Tybalt, worry in his tone.

"That's one of the later stages of iron poisoning," said Walther. "Her organs will start to fail soon. We need to get this done. She needs her magic to focus on keeping her alive, not split its attention between them. May?"

"On it," said May. I felt her hike my dress up over my hips, baring my stomach. "Do you have anything I can use to sterilize this?"

"It's Toby. Infection is the least of our worries."

"It's not *just* Toby."

"Don't cut the baby and you'll be fine," said Tybalt, voice gone as stiff as I felt. He sounded like he was talking through the veil of propriety and loathing that he used to pull around himself whenever we interacted, the one that said he was a king and I was nothing but the pebble in his shoe. I wanted to reach for his hand, to hold him tightly and let his presence comfort me, but even that much motion was beyond me at this point.

"I guess a gift from the sea witch won't need to be sterilized," said May, trying to sound confident. Under the circumstances, it was probably the best call she had.

Infection is a danger. Iron is a death sentence. People like the false Queen—and one presumed, Dame Altair—liked to claim that using it to restrain prisoners didn't violate the Law, because it wasn't *their* fault if those prisoners were noncompliant and came too directly into contact with the iron. Under the right monarch, that argument might even fly, and since it's not like we've had any higher authorities to make sure we were doing things the way Oberon would have wanted, that's been good enough up until now.

I didn't think Arden was going to be quite that chill about things if I died of iron poisoning. And even if she was, Oberon was back now—the useless asshole that he'd turned out to be—and the Luidaeg would make sure her father enforced his own damn Law.

None of which would make me any less dead, or Tybalt any less a widower.

"Careful," said Walther. "It's sharp."

"No shit," said May. There was a shifting sound, and then she added, "Don't hate me, okay Toby? This is going to suck so hard, and I just need you to not hate me."

I could never hate you, May, I thought. She was my sister, the girl I'd failed to save, and myself, all wrapped up in one large, colorful package. I loved her too much to hate her, no matter what she had to do.

The sharp edge of the shell knife was pressed against the skin of my belly, well below the apex of the curve and just above my pubic bone. It was colder than should have been possible, and I could feel it freezing my skin. I couldn't scream. Even with a knife that felt like solid ice pressed against me close enough to cut and freeze at the same time, I couldn't scream.

"Is she breathing?" asked Quentin.

"She's breathing," said Tybalt.

"I didn't realize she'd gotten exposed as badly as all this," said Madden, sounding like he was on the verge of panicking.

"Perhaps you should have," said Tybalt. He bit off each word until they were essentially their own little sentences, each one standing utterly alone.

"Can you stop tormenting poor Madden, please?" asked Walther. "He already looks miserable enough."

"Yes, he looks miserable, and my pregnant wife is possibly dying of iron intoxication, which suppresses her magic and makes her less than half as indestructible as she considers herself to be," said Tybalt. "Their conditions are exactly equivalent."

"Boys," muttered May, sounding disgusted. She pressed down a little harder with the knife, beginning to cut, and I discovered there was still something I could do, if shocked by enough sudden pain.

I could still scream.

What I couldn't do was stop myself from screaming, which would have required an amount of self-control that I no longer possessed. "Self-control" implies having a choice in the matter. May kept cutting and I kept screaming, until Tybalt pressed his hand down over my mouth and pushed me deeper into the bedding beneath me.

"Seek silence, beloved," he said solemnly. "We must not be found out, but must complete this action as quickly as we can, that we might escape into the shadows unharmed."

He only got that archaic and stilted-sounding when he was really upset about something, and my natural impulse was to try and make him feel better. I couldn't do that. I couldn't even stop screaming, although the sound was muffled by his palm. I never would have expected to be that relieved to have a man trying to silence me.

May kept cutting, like a line of fire up the length of my abdomen, until there was a clatter as she tossed the knife aside and began pulling at the edges of the wound she'd created. My eyes rolled back in my head, waves of pain threatening to steal me entirely from consciousness.

"Is there supposed to be that much blood?" asked Quentin anxiously. "Walther?"

"This is a reasonable amount of bleeding for abdominal surgery," said Walther. "Come help me measure this tubing."

"Okay . . . ?"

The feeling of May pulling at my flesh was replaced by the strangest sensation, both pain and pressure, as if she were reaching up *inside* of me and tugging. The pain and pressure receded, replaced by a terrible feeling of emptiness, like something essential had been stolen.

Tybalt took his hand away. That was all right. I had no more screaming left in me. I lay there, emptied out and spent, and listened to the others fussing around something at my feet.

Then a baby wailed into the gloom of the warehouse, and I understood what had been taken, and that it had been saved, not stolen. I closed my eyes.

The iron was waiting there, and as soon as I gave in, it had me.

TWENTY-ONE

THE DARKNESS OF THE iron's embrace was dark gray shot through with veins of gleaming red, not black, and it swallowed the world more comprehensively than I would have thought possible. I could move again, here in the dark, and so I turned where I was, trying to make out details. There weren't any. This was a void of light and shadow, emptiness made eternal.

I folded my arms and huffed.

This wasn't my first dance with iron poisoning: if anything, I'd dealt with the stuff more than any respectable changeling should be expected to—although that was at least in part because most respectable changelings would die after their first exposure to true iron. The low-grade, adulterated stuff is everywhere in human cities, burning and warning, but the true, pure, cold iron . . . that's mostly reserved to Faerie. Where it can do the most damage.

So this wasn't my first case of iron poisoning. But looking around this endless red-tinted darkness, I suspected it might well be the worst.

"Aunt Birdie."

I turned to find Karen standing in the dark. As was so often the case, having someone else to anchor myself against turned the space around me into something much more comprehensible: where she was standing was the ground, which meant that below her feet was down and above her head was up. She gave dimension and direction to the dark.

As always in my dreams, she was wearing a white dress like an old-fashioned nightgown, something long and lacy that wouldn't have looked out of place on a Gothic paperback. Her hair was long and brown, the color of birch bark, darkening to black at the tips.

Like some Cait Sidhe, her hair was naturally ticked, and didn't require any dye to achieve that somewhat startling two-tone appearance. Her ears were pointed and almost cupped, like they were something right between feline and fae, tipped with black and white tufts like a lynx.

Most startling were her eyes. When she was younger they'd been an unassuming shade of blue. Now, they were a pale yellow-green, as lynxlike as the rest of her. There was nothing feline in her family tree, and yet I wouldn't have batted an eye if I'd seen her in the Court of Cats. She looked like she belonged there.

"Hey, puss," I said.

"You're not dead."

I raised an eyebrow. "Blunt, but not unwelcome. Am I dying?"

"Yes. No. It's hard to say right now. Your body doesn't *want* to die, but there's so much iron in it that it's having a hard time *not* dying. You're more alive than you are dead?"

"And I'm dreaming?" Karen was an oneiromancer, capable of both reading the future in dreams and traveling through them to speak to the sleeping. As long as she and I napped regularly, we didn't really need phones to stay in touch. Of course, that implied that either of us voluntarily "slept," rather than being knocked unconscious.

She shook her head. "Not exactly. You're dreaming enough for me to reach you, but you're not dreaming so much that I can look around and tell your future from what you're dreaming *of*."

"I had the baby. Didn't I? They performed an emergency C-section on me to get the baby out and away from the iron, and to give my body a chance to put itself back together without diverting all its resources to protecting the baby."

Karen nodded. "That happened. The baby is fine, Aunt Birdie, breathing and crying and fine. Do you want to know—?"

"Tybalt and I were going to find out at the same time," I said. "Jin had some tests she could have performed that would tell us whether we were having a boy or a girl, but we wanted to be surprised. Well, I guess we didn't manage that one, did we?"

"No," said Karen. "He already knows, and it's not that important in the greater scope of a life. It's just the only thing I have to reassure you with right now."

"Then yeah. I'd like to know."

"It's a girl," said Karen, and smiled earnestly. "You need to get better so you can go and meet her. She's beautiful."

"I'm not sure I have much control over whether I get better, puss. There's all this iron I have to worry about before I can do that."

"Walther is doing his best," said Karen. "You'll see, when you wake up. It's going to be all right. Is there anything you need from me?"

"Yeah," I said. The Luidaeg had taken over Karen's education as soon as we realized she was a Seer, and while it had been odd at the time, we'd all allowed it to happen, because none of us had any idea how to raise a Seer, especially one who'd arisen without warning in a bloodline not known for producing them. Well, the Luidaeg's interest had turned out to be a lot more straightforward than any of us realized: Karen was the direct biological daughter of Titania, making her Firstborn, destined to be the mother of a whole new descendant line of fae.

Seers are rare. Firstborn are even rarer. As far as anyone knew, there hadn't been a new Firstborn since my mother, and she'd been hundreds of years old when Karen and her siblings were born. Titania had been having children the whole time she'd been in enchanted obscurity, but the spell she'd been under had compelled her to stay hidden, and she'd twisted that to mean killing her children every time they got old enough to start dating.

Nice lady, Titania. Nice like a knife to the kidney.

But the fact remained that Karen had direct access to the Luidaeg. Might even be asleep in her apartment right now, keeping her body safe while she moved through the dreams of her allies. Looking at her solemnly, I said, "Please tell the Luidaeg that Tybalt and I have accepted her generous offer, and would be thrilled if she would stand as godparent to our daughter. I know she'll protect my family if I can't."

Karen looked at me, expression turning complicated. "That's all you want from me? One message to the Luidaeg?"

"I—wait." I paused. "How much can you control what happens in dreams while you're inside them?"

"Real dreams, almost everything, if I try," she said. "I can change every aspect of what happens around me, and around the dreamer.

I can look however I like. I got this nightgown from a book Jessica had, about a girl having adventures in dreamland. It made her laugh the first time I wore it into her dreams, and I liked making my little sister laugh." She glanced down, picking at the lace on her cuffs. "She didn't do it enough. Not after Blind Michael."

"He did a lot of damage," I agreed quietly. "So if you can look however you like, could you look like someone else? If you knew them well enough to know what that meant?"

"I can," said Karen, glancing up again. "I do, when I visit the dreams of people who don't know what I can do. I make myself into someone else and move through their dreams without sticking out and getting myself noticed."

"Then if I *do* die here, will you visit her? My daughter? Not all the time, not every night, but often enough."

"You want me to visit her dreams and look like you."

"Yes." I nodded. "I want her to know what I looked like, not just from pictures. I want her to know what I sounded like."

"I can never be as obnoxious as you, Aunt Birdie," said Karen. "You're going to be fine. I won't need to haunt her dreams, because she'll be sleeping to get away from you. And no, I didn't See anything. I just refuse to let anything else happen."

"You're the best not-actually-a-niece a girl could ask for," I said, smiling fondly at her. "I hope you're right. I want to meet this kid."

"Well, then, maybe you should focus on waking up and finding out what Walther is doing," said Karen.

"And how do I do that?"

"Close your eyes," she suggested. "It's natural to run away from pain. That's what you're doing right now. Focus instead on running *toward* the pain. You want the pain. You want to find it, and when you do, you want to hold on to it just as tightly as you possibly can."

"I'm not running anywhere," I said staunchly—but when I closed my eyes and focused, really, really *focused*, like I was trying to find my magic after overexerting myself, I could feel a dull ache like a prodded bruise just on the very edge of my consciousness. Eyes still closed, I mentally willed myself toward the tender spot, and it got larger, and larger, until the pain was everywhere.

I opened my eyes, and Karen was gone, but the gray iron darkness remained. It might have been my imagination, but it felt like it was split with more veins of bloodied red, lighting up the area around me. The sight made me think that I was missing something.

Well, I had a body, or at least the idea of a body, and I was alive enough that Karen had been able to find me. I looked at my hands, memorizing them, then balled them into fists, closed my eyes again, and bit the inside of my cheek as hard as I could.

There was no pain, only the dull ache from everywhere. There was also no blood.

I bit myself again, harder this time—hard enough that I felt a crunch between my teeth, and the taste of blood, whether real or imagined, flowed across my tongue. I swallowed, and almost gagged as iron filled my throat. Coughing, I spat and spat, blackness into the dark, until the iron was gone.

More careful now, I bit myself a third time, and this time the blood that filled my mouth was only blood, bright and vital and animal. I swallowed it, and for a moment, the space around me was fuzzy and lit from above. I couldn't see anything clearly, but I could tell that there was something there to see.

I tried again, and again, until the blur began to resemble the warehouse, and there were voices in the distance, soft and wrapped in cotton that muffled and distorted them, but still absolutely, totally there. I closed my eyes and bit myself one more time, hard enough to hurt even in the void.

"—working?"

"I can't tell. It's not like I've *done* this before, and you're further away from her than I'd like in virtually every direction." Walther sighed. "I'm sorry, Quentin. I'm doing the best I can, all right?"

"Please, October. Please, my love. All I need you to do is open your eyes. Everything else can be negotiated later, if you'll just open your eyes for me now."

Tybalt sounded desperate, not like he was on the brink of tears, but like he was talking through them, like he was already weeping. There was a bright new pain in the world; not only could I feel the damage I'd done to my poor, chewed-up cheek, and the cuts May had made in my stomach, but it felt like someone had stabbed me in the bend of my right elbow, driving their weapon in deep and leaving it there for some reason.

"Please," repeated Tybalt. "Open your eyes."

So I did.

I was still on my back, and staring up at the unfinished stone of the warehouse ceiling. Tybalt was kneeling on my left, stroking my hair back from my forehead with one hand, and the tears I'd thought I heard in his voice were very real. He looked like a man in the process of falling totally apart. There was blood on his hands and arms, all the way up to his elbows, and the sleeves of his shirt were irreparably stained. There was even a smudge on his cheek, small and dark and silently accusing. *See?* it seemed to say. *See what happened because you wouldn't let me keep you safe?*

I closed my eyes again and pushed that thought away. There had never been a world where I would be content to be confined, to not fully be myself, and neither one of us should have believed there would be.

We wouldn't make that mistake again. I reopened my eyes and cleared my throat. It was a small sound, closer akin to a cough than anything else, but Tybalt reacted instantly.

"October!" he exclaimed, making no effort to keep quiet. Stealth had apparently been abandoned in favor of dramatics.

Having just been relieved of a baby and almost died, I wasn't opposed to dramatics. I forced myself to smile up at him. "Hey," I managed to whisper. "Did I miss the party?"

I heard people moving to either side, and May asked, "Toby?"

"S'me," I replied. "What's going on?"

Madden leaned over me from the left, towering over Tybalt. "You're not dead?" he asked, hopefully.

"Not yet."

"That's all thanks to Walther," said May. "He's been doing ridiculous things with blood since you passed out."

"Walther?" I turned my head to the right, guessing that he might be connected to the pain in my arm.

There was what looked like the shaft of a crossbow bolt sticking out of the bend of my elbow, attached to a long piece of clear plastic tubing currently filled with something thick and red. Walther was there, clearly monitoring the bolt and keeping it from shifting. He smiled thinly at the sight of my open eyes.

"Welcome back, Sleeping Beauty," he said.

I grimaced. "I appreciate you going with that fairy tale and not the glass coffin one."

"I don't want to attract her attention any more than you do."

I relaxed into the blankets beneath me.

Eira had a lot of names before she decided to spend a few centuries pretending to be Evening Winterrose. One of the earliest ones I'm aware of lasted long enough to leak out into the mortal world, where they made her a beautiful princess in a casket made of ice. Snow White. She's real, she's horrible, and she hates me. So that's fun.

Glancing back at the crossbow bolt in my arm, I asked, "Why is that there? Were you using me for target practice?"

"It's there because I am a genius and Faerie is so, so lucky to have me," said Walther. He shifted positions so I could see Quentin at the other end of the clear tubing, sitting upright with a second bolt sticking out of his arm. "Don't either one of you move, please. I need gravity to keep doing the work for me."

I blinked slowly. "What, exactly, is the work you're doing?" My head was feeling clearer all the time, like I was recovering from a hangover inch by inch.

"You and Quentin are both descended from Oberon," said Walther. "The Titania heritage on his side makes things a little hinky, but since you claim him as a son, and Simon as your father, I was counting on the sympathies being on our side. He's donating blood. Normally a human thing, but under the circumstances, it was that or sit back and do nothing."

"I would have had your lungs as a cradle-gift for my child," said Tybalt, voice very solemn. He was holding my left hand so tightly it felt like the bones were bending. I didn't try to pull away. After the day we'd had, he deserved to bend a few bones if that was what would make him feel better.

"Yes, yes, you're terrifying," said Walther. "Quentin's Daoine Sidhe. They're blood-workers, just like the Dóchas Sidhe, and they're incredibly good at borrowing other people's magic from the blood. So I give you *his* blood, which carries the borrowing, and you can use *that* magic to borrow healing from your own blood while your own magic recovers."

"All that blood loss was actually a good thing," said May. "It took a bunch of the iron out of your system with it. There's still more in you than is any good, but a lot of it wound up on the floor."

I turned toward her as she spoke, and my breath caught in my throat.

She was holding a very small bundle against her chest, wrapped in what had probably been a priceless tapestry before someone sliced a chunk of it off to use as a baby blanket. She followed the direction of my gaze and smiled, warm and welcoming as anything.

"Can we prop her up a little, Walther? Or will that mess with your transfusion?"

"We just need to keep Quentin higher than she is, so that gravity stays on our side."

"We can do that," agreed May. "Especially since she's still healing, and it won't do us any good to get the iron out of her organs if we let her turn around and dump them all over the floor."

Tybalt shifted positions, easing me up until I was reclining, half-lying down, half-sitting up. He left his arm behind my shoulders when he was finished, settling to the floor beside me.

"Okay," said May. "Don't try to move too much. We'll take care of everything for now." With this said, she leaned down and carefully transferred the baby to my chest. I raised the arm that didn't have a tube attached to it, getting it curled beneath her as best as I could. I was mostly drawing on muscle memory of having done the same with Gillian—that, and a much-reduced fear of dropping the baby, since I could be reasonably sure that she'd recover from anything that happened.

Not that I was planning to drop the baby. If anything, the exact opposite. I looked down into her tiny face, eyes closed and features just a little scrunched up, like the weight of being alive was still too much for her to stand. Her head was topped with wisps of thin, cottony hair, too baby fine for me to be sure of the color, but it looked as if it was going to be striped.

"She's beautiful," I said, looking up again and smiling at Tybalt. "Not how I wanted to do this, but still, worth the whole process."

"She is," he agreed, looking at me rather than at our daughter. "Like her mother."

"Sitting right here, bleeding to save my knight, not even going to get a glass of orange juice when this is over," said Quentin dolefully. "Can you maybe hold off on getting all sappy until she can stand up, and I can walk away?"

We both laughed, exhaustion and relief coloring the sound, then settled to just exist as a group, me leaning against Tybalt, the baby bundled on my chest, Quentin's blood flowing out of him and into me. Bit by bit, the pain in my guts went away, taking my various other aches and pains with it. I relaxed, sitting up straighter. The baby slept. That wasn't going to last, I knew, but while it did, I was going to enjoy it as much as I could.

After a few minutes of restorative silence, Madden scuffed his foot against the ground.

"I'm gonna go search the shelves some more," he said. "Maybe I can find a baby carrier or something."

Splitting the group seemed like an absolutely terrible idea, but Madden was clearly smart enough to want to give our little family unit some space. Walther was the only other semi-outsider, and he was occupied enough with maintaining the tubing between myself and Quentin that he wasn't going anywhere. I watched as Madden vanished into the warehouse with a speed that would have been insulting if he hadn't been so clearly terrified of overstepping and offending someone. "Poor guy."

"Not accustomed to infants?"

"Not accustomed to Cait Sidhe," I corrected. "You're sort of terrifying when you're upset."

"I have had more than sufficient cause to be upset," said Tybalt. He reached over and stroked a fingertip down my cheek. "The scratch has gone."

It took me a moment to realize what he meant. Then I blinked, turning to Walther. "Are we done?"

"Not quite," he said. "Give me your hand."

Over the years, I've learned that things go more easily when I just acquiesce to that sort of request. Under the circumstances, with a baby in my arms and what felt like an exsanguination's worth of blood pooled beneath me, I decided to be a little bit more cautious. "Why?"

"I need a blood sample so I can determine whether you're done recovering."

Hesitantly, I extended my right hand toward him, moving as little as possible to avoid dislodging the tube.

Walther produced a small knife, the kind normally used for slicing samples off of growing herbs, and sliced the side of my thumb, catching the resulting blood in a vial. The cut had already sealed by the time he leaned away. "You can have your hand back," he said.

I withdrew my arm, looking at my healed thumb with measurable pleasure. "Things are getting back to normal?"

"Seem to be," he said, adding a few pinches of something to the vial and swirling it like a sommelier trying to determine the vintage of a glass of wine. He chanted as he swirled, the smell of ice and yarrow lighting up the air.

A thin band of black formed at the bottom of the vial, leaving the majority of its contents bright and red and arterial. Walther nodded, looking satisfied, and held the vial up for the rest of us to see.

"There's still some iron in your system, Toby, but it's no worse than you'd get after a visit to a place with lots of 1860s architecture. I recommend a trip to see Jin and get it properly flushed out." He lowered the vial. "For all intents and purposes, you're fine."

Relief washed through me, cold and bright and refreshing. I looked down at the baby. "And her . . . ?"

"I did a blood test as soon as she stopped crying, and Tybalt agreed to let me take a few drops from her foot," said Walther. Tybalt narrowed his eyes at the reminder that he'd allowed Walther to cut his daughter. "No perceptible iron poisoning. She healed almost before I could take the knife away. She's totally fine."

"She's perfect," I corrected, looking down at her squished little face again. "She's going to need to eat soon, and that's going to be a problem—if there's any iron still in my system, I shouldn't be breastfeeding, and I never got the hang of that with Gillian, anyway."

"Then we should be going," said Tybalt. He leaned over, carefully taking the baby from my arms. I managed, barely, not to snatch her back as he stood, pulling her to his chest. Instead, I turned to Walther, holding out my right arm.

He smiled indulgently and plucked the crossbow bolt out of the bend of my elbow, causing more blood to well to the surface. This time, it stopped quickly, the skin sealing in its wake, and I relaxed a little more.

"All right," he said, turning to Quentin. "May, can I get a little help here?"

"On it," said May, moving to stand beside him. He handed her a strip of gauze and a wad of what looked like raw wool, muttering instructions I didn't need to hear.

When he pulled the crossbow bolt out of Quentin's arm, May was ready, pressing the wool against the wound. It began to turn red almost immediately, catching the blood before it could be fully spilled, and May wrapped the gauze around his arm, pinning the wool in place.

"Can you stand?" asked Walther.

He was talking to Quentin—of course he was talking to Quentin—but it was a good question. I pushed myself to my feet, tensing against the expectation of pain.

There wasn't any. For the first time in weeks, there wasn't any. My sheet-dress was stiff with dried blood, and I was sure it looked like something out of a horror movie. I reached down to feel my midriff, still ginger, and found nothing there that hurt. The damage had already been undone.

The pile of fabric where I'd been lying was like something out of a slaughterhouse. Even a Bannick couldn't have gotten those tapestries clean again. I nudged the mess with the toe of my foot. "Can we burn this?" I asked. "I don't like leaving this much of my blood around for people to find."

"Anyone who wanted to use it for magical purposes would get a nasty surprise when they encountered the iron," said Walther.

"You'd need a really good alchemist to separate the blood and iron after they've dried."

"Does Altair have access to a really good alchemist?" I asked.

Walther looked unsure. "She has money," he said finally. "She could probably hire one who doesn't know why she's not a safe employer."

"Then I ask again, can we burn this?"

Walther looked up at the ceiling. "I don't know what kind of ventilation we've got in here," he said. "We could suffocate ourselves. And without access to the Shadow Roads, that would mean *all* of us."

I grimaced, glancing to Tybalt and the infant in his arms. Not being pregnant and dying of iron poisoning was nice. Needing to worry about the safety of our child outside the comforting buffer of my body was less so.

Quentin staggered to his feet, wobbling. May hurried to relieve Tybalt of the baby, holding her with ease, and Tybalt moved to scoop my unsteady squire off his feet. Quentin started to protest, then relaxed against Tybalt, letting himself be carried.

"Did you see anything that looked like a way out of this place when you were looking around?" I asked. "I was pretty out of it while you were searching."

"Only you would call a raging case of iron poisoning 'pretty out of it,'" said Tybalt, with a sigh.

"Still."

"No," said May. "We didn't search the whole place—there wasn't time, and we had other priorities to worry about—but we didn't see anything that looked like an exit, or even a door."

Somewhere in the shelves ahead of us, Madden yelped. The sound was distinctly canine, even though I knew he was still on two feet: he had to be, or he wouldn't have been walking. Without a word, we collectively started walking, heading for the sound, leaving both my mess and Walther's alchemical supplies behind.

Really, it shouldn't have been a shock when we came around a tall oak shelf to find Madden standing next to Janet, who was holding a scabbard in one hand and a long kitchen knife in the other. The knife was a dull, poisonous gray, and she had the edge of it pressed against Madden's throat. He was watching her with wide, terrified eyes, the whites showing all the way around his irises.

She smiled at the sight of us. "There's my granddaughter," she said, in an almost jovial tone. "I found your dog, October. Time to make a trade."

"Trade?" I asked, feigning confusion.

"Yes. Give me my baby."

TWENTY-TWO

THE DEMAND WASN'T UNEXPECTED. It still made my stomach contort into a hard, unforgiving knot, rage flooding through my veins. I balled my hands into fists and shook my head.

"Not on the table, Janet," I said. "Try again."

"You know I deserve this child," she said. "You stole Gillian from me, but I can try again. I'll be the only mother the babe has ever known, and I'll be loved. Now and forever, I'll be loved."

"That isn't how love works," I said, keeping my eyes locked on the woman in front of me. Tybalt was to my side, still holding Quentin like he was an exhausted toddler after a day in the park; Walther was on my other side. May was somewhere behind us with the baby. I wasn't going to call attention to her if there was a chance she might be able to get away from here.

"You can't just demand that someone love you," I continued. "I know you don't want to be the villain in a fairy tale. That's what happens to people who snatch babies and take them far away from their families."

"I *am* that child's family! And I'm just doing to Faerie what Faerie thought it had the right to do to me!" Janet shook her head, scowling. "I lost one child because I saved a man who swore he loved me, and when I got another with the King of the Faeries, I thought I would finally be allowed to be a mother. But no. No, his wife hated me for being in his bower, and she swore to take my baby and twist her away from me, away from her own humanity. My lover listened, and while I slept, my baby disappeared into the mist. I searched and searched. For centuries I searched. And by the time I found her, she wanted nothing to do with the human world. She couldn't even see me as her mother."

"None of that makes this okay, Janet," I said. "You can't replace the children you lost with someone else's babies. It doesn't work."

"I replaced your mother with your daughter," she said. "For years, I was the only mother she knew, and if you hadn't known how to find us, we would still be happy together. You're the one who lured her away from me, back into Faerie, where she had no business being."

As if on cue, the baby began to cry. Not from directly behind me, as I would have expected, but somewhere off to the side. Janet's head snapped around, eyes going wide and bright with greed.

"The child is healthy, then," she said. "Bring it to me."

"Don't think I will," said May. "And I don't think you want her, anyway. There's nothing human about this baby."

"Liar," said Janet. "I know October's heritage. I know she still has humanity in her. The baby will as well."

May came into view ahead of us, walking toward Janet with a bundle in her arms. The baby wasn't crying anymore. Somehow, that didn't make me feel any better.

But something about the way she was holding herself didn't make me feel any *worse*. She was walking toward our enemy with my baby in her arms, and I was more curious than upset. It was an odd response, and it told me that something about this wasn't as it seemed.

"You know October's heritage, but you know the balance of it can change once magic gets involved. October's magic was willing to let her die to preserve her daughter's life. Why would it leave the girl human in the slightest? Humanity is a danger. It invites mortality in."

"Not for me," said Janet. She tossed the scabbard away, grabbing the bundle out of May's arms like she was grabbing onto the rope that would pull her to safety. Tybalt tensed next to me, snarling, but he didn't drop Quentin and he didn't lunge; whatever May was doing, he was trusting her to see it through.

Janet kept the iron knife pressed to Madden's throat as she pulled the bundle closer to her chest, peering into it. Her expression softened. "Oh," she said. "Oh, there you are. I've been waiting for you for so long."

"Give her back," said May, without commitment.

"You'd like that, wouldn't you?" demanded Janet. She stepped backward, removing the knife from Madden's throat, and shoved him toward us. He stumbled forward, already turning back and growling. She waved the knife.

"I'll see her dead before I'll see her back in Faerie's hands," she said.

I went cold. My baby could heal from almost anything, but iron was one of the few exceptions to that, as we'd just had brutally demonstrated with me. I glanced at Tybalt. He stood as if frozen, a stricken, horrified expression on his face, not even seeming to breathe. This was all my fault. I'd been too eager to get back to work, and now my cursed immortal grandmother was holding my baby while she was still too fresh to have a name.

I couldn't breathe. I couldn't breathe, and I couldn't move, because Janet had an iron knife and if I moved, she might use it, she might cut and cut and cut until there was nothing left of the child I had carried through so many trials, protected through so many dangers. She lost her baby after Maeve's Ride, but I'd held on to mine after Titania's. This wasn't right.

Janet took another step back, aiming her knife at all of us. "Stay where you are," she commanded, then whirled and ran away, heading for the farthest corner of the warehouse. I immediately moved to run after her—

—only to find May standing in my way, blocking me from my pursuit. "Stand *aside*," I snarled.

"Toby." She put her hands up. "Tybalt. Both of you stop, take a breath. Would I really hand my niece off to that asshole?"

"I—no," I said. "May, what's going on?"

"Promise not to run after her." She turned, walking back toward the shelves to our right, and took something off of a shelf, walking back toward us. The baby, who had been perfectly comfortable on the shelf, made an unhappy hiccupping sound followed by a thin whimper that sounded like it was going to escalate to full-out crying. May rocked her gently, murmuring nonsense syllables until the baby calmed down again.

"She's fine," she said, and presented me with the bundle. I snatched it away from her, staring down at my daughter, who quieted as soon as she was in my arms. I looked back up at May.

"How . . . ?"

May shrugged. "Night-haunt, remember? Or I was, before. I can still make manikins if I feel the need. I grabbed Walther's leftovers, and Janet stole herself a child made of leaves and bits of herb. She'll figure out something's wrong when the baby doesn't wake up, but by then, we'll be well away from here. Especially since she just showed us where to find the exit."

We all stared at her. Tybalt set Quentin gently on his feet, then reached over and grabbed May's shoulders, jerking her into a hard hug. May squeaked, then relaxed into his embrace, waiting until he let go before trying to step away.

He looked at her gravely. "Never again," he said. "Promise me, never again."

"It was a special circumstance," said May.

"Next time, I'll scratch your eyes out."

"They'll grow back."

"Not immediately."

I tuned out the sound of their bickering, focusing on the baby in my arms. She was awake and looking at me, eyes the muddy swamp water blue that always seemed to manifest in new babies. Gillian's eyes had been the same color. Her pupils were round. If she was going to take after her father, she wasn't showing it yet. No matter how closely I looked, I couldn't see any traces of humanity in her soft, round face. May might have been telling the truth. My magic could very well have removed her mortal blood while I was carrying her, not offering either one of us a choice.

The thought was almost revolting. Only almost, because nothing about my little girl could be truly revolting. I reached down to smooth a bit of hair away from her face, tucking it behind one wrinkly, pointed ear. Oh, she was perfect.

She was perfect, and someone was tugging on my arm. I looked up to find Walther next to me.

"If you're done with your beautiful bonding moment, we need to get out of here," he said. "Janet thinks she has what she wants, but we need to get past Dame Altair if we want to make it back to the mortal world."

The mortal world would mean cell reception and access to the Shadow Roads. We could get Madden and me to a healer, we could get the baby somewhere safe. Tybalt and I needed to talk about names—I couldn't just keep calling her "the baby," but somehow, picking names before she arrived had felt too much like borrowing trouble.

We could tell the Luidaeg we weren't dead, hopefully before Karen had a chance to relay my message—worse, the circumstances under which it had been given—and set her off. "Yes," I said. "Let's go."

This time, I kept hold of the baby, and Quentin walked on his own. May retrieved the scabbard that turned everything to iron, and carried it against her chest as she followed us. It felt strange to be following Janet's route through the warehouse, given everything, but it was the best clue we had as to where the exit might be found, and so follow her path we did, until finally we reached the wall.

There, between two large shelves, one loaded down with books, the other full of dishes for some reason, was a door. Either there was more here than just magical items, or a lot of people were distressingly fond of enchanting salad plates and drinking glasses. The door was tall and broad and made of what looked like solid maple, and when Madden brushed his fingertips against the doorknob, it swung open easily, unlocked and waiting for us.

"Good job," I said, letting May and Tybalt take the lead. My instincts told me to go first, but for right now, I had other priorities.

We stepped through, and we were back in the little house in the courtyard, emerging from the hall into the impeccable front room. It was empty. Either Janet had decided to keep running after she got outside, or she was elsewhere in the house. It didn't matter much, as either way, she wasn't in a position to stop us. We kept going, piling out the front door to the porch.

The courtyard was bright with morning light, the sun high overhead and illuminating everything.

Everything including Dame Altair and her brother, standing to either side of the small chicken-legged house, clearly waiting for us.

Fun.

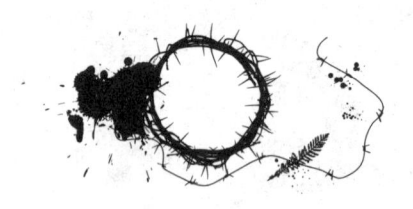

TWENTY-THREE

"I DIDN'T THINK YOU'D really give her the baby," said Dame Altair, focusing on the bundle in my arms. "She swore she'd succeeded, but I knew she was wrong."

I twisted, shielding the bundle in my arms from view with my body. "Don't you look at her," I snapped. "I don't want you looking at her."

"Fine, fine." Dame Altair put her hands up, showing me that they were empty. "I won't look at your precious baby. She wouldn't pay me for it now anyway, since she thinks she's already got it. Unless you were in the mood to make a trade . . . ?"

"Get the hell out of our way," snapped May, starting down the porch steps.

Dame Altair made a complicated gesture with one hand and briars shot out of the greenery around the porch, wrapping themselves around May's arms, legs, and throat as they jerked her to a halt.

"Uh-uh," she said. "Untitled little death omens don't get to talk to me that way. I'm a member of the nobility, remember."

"Queen Windermere is going to strip your title and banish you from the kingdom," said Madden.

"That assumes Queen Windermere is ever going to hear what happened here."

"Of course she is," said Madden.

"Don't threaten my wife," snapped Tybalt.

Dame Altair sighed. "You people are so fond of forgetting that the Daoine Sidhe are Titania's favorite children, which means flower magic as much as blood." She made another complicated gesture, and flowers all around the courtyard spread their petals wider as they released puffs of pollen into the air. Most were invisible, but a few were dense enough to rise as dusty plumes, easy to mark with my eyes.

"Just breathe and you'll tell the story I want from you," she said.

"Two problems with that," I countered.

"Oh?"

"First, that's a drug, and drugs don't stay in my system for very long. I'll shake it off while you're still figuring out what lie you want us to tell."

"That's one," said Dame Altair. "I'm willing to take the risk."

"Okay," I said agreeably. "Second, then: we're outside."

"And?"

"And whatever it is you've been using to block access to the Shadow Roads is *inside*."

Tybalt leapt from the porch, changing shapes as he went, and hit the ground as a tabby cat, racing for the shadows beneath the nearest tree. Dugan whipped around, trying to grab Tybalt's tail in one hand. He missed by inches, and Tybalt vanished into the shadow.

Dame Altair laughed. "He left you. He left his *child*. What purpose does it serve to reach the shadows if all he can do is *leave* you?"

"Tybalt never leaves me," I said. My head was starting to spin from the pollen in the air, and my tongue felt thick. That was fine. I bit the inside of my cheek, and the dizziness faded almost immediately. I tried not to let it show in my expression as I faced Dame Altair. She needed to believe that I was going under.

"He left you this time," said Dame Altair, tone mocking. She began walking toward me. "You look like you're going to fall over, October. Give me the baby. You don't want to drop it."

I held my daughter tighter, taking half a step backward. I managed to turn it into a stumble, maintaining the illusion of inebriation. Like hell was I giving her my baby.

"Come now. You won't even remember how willingly you handed the little bundle of joy over. You'll go to your grave convinced that you fought to the end to protect your child, and you can always have another one. If the cat truly never leaves you, as you say, there will be plenty of opportunities to repeat the breeding."

I tried to tune her out, biting my cheek again and counting the seconds as Dame Altair spoke. Distances were shorter on the Shadow Roads. It couldn't take Tybalt that long to reach Shade's Court, to leave the dark and the cold for the light of another Monarch's presence. Once there, he could save us. I knew he could.

So I glared at Dame Altair and shielded my baby with my body, stalling for time as she approached.

If she'd been quick about it, she might have pulled it off. I was unarmed and still dealing with a mild case of iron poisoning; Madden was too injured to shift into his more combat-ready shape, Quentin was weak from blood loss, May was wrapped in briars, and Walther wasn't a fighter. All of them were more impaired by the pollen than I was. If Dame Altair had been willing to do what she felt needed doing without taking the time to taunt me, this would all have ended in the open air of the courtyard, so close to freedom that I could taste it.

She reached me, and reached for my baby at the same time. I bared my teeth at her, a reaction I'd learned from Tybalt, and was about to reveal that I was shaking off the effects of her pollen, when the smell of blackberry flowers and redwood bark cut through the air, underscored by redwood bark and lightly crushed blackberries. More magical signatures appeared, layering themselves onto what was already there, as more and more Tuatha opened holes in the air and stepped through, filling the courtyard.

Dugan whirled, making a wordless croaking sound. Etienne, who had appeared behind him, gave his sword a lazy twirl. "I suppose we're doing this again?" he asked.

Dugan blanched, spun on his heel, and fled. Etienne pursued.

As this was happening, cats began to pour out of the shadows, swarming for Dame Altair and following after Dugan and Etienne. She screamed as they raced up her legs, and with her concentration broken, the flowers stopped pumping out pollen. Dame Altair whirled, slapping at the cats that covered her, trying to knock them away. Some did fall, but more promptly came, the combined population of two Courts of Cats attacking her mercilessly.

Raj flashed through the swarm, leaping up onto the porch to twine around Quentin's ankles and place himself protectively between my squire and the rest of the yard. His fur was puffed out until he seemed twice as large as his normal size—and he had grown to be a not-inconsiderable cat, lean and muscular, if not as bulky as his uncle. Abyssinian cats tended to be leaner than their domestic cousins, and he was an excellent exemplar of his breed.

Tail lashing, he glared at the flailing Dame Altair and hunkered down, taking up a clearly defensive position. Quentin smiled down at him, but didn't move. From the way he was wobbling, I wasn't sure he *could* move.

Dugan stopped running as Dame Altair's screams reached a fever pitch. He tried to lunge for his sister, but he was too far away to reach her. Instead, he almost ran into Etienne as the man put himself between Dugan and the house. Dugan recoiled, jumping back. Etienne grinned, looking almost feral at the prospect of a fight to come.

Dugan turned and sprinted for the wall that would take him back to the streets of Berkeley. Etienne started to pursue, then stopped, still grinning, and simply watched as Dugan ran straight into Tybalt.

Tybalt grabbed him by both shoulders, stopping him from jerking away, and smiled. It wasn't a friendly expression, more an illustration of just how many teeth could fit into a single jaw.

Dugan screamed. That, truly, marked the end to the fight, and as Raj shifted back into a bipedal form and Arden ran up the porch steps to help the rest of us down, I finally started to believe that we were going home.

TWENTY-FOUR

ARDEN INSISTED ON TAKING us all immediately back to Muir Woods to receive medical attention. I would have protested louder than I did, but the Cait Sidhe agreed to stay behind and secure the courtyard, with Shade taking temporary command of the entire group. A gathering of mortal cats is called a colony or a clowder, but watching her patrol the edges with her lieutenants close behind her, all of them feline form and fierce, I could think of a better word for a group of Cait Sidhe. A pride. Like mortal lions, they were as terrifying as they felt the need to be, and more than capable of making their wishes known.

Arden opened a portal back to her knowe and I stepped through, Tybalt close behind, with May and Quentin following him while Madden came through with Arden herself. When the portal closed we were standing in her throne room, empty and echoing in the absence of the Court. The baby gave one small, confused cry, then subsided. I looked at her anxiously.

"Shouldn't babies cry more than this?" I asked. "May?"

"She's early, and we know she was exposed to the iron; I'm sure it's fine," she said, walking over to stand near me and peer down at the baby, who was staring at the world with open eyes.

"Can we get Jin to come and look her over?" I asked.

"Etienne is already going to get her," said Arden. "Duke Torquill will surely allow for the loan of his healer in the service of his knight."

"Duke Torquill can eat me if he wants to argue about whether he wants to provide necessary medical care to his *niece* and her *newborn child*," snapped Quentin. I turned to look at him, surprised by his outburst. For all that his frustration with Sylvester had been growing for some time, he was usually too attached to the rules of courtly behavior to be so openly scornful.

He met my eyes challengingly, still wobbly from his own blood loss and earlier injuries, and I decided not to say anything. If he wanted to make this the hill he was willing to die on, so be it. Jin was coming anyway.

Then hands were gripping my arm, and Tybalt was guiding me to a chair, easing me down into it with exquisite care. I looked up at him, then blinked and grinned.

"You still have blood on your cheek," I said.

"Don't worry," he replied. "It's not mine."

I kept smiling as I chuckled and looked around the room. We looked like we'd survived a war. Madden, in particular, was covered in blood and scratches, in addition to the blisters on his hands. May was almost as bloody as he was, while Walther and Quentin looked mostly intact, if you ignored the way Walther was startling at every sound and Quentin was swaying where he stood.

"I'm going to kill my grandmother," I said philosophically, tilting my head back to look at Tybalt again. "I hope you're all right with that."

"If you must do so, you're committing to locating Maeve, as she was the one to curse Janet into immortality," he said. "Without her blessing, the woman lives."

"I've found two of the Three. What's one more?" I looked down at the baby. "Look what we made."

"She's perfect," said Tybalt.

"I don't know yet whether she's going to take after you or me, but I know there's no humanity in her," I said. "My magic . . . she's fully fae. Already."

"Then she was meant to be," he said. "Forgive a foolish father for not being too angry that his daughter was designed to live forever."

"I won't," I said. I sniffed the air, but there was so much blood and magic around us that I couldn't pick out anything about hers. That would be a surprise for another hour.

The throne room doors slammed open and I tensed, whipping around to see who had just arrived.

The Luidaeg stalked into the room. She still looked mostly like a human teenager, but her hair was unbound, falling around her face in thick, wavy curls, and her gown looked like it had been carved from the abyssal depths, blacker than anything else in the world, except at the edges, where it turned as translucent as the water that it was. Her face was twisted into an expression caught almost exactly between rage and grief.

Then she caught sight of me and it shattered, falling away to leave her momentarily exposed. In that moment, she looked heartbroken and older than any mountain left in the world, like the personification of all the centuries we'd scattered behind us on the path from there to here.

"Toby?" she asked, and her voice was a whisper and a shout at the same time. What little conversation had resumed after the doors slammed open died.

"Hi, Luidaeg," I said, mustering a faint smile. "Come meet your goddaughter."

"I am going to kill you," she said, striding across the room.

"Unless you have a timeline on that now, I already knew that," I said. "I'm guessing Karen talked to you?"

She looked at me, eyes still black with grief, and nodded.

"I didn't say anything to Karen that wasn't true while I was saying it," I said. "I really thought I was going to die. But I should have known better, and trusted my team to get me through the impossible."

"Yeah, yeah, you have good people who care about you," said the Luidaeg. She held out her arms. "Give me the baby."

What had been an obscenity from Janet and Dame Altair was a homecoming from the sea witch. I gingerly passed our daughter to her, and she pulled the baby to her chest, looking down at her face with a bittersweet, heartbreaking flavor of awe.

"Do you know her name yet?" asked the Luidaeg.

"We hadn't really talked about it much," I said, grimacing. "We were both trying to convince ourselves that there was going to *be* a baby. And after the last few days, I feel like the name I was going to suggest is in bad taste, so—"

"No," said the Luidaeg. "No, that's her name. It always was."

I sighed heavily. "Sometimes I forget how insufferable Seers can be," I said.

The Luidaeg looked at me and smiled. "Yeah, we're good that way."

"If you knew she was a girl, why didn't you say something before?"

"Because the future is very rarely absolute," she said, sobering again. "She was always a girl... if she lived. She was always going to be my goddaughter, if *you* lived. There were too many 'ifs' in the air until Karen came to me and they all collapsed, and then she was a girl and my goddaughter and an orphan inside of the year. Then I was raising her alone, and making enemies everywhere I went, and it was terrible, and I like this future better. But her name is still her name, and you should get on with it."

"Right," I said, slowly. I tilted my head back, looking at Tybalt. "What do you think of 'Miranda'? It's Shakespearean and I don't know any fae by that name. Janet's been using it for centuries, so it's technically a family name for me, because of my potentially evil, definitely kidnapping-prone grandmother."

"She tries to steal our child and so you'd name her in the woman's honor?" he asked, disbelieving.

"She failed," I said, shrugging. "I still like the name." I liked the fact that Tybalt's own birth name was caught in the middle of it, mired like a butterfly in amber, where we could find it any time we needed to look.

"It's not a month," he said.

"I've never been all that wedded to that naming scheme," I said, and he laughed, and Miranda yawned, and we were together, my strange little family. We were safe, and we were together, and we were going to be all right.

Isn't that what always matters?

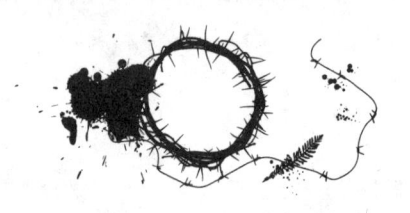

TWENTY-FIVE

IT WAS TWO DAYS before we were all given a clean bill of health and allowed to leave Muir Woods to go home. Jazz had returned before the end of the first day, feeding the cats—and Spike, who had returned from its own adventure none the worse for wear—taking care of Raysel, and calling Raj's cellphone what felt like every half hour to update May on the state of the house.

After six hours of constant phone calls, Raj had thrown his hands up and taken the Shadow Roads to Tamed Lightning to get new phones from April, who was always happy to have an excuse to upgrade our household technology to what she considered "acceptable" levels. With this done, he'd gone back to spending all his time with Quentin and Dean, watching them protectively.

Jin had arrived some twenty minutes behind the Luidaeg, diagnosing us all with varying degrees of iron poisoning—Madden's hands were the worst actual injury, but I still had enough iron in my system to have killed any two of my companions. Jin had been appropriately horrified, and all but ripped the scabbard away from May, deeming it too dangerous to be out in the world and demanding Arden secure it again right away.

The scabbard wasn't the only dangerous thing Janet had been hoarding, and that was why, when we were given permission to leave, the lot of us returned to Berkeley, accompanied by Etienne and Nolan, to go through the cavern beneath her house. Only May and Miranda proceeded onward to San Francisco, letting Chelsea portal them to safety. I suspected this was also Etienne's way of keeping his daughter away from the possibility of action, but I wasn't going to argue with him. Not about this. Not now.

The courtyard looked the same as it always had, perfect and unchanging, save for the cats who lurked in the underbrush and sat on the porch, watching our approach with unblinking eyes. Technically this land had been deeded to Janet, putting her adjacent to but outside Faerie. Kidnapping a King of Cats and a Hero of the Realm sort of called her sovereignty into question, and that was without accounting for the fact that Quentin was the Crown Prince of the Westlands. For the moment, both Shade and Arden were occupying this land.

The little chicken-legged house watched our approach without moving, shrinking down in its nest and trying to go unnoticed. Danny looked at it and snorted.

"If nobody wants to take the little hut, I will," he said. "It's cute."

"And what will your Barghests think of that?" I asked.

"Probably that it looks like something fun to play with," he said.

Dame Altair had convinced Danny to leave us behind with a combination of illusions and compulsion charms, something that the stoic, loyal Bridge Troll was taking very seriously. He'd arrived at Muir Woods only a few hours after our rescue, and hadn't left since. It was a bit much, if I was being honest, but he was so desperate to make up for what he saw as his failure that none of us were going to order him away.

As a group, we entered the house. Arden's guards promptly scattered, going to search all the rooms we hadn't checked before, while Arden and the others followed me down the stairs in the kitchen, all the way to the basement.

The smell of blood and iron trapped underground made my nose wrinkle, and Tybalt held my hand a little tighter as we started down the hallway. Walther made us stop at the room where he'd been held with Quentin, long enough for him to go in and retrieve some of the previously abandoned alchemical supplies, but otherwise, we made straight for the cavern, passing empty rooms and dead-end halls without hesitation.

I didn't have Walther or Tybalt's ability to sniff out a trail, but I had bled all through this place, and the scent was enough to guide me easily through the dark. We stepped through the last door into the cavern and Arden started swearing, seeing the treasures of her kingdom piled up like they were the contents of a junk shop.

Her swearing only got louder as she began going through those shelves. "Some of these things disappeared while my *father* was King!" she said, sounding endlessly offended.

"And now they've reappeared," I said. My feet had carried me back to the nest of blankets and tapestries where they'd cut Miranda out of me, a bloody horror in the midst of all these treasures. Tybalt squeezed my hand.

"Can we burn it now?" I asked plaintively.

"We can do anything you like," he replied.

"Hey!" barked Madden.

We all turned to look at him. He was standing next to a marble plinth, unremarkable in its surroundings, topped by an ornately carved wooden box. He pointed at it with one shaking finger.

"This wasn't here before," he said, sounding puzzled and almost offended.

I walked toward the hope chest, Tybalt still holding on to my hand, and tilted my head to the side. "No," I agreed. "It wasn't. So what's it doing here now?"

"Nasty human lady didn't come back," said Madden. "Neither did mean purebloods lady."

Janet's failure to return was news; Dame Altair's was not. Both she and her brother had been taken captive by Arden's guard, and were currently in custody, under twenty-four hour watch. They weren't getting away again.

The same couldn't be said for the false Queen. As far as anyone had been able to tell, she'd left the Kingdom as soon as her loyal vassal freed her, leaving him behind to face his fate. Not a very good boss, if you asked me.

"So who *did* come back?" I asked.

Madden looked to Arden for permission, then picked up the hope chest, turning it over in his hands like he thought our reverse thief might have left a note.

The smell of wild roses filled the air as he disturbed the handful of rose petals that had been scattered under the hope chest. I gasped. I knew that smell. I knew those roses.

Maybe whoever returned the hope chest had left us a note after all.

Turn the page for a brand-new October Daye novella
by Seanan McGuire

SEAS AND SHORES

Copyright © 2025 by Seanan McGuire

SEAS AND SHORES

February 1, 2016

But truth is truth: large lengths of seas and shores
Between my father and my mother lay . . .
                —William Shakespeare, *King John*

THE HOSPITALITY OF DEAN'S knowe was as pleasant as it had ever been, but my recent memories painted the place as the property of Countess Evening Winterrose, my former owner and forever nightmare. October's presence leavened it somewhat, reminded me that this was the place where I had been reunited with my Patrick, where I had been reborn in love and family's embrace. But soon enough, she had to depart from us on her own errands, and I was left in my stepson's company, with no one to play buffer between us or distract me from the decades of memory the knowe contained.

Dean looked at me, making no effort to conceal his own discomfort. That helped, somewhat: I wasn't the only one on the verge of violating etiquette with my squirming. "Is there anything I can do to make your time here more comfortable?" he asked.

"I should eat something before I undergo my journey," I said. "I have both the potion that will allow me to breathe underwater, and one half of a coral scallop's shell. When I enter the water, it will send a pulse to its partner, and Anceline will come to meet me and tow me down into the depths."

Dean nodded, as if all of this was completely reasonable—and to him, perhaps it was. We were two sides of the same coin, and had far more in common than most people realized. He was the son of a Merrow who couldn't breathe below the waves; he had been sheltered but confined in Saltmist, unable to live freely until he made the choice to leave. Now he was the captain of his own destiny, able to go where he liked and do as pleased him, but was denied the ability to return home without aid.

I had been supposedly free when I lived in the Mists. All my chains had been invisible ones, gifted to me by the woman I called mistress and locked with my own hands, for the sake of finding and protecting my beloved daughter. For me, true freedom had come in Saltmist, where I couldn't leave the safety of the knowe without magical aid, but no one sought to claim or control me. I was allowed to live, work, and love as I desired, and that mattered more than all the open spaces that had ever been.

It would have been nice to live closer to my younger daughter, but I knew Dean felt much the same about his parents and his younger brother, all of whom were denied to him by his choice of residence. We were part of the same strange, separated family, and as long as we shared that commonality, we could be friends, or at least not enemies.

"Marcia is in the kitchen," he said. "She would be more than pleased to make you something before you begin your journey."

"Marcia," I said politely. "She's the changeling who stands as your seneschal, no?"

"Yes," said Dean, shooting me a challenging look. "Are you going to object to her bloodline?"

"No," I said, putting up one hand to ward off his visibly burgeoning offense. "My younger daughter is a changeling. It seems likely my first grandchild will be as well. I, myself, was born a changeling child, and I have no objection to the interlacing of mortality with Faerie's roots. It might serve us well, to have less time to conspire against the future."

Dean blinked, visibly taken aback. "I . . . was unaware of that piece of your past."

"Most are. My brother prefers that we not speak of it. I don't know whether he's ashamed of our mother or whether his wife has asked him to keep it as quiet as he can, but the reality of our origins has long been as veiled as he can bring it to be. For too long, I allowed him the deception—it seemed to hurt no one, and both our mothers have long since stopped their dancing, the one from mortality's sting, the other from the pains of war. I only wanted to be sure that

I was thinking of the right person when I spoke of your seneschal. It is . . . surprising for a landed noble to allow one of the thin-blooded such a high position within his court. I respect you for the choice."

"It wasn't really a choice," said Dean. "Marcia sort of came with the title. She'd been filling the same role for Toby, and I figured well, if she's good enough for the bravest person I've ever met, she's got to be good enough for me."

"Then I will be honored to receive a meal from her," I said gravely. "Has the kitchen remained where it was when I was last here?"

"This isn't Shadowed Hills," said Dean. "I'm not hiding anything, and so my knowe isn't either. It's opened a few new rooms, according to people who'd know, but it hasn't really moved any of the old ones."

"Excellent," I said, and offered him a shallow bow before turning to leave the courtyard and proceed to the hall that would lead me to the kitchen.

Goldengreen had always been a beautiful knowe, and in the absence of Evening's cold insistence on absolute perfection, it was beginning to blossom into what it had always held the potential to be. The air was lighter, the skylights high above us open to allow the creamy golden moonlight to shine through, the stone walls softened with tapestries and hanging coats of arms, many of which were unfamiliar to me. Quentin had no proper coat of his own, not under his current circumstances, and so the space next to Dean's own arms was occupied by the arms of Shadowed Hills, modified by the addition of a sprig of heather crossed with a stylized oar down at the bottom. Somehow I wouldn't be surprised if that little symbol was a part of Quentin's actual arms when the time came for them to be revealed.

Young love has its attractions. It burns hot and fast and intense, without perspective, without comparison. The early days of my love for Amandine were glorious, bright, dazzling things, where a smile was my salvation and the touch of a hand was all but overwhelming. But those days passed. For their sake, I hoped the boys had something between them beyond that fire. Fire isn't sustainable forever.

With Patrick and Dianda, I was experiencing the kind of love my parents used to wish for me, a mature, considerate love that warmed but didn't burn, progressed but didn't hurry. We were immortal. We had all the time in the world.

I walked along the hall, listening to the bogeys scurrying in the rafters above, and stopped when I reached the open doorway to the kitchen, looking inside. Marcia was there as promised, moving between a pot of something on the stove and a wooden island where she was slicing some sort of roast in quick, easy strokes. She wasn't alone: two other members of the staff were there with her, a dainty Hob scrubbing out one of the ovens, and a sturdier-looking Silene sorting through a pantry that was apparently used entirely for the storage of root vegetables.

All three of them looked around as I entered the room. Marcia pursed her lips.

"Ah, the infamous Baron Torquill. Are you here today as the father of my liege, or because you've decided to enchant us again?"

The Hob made a frightened squeaking sound and lurched to his feet, abandoning his efforts at cleaning the oven as he scurried behind Marcia. It was almost comic: neither of them was particularly tall, but the Hob was much broader-bodied than Marcia, making him look like a human child trying to hide behind a telephone pole.

"I come in peace," I said, raising my hands to her, palms out, to show that they were empty. "As you say, I am the stepfather of your liege, and this is one of the easiest passages between your realm and the one I inhabit. I mean no harm now, as I meant no harm then—my actions were not my own."

The Hob glanced around Marcia, looking conflicted, while the Silene turned to face me, tail swishing wildly.

"When the Lady of the Flowers made us think as we were people we're not, I did some things I'm not full proud of," she said. "Bad decisions that looked like good ones because they were being made through me by someone else. From what I hear, same thing was done to you the day you come and made us all be trees and flowers and things."

"Yes," I said, with some relief. "I don't want to name the woman who enthralled me, for fear that she might hear us, but yes. I had no desire to do those things. I regretted them as soon as I was returned to myself again."

Marcia frowned, looking unsure. "Why are you here?"

"I came to land to attend Queen Windermere's Court. I came to Goldengreen to begin my journey home to Saltmist. I came to the kitchen because it's a long swim home, and I would rather not undertake it on an empty stomach." I gave her a beseeching look. "Your Count informed me that a hungry man might be able to find a meal here."

For the first time, a flicker of amusement worked its way through her expression. "Well, far be it from me to make a liar of my liege, or throw his hospitality into question. We haven't got anything fancy right now—just bread and cheese, if you'd want a sandwich, or a beef stew I've been working on for the kitchen staff."

"I will gladly eat whatever my lady wants to set before me, and consider myself privileged by the flavor," I said, and moved toward the kitchen table. Many nobles won't allow their household staff to dine with them, considering it "improper," and so almost all kitchens are fitted with a sturdy table intended for eating rather than food preparation. I settled myself, folding my hands at the table's edge, and leaned back to wait.

The three kitchen staff in evidence resumed their tasks, some with more enthusiasm than others. The Silene seemed to take pleasure in hefting heavier and heavier burdens, making sure I saw how much physically stronger she was than me, while the Hob was slower to creep back to his oven and kneel to collect his cleaning tools. As for Marcia, she crossed to one of the stoves, removing the lid from a large pot, and filled a bowl with two ladles of thick brown stew, which she carried over to my table.

"Stew," she said. When I looked avidly at the bowl and didn't recoil from its lumpy, mixed-together contents, she smiled. "I'll get you some bread."

"I appreciate your efforts on my behalf," I said, and smiled as she waved my words away as unimportant. The rituals of dealing with kitchen staff have remained fairly consistent for centuries—be polite, don't touch things without invitation, and appreciate their stew, and you'll be on solid footing.

The stew was beef, as promised, with chunks of carrot, potato, turnip, and beet bobbing in the thick gravy. There were onions as well, and a mixture of herbs that was at once familiar and surprising to my tongue. I didn't have to feign pleasure as I began to eat, and my mouth was full when Marcia returned with a small loaf of crusty bread and a pot of butter, both of which she set beside my bowl.

"What's the matter, Baron? Do they not feed you in the Undersea?" she asked, almost laughing.

"They do, but rarely beef," I replied, after a hasty swallow. "The chefs in Saltmist are both excellent and understandably focused on seafood. Any taste of the land is a pleasant treat to receive. There are nights when I think I would contemplate crime for the sake of a chicken and mushroom pie."

I smiled to show that I was kidding. When one is considered a criminal, jokes about crime must be made with the utmost delicacy if they're to be made at all. There was a time when I would have joked about self-harm instead, but the efforts of my therapist and my spouses have convinced me that it's better not to behave as if my life were a coin I might choose to spend at any moment.

Marcia *did* laugh then. "I'll get you a piece of cheese," she said, as if she were conferring some impossibly large favor, and wandered deeper into her kitchen, leaving me to eat my fill.

It was strange to be sitting comfortably in the kitchen of a land-based knowe. It would have been strange anywhere, but here, where my lady had so recently kept her courts, it was almost an impossibility. I ate my stew and thought of other kitchens, all the way back to the ones I'd known in childhood, when my brother had been always at my side and our futures had still seemed impossibly distant.

Sylvester had already been fond of racing at things headlong, unable to conceive that he might be putting himself in danger, and had taken to picking up all manner of sticks and such to use as swords until the day when our father allowed him a weapon of his own. I had been quieter almost from the beginning, fond of reading, of gardening, of understanding the way things could be put together. The first time I remembered one of our mothers saying that Sylvester would break things and I would fix them, I had been scarcely five years old, and had taken those words as my personal creed, throwing myself against them until the thing that broke had been my sense of self-worth. Sylvester had armored himself and ridden off to do battle, leaving me behind, and I'd been grateful for his abandonment, because if I wasn't meant to be protecting my brother, I might be able to devote some effort to protecting myself.

Raising children was so fraught. There were so many ways to do them harm without even realizing the risk was there. I remembered the raising of two daughters, but had only truly been involved in raising one—and that child, not half so much as I should have. In the real world, Amy had shut me out of August's childhood as much as she could, reducing me almost to an affectionate uncle who would sneak her cake and encourage her to grub about in gardens, nothing meaningful. Nothing *present*.

But August had still chosen me in the divorce, because my absence had been less destructive than Amy's presence. That terrified me.

There was a scrape across from me as Marcia pulled out the other chair and settled, setting the plate with my cheese in front of me and a bowl of peapods in her lap. She set a second bowl in front of her, looking me directly in the eye, as if she were waiting for me to object to her presence. When I didn't, she began briskly shelling peas into the second bowl, still watching me.

"Where'd you go, Baron?" she asked. "I know it can't be the bread. I baked that myself this morning, and it's excellent."

"No false modesty?"

She shook her head, still shelling peas. "Never much saw the point," she said. "It's always been easier to own what I've done brilliantly than it is to pretend I can't see good from bad and wait for someone else to tell me how skilled I am."

"A healthy outlook," I said. "I apologize. The stew is excellent, and eating it here reminded me of my childhood, which brought up some thoughts that might be better contemplated elsewhere."

"Londinium, wasn't it?" she asked.

I blinked at her. "Yes, but I thought I was well-shed of the accent. How did you . . . ?"

"Well-shed isn't the same as 'free,'" she said. "There are traces, if you listen long enough. And no, I haven't listened to you long enough, but you have a convenient brother who used to associate with my mistress, back when I still served Lily. I've heard him say all manner of things. Plus, well. I serve in a Daoine Sidhe's Court. I can name the origins and bloodlines of every Daoine Sidhe in the Mists. It seemed safer to do my homework."

"Fair enough," I agreed. "I miss it sometimes. Not the city, so much, but the land. The country. The fae have lived in England as long as the humans have, and the land knows us. We followed their ships to the Americas, and this land has never been as familiar, or as welcoming."

"Doesn't have to be," said Marcia.

"No, it doesn't."

"What thoughts came that put you a million miles away and leaving your stew to cool?" She snapped another peapod. "Maybe I can help."

"I don't—" I paused, then sighed and swirled my spoon in the stew. "Have you ever had children?"

Marcia went very still. "Yes," she said finally. "But it was a long time ago, and I don't particularly want to talk about it. Their father and I are not presently together."

"I apologize, my lady, and didn't mean to cross any boundaries; I ask only because I am pondering parenthood, and how difficult it is, and how great a thing to undertake."

"Ah," said Marcia, nodding. "You took your two daughters and married into a family with two sons. I guess that's plenty of parenting for one man."

"Yes, and during Titania's enchantment, when I was given what I desired most in all the world, I was able to raise both my daughters in peace and comfort, with as few dangers as possible coming anywhere near to them."

Marcia blinked. "When you were—pardon me, Baron, but that's not how I've heard anyone else describe that liar's reality. Most people were being punished in some way. What do you mean?"

"I mean that my ex-wife had volunteered me as a sacrifice to the planned Ride that would solidify that world in place of our own, and in order for me to qualify, I had to first be given seven years of paradise. I suppose that since there wasn't time for a true seven years within the enchantment, they opted instead to give me a lifetime of pleasant memories shared with my family. It was a gift, and as long as I don't allow myself to consider the strings attached to it, I'm able to appreciate the moments of sweetness it provided to me."

Marcia blinked again, expression turning horrified. "I . . . no one told me that," she squeaked.

"Put very little past the Lady of Flowers," I said gently. "She has shown us her true colors, and I would rather they not be forgotten again. I can only hope the Lady of the Waters will be better, if she ever chooses to return to us."

"She will be," said Marcia, with a quiet, terrible conviction in her voice. "She has to be better than that, or why are we even trying?"

"Indeed," I said. "And on that note, with a full stomach, I must praise your hospitality and be on my way." I rose, picking up my empty bowl. "Where shall I put this?"

"Leave it, leave it," said Marcia, still looking disturbed. "The Count has so little work for us to do, it's shameful. Let me have the pleasure of doing one of the things I'm paid for."

"Very well," I said. "Am I forgiven for my actions while bespelled?"

"Right now, Baron Torquill, you're forgiven for everything you've ever done."

I smiled. "If only it were so. Good night, Lady Seneschal, and may you have open roads before you."

"Kind tides to carry you home," she replied, and watched as I walked away.

Back in the hall, feeling much better for having eaten, I proceeded to the winding stairway down to the receiving cove. It was a gloriously impossible space, a single set of stairs anchored to the sand at one end and to the free-hanging door on the other—the wall the door was actually set in not being visible once you were on the stairs. At the bottom, a wide expanse of sand extended to a small boardwalk before giving way to the sea, which lapped gently against the contained shore.

There were no riptides here, no storms. The water was always warmer than the Pacific ever deigned to be, because this was a slice of the Summerlands sea, provided for Dean's sake, to make it easier for his family to visit.

I would never forget the first time I had seen this room, hauled along by October and her King of Cats as they presented me to the people who had arranged for my salvation, who had looked at a broken man and seen that there was still something there to save. Up until that moment, I had given up daring to hope that I might someday be free of the chains I had willingly wrapped around myself, of the terrible people who would only ever use me for terrible things.

I walked across the sand to the boardwalk, stepping onto it and looking out across the water. I had a home now, a true home, for the first time in centuries. I had a family that loved me, not only because they felt they could use me, but because they looked at me and knew that I would return their love enough to keep us all afloat.

I walked to the edge of the boardwalk, looking down. For some men, that would have been a pose of despair. For me, in this moment, it was a pose of greatest hope, and acceptance.

I deserved what was waiting for me in the water. I might not always believe that, but I accepted it now, and I was going to let myself have what I deserved.

Pulling a flask from inside my shirt, I popped the cork out with my thumb and swallowed its contents in a single fierce gulp. They were bubbling and faintly acidic, like drinking a shot of lemon juice mixed with absinthe. While I had been able to refine the water-breathing potion beyond what Dianda's alchemists had achieved before I came along, I had yet to stabilize the flavor. Every batch was different, and none were what I would call truly pleasant. Still. Putting the flask back inside my shirt, I stood up a little straighter, waiting for the potion to take effect.

When my former mistress had ordered me to remove October from our world, she had done so in vague enough terms that she would have deniability if somehow I was caught, if somehow I was forced to give her up. And because of those vague terms, I had been able to twist what I knew full well was an assassination order into a transformation, changing the girl who was my child in the eyes of the law into a fish's form and leaving her to the waters. When the change had taken hold, I'd watched her start to suffocate, no longer able to thrive in air. And I had laughed.

I could say that it had been part of a performance, that I'd been trying to keep Oleander's suspicions at bay—she would respect cruelty where she would have crushed kindness—but I had still done it, and the last thing October had heard with her true ears for fourteen years had been the sound of the man who should have cherished and protected her laughing at her pain.

So I stayed where I was until my own breath began to catch in my throat, my lungs laboring against an atmosphere turned alien to them, and when I felt myself on the verge of suffocation I allowed myself to fall forward into the water, gracelessly returning to the sea.

My breathing resumed immediately, oxygen-starved body taking what it needed from the water without hesitation. I inhaled gratefully. The point hadn't merely been self-denial, for all that I found peace in paying pebbles of penance into the sea; it was easier to fill my lungs with water when they already ached for air. Without that pause, I would wind up holding my breath anyway, unable to quite relax enough to inhale below the waves until it was almost too late.

The shell in my pocket glowed a bright and enthusiastic green, marking my place in the sea. I turned and began swimming toward the cove exit. Anceline was small, as Cetacea went, but she was still more than twelve feet long, the mermaid melding of Daoine Sidhe and killer whale. It would be easier for her to take me in open waters.

So I swam, only slightly hampered by my shoes and court clothes, head kept well below the water, until I passed below the cove wall and all the glory of the Summerlands sea unspooled around me. It was warmer than the mortal ocean, yes, but also brighter, filled with shafts of coruscating light that pierced deeper than the sun ever could, illuminating the scales of bright-bodied fish and the occasional passing turtle. We were close to the California shore, even here, but the waters around me were more like those of the mortal tropics, welcoming and calm.

And dangerous, of course. I couldn't be trusted to swim home on my own, even had I been able to find my way, because there were predators in these waters, sea monsters doing as sea monsters did and serving their natural ecological niche. The sea dragons and Kraken were as natural a part of this ocean as the Cetacea and Merrow, but that wouldn't make it any more pleasant to be devoured by one if I tried to make my way alone.

So I stayed where I was, near enough to the shallows that the truly massive predators were unable to come close, treading water and waiting for my ride.

A vast, dark shadow began to rise below me. I looked down upon it, the first stirrings of fear beginning to tangle in my breast, and watched the way it moved. It was approaching slowly, almost leisurely, not with the speed of a closing predator; I held my position. Attempting to swim aside wouldn't do me as much good as I might hope, given how slowly I moved compared to most things residing in these waters.

A hand reached up from the depths and grabbed my ankle, jerking me briskly downward. I didn't fight or struggle. Anything with hands would be a friend, this close to shore. Dianda's borders were too well-defended for me to fear anything else.

Anceline dragged me down and level with her face, looking disappointed. "Aw," she said, voice distorted by the water. "I was hoping to scare you a little. Do you not scare?"

I answered with an exaggerated shrug, spreading my hands. The potion allowed me to breathe below the water, but didn't give me the ability to filter air sufficient to speak. It was a small limitation, and one which rarely chafed.

Anceline laughed. "Well, then, fearless one, it's time to go home. Did you achieve everything you needed?"

I nodded.

She smiled. "Then hold fast," she advised, and drew me close to her before diving down, moving faster than I could ever have accomplished on my own.

I wrapped my arms around as much of her torso as I could manage and held fast, watching avidly as the sea whipped by. This was my favorite part of the journey between Saltmist and the shore: the return, when I could see all the sea unfolding to surround us in a brilliant tapestry of life and color. We dove, and the sea scintillated around us, prismatic and glorious, until we broke through the last barrier between the open water and Saltmist itself.

We entered above the fields that were tended by Dianda's subjects, growing sea fruits and grains, as well as shellfish and mollusks. Abalone farming was remarkably akin to potato farming in many ways, although I was under the distinct impression that potatoes moved less. Farmers and field hands looked up at us as we passed, some waving, while others merely returned to their work.

Herders and hunters also passed below us, the former with their schools of fish or fevers of rays, the later with their nets and latest kills. One young Easgann we passed was herding a full shiver of sharks, and I was very impressed by his calm as he directed beasts even larger than he was, but couldn't stop to say so. The palace had appeared in the distance.

We were almost home.

The first time I had seen the palace of Saltmist, it had felt like something out of a dream, a fantasy I would doubtless destroy by reaching for it. It still felt like a dream, a confection of mother-of-pearl and coral rising up from the seafloor, but now it was a dream I could attain, a place I could—and did—belong. Anceline pulled me closer and closer, her mighty tail beating against the tide. When we were close enough that I could have reached out and touched the walls, she stopped, hovering in front of an opening in the wall as she released me.

I paddled a few feet away, then turned back to her and made the sign I had learned meant appreciation before ducking into the opening, which led to a tunnel well wide enough to let me pass, but could never have accommodated Anceline. There were handholds built into the wall. I grasped them firmly, pulling myself upward without giving in to the urge to float. My lungs were empty of air; I was nowhere near so buoyant as I naturally assumed myself to be, and my potion would only last for so long.

A claustrophobic person would have extreme difficulty with the last stretch required to enter the palace of Saltmist. I pulled myself further upward, head breaking the surface of the shallow pool in the arrival chamber. Spitting water in as decorous a manner as possible, I inhaled, and promptly started coughing.

The potion which allows us to breathe water cannot change water's essential nature; it is a liquid, and our lungs are built for gasses. When I breathed in, water and air met in my throat, and each attempted to assert their dominance. Still coughing, I pulled myself over to the edge of the pool and leaned against the rim, waiting for the tail end of the potion to wear off and my body to sort itself out.

It was always more comfortable to wait in the water for the potion to finish its work. It came with no physical changes—yet; I was working on that—but still, the body preferred to remain damp while the potion was in effect. I wasn't the only one to feel its effects so. Patrick and August both reported the same. I had yet to sit down and discuss the experience with Dean, but I would be truly surprised if his was not something similar.

The coughing got worse as I waited, and then, abruptly, the water in my lungs became an aching irritant, heavy and painful. I lurched from the pool to the basins against the wall, vomiting up the water I had inhaled. That, too, was part of the potion, its last attempt to protect its users: when it wore off, we expelled all inhaled water immediately. We did not drown, and we did not risk aspirational pneumonia. Truly, it was a well-designed tincture, and I was a fool to think I could improve upon it. I was—

I was not going to indulge in self-hatred, not even within the privacy of my own mind. Cruel thoughts were acid for the bedrock of the self, and they aided nothing. I pushed myself away from the basin, wiping the water from my chin. There was nothing to be done for the water dripping from my clothing. I have my talents, but I'm no Naiad, to sculpt water to my desires, or even a Merrow, to convince the water to flow away from me when I need it to. I would simply have to drip until I found my way to someone who could dry me off.

No one had yet come to greet me. That was odd, but not entirely unheard of; Patrick knew I didn't like it when people watched me vomit, and would sometimes allow himself to be distracted from my returning, and August was not yet so attuned to the palace wards as to know all my comings and goings so precisely. Still, it was difficult not to feel a small twinge of sadness as I left the room for the empty hall behind.

I am not ashamed to admit that I am a social creature, choosing solitude only when necessary for my work, preferring the company of friends and family to my own. I like to talk, to understand and be understood. After I began seeing Dr. Voss, Dianda said the first true sign of my recovery was the way I never stopped talking. There was a time when I would have taken that for an insult, but she had been smiling as she said it, and had kissed me later that night with all the tenderness a heart could hold, still smiling all the while. I had married into a family that liked to hear what I had to say and actually wanted to *talk* to me, and that was perhaps the greatest and most unearned blessing of them all.

Sorrow nearly killed me. But it was silence that came closest to destroying me.

I walked briskly down the hall, shoes sloshing with every step, confusion growing as the absence of my family became more and more noticeable. We weren't under any sort of attack; Dianda wasn't bolstering the defenses or singing in storms to sweep her enemies away. Patrick was fond of tinkering in his lab, and could easily lose track of time that way, but had never shown any inclination to do so when I was out of the Duchy, preferring to fret over whether or not I would be able to safely return. And the children . . .

Peter was not yet overly concerned about my whereabouts, but August was prone to panic attacks when she didn't know precisely where to find me, and had been known to use the viewing window in her room to keep tabs on my location, reassuring herself that I was safe. It wasn't the healthiest behavior, but as long as it didn't become obsessive enough to be self-destructive, it was allowable. She was an adult, and she had good reason for her fears. I wasn't going to interfere.

She should have been at the arrival chamber, or nearby, when I returned. That she hadn't been was both strange and concerning. I walked a little faster.

Voices drifted back to me from somewhere up ahead, familiar but too faint for me to immediately recognize them. I relaxed; the knowe wasn't deserted. I didn't slow down, however, and in short order was turning to face an open doorway, an organic arch in the nacreous wall of the knowe, leading into a chamber that appeared to have been carved from living coral, with polished lilac walls and furniture grown of the same stuff, its arms and branches allowed to retain their original shape.

Two women occupied the room, both seated in cupped chairs of coral. One, blonde and whisper-thin, with enormous blue eyes that seemed to make up more of her face than was physically possible, the other dark-haired and lushly curved, with shark belly–pale skin speckled with tiny scales and two long, sinuous tails where most people's legs would have been. They each ended in fins, rather than tapering off like tentacles, and that marked her as more sea monster than serpent. Not that she would have rejected either title.

Both were wearing simple, almost Grecian gowns that would have been out of fashion in any land court, but seemed perfectly reasonable here. Perhaps such things had changed more slowly beneath the sea, where human taboos had been less successful in penetrating, and covering one's nakedness was more a matter of preference.

I recovered from my shock with what felt, to me, like admirable quickness, and dipped into a bow. "My Lady Amphitrite, it is an honor," I said.

"That's Captain Pete to you, landlubber," she said, almost laughing.

"Ah, but you come not in a captain's bold array, but in a courtly visitor's attire, so I assumed you bore the associated title."

"Am I not allowed to gown myself more comfortably to meet my heir?" she asked, almost laughing.

I froze.

Like October, Dianda had been pregnant when Titania's spell consumed us; unlike October, she had not yet been aware, and had thus not informed me of her condition. Upon realizing that she was with child and I was prisoned in an enchantment that robbed me of knowing who she was, she had gone to her Firstborn, Amphitrite, known also as the Mother of Sharks and the Devouring Deep, to ask for aid.

Unsure of what would be needed to bring me back to them, Dianda had given her pregnancy over to her ancestor to protect until such time as she was able to reclaim it, which she had done after my return, after first explaining the situation to me in the clearest terms she could manage. "I didn't want to have a baby when one of the possible fathers was unaware of who we were to each other, so I gave my pregnancy to one of the Firstborn to carry, and now I'm ready to be pregnant again" was an odd sort of thing to hear from one's wife, but far better than many of the alternatives.

But while Amphitrite was not her sister, the sea witch, asking her to carry the child did come with a cost: namely, she needed an heir for the Duchy of Ships, being done with the process of conceiving and raising her own children. I had negotiated the point as best I could, convincing her not to take the child until their seventeenth birthday, and not to hold them against their will if they wanted to come home, but the end result had been her desire. Our child would be born already tithed to the Duchy of Ships, sworn to Amphitrite before they drew their first breath.

Sometimes it is a terrible thing, to be born of Faerie.

The blue-eyed woman turned to me, all smiles. Her expression was slightly vacant, as it almost always was. "My Pat is with his lady even now, to herald the arrival of a new daughter of the sea," she said, happily. "If you hurry, you may be able to arrive before Hydor floods the birthing chamber. You're already quite drenched, so it won't damage your clothing either way."

"Oh—oh!" Hydor was the name of the Naiad colony that lived here in the knowe. They kept the air-filled chambers where Patrick, August, and I spent most of our time dry and safe for us to use. Without them, we would have been at the mercy of the deeps—and the deeps are very rarely merciful. I took a step back, heart pounding. "I—which way do I go?"

This wasn't a discussion we had yet had, either individually or as a family. The woman smiled serenely.

"Go to the hall and all will be answered," she said.

"You are a miracle, Mary. I won't forget this," I said, and ducked out to the hall.

Mary was the oldest Roane I had ever met, old enough to remember Cailleach Skerry, where her descendant line had originally lived with their mother, the Luidaeg. I didn't think she was one of the Luidaeg's children, but a grandchild, perhaps? It wasn't outside the realm of possibility. Because of her nearness to her line's beginning, she held the gift of prophecy in both hands, and sometimes it threatened to consume her. If she said we were heralding a new daughter of the sea, then August was to have another sister. I remembered the look on her face the first time she'd been handed the infant October, and I couldn't wait to see that expression again.

For real, this time, with none of Titania's involvement. Everything that was about to happen was real.

I stepped back into the hall, looking anxiously around, and was unsurprised to see a woman with cherry-red hair and the lower body of an octopus racing along the ceiling toward me. "Master Lorden!" she exclaimed, as she drew near. "You have to come with me!"

"I've just been waiting for someone to show me where to go," I said.

She passed overhead, one tentacle whipping down to wrap around my wrist, and continued onward, clearly set on dragging me along. I didn't fight, but ran behind her, letting myself be pulled.

"How are you, Helmi?" I asked, as I ran.

"Exceeding cross with you, that you felt the need to depart so near to the birthing!" she chided.

"I thought we had another month," I said.

"The babe was carried by one among the First for *weeks*," she said. "How could we expect anything so common as a predictable timeline?"

It was a fair enough question, and I decided not to argue with it, but to focus on running without my wet shoes slipping on the floor.

We ran until we reached a door I didn't know. Peter and August waited outside; Patrick was nowhere to be seen. Helmi released my wrist, slithering down onto the wall and producing a flask from inside her wrapped top. I took it without hesitation, offering her a shallow bow in thanks, and turned to the children.

"What have I missed?" I asked.

"Oh, *Papa*!" shouted August, throwing her arms around my shoulders and crushing me into a swift embrace. "Dianda's been in labor for the past hour. We thought you were going to miss everything!"

"Do Merrow have their children so quickly as all of that?"

"Often," said Peter. "But Mom's fifty-fifty for kids being born with legs and with tails, and legs slow everything down. Still, you should probably get in there."

I looked at the flask in my hand. "Am I to assume they've flooded the room?"

"They had to," said August. "If the baby isn't born in water, they may never learn to breathe it. They may never learn to breathe it either way, but a water-born baby can be taken quickly to the air if needed. An air-born baby who *could* have breathed water may never get the knack."

"Truly?"

"No one knows," said Helmi. "Mistress Mary ordered the chamber flooded for Dean's birth, even though he would never have the knack of breathing wet. Said his parents would wonder forever if they'd done something wrong if they birthed him dry. And these are all very good things to wonder and ask, but do you think you could do that *later*? Perhaps?"

"Oh!" I turned back toward the closed door. "How am I to . . . ?"

"Doors can open, Papa," said August, almost teasingly. "Hydor will hold the water where it belongs."

"How many of her are in there?"

"Five that I counted," said August, giving me a little push toward the door. "Come on, Papa. I want to meet my new sibling before Peter weasels his way in there, so they'll like *me* best of all."

"Hey!" objected Peter.

"Hay is for hippocampi," said August primly. "Are you a seahorse?"

I left them squabbling, swallowing the contents of the flask—lemons and salt this time, with a thin but not unpleasant ribbon of treacle—as I pushed the door open to reveal the flooded room beyond. The water stopped at the doorframe, politely remaining confined rather than rushing out into the hall.

Dianda, in full Merrow form, was stretched out on the bed at the center of the room, her hands knotted through loops of kelp that both gave her something to hold on to and kept her from floating away. She turned toward the sound of the door swinging open, face relaxing into a pained, exhausted smile when she saw me.

"Took you long enough," she said. "Close the door, we've got spies."

I glanced back at August's and Peter's inquisitive faces, then closed the door, blocking their view of the birthing chamber. I returned my attention to Dianda. The swell of her belly had grown even in the past few days, until she seemed to be almost more stomach than mermaid. I hadn't seen her legs in well over a week, as she preferred to stay in the water as much as she possibly could, letting it take the weight off her back. Now, seeing her stretched out like this, it was less surprising that she was already in labor. If anything, it was surprising that she had managed to wait this long.

Patrick was on the other side of the bed, clearly worried, his bronzed hair floating gently in the currents moving through the room. Aster, the ducal healer and an Undine of some skill, was standing next to him. Despite the water filling the room, her hair was perfectly still, lying flat over her shoulders and not reacting to the current in any measurable way.

Five women stood around the edges of the room, identical save for the shades of their hair and skin. All of them had blue hair, ranging from pale sky blue to deep sapphire, and while the palest of them was white enough to pass for someone who had drowned, waxen and translucent, the darkest had skin the color of the spots on a cowry shell. Their faces and figures, however, were perfectly matched.

That was always the way with Hydor and her sisters, all of whom were also Hydor. Naiads aren't very creative when it comes to little things like names, viewing them as a distraction from the more important aspects of life, such as the movement of water. I suppose importance is weighted differently, when one is a Naiad.

I hurried across the room to Dianda's bedside, kneeling beside her. She pulled one hand from its loop of kelp and offered it to me. I grasped it with both of my own hands, kissing her webbed fingers until she laughed and pulled away.

"We should silence you more often, if you react like that," she said, and winked to show that she was teasing. Much like my October, I have a strong dislike of things being forced upon me, and threat of muzzle or restraint could at times trigger a panic attack.

Not now. Not here, in this moment, that I felt like I had been awaiting my entire life. In no version of my life, not the real one and not Titania's pretty lies, had I been allowed to attend the birth of one of my children. August had been born alone, with only Amandine to attend to her, and October had been born in a human hospital, her mortal father looking on. I had pitied the man more than I hated him, for while he had been given the joy of seeing her beginning, he had also been given the all-consuming grief searching through the ashes of the home they'd shared for the remains of her small body. Not that she had died there; all he'd been able to find was a night-haunt construct, left to give him something to weep over while her mother whisked the real child away to Faerie.

This child would never be stolen in such a way. She might be destined for Amphitrite, but we would have seventeen years of her before that unhappy hour, and she might not stay gone from us forever. So much was yet unwritten.

The door opened and closed again behind me, Helmi making her way into the room. She positioned herself at the foot of the bed, wrapping two tentacles around Dianda's flukes and pulling them straight.

"You're doing so well, my lady," she said. "So brilliantly, beautifully well. Now, shall we meet this child of yours?"

Dianda pulled her hand out of my grasp and slid it back into its loop. Once this was done she yanked down on the kelp ropes and *howled*, the sound long and loud and carrying even below the water. I grimaced. I needed so badly to continue working on the breathing potion, that we might also make our voices heard beneath the waves. Hearing my wife in such evident pain and being unable to soothe her was ... trying.

On the other side of the bed, Patrick appeared to be having the same difficulty. He had turned his face away, hands balled into white-knuckled fists. We could do nothing to lessen her pain, but were the room filled with air, we could at least have tried to offer some encouragement or distraction. Here and now, we could do nothing as she writhed on the bed, gills flared open in agony, entire body straining.

The moment passed, and she relaxed back into the bed, going limp. Helmi kept hold of her tail, reaching up with one tentacle to stroke the scales along her flank. "You're doing wonderfully, my lady," she said. "So very, very well. This is the greatest of battles, and for you to join it not once, but three times speaks so grandly of your bravery and fierce nature. Only win this battle, and all the fighting is done."

Dianda jerked down on the kelp and howled again, and Helmi continued to make encouraging noises, even as a ribbon of blood rose into the water, whisked quickly away by Hydor, who formed the bloodied water into a sphere and shunted it to the corner of the room. I had been warned that they would be doing this throughout the birth. When everything was finished and done, they would take the blood to the court alchemists to be mixed into potions that would help the babe grow in stability and strength. Such was the tradition in the Undersea, and I had no interest in defying it.

I could not help her. My wife was suffering, and I could do nothing to lessen her pain. And this moment wasn't about me, but in my inability to help in any way, my thoughts were beginning to chase themselves in circles through my mind, like rabbits fleeing from the shadow of a hawk. I took a deep breath, trying to center myself as Dr. Voss had suggested, to throw down anchors in the moment and live only here, not in might-have-beens or self-recrimination. Dianda needed me here.

So here I would stay.

She pulled her hands out of the kelp loops, reaching for me with the right and for Patrick with the left. We took them, not hesitating, and she crushed our fingers as she screamed again, the three of us momentarily united in the agony of the moment.

More blood plumed out into the water, and a heartbeat later, a baby followed it.

Helmi was quick to snatch the child from the water with three of her tentacles, drawing it to her breast so quickly I had time to see little more than fins and scales and a full head of hair in some dark shade. A flash of disappointment flared behind my heart. It had been wrong for me to hope that I was the biological father, not when we'd all agreed it wouldn't matter; that no matter who the child resembled, the three of us would raise them together, in love and safety.

And we would do that, we would. I had raised October, knowing all the while that she would never be mine. But I had hoped, and Torquills are always born with red hair. Even my August, whom Amandine had worked so hard to strip the Torquill blood away from before she could be born, had entered the world a strawberry blonde.

In the story of Dean's birth, the room had been drained immediately upon his arrival, when they realized he couldn't breathe underwater. Here and now, Helmi swept a tentacle across the baby's face, clearing away blood and mucus, and the child wailed. The sound was short, sharp, and carried well below the water. I relaxed. Our daughter could survive the deeps. She wouldn't have to leave us as Dean had. It was a relief even greater than my momentary disappointment had been.

"You have a daughter, my lady," said Helmi, releasing Dianda's flukes and moving around the bed with the infant, only to stop when Dianda bore down on our hands and screamed again, her cry even louder than the child's.

"I'm not done yet!" she howled, letting go of our hands and shoving her own back through the kelp loops for stability.

I blinked, straightening. Twins were something that *did* run in the Torquill bloodline. My biological mother, Celaeno, had been unsurprised when we arrived, remarking that she had two uncles as alike as hares in the morning, and twins were always a blessing. Perhaps my disappointment had been premature.

And then Helmi was shoving the baby into my arms as she moved swiftly back to the foot of the bed and caught hold of Dianda's flukes once more, jerking her tail back into a straightened position. Startled, I let go of Dianda's hand and wrapped my arms around the small, pudgy bundle I had been handed, so like and so unlike the other infants I had known.

Like her mother, she was shaped like a fish from the waist down, finned and scaled, although her scales were barely large enough to be worthy of the name. They were dusted across her skin like flexible sequins, so pale they had barely any color at all. Her flukes were short but diaphanous, and a rich copper color with glints of silver toward the base. The fins on her hips were similar, much shorter than they were on any of the adult Merrow I knew, or even Peter. I had to assume they would grow as she did.

She was still crying. I pulled her close to my chest, careful to support her head, and her wails tapered off, replaced first by confused whimpers, and then by silence. She opened her eyes to blink at the world around her, and my breath caught in my throat, leaving me even more silent than the water.

Her eyes were the deep golden color of fireweed honey, even as mine were closer to clover. Looking closely at her now, I could see the red undertones in her hair, like black cherrywood. She looked back up at me, and I offered her a smile, even knowing she wouldn't understand it. I knew I would have loved her all the same, but still, it was a joy to know that I had contributed something to this family, something that would last as long as we could keep her safe and home with us, here in her land below the sea.

Dianda screamed again. My head snapped up, baby still cradled close to my chest, and as I watched, her screams became a howl of rage, and our second child slid into the sea. As before, Helmi was there to catch the baby straight away, wiping blood and mucus from the infant's face with one tentacle.

Had this baby been born first, there would have been no moment of confusion as to whether I had been the biological father, nor were these two ever going to have to deal with being confused for one another, as Sylvester and I had. This child's hair was a bright wine red, darker than my own, but still as vivid as a signal flare, if not quite as bright as Helmi's hair. Dianda groaned, slumping back into her pillows.

Aster moved to start massaging her stomach, while Helmi kept hold of Dianda's flukes. "Almost there, my lady," she said. "Give me one more push."

Dianda glared at her, huffing, then screamed as she bore down, the tendons in her neck standing out as her gills flared wide and the afterbirth came free, gathered by Hydor as quickly and efficiently as the blood had been. Dianda collapsed bonelessly back into the bed, pulling her hands out of the kelp and shoving her hair out of her face.

"Great, now the redheads outnumber us," she said, words slightly slurred from the pain. "Give me my babies."

Aster continued massaging her stomach, muttering as she did, until the bleeding stopped entirely—something which didn't take very long at all, although whether that was the Undine's magic or a biological adaptation to keep Merrow mothers from bleeding too long into open waters, I had no way of knowing.

"Overachiever, aren't you, my lady?" asked Helmi, extending a tentacle to take the babe from my arms. For a moment, I considered fighting her, but I let the child go, let her carry them both over to their mother. "You have two beautiful daughters, even as you have two beautiful sons. Are you ready for them?"

"Give me my babies," repeated Dianda, reaching out with both arms. Helmi slid the babies into them, and Dianda laughed as she pulled them to her chest. "How am I supposed to deal with *daughters*? I never even had a sister. Not that my brother was much of an example for raising my sons." She lifted her head to offer me a weary smile. "You're going to need to step up, sailor. You're the only one of us who's raised a girl."

I smiled back, silenced by the water, but still able to tap my hand above my heart, trying to remind her of what mattered most. All we had to do was love them. As long as we could manage that much, everything was going to be just fine.

Hydor finished gathering the blood into a series of crimson spheres, which she collected with the aid of two of her sisters before heading for the door, bloody burden in hand. They slipped out through the wall of water, and I caught a glimpse of Peter and August straining to see what was happening inside.

Dianda laughed a little, sounding utterly exhausted. "You can let them in now, Helmi," she said.

"My lady?"

"The children. Let them in."

"Ah," said Helmi. She waved a tentacle at the two remaining Hydors, who nodded and closed their eyes. The tension that had been holding the water in place around us promptly shattered, and when Helmi opened the door, the water went rushing out into the hall.

Patrick and I promptly started coughing as the air met the water in our lungs. Helmi sighed. "Hydor?" she asked.

Each of the Naiads moved toward us, putting their hands on our shoulders and locking their eyes with ours. "Exhale," they said, in eerie unison.

I struggled to do as I was told, and managed not to choke as the water in my lungs was pulled upward and exited my lips like a ribbon of shining light. Hydor wound it around her hand. I gasped, still not quite ready to breathe air, and she sighed, repeating the process of eye contact and steady pull. This time, the ribbon was pale orange swirled with red, and I knew it for the remainder of the breathing potion.

"Remind me never to anger you, my lady," I said, still gasping a little as my body remembered what it was to breathe.

"Why should I remind you?" she asked. "I trust you will remember." She turned, carrying the water from my lungs and the potion from my gut, and walked out of the room. Her sister did the same.

As they exited, Peter and August came creeping into the room, moving cautiously, like they expected to be thrown out at any moment. Peter was on two legs for now, holding tight to August's hand, and both of them were focused on Dianda and the babies in her arms.

"It's all right," she said. "You can come over here. Just be quiet. Your sisters are sleeping."

"Sisters?" asked Peter.

"Sisters," she confirmed. "No names yet. The one with the darker hair was born first, and the second was a bit of a surprise, since I didn't realize I was carrying twins."

"We probably should have suspected, with the size of you, and the fact that Simon was involved," said Patrick. "He's a twin."

"Doesn't mean I was expecting to have a litter," said Dianda.

"They're beautiful," said August. "Are all Merrow babies born with fins?"

"It's our default state, so yes," said Dianda. "Dean wasn't born with proper fins, and that was part of how we knew he'd never be able to shift well enough to protect himself under the sea. Peter was born with a bifurcate tail, even though he shifted into a single tail, like mine, when he first started his changes. These two, though... they look as Merrow as I am." She sounded relieved.

I couldn't blame her for that. Our girls would have easier lives because they were suited to the sea, and that was something I suddenly wished for them with all my heart. Easy lives, kind tides, and no knowledge of the dangers of the world. I had wished the same for August, and for October, but I had known from the beginning that I wished in vain. Their mother had been Amandine. Ease had never been their destiny.

August was inching closer and closer to the bed. Dianda offered her a weary smile. "Did you want to hold one of them?" she asked.

"I do," said August. "Is it safe?"

"Babies are fragile, but not *that* fragile," said Dianda reassuringly, and offered August the older of the two, leaning carefully closer. August bit her lip, then leaned down to take the infant Merrow from her mother's arms, lifting her until she could cradle her close against her chest.

The baby opened her eyes. August gasped.

"Papa! Her eyes are like ours!"

"They are, poppet," I said, watching as Patrick took the second baby in his arms, holding his daughter with exquisite care. I moved closer to the bed, sitting on the edge and reaching for Dianda's hand.

She turned her weary smile toward me, even as she slid her hand into mine. "Couldn't resist getting all those redhead genes all over my beautiful babies, could you?" she asked.

"I apologize for any inconvenience," I said gravely. "But you'll be able to find them easily in the dark, and my own mother always told me that was a benefit of having highly visible children."

"Two," said Patrick. "How are we going to care for two babies?"

"The same way you would a single babe," said Helmi, now hanging from the ceiling with her hair dangling straight down in a cascade of curls. "By handing them over to me for their care and feeding, and spending as much time with them as your duties allow. I care for the children of this house. It's my pleasure and my purpose and you won't have it away from me just because you've gone and acquired slightly more than you expected."

"We would be lost without you, Helmi," said Dianda.

"Yes, you would, my lady," agreed Helmi. "But as you have me, you're quite well found. I'm going to fetch a chair for Master Peter." She undulated quickly across the ceiling and out into the hall.

Peter shifted his weight excitedly from foot to foot. "I can't hold a baby until I'm sitting down, but can I once I am?" he asked, eagerly.

It wasn't cruelty: it was simple common sense. Peter was only half-Merrow, and at times his ability to remain in a bipedal state failed him without warning. That would have been difficult enough, but at times his transformation failed in the other direction, making it unsafe for him to swim too far afield or linger too long in the flooded chambers of the knowe. He was as much a captive as his brother had been when he dwelled in these halls, without even Dean's option for escaping.

August had mused about speaking to Patrick and Dianda, asking them for permission to approach Peter and offer to shift the balance of his blood more toward one direction or the other, just to give him the ability to hold a form for longer. She had yet to do it, but watching the wistful way he was looking at his baby sisters, I suspected the offer would be made quite soon.

The baby in Patrick's arms yawned enormously. I squeezed Dianda's fingers.

"Do we need to go and let you rest?" I asked.

"She can stay awake long enough for the boy to meet his sisters, but then yes, you do," said Aster firmly. "This is a bit more on the wild side than I prefer my delivery rooms to be."

"Come now," said Dianda with a yawn. "You know you love it. How many babies do we get around here?"

"Not nearly enough," said Aster. "You've done more than brilliantly, my lady. Four babes, all born alive and breathing, is a wealth beyond all measure. Your household is well-favored."

"Twins are a risk, though," said Dianda. "Too many fools in need of heirs are likely to come with arms in hand, thinking we won't fight as hard when we have a backup daughter."

"We'll fight all the harder," I said, squeezing her hand again. "I would have killed for my brother's sake when I was a boy. I'm sure they'll feel the same. To be a twin is to walk inside and outside yourself at the same time, and know that you will never truly walk alone. Anyone who comes here seeking to take an heir by force will suffer for it."

An awkward silence fell following my words. We were all doing our best to ignore the blue whale in the room. Amphitrite, First of the Merrow, was sitting calmly in our halls, waiting for the word that her claimed heir had been born. We had bartered one of our daughters away before she drew her first breath.

And if we hadn't, she might not have drawn breath at all. Dianda had been brave, passing her pregnancy to her First for keeping and protection. She had been mazed by fear and grief, and had not inquired closely enough as to what that protection would cost. No matter how dearly we loved our daughters, we wouldn't be able to keep them both.

Not forever, anyway. For seventeen years, this would be all the home and safety they knew, or needed.

The door rattled in its hinges as Helmi shoved it open wide enough to undulate her way inside with Peter's wheelchair, pushing it up behind him. "Sit, so you can hold the baby and we can let your mother rest," she commanded.

Peter sat. Patrick walked around the bed to lower our wine-haired daughter into his waiting arms, and he laughed, absolutely delighted, even as his control over his shape finally gave way and his legs blurred, becoming a silver-scaled tail. The smell of stonecrop flowers and kelp briefly wavered in the air.

The baby in his arms yawned, then blurred, her own tail vanishing, replaced by chubby infant legs. The smell of rowan flowers and some variety of lotus drifted from her even as she yawned again and closed her eyes.

Patrick looked up, staring at me. "Did you see that?" he asked.

"I did," I confirmed. Our darker daughter had shown no signs of transformation, but seemed content to rest in August's arms. August, for her part, didn't seem to have noticed anything out of the ordinary. She was too busy staring at the baby, seeming utterly enchanted.

"And with that, please give your mother back her babies, and get out of here," said Aster. "That goes for the husbands as well. The woman has just given birth, twice, and she needs peace and quiet, not a welcome home party in all but name. Save that for the presentation."

Urged onward by Aster, we collected ourselves and were swept out of the room, Dianda beaming and weary with a baby in each arm as she watched us go. August hugged me as soon as we were outside the room, laughing.

"Oh, Papa, they're perfect," she enthused. "And to give them each the gift of a sister her own age—oh! They can grow up together, as—as some sisters do." She caught herself, tone turning sadder as she remembered that she and October had never truly grown up together, whatever her memories tried to say. "What are they to be named?"

"You'll find out at the presentation, along with everyone else," I said.

She huffed, stomping her foot like a much younger child. It was my turn to laugh at that. She had taken our arrival in the Undersea as an opportunity to behave like the child Amandine had never truly allowed her to be, racing through the halls with Peter and throwing herself joyfully into the role of child of the house while she learned the ways of life in the Undersea. Then, during Titania's spell, she had been forced into the adulthood her life thus far had failed to prepare her for, and when she was restored to her true self, she had once again embraced her position in the house with joy.

When you have forever to grow up, and a parent who missed years of your life and yearns only to indulge you, I see nothing wrong with a little time spent in being indulged. As long as, when necessary, maturity remains a cloak that can be donned for polite company.

"I love you, pigeon, but we follow the rules of the Undersea, and the rules of the Undersea say the babies will be named to all save the parents when they are presented," I said. "Now take Peter and find something else to do. We have company we need to attend upon."

Patrick gave me a confused look as August took the handles of Peter's chair and pushed him down the hall, him chattering a mile a minute about his new baby sisters and her smiling indulgently, clearly still delighted with what she'd seen since the birthing room door was opened.

"Company?" asked Patrick.

I blinked. Was it possible he didn't know? "When I arrived, I was met by Mary . . . and by Captain Pete, who came to attend upon the birth of her heir."

"Mary's been at the Duchy of Ships for weeks, helping the new Roane adjust to their powers," said Patrick. "She said the Sight didn't come on all of them at once, and some of them aren't doing very well with the change. I'm glad she made it home for the babies to be—I'm sorry, did you say *Captain Pete*?"

"I'm glad you've caught up," I said, sincerely. "Yes, Patrick, the Merrow First is in one of our sitting rooms with the Court Seer, both of them waiting for word of the baby. She was only expecting one."

"We're supposed to have until she turns seventeen," he said, grabbing my arm in desperation. "Simon, Dianda will kill us if Pete's come to take her baby before she's even out of the birthing bed. *Kill* us."

"Yes, well, I'm sure Amphitrite keeps her word better than that," I said. "The only question is which child she'll lay claim to. The first born, or the first to show her magic."

"Simon . . ."

"They parallel Sylvester and me in that regard. He was the first to arrive, and I was the first to call upon my gifts."

"Oh? And did your Firstborn attend the birth, ready to spirit one of you away?" His voice was bitter. I couldn't blame him for that.

Nor could I stop my own unhappy frown from forming. The image of Eira attending on *anyone's* birth was horrifying, all the more so because I had reason to believe she'd done it at least once—I had long suspected that was how Dawn had come to her, stolen scion of her own descendant line. And in the end, Eira had been able to have me, even if she hadn't attended on our birthing bed. Was this situation an echo of that?

No. It couldn't be. Amphitrite was Firstborn, but she was no Eira Rosynhwyr. She might be so powerful that the rules no longer applied to her: she wasn't *cruel*. "Come with me," I said, beckoning for Patrick to follow as I turned and started down the hall.

The more time I spent in the palace, the easier it became for me to navigate. When I first arrived, I'd been lost as often as not, especially when I dared to venture beyond the landmark of my rooms, which were always static and welcoming to me. Now, I was learning how the striations in the walls could tell me what level I was on, what I was likely to encounter as I walked. They were subtle, and half of navigation within the knowe seemed to depend on subconscious recognition of the architectural cues, but they were enough.

We walked along the hall, passing a few Cephali at their work, hanging from the ceilings with dusters in their hands—there is dust even deep beneath the sea, which is entirely unfair if you want to ask my opinion. Patrick stayed close by my side, radiating a tension that seemed inappropriate for a man whose wife had just been successfully delivered of two healthy babies.

By the time we reached the sitting room where I had left Mary and Amphitrite, he was walking close enough that we might as well have shared a single shadow, his hands trembling with the anxiety of it all. I reached back and claimed one of them in my own, offering him as reassuring a smile as I could manage.

"Stand strong, my love," I said, voice low. "We have weathered worse storms than this one, and we will see the harbor soon."

Patrick gave me a grateful look, and together, we stepped into the room.

Mary and Amphitrite were both as I had left them: indeed, it would have been easy enough to convince myself they hadn't moved at all while I'd been gone. A small rolling cart holding the remains of an afternoon tea service put lie to that impression, crumbs and empty teacups making it clear that they had moved at least once. They both looked around as we stepped inside, and Amphitrite stood, her twinned tails melting seamlessly into legs as she asked them to hold her weight.

"Well?" she asked. "This useless Seer"—she indicated Mary with a sweep of her hand. Mary cackled, clearly charmed by the description—"refuses to tell me whether the baby has been born."

"Untrue, Petey," said Mary. "I refused to tell you whether *your heir* had been born, because there is yet no way of knowing. She'll have to make up her own mind, and so much of that decision hinges on your behavior, alongside the behavior of her parents, that she could really go either way."

"My lady has been delivered of her precious cargo, and is recovering now, while cradling her efforts as any mother might," I said, choosing my words with absolute precision. It seemed that Amphitrite didn't know yet that there were two infants born and alive: I was willing to extend her ignorance as long as I could without verging into insult.

"I want to see them."

I raised an eyebrow, keeping my attention firm on Amphitrite. "My lady Firstborn, my beloved wife is only now done with her labors. She is no Firstborn, and you know well that your line has no accelerated healing in them. It will be some time before she can transform herself without pain, or rise from her bed without regretting it. Can we perhaps arrange this meeting for another day?"

"The presentation of our new family to the sea will take place in seven full tides, as is the custom," said Patrick. "It's also traditional that we invite the Firstborn of the parental line or lines to the ceremony. Normally that's a formality, but in this case, my lady, might I hope for your attendance?"

"You might," said Amphitrite. "Seven full tides, and I'll return to meet my heir." She drew herself to her full height and strode toward the door, apparently intending to make her farewells.

I paused, then turned toward her again. "Wait?" I asked.

She stopped, looking back at me. "Yes?"

"My Firstborn is mercifully unavailable," I said. "As is Patrick's. But my mother was human, once, and so I am not entirely of our shared descendant line. I would beg your consent to invite a proxy to attend our presentation, if you would be so kind."

"My consent isn't needed to invite a guest to your own halls," said Amphitrite coolly.

"No, lady, nor is the Duchy of Saltmist a part of your demesne. But I would hesitate to risk insulting you as our ally by asking someone you are not currently on the best of terms with to attend upon us here."

Amphitrite stilled like the water following a storm, becoming so profoundly motionless that it was difficult to credit. Finally, slowly, she said, "You want to ask my sister."

"She *is* the Firstborn I've known longest and best," I said. "Technically I've known Amy longer, but I would no more invite that woman into my home than I would try to swim for shore without the potions that protect me in deepest water."

"As if I'd *let* you ask her here," countered Patrick. Then he paused, thoughtfully. "Actually, I might. Dianda gets irritable when she's nursing. Having your ex-wife to throw things at might improve her mood enough to make up for the inconvenience of being required to show hospitality to the b—"

"Still my sister," said Amphitrite, in an amused sing-song tone.

Patrick paled. "Apologies, my lady. I simply find your youngest sister somewhat . . ."

"Intolerable, yes. Most of us who've met her agree. But that doesn't mean I can stand by while you insult her. It reflects badly on me if I do that." She smiled, showing a mouthful of serrated shark's teeth.

"Of course, my lady."

I cleared my throat. "If I may: my lady Firstborn, Saltmist is not a part of your protectorate, but we are near enough that our affairs sometimes spill over onto one another. I would be well-pleased if the sea witch, Antigone of Albany, were able to attend the presentation of my youngest daughter to the sea. I know she's been banned from your waters for another five years yet to pass. Will you take offense if we ask her here?"

Amphitrite's expression softened. "Not in the slightest," she said. "If anything, you will please me by creating an opportunity for me to break bread with my sister, whom I dearly miss, for all that I was required to banish her for honor's sake."

"Then the invitation shall be sent," I said gravely, and bowed. "Do you need an escort away?"

"No. I know which way to go." She smiled at Patrick. "Be watchful and wary, and I'll see you at the presentation."

She swept from the room then, majestic as a ship under full sail. As soon as she was gone, Mary flung herself from her own chair into Patrick's arms.

"Both our girls are here!" she squealed. "Oh, I never thought I'd see the day. Such good girls they'll be, and such delights below the tides, and such a blessing to a household already three times blessed!"

"What do you mean, Mary?" asked Patrick.

"She's been telling me for years that there was a girl who would sometimes come and sometimes not, depending on the tides," said Helmi from behind us. I managed not to flinch or whirl around. Her comings and goings were still difficult for me, but I was adjusting to them tide by tide, and more and more she felt like a normal part of living. "It was a long time before I understood what she meant, and then I thought the girl might be August, who was a daughter of this house from the moment she entered the water, but shortly after Master Lorden disappeared, she told me the girl was coming, and I understood."

Mary cackled.

Helmi moved forward, stopping next to me. "She used to say the strangest, most contradictory things about 'the girl,' who never had a name."

"She'll be named soon enough, she will, and no one will be shocked," said Mary lightly.

Patrick sighed. "You already know the babies' names, don't you?"

"Not until you conceive and speak them, my Pat," she said. "I haven't the naming of these children. If I did, you would know by now. If I spoke their names as I've heard them in the water, before you decided on those names for yourselves, I would make myself a liar, because another name would win. Apples and oranges, sea buckthorn and saltberry, we mustn't rewrite the future in the process of observing it. Naughty to do that, upsets our mum, doesn't it?"

"I'm sorry, my lady, but you've lost me," I said politely. "You saw the coming of our daughters?"

"Almost always only one, with hair like wine and magic that smelled like whitethorn flowers and water lilies," she said. "Sometimes two, and once, for a moment, three, but the third babe was pale as seafoam and couldn't linger long. I'm sorry not to see her born, as I would be sorry for any lost tide, but it may be more a mercy than a burden that she does not arrive." She let go of Patrick and leaned over to touch my arm. "I saw you'd ask my mother's attendance if you could, and that if you did, now would be the time to greet her. So I thank you for that, even as everything else is in flux."

"I—what?" I blinked at her. Fortune-telling has never been one of my gifts, and has never been one I envied. The things they see try them so. I couldn't imagine the moment when the vision of an as-yet-unborn child forked to become a different child, or to show one who would now never be. Dianda would never bear again, not after her bargain with Amphitrite, and neither Patrick nor I was going to lie with another woman for the sake of a child, not when we each had four to call our own. Even my parents never managed such a genuine embarrassment of riches, and there were those in Faerie who believed either my brother or I should have been given to another household to serve as their heir.

Even as we were going to give one of our daughters to Amphitrite. The thought had been terrible when there had only been one baby in the equation, when we would be left alone by the captain's claim. Now it was one of two, and her sister would be left behind no matter who Amphitrite took from us.

Dealing with the Firstborn is always bitter. You'd think we would have all learned that by now.

Mary leaned over to hug Patrick again, tightly. "You have done so very well, my Pat, and all without knowing the lines you walked along," she said. "I could never tell you how much you meant or mattered, but only that I loved you, and had loved you since the day I Saw you coming to us. You were the first link in a chain that made so many things possible, and you have performed your part in all things brilliantly."

"So you always say, but you never explain," said Patrick, stroking her hair with one hand. "I love you too, Mary, oblique creature that you are, and I'm glad you'll be here for the presentation."

"Oh, do not sorrow so for the Devouring Deep's attendance," she said, lightly chiding. "She's a fine guest to grace your halls, and any who knows she came will think twice before they trouble you in future. What's more, she's to come from the Duchy of Ships, and that means she'll bring you such a cake as you have only dreamt of."

"Forgive us, but we've had Aldridge's cakes before," I said gently.

Mary laughed. "Not like this, you haven't!"

She let go of Pat and spun, still laughing, before she drifted out of the room, leaving Patrick and I to look at one another in bafflement.

"Is she always like this?"

"Since I met her," he said. "She's one of the older remaining Roane in the sea. She always calls the sea witch her mother and disappears before they can see each other. So maybe she means it, and we're to host a family reunion."

"An unpleasant but fascinating thought." I looked around the empty chamber, then turned back to him and smiled brightly. "We have *daughters*."

"Two of them," he agreed, the corner of his mouth twitching with the effort of restraining his own smile.

"Two beautiful little girls."

"And Dianda was right—those damned redhead genes of yours get all over everything." He stepped closer, sliding his arms around my waist and tugging me toward him. I allowed myself to be pulled, until our stomachs were pressed against one another. I slid my own arms around Patrick's waist in turn.

"Are you angry?"

"Not in the least." He finally allowed himself to smile, and it was the sweetest thing I had ever seen. "I remember the way you described your family, when you were younger. You had two mothers. You knew which bore you, and it made no difference to your love for them. They were both your parents. Well, our daughters will have two fathers. We'll both love them, we'll raise them together, and they'll never know the difference between us."

My own smile faded. "If you're looking to my own upbringing for our map forward, you should know that as we grew older, my brother became ashamed of our mortal origins. Our blood had already been transformed, long before we were old enough to have had a part in the decision, but he feared loving Celaeno too openly would mark us as tainted by our lost humanity. By the time she died, he insisted only Glynis had had any part in the making of us."

"Ah, my love." Patrick kissed my cheek. "Neither of us is mortal. Nothing has been changed within our children, and legally, they belong to all three of us. There's no need to fear that a shock of red hair will isolate me from our children."

"Fair enough," I said. "I worry, my love. You know I worry. If I stop worrying, I'll be someone else altogether, and as this version of me is only now learning how to be happy, I'd prefer to remain the man I am."

"I also prefer the man you are," he said, and this time, he kissed me properly, slow and sweet and deep. I released his waist to slide my arms around his shoulders, and let him push me back until I was pressed against the wall, still kissing him, as he was still kissing me, and for a time, I forgot to worry about the future, or the present, or anything beyond the wet clothing still clinging to my body, and the difficulty presented by his buttons.

August and Peter were safely in their quarters, well away from here, our wife was resting peacefully, and for a little while, all we had to worry about was one another. And for the moment, that was more than enough.

Passing messages between the land and sea can be far more difficult than it has any right to be. Before the Convocation which removed most of the Selkies from our waters, they had been used as messengers, allowing them to make use of our air-filled chambers where they could rest. Now, however, they had all the sea at their disposal. They could swim forever and sleep below the surface, wrapped in magically generated bubbles of breathable air. Much like the Merrow, they could call and control storms—although almost none of them knew how that magic worked, which was making oceanic weather patterns temporarily *fascinating*. Some of them had taken refuge in more heavily Merrow-occupied domains, where they could learn about their evolving magic without accidentally unleashing a hurricane on San Francisco.

Without the Selkies to carry messages for us, I needed to figure out how to invite the Luidaeg to our presentation without actually making the journey all the way back up to the shore. I returned to my chambers after Patrick and I separated, moving toward my laptop computer as if drawn by an invisible string. It had been a gift from Dean, modified by his friend April—his friend, my great-niece. She had originally been a normal Dryad, but my niece, January, had managed to transplant her into a computer server, which had changed her nature in some essential way, making her a unique creature. She spoke to computers now, the same way that a normal Dryad could speak to trees.

When she modified a piece of electronic equipment, she did it in a way that left it able to function even in deep Faerie, meaning my laptop not only worked, but was able to communicate with the mortal internet—something I would otherwise have assumed impossible. I turned the machine on, and while it was booting up, removed the last of my wet clothing and replaced it with dry clothes from my dresser.

By the time I was dressed, the computer was ready for me. I sat down at the desk, opening the video call program I used to communicate with my therapist. Several seconds passed, broken only by the sound of digital ringing.

Then, with a beep, the black screen disappeared, replaced by the worried face of Dr. Isobel Voss, the changeling woman who had been tasked with the problem of putting my battered psyche back together. She looked at me, eyes wide and anxious.

"Simon?" she said. "I didn't think we had an appointment today. Are you all right?"

"Did I catch you at a bad time?" I asked, politely. "I do apologize for calling you outside of our scheduled hours, but it seemed like a viable reason."

"I was between appointments," said Dr. Voss. "It's fine. Are you all right?"

"I am gloriously well, better than all right by all known means of measurement," I assured her, and blinked as she didn't look reassured. "Doctor?"

"That level of effusion can signal severe emotional distress," she said. "What's going on, Simon?"

I took a deep breath, forcing myself to calm. "I'm not in distress, I promise, and I didn't call you to try for an emergency session. I called to ask if you would be willing to carry a message for me, and whether you would be willing to consider a visit to Saltmist in a week's time."

Dr. Voss frowned at the camera, looking bewildered. She was a handsome woman, half-human, one-quarter Siren, and one-quarter Daoine Sidhe. The combination had given her lush, dark curls shot through with silver, like foam dancing on the surface of the waves, and silvered eyes that had to be hidden behind illusions before she met with the human clients who made up the majority of her business. I didn't actually know how well she could travel under the water, as she had never come for an in-person appointment.

"A week's . . . Simon, are you inviting me to the presentation to the sea?"

"Yes," I said, with a wide smile. "Dianda has had the baby—the babies, in fact. Two girls, both born alive and well, finned and scaled as anything, although the younger of the two has already demonstrated magic enough to transform herself into a bipedal form."

"And how does this make you feel?"

"I'm relieved that they're here, that they were able to arrive healthy and hale after the circumstances of their gestation, and they're beautiful. Not that beauty is what matters where a baby is concerned, but still. It was a wonder to watch my children enter the world, and in a week, we'll present them to the sea and name them for the tides to hear, and I would like it if you could be in attendance. If you can't make the journey under your own power, I can have someone sent to collect you from the pier, and guarantee your safety upon your return."

"I'll . . . think about it, Simon," she said carefully. "We have an appointment tomorrow. I should be able to give you an answer then."

"All right."

"And the message?"

This was the trickier bit. I smiled again, more politicly this time, and asked, "Can you go to Half Moon Bay and ask Elizabeth Ryan if she would come down to Saltmist? I have some messages I need to ask her to carry for me." Elizabeth Ryan had been the leader of the local Selkie clan when they were still something that existed. She knew all the remaining Selkies, and all the new-made Roane, and would be able to find me messengers.

It might have been easier to ask Dr. Voss to go and invite the sea witch on my behalf, but I suspected the outcome of that might be my needing to find a new therapist. I had been with this one for well over a year—possibly longer, but I didn't count the four months I had spent captive inside Titania's enchantment—and she knew me well enough at this point that I no longer needed to explain things a new doctor would absolutely have needed me to go into in more detail. There is a certain relief that comes from no longer needing to explain one's inescapable trauma. It has made therapy far less upsetting.

No. The Roane would make things easier, and inviting my doctor to our presentation would be a beautiful side benefit. Dr. Voss looked at me suspiciously.

"Is that all?" she asked.

"It is," I assured her. "I'll call my daughter myself, in a few hours—she was busy when I returned below, and I doubt she's done so quickly. After the messengers arrive, I'll be able to notify the others who will need to know."

Peter would doubtless already have called his brother, and Dean would inform Quentin, which meant waiting to tell October until she was done with whatever errands Arden had for her wasn't really an option. That was fine. I didn't object to speaking to my second daughter. In fact, I generally relished the opportunity.

Titania's enchantment had left us with a much more stable relationship, and left me with a head full of memories that told me she had lived at home until very, very recently, when she was actually a grown woman with a husband and household of her own. It was sometimes difficult not to take every possible opportunity to check up on her, even more so now that she was pregnant. I knew she'd been pregnant once before—her daughter Gillian was proof of that—but a father worries.

Dr. Voss smiled at me. "You clearly enjoy referring to October as your daughter. How does she feel about it?"

"I do," I said. "I've always thought of her as such, but wasn't allowed to acknowledge it until my divorce from her former mother was finalized. To be able to claim her openly is a gift, and one I treasure. As to October herself, we were moving toward her comfort with the notion when we were enspelled and it became her normal. She has allowed at least a portion of that feeling to linger, to my great delight and satisfaction. I think she'll be glad to hear of the birth of her sisters."

Dr. Voss nodded. "Excellent. In our next actual session, we can talk about how Faerie forms and denies family bonds. October isn't related to you, and yet you're her father; she *is* related to Amandine, but is no longer considered her daughter. I'd like to better understand how this is affecting your relationship."

"But not right now."

"No, not right now. Right now, you need to be focused on the present, on the family that you have with you in the Undersea. My questions can wait." Her smile softened, becoming less the impersonal approval of a clinician and more the warm, happy smile of a friend. "I'm so happy for you, Simon. Go be with your wife and daughters."

"Yes, Doctor," I said, and ended the call.

Rising, I left the room for the central room which connected my chambers with Patrick's and Dianda's. The Undersea had some fascinating traditions around rooming: each of us had our own bedroom, and a second room to use for whatever we liked, as well as the large room we all shared on the days when we chose to sleep together. Those days were more common now than they'd been when I first married them. I still couldn't handle that sort of closeness on a nightly basis, but every other? Every third? Their welcome had never wavered, and they had allowed me to approach them in my own time, never forcing me into anything.

A new door had joined those that I was used to, the central chamber expanding accordingly. I approached it, pressing my hand flat against the polished coral, and was unsurprised when it warmed beneath my touch, the wards welcoming me. This was not yet a private space.

I opened the door. On the other side, a cozy, comfortable room had been prepared, decorated in reds and golds, like a forest in autumn, with all the furnishings one might require for a newly arrived baby, or pair of same: two bassinets, a dresser with rounded edges, a changing table. Several soft toys with embroidered eyes sat atop the dresser, ready to be needed, and the walls were papered in a pattern of changing leaves that rustled when I approached them. The rug looked like a slice of the forest I saw echoed all around me, and when I looked closely at the wall, I saw a fox slipping just out of sight.

I was suddenly gripped with the longing to have seen Peter's and Dean's first nurseries, the ones where they would have slept until they were weaned and moved into their own suites of rooms. Peter still lived comfortably in his, and August had her own, but I had fond memories of her first room, even as it had been white and all but featureless, at Amandine's request. She had feared that excessive stimulation might upset the baby.

There were clearly no such concerns here. I could have stood and watched those leaves for hours.

There was a soft scuff behind me as someone approached. Voice soft, as if he were speaking to a wild beast that might yet startle, Patrick said, "The knowe decorates the infant rooms on its own. I've never been sure how it knows what to do. Peter's room was a coral forest. There were living fish in the walls, darting in and out of safety, and some of the same fish showed up over and over again. They remembered us. Never was quite sure how the magic worked, or what happened to those fish after the knowe closed off the room. Dean, now. He had a beach at sunrise, all little waves and endless mist. The only thing they've all had in common was that they were peaceful. I can see us spending a lot of time in here."

"Two babies—we're going to have to," I said. "How's Dianda?"

"She's finally awake. That's why I came looking. She's asking for the both of us, according to Helmi. I don't think it's a good idea to leave her waiting if we don't have to."

"No, probably not," I agreed. "How are . . . ?"

"The babies?" He reached over, threading his fingers gently into mine. "They're both fine. Helmi says they're strong and perfect, and that's the only thing I need to know."

"Helmi is biased."

"As are we." Patrick smiled at me, tugging gently on my hand. "Come along. Let's go see them."

I smiled, and let myself be led away.

Dianda, still finned and scaled, was reclining on a long bed in an unfamiliar room, one which probably hadn't existed before she needed it and doubtless wouldn't exist anymore by the time the tide rolled in. Helmi was dangling from the ceiling above her, holding our darker daughter. Her brighter counterpart was in Dianda's arms. Both girls were sleeping. Birth was an exhausting exercise, it seemed. Even Dianda was clearly weary, and I'd seen that woman wrestle a sea dragon without so much as a hint of fatigue.

She lifted her head as the door opened, and found a tired smile for the two of us, freeing one hand to beckon us forward.

"Did you speak to the captain?" she asked.

"I did," I assured her. "Amphitrite will return for the presentation to the waters, and any case she has to press will be held until that time. She has further agreed that the sea witch should be permitted to attend the presentation, and I have sent word to Elizabeth Ryan that we have need of messengers."

"Have you called Toby yet?"

"Not yet. She was busy when I left the land, and I'd rather give her time to finish her business before I interrupt her."

"The announcement of two new sisters isn't 'interrupting' her, Simon," said Dianda. "It's a grand and glorious gift that too few in Faerie are ever able to receive."

"I was never close to my brothers, but I was still thrilled to know they existed," said Patrick. "You need to call her."

"I will," I said. "I promise. We'll want her here for the presentation, if nothing else, and that means working around her pregnancy."

"Tybalt's not going to let her travel to the Undersea when she could deliver at any moment," said Dianda. "We were supposed to be due around the same time. Probably would have been, if I hadn't been carrying twins and thrown the whole timeline off. That means a week from now, he's going to be even more overprotective than he usually is."

"I'm still inviting her," I said firmly. "Our memories may be scrambled compared to what they should be, but even before Titania's spell, she would have been rightfully hurt if she wasn't asked to come and welcome her sisters to the world. Amandine never showed that girl a drop of love she wasn't required to."

"I know," said Dianda. She looked down at the baby in her arms. "What are we going to call them? I never considered names in pairs."

"Nothing with the same initial, and nothing that rhymes," I said, firmly. "I've been a twin, and I can tell you the initials are annoying, but rhyming, I'm fairly sure either Sylvester or I would have committed fratricide just to make it stop."

"They named you both with 'S' because of your sister, didn't they?" asked Patrick.

"You know they did."

"The land can afford to have stricter naming rules than the sea," said Dianda. "Down here, we try to avoid duplicating names within the same Kingdom, but we know people stop swimming, sooner or later, as long as they move through mortal waters; we can't afford to retire every name forever just because it's been used. So we have options."

"There are always options," I agreed, sitting down on the edge of her bed. She promptly passed me the baby she'd been holding, reaching up to take the other from Helmi. I looked down at our daughter, entirely besotted.

Her eyes were open but unfocused, and as bright as they'd been at her delivery. Red hair and golden eyes and it was like holding a freshly born August all over again, the future contained in the safe circle of my arms. The fins were new, but no less welcome than any other aspect of my daughter. She was perfect, in all ways. I looked at her, and it was like I'd always known her, like I'd always been waiting for her to arrive in this world.

"It was worth it," I informed her, in a low voice. "All the fuss, all the Firstborn, all the terrible curses and awful enchantments... they were all worth it, because now you're here."

"Now they both are," agreed Dianda. I glanced up and she was watching me, eyes wise and weary. "Our littlest jewels of the sea."

"No jewel names, please," I said, wrinkling my nose. "Oberon's original plan for his youngest daughter was the name of a kind of garnet. I would prefer to avoid even the appearance of honoring her in our naming."

"I wasn't thinking jewels," said Dianda. "I was thinking of your sister. I never met her."

"Neither did I," said Patrick. "But we know how much she meant to you."

My breath caught in my throat. "September was the best of us," I said. "She was better than our house deserved. My parents named her for our father, and then named us to honor her, and every daughter of our line has been named in her honor ever since."

"Running short on calendar months by now, aren't you?" asked Dianda.

"February seems an unkind name for a child, but it hasn't been used," I said. "Neither March, nor June, nor July in truest sense of the statement—October's Gillian is a sideways July, not a direct one. November and December remain as yet unclaimed."

"What of October?" she pressed.

"She has no intention to name her second child for the calendar;

I believe she'll be looking to Shakespeare, if anything. She's made her additions to the tradition, with Gillian and May, and she never knew September."

"Then why don't we?" asked Dianda. "Until the presentation these babies have no name outside of this room, but we'll need something to call them until the time arrives. The end of the year seems like a decent enough place to find a name, and there's two of them together, for two months as yet unclaimed."

My breath caught. Amandine had allowed August in part because it began with the letter "A," which had allowed her to claim it was in her own honor that our child was named, and in part because August came before September, and she'd seen it as a way of replacing my sister in my affections, forgetting that the year is a wheel, and nothing is truly before or behind anything else. It has an end and a beginning, but even as October will ever follow August, the reverse is also true.

"Are you sure?" I asked.

"November and December seem like fine additions to our family tree," she said, and smiled at me, as warm as she was exhausted. "Let me have this."

"I can deny you nothing," I said, taking her free hand and kissing it, aware all the time of the babe in my arms, the babe in hers, the space between us that had once been so empty and now grew so very, beautifully full.

Then November, firstborn and darker-haired, began to wail, and the momentary peace was shattered as we saw to the needs of babes, as parents have done since time began, as parents will continue to do until all time is ended.

The presentation to the sea did not exactly match any tradition of the land, which made sense, as the needs of the environments were not the same. For a week after any birth, parent and child would be sequestered from the rest of the Undersea, taking that time to rest and recover. Even the notoriously warlike Merrow respected that period: no Merrow would attack someone who was in seclusion following childbirth. Dianda was not allowed to appear at court functions or outside the private areas of the palace. Patrick and I were afforded a bit more freedom, and we were expected to coordinate with the staff and guests to ensure that everything would be just right for the presentation itself.

Not that Helmi was letting us do much in the way of coordination. This was far from her first, and she was worried, in her brisk, efficient way, that we would make a disaster of it if we were allowed to do much more than expand the guest list and keep Dianda from throwing things in frustrated boredom.

We were two days into the preparations before she thought to inform me that, had Dianda died in childbirth, Patrick and I would be expected to stay in isolation with the babies. It made sense, but it was also slightly horrifying that they had plans and patterns for the death of the mother. I could have gone centuries without hearing that the Undersea was so prepared for sacrifice.

Dianda explained later that the tradition dated from the early days of the Undersea, when there had been fewer palaces beneath the waves, and more childbirth had happened in open waters, where sharks and worse could intervene. It was still a horror.

I had called October that same night, or tried to, anyway; she wasn't answering her phone. She wasn't answering the next day, either, or the day after that. Now, two days after the arrival of her sisters, I was sitting at my workbench and trying again, forcing down the narrow column of fear that threatened to expand and overwhelm me. It never means anything good when October isn't answering her phone.

To my relief and delight, she picked up. "Hello. October Daye speaking. Did you not get the memo that I'm on medical leave for the next three weeks?"

"Medical—October, what are you talking about?"

"Dad?"

"Yes, sweetheart, it's me. Are you all right?"

"Oh, I'm fine, honest. Just got kidnapped a little, and iron poisoning, a little, and cut open, kind of a lot. You know. Normal stuff." The way she said it, it sounded like her definition of "normal stuff" was perfectly reasonable, even though I knew it wasn't. I was fairly sure she was counting on that tone to keep me from getting upset by the sheer horror of what she was actually saying.

Sadly for her, that "oh no don't worry everything's fine" tone was something that had persisted during Titania's version of our world, and I was well-familiar with what it meant. "October. What happened?"

"Oh. Um. Dame Altair turned out to be Dugan Harrow's sister, and was working for Janet, who wanted my baby as a replacement for Amandine or maybe Gillian, it's not completely clear which one it was, and she had me restrained with iron, which made me really sick, and um, May had to deliver my baby in a secret underground warehouse full of stolen magical items in order to keep us both from dying? Congratulations, Granddad, it's a girl."

Joy and horror briefly warred for ownership of the moment. I sat in silence, open-mouthed and unable to formulate a single coherent reply.

"Simon? Are you still there?"

"I . . . yes, October, I'm still here. You're all right now? And the baby?"

"Oh, we're both fine. She's with May at the moment, since May's more comfortable wearing an infant around the house, and everyone's sort of afraid I'm going to go do something stupid and heroic at any moment."

"They've met you, then."

"Yeah."

"You sound happy."

"Oh, I'm exhausted, but I'm thrilled. Last time I did this, I only healed a little faster than most humans, and my baby was so much more human than I was that we never seemed to sleep on the same schedule. Not that she really has a schedule yet, as such."

"I can't wait to meet her."

"Isn't that why you're calling? To set up a visit."

"Yes, dear, but not in the direction you're thinking. Duchess Dianda Lorden of Saltmist has been delivered of two healthy baby girls. Both are thriving, and are to be presented to the sea in five tides' time. I was hoping you might come to the presentation."

"I know Tybalt can use the Shadow Roads to get to you, but I don't think he's going to be willing to take the baby through a space that doesn't do air," she said, slowly. "And she certainly can't swim it yet . . ."

"We've invited the sea witch to attend, and I know her apartment is able to open a door directly into our receiving room," I offered. "If you could accompany her, you might be able to ease the journey."

"Oh, *excellent* point. Five tides—is that five days?"

"It is. Around four o'clock in the afternoon, I think. Come and let me meet my granddaughter, and meet your new sisters at the same time."

"And that won't be rude? Like announcing your pregnancy at someone else's engagement dinner?"

"Family is always welcome here, even if the timing is less than absolutely perfect," I assured her. "Our girls will share the treasure of their childhood, and grow up as tangled as briars."

"That sounds like a promise."

"Because it is."

In the background, a baby yowled. October made a sound that was somewhere between a chuckle and a sigh.

"Miranda's hungry, and I have to go," she said.

"You named the baby Miranda?" I asked.

"Yeah. Janet was using the name, but it was never hers. Shakespeare was the one who decided it should be a first name, and she snatched it so quickly that as far as we can tell, it's never been truly used in Faerie."

"So not a month this time."

"No. No more months for me."

That was a relief. I smiled. "I'll see you in five days, October."

"If the sea witch lets us use her door, yes, you will."

"I believe she will," I said. "I love you."

"Love you too, really gotta go, she has some lungs on her," said October, and the line went dead.

I put the phone down, still smiling. Time to resume preparations for the presentation, which was, after all, a party the size of which I did not commonly involve myself in.

The evening of the presentation arrived cool and dark, as evenings in the deep sea usually were. I had no talent for reading the tides, and had to take my time from the clocks scattered around the knowe.

Dianda had emerged from isolation an hour or so prior, returning to her rooms to dress and prepare for the gathering to come. Helmi had the girls, as she was wont to do any time Dianda let her guard down; Helmi took her responsibilities as nurse to the household's children very seriously indeed.

According to Patrick, people were beginning to arrive, and the grand reception hall had been opened for the occasion, giving them a place to gather. The space had been decorated in garlands of kelp and flowering sea plants, all wrapped in veils of living water to keep them moist and thriving. Arrangements of dryland flowers dotted the tables, a nod to myself and Patrick, scenting the air with whitebeam and rowan. Water lilies and lotuses dotted the surface of small pools, and I wondered how October and her hydrophobia would handle the décor. Not that it mattered; it was too late to change anything now.

Darker-haired daughter in my arms and Dianda by my side, I walked toward the receiving room. Patrick walked to Dianda's other side, our brighter child held against his breast. Both girls were awake but quiet, watching the world around them with wide eyes. They had so much yet to see.

We entered the receiving room as a door that wasn't normally present opened and the sea witch stepped through. Her hair was loose around her shoulders, and her dress was sliced from shallow water, clear and ever-shifting as ripples of foam and tide ran across its surface. Despite its clarity, she wasn't exposed in the least. She looked at the five of us and smirked, then stepped to the side to let October and Tybalt enter.

October was holding a baby bundled in her arms, and Quentin and Dean came close behind them, walking hand in hand.

Dean brightened at the sight of his parents. "Mom!"

"Come meet your sisters," said Dianda.

He beamed and dropped Quentin's hand, hurrying to coo over the babies. October walked forward at a more sedate pace, stopping a few feet in front of me as Dean took the infant from my arms.

"Hey, Dad," she said.

"Hello, my pigeon," I replied, unable to look away from the child she carried. The little girl had thin, pale hair, banded with darker streaks. It was almost certainly her father's heritage expressing itself, but it looked less like a tabby's fur than it did like the feathers of an eagle owl's wings. Her eyes were open, taking in the room around her, and pale as her mother's, the color of morning mist.

October followed my gaze to her little girl and smiled. "This is Miranda."

"We can't offer your sisters' names in return," I said apologetically. "Not until they're given to the whole sea."

"We haven't told Peter or August," said Patrick. "They're in the main reception room."

The Luidaeg cleared her throat. "And are we about done ignoring the undying sea witch, or should I patiently ignore etiquette for a little longer?"

"Apologies," said Dianda, and curtseyed deeply. She was the only one of us who could do that without risking dropping a baby in the process. "We are honored by your attendance."

"Damn right you are." She looked at the girls with sharp-eyed interest. "Pretty things. Glad they're your problem and not mine. Kind of missing the days when you met me with worship and adulation, but I guess familiarity breeds contempt even when it shouldn't."

"Mháthair?" asked a voice behind us.

I turned. Mary was standing in the doorway, one hand clasping it like she was fighting to keep herself upright, eyes fixed on the Luidaeg. I looked back. The Luidaeg was staring at her, eyes bleeding slowly to Roane green, cheeks pale.

"Máire?" she asked.

"Always and still," said Mary. She let go of the doorframe. "I waited. I said I would wait, and I stayed clear of your path as I waited, and now the moment is here, and you're here, and I'm here, and we're both here together."

"Máire," the Luidaeg repeated, in a voice filled with wonder. She jerked away from us, moving unsteadily, and lurched across the room to collapse into Mary's arms. The two women clung to each other, and watching them felt vaguely obscene, like this was something we should never have witnessed. I turned back to the others.

"We should go," I said. "Mary knows the way, if they want to attend. I get the feeling they may not."

The group of us shuffled awkwardly out of the room, leaving Mary and the Luidaeg where they were, and made our way through the knowe to the reception room. When we arrived, it was indeed full of people, some familiar, most not. Representatives from all the local Undersea domains had come, and those who couldn't fit inside the hall were poking their heads up through the pools in the floor. Cephali hung from the ceiling, a forest of bright colors and waving tentacles.

Peter and August moved quickly to join us as we entered, followed at a more leisurely pace by Amphitrite, now fully in her Captain Pete guise, complete with oversized plume in her overlarge pirate hat. She eyed us, then the babies.

"Two?" she asked.

"Three, if you count mine," said October.

Pete shook her head. "Yeah, but yours isn't my problem."

"We may need to discuss our bargain in more detail," I said.

"Yeah, looks like it," said Pete. "But we have time."

We did. We had all the time in the sea. Dianda turned to me and Patrick, holding out her arms, and we tucked the babies into them, letting her carry them with her to the top of the coral dais that had been established for just this purpose.

"I know you all want cake, so we'll keep this simple," she said, to a ripple of laughter from the room. "By reef and rock, by tempest and tide, I, Dianda Lorden, Duchess of Saltmist, bring my daughters now before you. Welcome to our waters November and December Lorden, born of our union, beloved of our halls, and heirs to all the glory of the sea."

This time the ripple was applause, rather than laughter. She held the babies higher for all to see, and whispers and cheers joined the sound of hands clapping together.

October smacked me in the shoulder. "Couldn't resist, could you?" she asked.

"It was Dianda's idea," I said. "But I think it suits them."

"It does," said Patrick, putting an arm around my waist and pulling me closer.

"I was promised cake," said August. "And I need to meet my niece." She took October by the arm, pulling her into the crowd with Tybalt following predictably behind, and this was my family, this was my future, this was everything I'd ever wanted in the world.

This was home.

ACKNOWLEDGMENTS

And here we go again: book nineteen. We're almost out of our teens, we've been through a parallel reality, a lot of blood, a wedding, and a pregnancy. This series now has as many volumes as I had years when I started writing it: I was nineteen and didn't know much about what I was going to grow up to be, but I knew it would involve writing. (The books were not sold or published when I was nineteen: I never gave up on Toby, and *Rosemary and Rue* was released when I was thirty-one.)

I am so incredibly grateful that we're still able to keep on going, nineteen books and two publishers in. These are challenging times, and being someone who tells stories for a living can be hard when it feels like reality weighs more than the atmosphere of the entire world. Biggest of thanks to everyone who's supported and tolerated me through this process, including my D&D group (We blend! We really do!), the Machete Squad, the entire team at Tor Books, and everyone who reached out during our year-long break from the series to tell me how much they hoped it wasn't ending, that I would return to October and her friends and finish out the story. Thank you for having faith in me. It means the world.

Thank you to my most beloved Amy, who remains one of the rocks of my reality; to Terri, who manages the administrative side of my life as best as possible; to all the bookstores and conventions who have welcomed me in the past year; and to Dr. Gauley, for her incredible veterinary medical care. Thanks to everyone who's tolerated my current unending need to drag them to *& Juliet*, especially Scotchy and Marnie, who were with me for the discovery of the show, and to the entire crew at Dispel Dice. Thanks to Shawn and Jay and Tea, to Margaret and Mary and Natalie and Roy and Kate and everyone else who needs to be mentioned here. I adore you all.

Thanks to my editorial team at Tor, Lee Harris and Oliver Dougherty, for making the adjustment to a new publisher as smooth as it could possibly have been. To Diana Fox, my agent, who probably understands how to manage me better than anyone else, while Chris McGrath's covers and Tara O'Shea's dingbats just get better and better. All my cats are doing well, although Kelpie is continuing to grow all out of reasonable expectations. Finally, thank you to my pit crew: Christopher Mangum, Tara O'Shea, Terri Ash, and Alec Fowler.

My soundtrack while writing *Silver and Lead* consisted mostly of *& Juliet, Cinderella's Castle, Ruin* by The Amazing Devil, endless live concert recordings of the Counting Crows, and all the Ludo a girl could hope to have (eternally waiting for a new album). Any errors in this book are entirely my own. The errors that aren't here are the ones that all these people helped me fix.

Let me show you what's waiting down by the edge of the water. I think you're going to enjoy it.

ABOUT THE AUTHOR

Beckett Gladney

SEANAN MCGUIRE is the author of the Hugo, Nebula, Alex, and Locus Award–winning Wayward Children series; the October Daye series; the InCryptid series; and other works. She also writes darker fiction as Mira Grant. McGuire lives in Seattle with her cats, a vast collection of creepy dolls, horror movies, and sufficient books to qualify her as a fire hazard. She won the 2010 John W. Campbell Award for Best New Writer, and in 2013 became the first person to appear five times on the same Hugo ballot. In 2022 she managed the same feat again!